# PALOS VERDES BLUE

# JOHN SHANNON

# PALOS VERDES BLUE

## A JACK LIFFEY MYSTERY

PEGASUS BOOKS
NEW YORK

PALOS VERDES BLUE

Pegasus Books LLC
80 Broad Street, 5th Floor
New York, NY 10004

Copyright © 2009 by John Shannon

First Pegasus Books cloth edition 2009

Library of Congress Cataloging-in-Publication Data is available.

ISBN: 978-1-60598-037-9

Printed in the United States of America

Distributed by W. W. Norton & Company, Inc.

www.pegasusbooks.us

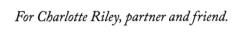

*For Charlotte Riley, partner and friend.*

"Whenever there are great virtues,
it's a sure sign something's wrong."
—Brecht, *Mother Courage and Her Children*

# PALOS
## VERDES
# BLUE

# 1

# THE WRONG CURRENCY

A SMALL BOY STOOD IN FRONT OF THE PICKUP HOLDING A PLASTIC MACHINE GUN THAT FLASHED ITS RED TRANSPARENT BARREL AS IT CLACKED AWAY GRUESOMELY. Die, motherfucker, the boy mouthed clearly at Jack Liffey through the windshield, bracing his short little legs for the imaginary recoil, like some TV he-man of death. Then he ran off, squealing. The mock attack didn't upset him. Because of his job, he dealt regularly with the excesses of childhood.

What did unsettle him was returning to the neighborhood where he'd lived long ago, had actually owned a house. He guessed it was some root phenomenon of consciousness stirring. Inside himself, he sensed a whisking-up of inner confusion about who he really was. For instance, Joe Wells, who'd lived in the ranch house directly across the street—now repainted a nameless beigy earth tone—would never have let anyone park a boat on the block, let alone right in front of his own home. He'd have gone ballistic, called the cops, probably even torched it late at night.

Meanwhile, on this side of the street, the Shelling house was just plain gone, now denuded land ready for something new. A *scrape*, in the Realtors' lingo. Even though this area of Redondo was over the crest and inland from any ocean view, values still had risen astronomically. Down the block there was already one three-story McMansion. You couldn't take your eyes off the poor botched structure, lost between two incompatible waves of banal suburban longing—stylistically somewhere between Taos and Normandy. Parabolic window in front, pseudo-Vegas jutting out above, diamond-shaped medieval mullions on the upper windows, and a red tile roof so steep it would just have to go on waiting vainly a very long time for the snows. The thing was beyond critique, like a madman's tiny fanatical runes on a cramped sheet of paper.

And where his then-best friend, Dale Nichols, had once parked a well-loved MG TD, a young man with Buddy Holly glasses could be seen spraying water on a new concrete driveway. Was he expecting it to grow? The neighborhood had become a checkerboard of astonishing tax deductions, he thought. Every one of them nudging a million dollars from one side or the other—probably even Kathy's. "His."

At least his ex-wife's simple frame bungalow was unchanged, except for the creep of entropy. It obviously needed paint and a reroof, but it still looked comfortable. Once his dark tower of retreat . . . but no more.

Kathy had left a message on his machine across town in East L.A., where he lived now with Gloria, a Latina cop. Her words conveyed an ambiguous SOS, and he had to assume it was about their daughter, Maeve. Maeve had just had an abortion after beating herself up for weeks about making the decision. He was in fact relieved that she'd done it, though he'd never let on to her which way he would have voted. She was just finishing up at Redondo High, and she'd already been admitted to three colleges, and what parent wants to see a child turn her back on all that to pin diapers on the kid of a thirty-year-old gangbanger who'd briefly infatuated her and then dumped her?

Kathy peered out the front window and noticed him, so he had to pretend he'd just driven up, yanking again on the parking brake and waving casually to her. She did not look happy. She looked instead like someone who'd been kicked as a puppy and had slowly grown ill-tempered.

*I will endure,* he thought.

She opened the door for him as if he'd never been away and he smelled it right away. Frying fish sticks, probably the cheapest generic brand, Captain Pegleg or something similar. It was her secret food vice that she ate whenever she was alone or in need of comfort, dunked bite by bite into sweet tartar sauce. By deduction, it meant Maeve was away or locked in her bedroom. I guess I really am a detective, he thought.

"How could she be in trouble already?" he asked after their perfunctory greetings, imagining some complication of Maeve's surgery or more likely a calamitous depression. Even an attempted suicide. Stop it, he told himself.

Kathy's forehead wrinkled for a moment before she realized what his question meant. "Oh. I'm sorry, Jack. It's only natural you'd think it was about Maeve. She's still pretty sad but she'll work through it."

"Can I see her?" He followed her out of the entranceway into the living room, radically rearranged now, unable to stop himself from looking for signs of a man—whatever that would be. A leather box, a pipe, a pair of athletic socks casually discarded, *Esquire*? He wanted it for her, really. He honestly did wish her well. Just not that creep Brad she'd lived with, then married, and eventually had to chase away. The man had slapped Maeve once, and Jack Liffey still wanted to frogmarch him out a very long dock and strangle him over open sea.

"The princess is not receiving today," Kathy said. "Not even her beloved dad, so she told me. She said she needs a few days off from normal life to meditate and heal. I started by leaving trays of food outside her door, but she never picked them up, so I've been feeding her flat foods I can get under the door. Swiss cheese. Cooked Pop Tarts—you know how she loves them. Unfortunately, baloney won't work since she's still in her veggie period and you can't really get tofu to hold together."

"She likes Ryvita with peanut butter," he said, and they both laughed a little. It was good to see Kathy lighten up some. "Think of it as a whole new flat cuisine," he suggested. "You can write it up for other moms with stubborn girls. Hey, hadn't you better go save the fish fingers?"

She blushed. "You still know my secrets."

"If you find them not within this month, you shall nose them as you pass the kitchen."

"*Hamlet?*" she asked.

"Bad *Hamlet*. Get them off the stove before they burn. And let me try to have a word with Maeve."

"Don't be discouraged. She's clinging to her hurt."

He made as much noise as he could going down the hardwood floor of the hallway, hoping that way to announce himself. Jack Liffey knocked softly at the door where a hand-lettered sign warned, *If you don't sprout, stay out.*

"Hon, it's me. I'm not here on a rescue mission, I promise. I came over because your mom has something else to talk about—nothing to do with you. But I'd love to say hello as long as I'm here."

"Hi, Dad." The voice came softly through the door, causing his legs to go all rubbery with affection. The yearning to protect was powerful and had its own etiology.

"Are you okay? I know I can trust your word."

"That's some kind of reverse blackmail, isn't it? I'm not crazy, Dad. I just need to be alone for a while. Can you do that?"

"Of course I can, hon, but your mom is running out of flat food, and she's worried. Do you think you could put in an order and then whisk a tray of something nourishing into the room if we stay out of the way? Just for my peace of mind?"

"There're some cooked edamame beans in the big brown bowl in the fridge. Could you nuke them a little and sprinkle Tabasco on them?"

"You mean soy beans?"

"Uh-huh. They're great for phosphorous and vitamin A. Protein, of course."

"Sort of pre-tofu," he said.

"Don't joke right now, okay?"

"Sorry. You know I'll talk about anything you want when you're ready. I love you very much, honey."

"I know that, Dad. Thank you."

"Don't go on living with pain for too long, that's all. Proust said a little pain is good for the soul but too much starts closing off paths you may need."

"Wow, I'll have to think about that. That's profound. But go away now, please."

He headed back to the kitchen. As far as he knew, Proust hadn't ever said anything of the sort, but a little extra authority never hurt with Maeve.


At the table he declined a share of the fish sticks. He had a secret food, too, but it had nothing to do with the ugly bug-eyed crap left over in the bottom of commercial fishing nets. He could barely look at the kitchen table, green Formica with little flying kidney shapes, the perimeter wrapped with three-ribbed aluminum. It had been his mother's and it screamed of the early 1950s.

Kathy held a small portion of fish up on her fork, liberally daubed with lumpy white sauce, as if she were just coming awake to what she was eating. "I'll tell you a secret, Jack. You were always the strong one. Even in the bad days."

The bad days meant all the drugs and booze right after he'd lost his secure aerospace job, and she'd had to go back to work as a substitute teacher. That was over a dozen years ago now, and he wasn't proud of any of it. However, he knew better than to reply.

"You know how I've always said I disliked your newfound . . . profession. Well, hell. You've turned out to have a talent for it. And Gloria's a good woman—I admit that, too—unlike some you've been with."

This ticked him off a bit. Especially after Brad the asshole had all but insisted she get a breast job and have her pussy stitched tighter. Jesus Christ. But all in all, she seemed pretty mellow now, for Kathy. Somehow she intuited that that he was thinking about doing Brad harm.

"I wanted to hurt him, too," she told him. "You know, he left a lot of his stuff in the closet. A few months ago I took all his eBay-ready baseball cards up the cliffs in P.V., and sailed them into the ocean, one by one. Until it got boring, and then I just dumped what was left. I had help, actually. It was a kind of coming-aboard ritual to a divorce club I go to up in P.V. every two weeks. A book club, really, but with an edge."

"Edge—yeah, I get it. Kill the scrotum, the head dies."

She smiled. "Thanks for that. My best friend up there is Helen Hostetler." She took another forkful of Captain Pegleg, dipped it, nibbled, and sighed. "Her daughter's missing, Jack. It's right up your alley."

"Which town?" San Pedro, where he'd grown up, was the far eastern flank of the peninsula, down at sea level around the port, a working-class town to the core. All the rest of what, back then, they'd basically either hated or ignored—but called The Hill, when they had to call it anything—was made up of five interlocking horsey 'burbs of an ever-increasing wealth that oozed uphill toward the crown of Rolling Hills at the top. This was a gated town he'd never set foot in, one where local jokes had it that even the maids were rich.

"Helen lives just west of Lunada Bay. I guess that's Palos Verdes Estates."

All he remembered about Lunada Bay was that the Greek freighter *The Dominator* had gone aground near there when he'd been in high school, and they'd all delighted in hustling around P.V. Drive every few weeks in their beat-up jalopies to watch as the grounded freighter broke up and began rusting away on the rocks. He wondered if anything was left of it now. Then he remembered that Lunada Bay was also where the spoiled rich surfers who lived nearby had tried to drive away all outsiders, slashing tires and beating up what they called flatlanders, until even the sheriff had had to intervene. Bayboys—that was what they'd called themselves. An angry whiteboy *gang*. He smiled to himself. Like hamsters with ostentatiously evil tattoos.

"What can you tell me about the girl?" he asked.

"I'd rather let Helen brief you."

"Okay, what can you tell me about Helen?"

Kathy thought for a moment. "Remember, this is a good friend I'm describing so you'll have to consider the source. Hel was a junior tennis champion once, really very, very good, but she broke her ankle in about six places coming off the back of a boyfriend's motorbike and that was that. She was already at Loyola-Marymount on a tennis scholarship, and she switched from whatever she was studying to

French. After she graduated, she was a secretary for some import-export company down in the harbor where she met Freddy. He was a broker or expediter—no, a freight forwarder—one of those strange-sounding jobs. I never met him. They got married and moved up to where he thought they belonged, among all the fancy folks. Don't make a face. Her place really isn't that pretentious. Biggish but, basically, just your standard upscale L.A. ranch house."

"I remember P.V. It's the zoning covenants up there that keep them from building those horrid pretentious sugar cubes. I guess that's one of the perks of old money."

"*Old* money?"

"Well, it's all relative in L.A., isn't it? I guess I just mean before color TV."

He saw she wasn't really registering anything but her own worry. "Hel's a good woman, Jack, who never really got her due in the world. She kept the household together and raised her kids as well as she could after he ran off with some young cunt. She worked part time back at her old company and volunteered a lot at the library. I met her at the Divorcee Book Club. We had very similar tastes. We both hated *Snow Falling on Cedars* and we voted down *The Bridges of Madison County*."

"Okay, what's in the other column?"

Kathy made a face. She took her time before answering. "All right, I get it, but you didn't hear this from me. Antidepressants, for one thing, but then, that's everybody on the hill, really. They may as well put them in the water. Prozac, Zoloft—it's a shifting reality. And since the world gets awful cold and lonely after a while, she had an affair with a married neighbor. It happens. Right now I think I'd even have a fling with you."

He avoided her eyes. "Man, that is desperate," he said as neutrally as he could.

**Maricruz Olivares**
**Behind Aztec Market**
**Huépac, Sonora**

Dear Maricruz*,

*This is Jaime and I do not know if I will ever be able to post this letter. It may be better for people in the* poblano *to think I am gone off the face of the earth. I am trying to make my English better but I am going to write in Spanish for now because we will both be more comfortable that way. On that terrible day when I knew I had to leave, I also knew the events of that day would transform my fate completely. Maybe if we were not such a dry country of poor farms there would not now be just a few large industrial farms owned by rich men or by powerful* norteamericano *companies. No matter what you heard, on that day the* patrón *of the chicken farm, Don Ignacio himself, came to me and asked me to procure you, yes you, to work as a maid in his home. I knew what he wanted and so do you because he is famous for abusing women whom he employs. I told him to his face he was a* gran pendejo [it just means a big jerk, I am trying to preserve some of the flavor of Jaime's Spanish —ML.] *He said I was fired at that moment, and he had his bodyguards rush me off the farm. As you know, there would be no other work for me in Huépac after that. I realized I would have to go to* El Norte. *I could have feared this, but I have studied hard and I speak English well, as you know. Mari, I am trying to look upon my fate as a great adventure now. Please remember me fondly.*

With all my fraternal love, Jaime

*These letters translated from the Spanish by Maeve Liffey.*

Since he knew it was Gloria's early day home, and that there was already some trouble on that front, too, he drove his old pickup straight back to Boyle Heights after he'd grabbed a fast-food lunch in Redondo. He'd catch up with Kathy's friend Helen Hostetler in the evening. You weren't supposed to say it, but the comings and goings of divorced housewives were pretty easy to predict. And so were those of cops—sometimes.

Gloria Ramirez was in her favorite reclining chair with a beer and a mail-order catalog open on her lap. Her feet were up on an ottoman and her eyes were closed. He glanced at her thick legs and felt an ache for her. She must have heard him come in the front door. "Love can be a kind of loss," she said without opening her eyes. "You know what I mean?"

Her .40-caliber Glock in its clip-on holster was on the sideboard not far away, and there were a lot of things you didn't say to someone within reach of a gun that powerful. The LAPD had carried 9mm Berettas until they found out you had to shoot a drugged-up attacker as many as twenty-six times with a 9mm to make him go down. It was then the police union started calling the old weapon a poodle-stopper.

"Maybe you could tell me."

"I don't mean you taught loss to me, Jackie. No, not that. It just happens."

His aging dog Loco, allegedly half coyote, wandered in and sniffed at him in a way that made him wonder if the animal was going a bit blind. Don't you dare, he thought. He sat opposite Gloria, and Loco collapsed across his feet.

He nudged the dog off, heading into the kitchen for a ginger ale, which he sipped at. He'd fought his way by himself out of a bad drinking period and been sober ever since, over ten years now—but he knew a lot of folks would call him a dry drunk and not trust the change. There still wasn't a day he didn't want one of those nice cold beers. Especially when Gloria was in a mood like this.

"Shit happens, they say," she said.

A month earlier, she'd driven up to Bakersfield to help him out on a case, and he knew that up there she'd met a man that she'd fancied quite a lot. But he didn't think she'd done anything much about it, and he wasn't even supposed to know the whole flirtation had taken place. He guessed it was a dry affair.

"You upset?" he asked, sensing that anything he said was destined to be a bit idiotic.

She traced her finger around something on the catalog page. Outside he heard one of the Gomez kids across the street banging hard on a part of the engine under the hood of their family's old Chevy Biscayne as *banda* music played faintly, pumping out its polka beat. These noises had become the ordinary consoling sounds of the neighborhood.

"I feel a little detached," she said. "Like that woman who gets dressed every morning and then puts on her weapon and goes down to the Harbor Police Station isn't me at all. But cops aren't supposed to have weird feelings like that. Everything's meant to be dialed in for us, hard-ass only, twenty-four/seven. If you ever want to make L.T., that's for sure for sure."

I wonder what we're talking about, he thought.

"It's rough," he said. "You're not a hardass inside."

Her eyes came up as if she were just noticing him.

"How do you know that?"

There was no answer to a question like that, but he felt certain he'd better not joke. "I just do. I know you're a good woman."

"That's a real trick, Jackie, if you can know that. Uh-huh. You're full of real tricks." She took a long pull on her beer, finishing off the bottle.

There was a louder clang outside on the car and then an angry complaint in Spanish. A helicopter pounded noisily overhead, though it seemed a bit early for that. The police buzzed their neighborhood off and on all night, occasionally flicking on their godawful Nightsun searchlight.

Gloria set her empty bottle down on the table and ran it idly in little circles. She never came to rest, he thought. Even several beers in, her hands fidgeted and her attention was clamorous, her black eyes fierce as lasers when they came to focus. At night, she turned over fast in her sleep every few minutes like someone hit by a cattle prod, each time tightening quickly into a new defensive pose. She even yelped once in a while and talked out loud, but too fast to follow. She always woke up fuming.

Loving her was a workout, but he did, and he meant to make a stand on it.

"Can I bring you another one?" He leaned forward.

"Freeze, motherfucker!" she snapped. He couldn't help but flinch as Gloria stuck out a finger to make a pistol aimed at him. She laughed. How funny was it? It was a private laugh, containing more layers of irony than he could access. "Sorry, Jackie. Go ahead, I'd like another one." She shook her head. "You're so nice to me, your balls should fall off."

"Only women get to be nice?"

Her grim smile softened. "I remember when I first wanted to be your girlfriend. On Terminal Island, remember? All that danger, but you stayed nice to Steelyard even when he was being a asshole to you. I thought, hey, that's the way a wife's supposed to act. I want a wife.

Why shouldn't *I* have a wife?" She laughed again. "Now I'm being a asshole, and you're *still* nice. I don't get it, and I'm not gonna try."

As he extracted his feet from under Loco and got up, she added, "You looked a whole lot younger back then, boyfriend. It's only been a couple years. Is it being with me makes you look so old now?"

"This is just what I look like now. Sometimes it happens fast." He knew he'd gone mostly gray and his neck was starting to wrinkle up and he had ugly white keloids on his arms, but it wasn't what she was really talking about.

She grabbed his sleeve as he walked past. "You up for a matinee?"

"We didn't use to ask," he said. "We'd just start kissing."

"Last one undressed's a chickenshit," she said.

In a cheap gas station that evening, a panhandler who looked as if goats had been eating his hair tried to pump Jack Liffey's fuel for him under the glary light. He gave the old man a dollar and sent him on his wobbly way. He probably needs it more than me, was his automatic thought, but he was really still thinking about Gloria.

After the late-afternoon sex, for dinner they'd had a supermarket-cooked chicken, and he'd made a big salad and some garlic toast, and she'd finally become more cheerful. Yet he sensed that, underneath, there was still something more than her normal disaffection eating at her. Gloria was three-quarters—maybe more—Paiute Indian, and she'd been raised by foster parents to think Hispanics were the bees' knees and *indios* were dirty and hateful, and she'd never really recovered from all that toxic rancor, not to mention her years as a rebellious delinquent. It was amazing, he thought, that the police and their natural enemies were so genetically similar that she could have crossed that bridge to become one of the keepers of order with so little difficulty. He'd seen her work and she was a very good cop; she remained in charge without swagger, staying sharp and full of empathy just when it was required.

He wondered if the good-humored guy in Bakersfield whom she'd fancied still held an attraction for her, if he was a lost opportunity for a little more of the loving that she needed so badly. He was sure it wouldn't have helped for long. But he wasn't sure whether there wasn't even more balm he could apply to that terrible open wound in her psyche. All he could do was keep on trying.

On his way to meet Helen Hostetler, he was distracted by a platoon of men in Davy Crockett coonskins and fringed suede jackets carrying a seemingly weightless full-size log cabin across the boulevard in front of him. They had the green light and were hurrying a bit. There were two extra Crocketts carrying big signs in advance and behind the cabin that said: WIDE LOAD and I WOULD VOTE TO PLOW THROUGH ANY GENTLEMAN'S ESTATE WITH A ROAD OR A CANOE.

Jack Liffey gave them a V-sign out the window. He had no idea who they were, but, for him, any madness like that demanded unquestioning encouragement. Whoever you guys are, you're probably going to be sorry, he thought.

*Dad. This is all just so wussy! I shouldnt show you how much I miss you but I cant help it. Dad Im sixteen in a week please dont forget.*

*I come home today and ask if you called and mom just hands me some boring official letter I stick in my pocket. You know really heres the picture of the way it is now—shes stuffing Oreos in her mouth with both hands and brown crumbs dropping all around her all day. Jesus. Its been like this since you left. Shes really puffing up toward that awful woman on TV.*

*She goes your lucky to be so thin but its just a lot of unnecessary crap. To me you know. Shes really bitter I think.*

*And I go its smoking dope keeps me light on my feet Mom. You ought to try it. And I do a little tap dance to the fridge to show off and get me a Corona. All she drinks now are these G and Ts one after another.*

*So she goes if your going to drink make me a gin-mint sweetie.*

*I go that stuffs poison.*

*She goes will you play scrabble with me later?*

*And I go I got to meet the Bayboys. Im important in the Bayboys dad. Its our duty to guard the bay and keep the best surfing spot in California for us. And I mean by any means necessary.*

*I go to Mom the tides at six-o-six and theres a weak onshore so it wont blow off the waves. Itll be super surf tonight.*

*She goes in that baby voice just one game and what about your lessons?*

*You know everybody up on the hill has to have these dum lessons thats the rule we all guess. Tennis and dance and piano and all that shit. I stopped going to violin months ago but Mom doesnt know it. I can tell you tho.*

*And I go to her that the Surfline on the phone is announcing eight footers. I gotta represent. Ill write more later. Please send me a address to write you Dad.*

"You must be Jack." The woman looked older than her age and plain in a faded print housecoat. For some reason the blond in her hair seemed to have been shot dead, leaving no highlights at all. "Helen Hostetler. Nice to meet you." They shook hands decorously, and she beckoned him in.

He bowed his head and pointed out the bald spot. "No horns. No matter what Kathy's been telling you about me."

She gave a half laugh, as if unsure what he'd meant to convey. "She doesn't talk like that about you, Jack. You'd be surprised."

He raised an eyebrow, but pleasantly, to keep her at ease. "Please have a seat in here. I know better than to offer you alcohol, but I have coffee."

"That'd be great."

The furniture was a bit beat-up for Palos Verdes, and paint was starting to peel at the baseboards. There was something about her that he liked. A little what-the-hell attitude, he decided. There was an oil portrait of what must have been her—younger, naturally blond, with two teenage girls. No dad included. But the odd multipart background included a Corvette and a dog and a sailboat and the house itself. All the objects the man had once possessed. It gave Jack Liffey the creeps.

In the living room, there were two bookcases that he gave the once-over. The first held a lot of women writers, and some damn good ones—Nadine Gordimer, Marilynn Robinson, Katherine Dunn, Muriel Spark. Classics, too. And not a single cozy mystery about a great-aunt who let her chihuahua solve the crimes. The second bookcase was all nonfiction, which he never much read, on principle—he just wasn't sure of the principle.

She soon brought them coffee with all the trimmings, and he took a cup untrimmed. It was damn good, some kind of intense French Roast.

"I guess Kathy's already told you something," she said.

"Let's say she hasn't."

So, laying out her story in a straightforward enough manner, she explained to Jack Liffey that her seventeen-year-old daughter, Blaine—named for a grandmother—had gone missing two weeks earlier. There'd been no insinuation at all that anything like that was coming. No drugs, only a few innocuous boyfriends, no acting out at home or school, as far as she knew. Blaine was nothing but utterly wholesome, fresh-baked whole-grain bread.

"Tell me more about her."

"She's been working with a group that's trying to save an endangered butterfly, the famous Palos Verdes Blue. I mean, how can a girl trying to save a butterfly be into anything disreputable?"

There was no point telling her about the other innocent girls whom he'd eventually found banging the whole high school football team out of some unspoken need, or mainlining heroin, or burning brands into their arms with kitchen forks. Teenagers had psyches stranger and more convoluted than most adults could imagine.

Carefully edging away from the subject at hand, he nudged her toward talking about herself, which he often found a lot more relevant.

"Do we have to talk about me?"

"If you don't trust me, I can get you somebody else."

"Okay, sorry. I'm an anxious person," she said flatly. "I don't understand why. I used to ride a gutless Solex all over France, no worries at all, and now I can't help feeling apprehensive that I might not be able to pay next month's mortgage or even find a parking place at the supermarket. That's a caricature of myself, but little things have begun to worry me more than they should. And if you're that nosy—recently, I've become horny as hell."

"Which antidepressant are you on?" he asked.

"Kathy told you that?"

"No. Everybody is. Some of them are better against anxiety. Paxil, I think. Ask your doc. Do you self-medicate with alcohol? I ask because I once knew all about that."

"I'm not on anything but Prozac."

"Does your daughter know you have affairs?"

"I beg your pardon!"

"You mentioned the horniness, Mrs. Hostetler."

"It's not like I'm hanging out at one of the cougar bars." She sipped her coffee decorously. "I've been discreet. No, I don't think she knows. And, by the way, it's in single digits."

"Single digits could be *nine* boyfriends," he said.

"It's *three*. In the twelve years since Freddy left me. None very recently. Can we move on?" This was all imparted in a tone that seemed a bit beyond her natural range. Ease of manner was apparently unavailable to her now.

"I'm sorry. I have to ask things I'd rather not know. The other daughter?"

"Beatrice. She's three years younger than Blaine and into engineering. It's like she has something masculine to prove."

"Girls aren't supposed to be engineers?"

"How many have you known?" she asked sharply.

She was right. "A few, and they were mostly stuck in ancillary jobs."

"See." A placid black Labrador strolled out of the back of the house, demanding attention, and Helen scratched between its ears.

"What was Blaine's major?"

"Biology. I don't know where that goes. Medicine? Teaching biology to other kids?"

"Can I see her room?" he asked.

"Is it important?"

"Yes, it's important. I'm sure you can see that."

"Well, I've poked around in there but it didn't get me anywhere."

The dog looked up at him quizzically and sniffed, as if detecting Loco.

"Not to have a look at her room would be odd, wouldn't it, Mrs. Hostetler? If I'm really a detective. And I'm going to have to ask you for money in advance. A retainer."

"Fine," she said. "I think you can call me Helen. I'm not your mother. And I can pay you in cash. Real dollars."

That was good, he thought. Most of his life had always seemed to be spent in the wrong currency.

# 2

# CLOUDED MIND

A LARGE POSTER OF A HANDSOME BLOND SURFER ON A STEEP WAVE, ARMS LANGUID AND CONFIDENT, WAS TACKED UP OVER THE BED, BUT THAT WAS HARDLY SURPRISING IN A HOUSE THAT WAS WITHIN A SHORT JOG OF LUNADA BAY. Just disappointing. He'd have preferred Beckett or Camus—maybe Che. But there was a small typed card over her desk that made up for a lot of it:

**We must be the change we wish to see in the world.**
**—Gandhi**

There was a tidy single bed with pink frills and too many pillows. An iPod rested in a cradle next to her computer and he tucked one of the earbuds into his ear and tried to get the hang of the control ring. Second nature to every teenager in the country, he knew. He caught snatches of some shrill music and shut it off. The drawers had little more than what you'd expect—Post-its, a jokey rubber stamp that said DESTROY BEFORE READING, color inkjet cartridges, old CDs, an empty eyeglass clamshell.

Beside the laptop was a stapled sheaf of paper titled *P.V. Habitat*

*Restoration.* He thumbed through a long list labeled Invasive Plant Species, each one illustrated by detailed drawings of the leaf and the flower, along with a little silhouette view of the whole plant. There were pages of native species, too. And a list of plants favored by the Blue butterflies for depositing their larvae. Someone had hand-written in the margin—apparently before the document had been photocopied—*At any locality a Blue is almost always restricted to a single plant species.* Afterward, another hand had written in blue: *Milk vetch (locoweed).* That was good to know, he thought. Like knowing a missing child always hung out at Del Taco.

As he set the dissertation down, a miniature Mexican flag fell out of it, glued to a toothpick of a pole. He turned it back and forth and decided the red-white-green was really rather a beautiful combination, if you could get over the fact that right in the center a pitiless eagle was chowing down on a rattlesnake. He'd read that for the fourth redesign of the flag, commissioned in honor of the Mexico City Olympics in 1968, they'd made the eagle look a lot more predatory. Just in time, apparently, so the cops could shoot down the protesting students carrying it. He pocketed the tiny flag.

In the closet her clothes seemed tomboyish, lots of jeans and hiking pants and cowboy shirts. There was a section off to one side for plaid skirts and white blouses, obviously a school uniform. He felt pockets and groped around among the tennis shoes and hiking boots. There was one pair of plain riding boots, scuffed up the insteps from stirrups, worn from actual riding.

Most of the books in her bookcase bore serious-sounding scientific and botanical titles. There were also a handful of romance novels and assigned-reading classics exiled higgledy-piggledy to the bottom shelf, with the middle shelf set aside for small objects of sentimental value. He squatted for a closer look. A crude but cheerful Latino folk-art bus with a devil lying full length on top and blowing a trumpet. A nautilus shell neatly lasered in half to expose all its logarithmic septa. He'd had one just like it himself in an earlier century but had grown to dislike the too-rigid geometry.

A scuffed softball with signatures. A Slinky spring took him back a ways. It was nice to know they were still around. A tooled silver frame held the photo of a square-jawed boy that he would have to ask about. He wondered if Maeve would like this girl. There were points of argument on both sides.

He waited for last to pick up the big-earring-size cardboard box in the middle of the shelf that contained exactly what he had expected. Under a celluloid top, on a pouf of absorbent cotton, a pin impaled an iridescent blue butterfly the size of two thumbs. The wings shone with unpredictable highlights of lavender and silver as he swayed a little under the room light, then squatted down on his ankles. The lobed wings were bordered by a perfect rim of black and then white. It was remarkable that such a small and delicate creature could stir up so much fuss.

A tiny label inside the box said *Glaucopsyche lygdamus palosverdesensis*. *Glauco . . . psyche*, he thought, dredging hard through his high school Latin. Something like clouded mind? Strange name for a butterfly.

He stood at the door for a moment, listening for ambient sound in the house, and then left Blaine's bedroom. The first door along the hall was a bathroom but the next was clearly another girl's room, certainly Beatrice's, as unalike the first as the abodes of sworn enemies. The posters included an ethereal girl lying in a stream and drowning herself (what else but Hamlet's Ophelia?) and a large reproduction of a Tarot card, The Hanged Man—the poster pinned to the wall upside down. He'd always preferred The Skeptic himself.

The clothes closet was open and he saw at a glance enough black clothing that he had little need to look further. He'd dealt with Goth kids before, and he had a grudging respect for them as America's last truly outsider, uncoopted subculture, rather like the Beats of his own day. The ones he'd met had been quiet and smart, a bit self-important, and rather astute about their tangential place in the scheme of things. None of them had carried guns.

Already he'd seen enough to know that the two girls, three years apart, would probably have a very strained relationship. He guessed that Beatrice—before adopting her new persona—would have been seen by all as the "good" daughter, ascribed all the upbeat, great-aunt-beloved traits—kind, generous and affection-ate. Though, in fact, it was probably the older sister who embod-ied those traits, only in a less showy way. He'd learned that adults could be so damn wrong-headed about kids. Beatrice would know far more about Blaine than the reverse; she would be shrewd and calculating, an accomplished actress, maybe even a bit pitiless. He would have to talk to her. She was the true five-star survivor in the family.

No, he thought, maybe not. Beatrice would have to pay in the end, too, if her sister did. He stared at the classic feminist novels aban-doned across her small desk—*The Golden Notebook, Jane Eyre*, and a couple of Anaïs Nins. There really are no survivors in a shattered family, he thought. Time brings them all down. How had Maeve managed to do it?

"What are you doing in here!"

Helen stood adamantly behind him, having swung the door wide open, glaring as if she'd caught him peeking into her bra drawer.

"I meet all flights," Jack Liffey said. "It's my job. I'll need to talk to Beatrice."

"Bea's with her father. Blaine would never go stay with him. She's too loyal."

He thought of Maeve again, wondering if every fractured family became a power struggle. His had certainly been, for a while.

"I need names and addresses. Friends, her father, boyfriends."

"Can you be discreet?"

"No, not really. Do you want your daughter found, or should I just wave discreetly as she's carried off into white slavery?"

All at once the woman began weeping. "Oh, Jack, I'm sorry. I'm just so scared and alone." She held on to him awkwardly and he let her because there was nothing else he could do. Her forehead rubbed slowly against his shoulder. She wore a potent perfume, something animal he knew from years ago. He didn't want Gloria to catch a whiff of it, but there wasn't much he could do.

She squirmed against him until there was little doubt what was going on. A few years earlier he would probably have bedded her. He'd still subscribed then to the notion that you only regretted the things you *didn't* do, not what you *did*. That attitude hadn't survived his own daughter's fierce opprobrium—nor any number of bad experiences. These days he was several hundred years older, and he just wanted to find a way of pulling away from this sad woman without insulting her.

"Kathy tells me you're a strong woman—raising your daughters alone."

"I never wanted to be strong, Jack. I wanted a helpmeet, someone with real character."

"Me, too. But we got daughters instead, and we owe them," he said.

"In her calm moments now, Kathy calls you a real mensch."

He wasn't sure he believed Kathy'd ever said such a thing, or if it was just more of the woman's running on V-eight, overrevving.

"Let it go, Helen, nobody's a mensch. We're all broken at the weak places the way they say, and the strong places, too, or whatever it is. I drank. I left Kathy, and I left other women, too. I let people get hurt because of things I failed to do. Forget the divine plan. All we can do is hang on like hell to the best that's in us."

Somehow they ended up side by side with their arms around each other, which was a big improvement. Still, she had very large breasts that had been rubbing all over him.

"Can you find Blaine?" she asked.

"I'm pretty good at it. But I won't make her come home if she's desperately unhappy here."

"Christ, Jack! That's mean."

"Yeah."

From where they stood on the upper landing, a long band of windows looked out over the grassy field that separated Paseo Del Mar from the cliff above the Pacific, and all at once, astonishingly, they saw a skydiver land near the cliff, roll once and quickly gather up his bright-red chute before the wind could tug him over the edge.

In a moment a second parachutist came down farther from the cliff. Then another and another, until one hit hard in the street out front. Finally, a late arrival crashed awkwardly into the shrubbery next door, spooking a big peacock that fluttered up with a cry that sounded just like a human baby stuck with a pin. It was all too damn much.

"This is a strange world up here," he said.

She let go of him, supremely uninterested in the skydivers. "Thanks for saving my feelings, Jack. You can still have me anytime you want, but please don't say anything to Kath." She went up on tip-toe to kiss his cheek.

"Of course not."

**Maricruz Olivares**
**Behind Aztec Market**
**Huépac, Sonora**

Dear Maricruz,

*We must both try to remember all these experiences of good and bad of our life. The way we slept at every angle on two old mattresses in the back room. Our father Santiago dying trying to cross. The* migra *finding him too late on the edge of Organ Pipe Cactus National Monument in Arizona. Remember Diego, the local* judiciale, *telling us there had been five days of very hot 45-degree weather.* [That's 110 Fahrenheit! —ML.] *They said that his* compañeros *argued with the coyote against leaving him after he sprained his ankle, but the coyote insisted and said he would send someone back, and they left him most of their water and hurried on to the highway where a truck was waiting.*

*There must be no more abandoning! Though I leave you all for now.*

*When I had to go, you were out with your friends. There wasn't much for me to collect into my old backpack, as you know, only my old clothes and underwear, and the Milton book.*

*Mother came in very angry and asked why I had insulted Señor Don Ignacio. She almost broke my heart standing there with her arms crossed, and I wasn't sure I was ever going to see her again.*

*How could I tell her what Don Ignacio had intended for you? You know the* patron's *house is famous all over Huépac for losing its* mozas *one after another.*

*—You're too hot-headed, Mother said.*

*—You know I'm not. I am a rock. It's just my turn to go to* El Norte *for us all.*

*We both crossed ourselves, thinking of father.*

*—It was about Maricruz, wasn't it? Mother said.*

*I didn't say anything because I was choked up. Now, this is a great secret I am about to tell you, Maricruz. You must not reveal this.*

*—*Mijo, *wait, Mother said to me. You think because you speak good* Inglés *and you know maths and I left school young that I'm a simple woman. Nothing is simple in* la vida.

*I was ashamed that she thought I gave her such disrespect, but maybe I had been thinking her rural and maybe simple a little,* una pueblerina.

*Then I saw that she was crying.*

*—How do you think we bought tortillas and beans when your father was gone the last time and he couldn't send us money?*

*Mari, I felt a terrible shaking but I didn't know why.*

*—Don't blame Don Ignacio,* mijo. *I went to him of my own free will. You must learn this: it means nothing at all for a woman if you feel nothing in your heart.*

*O, Maricruz, do not tell anyone about this! I could kill the whole world. But not you or* mami. *I will not abandon you.*

**Your loving brother, Jaime**


Maeve picked at the edamame, but she had no real appetite at all and finally pushed the bowl aside. She'd been despondent for days and lay on the sleeping bag on the wood floor, using abstemiousness as a kind of Buddhist-inspired self-punishment, a peculiar trait she'd probably inherited obliquely from her dad. There was only a half bath attached to her bedroom, a toilet and basin, and she'd been taking sponge baths for almost a week now. She'd tried reading the most miserable of Dostoevsky's novels, when she could focus at all, or listening to the darkest old-school rock like the Stones doing *Paint It Black*.

She felt utterly hollow inside. Oh my god! she thought. I'm literally and truly hollow inside. And she felt a pang of guilt, rationalize how she might. Her vision went pink for a moment as she clenched her teeth. This was something else new she'd discovered, a trembling anger in herself—a will to break things or spoil things that she'd never had before, though she never seemed to follow through on it.

"Basically," she whispered, "you're just depressed, girl, you're depressed from staring at your own navel for too long." She knew she could go to her mom's shrink and get some Prozac or whatever, but it wasn't her style. Besides, when she was seven years old, she'd seen her dad ride the drug train pretty far down the rails to wherever it went, and she'd sworn to limit herself to the perfectly ordinary mood-lifters like marijuana and beer.

That was just what she'd done when she'd been hanging with her baby's father, Beto, though she was afraid his *klika* of *carnals* had sneaked something like Angel Dust into the wooze-inducing Shermans they'd insisted she smoke. "The baby's father," she thought aloud, with a little sardonic rage. The *ex*-baby's ex-father. Wherever you were politically about abortion, she thought—and she supported the right fiercely—going through with it hurt you and then hurt you some more.

She caught a peek at herself at the very bottom of the full-length mirror. There was no color to her skin, the bones showed in her emaciated face like a skull, and her hair still had the gloss black out at the ends from all that dye. Playing Latina, as if she'd been dipped in another world. Luckily she couldn't see the Olde English Ⓖ they'd tattooed crudely on her breast.

Enough of this. Self-pity sucks. It'll drive you nuts. She stood up and put on a blue work shirt, and then tugged and hopped to force her hips into some retro pedal pushers. She heard noise down the hall, her mom on the phone. It was her mother's special telephone voice, overhearty and punctuated with fakey laughter. But she'd stopped blaming her mother for it. We all had a thousand social faces, she thought.

She pushed up the old sash window. If she wanted her escape to remain discreet, she'd have to leave her car behind, which meant either the bus or heading for a friend within walking distance. Imogen Mendez came to mind. If she was home, it was about three-quarters of a mile. They had studied Krishnamurti together for a while and read Hesse, but last summer Imogen had got involved in a pyramid selling scheme called HerbaVigor. She'd been what they called a Bonded Associate Partner. Imogen had thrown dinners that were really high-pressure sales events for things like L-arginine, the fatbuster, the perfect route to weight loss without even trying. The whole business had embarrassed the hell out of Maeve. Imogen had seen her a few times since and cried on her shoulder once but avoided any more herbal pitches like the plague. Maeve was pretty sure Imogen was over the summer mania by now.

She lowered herself to the grass and then jumped the hedge into the Robbins' backyard. She tiptoed past the side window just in case their cleaning lady was in. In less than a block she realized she was still a bit weak and woozy. It couldn't have helped that she'd eaten only under-the-door foods for several days. She burped a few times as she walked and then, happily, her mood seemed to lighten. School would be starting soon, her last high school year, and there'd be all those decisions about college. For some time now she'd been torn between going to someplace fancy and far away like a lot of her friends—Brown, Harvard, Princeton—or sticking close to home at one of the Cal schools. Maybe even a private school out West, if she could get a scholarship. Her dad promised to finance it, but she knew he had no real money.

It would help a lot, you dunce, if you knew what you wanted to study. Photography and marine biology and veterinary science had all faded out of her hopes and dreams, leaving her essentially clueless about a plausible future.

"Hey, hey, hey! *Güerita!*"

She glanced up to see an idling early '50s Chevy coupe, patched in gray primer. The Latino kid leaning out the window was slapping the outside of the door with his palm as the car inched along beside her.

"Wanna go for a ride? We won' hurchou none."

"*Que vaciado, caballeros. No seas gacho.*" It was a fairly mild rebuff, but so slangy that it made the boys' eyes bulge out in surprise.

"Where you from, *chica?*"

Where was she from? Always the big big question. "East Los." She almost threw the Greenwood sign, but she just waved the car on, and the boys laughed and gave her back a local gang sign. Wannabes, that's all they were. The driver now hit his hydraulics so the rear jacked up three feet quickly and then dropped, and the old beast rumbled slowly away. The whole encounter gave her a terrible pang of regret, or something like it. *I guess I've got a past now,* she thought.

Jack Liffey was surprised that Blaine's boyfriend, the handsome boy in the silver picture frame, had wanted to meet him in San Pedro instead of somewhere up on The Hill. "Do you know Bessie's?" the boy had asked on the phone. It was a beer bar facing the old clap-board Victorian lighthouse at Point Fermin. The name over the door was Walker's, but San Pedro was the kind of town that clung to its past, and most people still called it Bessie's.

Jeremy Kingston was as big as a rugby player but so combed and immaculate he looked like he was just off to teach Sunday School.

They took their Cokes and walked away from the bikers and the other belligerents who filled the place. After crossing the street and then the broad grass park, they sat on the ornamental concrete wall overlooking the agitated Pacific far below. Skydivers had once used these cliffs because of their permanent updraft, but too many had died and they'd been banned. The wind off the sea was cool and gusty, almost a third presence with them. Kingston spoke so softly that Jack Liffey had trouble hearing him over the wind and the ram-bunctious kids nearby who were hurling radio-controlled gliders out over the updraft. At their age, he'd have given an arm and a leg to have had radio control.

"Why'd you pick San Pedro?" he asked.

"There's really nowhere comfortable up on The Hill. Not for me. Rich people's hangouts or that awful mall on top. I like Pedro." He'd pronounced it just the way most of the town's Anglos did, as Jack Liffey had himself all his life, *Pee*-dro. Most of the Latinos in town had given up long ago and followed suit, but a few still held out for *Pay*-dro.

"I grew up in Pedro," Jack Liffey volunteered.

"By gad, sir, and you're really a detective?" the boy said in a funny accent.

Jack Liffey turned to look at him carefully.

"Sorry," the boy said. "I just saw *The Maltese Falcon* on Netflix."

"The Sydney Greenstreet accent is a little out of your range.

What I do is I find young people who've gone missing. I'm not a detective. Blaine's been gone awhile now. Do you have a theory?"

The boy looked puzzled for just a moment. "Ah, you mean *Blue*. Nobody calls her Blaine—maybe at her private school."

A fat man went running up to the wall near them, whacking a remote control box that sprouted a long antenna. "Come back here, you fuck!" A big red glider seemed to be determined to head straight out to sea.

"Where do you think Blue is?"

"I've burned out half my brain cells trying to answer that question, Mr. Liffey. You know, we weren't sleeping together, if that's what you're thinking. I was crazy about her, but she was pretty . . . celibate with me. Is that a word?"

"It's a word, and call me Jack. There's a Mr. Liffey living in downtown Pedro facing Terminal Island and he's my dad. I'm sorry to have to ask this. Do you think she might have suddenly fallen madly in love with somebody and run off somewhere? It happens."

Jeremy thought about that. "I shouldn't say this, but I think she was a volcano of really amazing emotions just waiting to boil up inside."

"Dangerous emotions? Like the Earth First people?"

"No, no, no. She'd never do anything that could hurt anybody. Nothing alive."

"Four hundred bucks! I'll *kill* you!" The fat man leaned far out over the concrete railing, slapping his joystick over and over as the tiny red plane diminished out over the ocean toward Catalina.

"Any kids hate her? I know how tribal it can get in high school."

The boy smiled. "At my school—not hers. It's such a joke. You may not believe me. If you want snobbery and all that rich-kid clanning up, just go to any public school up on The Hill. Her mom took her out and put her in Prestwick to escape all that. For an extra thirty grand a year you get to go to school with some scholarship kids from down in Pedro, even a few blacks, and the school insists that everybody do community service. I really envied her. We met on the habitat restoration project. You know—the P.V. Blue butterfly."

"Is that where her nickname comes from?"

"Maybe partly, but I've always seen her as kind of blue, by nature, you know, kind of sad. But a really profound kind of sad. Like when someone reads a lot of existential philosophers and finds life deeply disappointing. Like that."

Like you're going through a fairly normal adolescence, with an intellectual twist, Jack Liffey thought. "You're not sad?"

"I tried to be," Jeremy said, as if he'd failed an important test. He gave a small shrug.

Nothing better than a well-mannered teenager with an appreciation of life's weirdness. Jack Liffey had thought this model had been discontinued. But expressing affection for the boy was not part of his job, not now.

"If I'm going to find Blue, what do I need to know? Help me. There's got to be something you know."

"Gosh. I guess it's sinister if I don't have an idea, isn't it?"

"Damn right. And if you don't give me another target, *you* stay in my sights."

The fat man stood with his mouth open, pounding one fist slowly on the rock wall, then he hurled his control box out into the rocky surf below. Jack Liffey watched it descend and burst open far below.

Jeremy Kingston took a long time contemplating Jack Liffey's question. "I found out Blue went to a hookup party—at least once. The idea made me sick to my stomach. I actually puked. You know, all those soches, drinking and passing around plates of drugs and choosing up for meaningless sex. This one was at Duke Manning's house while his parents were away in Italy. He's one of the Bayboys."

"What's a soche?" Jack Liffey asked, though he knew.

"I don't know if the word really has a meaning. Socially desirable person? I mean the popular kids. Screw them."

They really had discontinued this model, Jack Liffey thought.

**Dad,**

*I wish I could take you out there. I can feel the ol feeling just going from the house to the path. I relax all over when the board is under my arm and Im just walking along toward the hill and the break. From the cliff yesterday I could see a bunch of the honeys came out to watch because they heard its good out there. Their all on their Bill Blass towels to catch the last of the sun and poking fingers into their hair. I cant wait but for some reason I do. I love to see the hole scene 100 feet down there. Theres a double row of the guys on the water waiting to drop in. The regulars are all set up near the point for the best take-off and I can see a few outsiders for sure in their bright shorts and long hair. Were keeping them pushed away from the barrel and keeping them out of the rotation.*

*Then some voice close by goes Twitch! I see that its Deputy Dawg Gordon. He goes no trouble tonight please! I dont feel like climbing all the way down there to bop you boys.*

*I smile and go sure thing Dawg. Well just have to leave those ol grommets alone today.*

*And he goes I swear to you kid if I catch the Bayboys harassing anybody Ill get a meatball planted on this beach for the rest of the year.*

*Do you remember dad? It's a yellow flag with a black circle that means surfing is taboo.*

*I go mondo dawg and walk down the path toward our bay.*

That offshore reef always makes awesome surf. I been around with the guys and seen em all and the only thing close is North Trestles way down south on the edge of Camp Pendleton in OC.

When I make it down a girl goes hey there Twitch. Catch us a gnarly one man.

Another girl goes look at all the Vals out there. I can tell shes egging me.

I paddle out and I tell you its a real hairy job against that break. When Im past the soup I can hear Duke talking tough to one of the Vals. He goes dont none of you fuckers drop in on our waves. The best you get are the betweens we aint using. Duke is what you might call an angry guy.

The Val hes talking to is a big guy and he goes next time well you best come strapped or we take care of you horsefucker pussies up here for good. Its a free country.

I come up on Duke and go real soft dude. Pretty soon I got it all backed down and I get the Bayboys to make a tight group so I can say what I gotta say. Everybody knows were under a court order I go. Bras be cool. Deputy Dawg is up there watching. Its careful time.

We didnt have no straws to draw straws of course and Ledge says we should just measure dicks and everybody boos an laughs. Hes fifty or even older and we already know hes got a dick as big as a brother. So we go for rock paper scissors and after a while it comes down to me or Ledge. The Legend looks like hes made out of nothing but rubber bands under skin thats too tight but hes our last connection to the old school Bayboys and we all love him to death. Those guys back in the day.

I go Ill do it Ledge.

And he goes fuck you gremmie. I do my share. Slap my hand.

And we do two out of three and I get the job with my scissors cutting Ledges paper. Im stoked and I grin like a crazy chimp and the

*Bayboys all pull apart to let me ride the next heavy one in. And after the wave standing up on the sand I stick my board next to the girls and I know theyll say I was there all night with them.*

*I go up the cliff the long way to stay away from dimwit Dawg. I know by heart which cars belong on Paseo and I can tell which have been driven up here by Vals. If you dont know the word Vals it started to mean all the dweebs who live far up in the San Fernando Valley but for us now it means anybody who hasnt grown up on the Hill. Were homies just like the brothers over in Watts and we got our rights.*

*Dad dont judge me. We got to do this stuff. I got out my Swiss Army and opened that punch thing on the back side. Man the sound made me scrunch my shoulders. It was a terrible screech as I keyed the green paint of a big Suburban Chevy down the whole side. Then I got low and punched a BMW X5 in the side of the tire. I swear to god it hissed down like a elephant on TV whose got shot and falling down on one knee.*

*Dad please give me a REAL place to send letters. I dont want to go through no lawyer.*

Things were getting more ragged and disagreeable in her life, and Gloria knew it. She'd just tried to bonk the cap off a beer bottle on the edge of the kitchen table, the way they did in the movies, and it had chipped the Formica and hadn't budged the cap. Her thoughts were not comforting at all, try as she might to find a silver lining to the clouds overhead. She knew she was getting meaner to Jack, without wanting to or knowing why, and also without being able to stop herself. And that was just the background noise. It wasn't what had set her off today.

She'd been given the afternoon off. Without pay. It was like getting swats in high school in the old days, or detention, or having to run extra laps in gym. She wondered if it had begun a week ago when she'd refused to put money into the office pool for the Dodger game. She knew some of the guys thought it was a little like a New York cop refusing to go on the pad. It made you a goody-two-shoes, a geek who might break the code and turn you in.

Captain Francis X. O'Reilly. New to Harbor Division this month. He'd once been the big chief's chauffeur and confidant and something had gone wrong with his career so he'd been spit sideways in the department like a watermelon seed. The rumor mill said alternately that he'd fucked somebody's wife, or somebody's *son*, or failed one of the new anger-management evaluations. The story she'd liked best was that he'd been given a high-level policy assignment to make sure "community-oriented policing" looked like it was actually working. He'd gone to the First AME Church and blurted out that some of his best friends were "colored guys." Gloria knew she'd never find out for sure.

What she did know was that he'd landed at the Harbor Division with a wild hair up his ass. About neatness. *Neatness*, for Chrissake! Next to godliness, he'd announced. Who'd believe it? It was apparently the way he thought he'd work his way back to the Glass House downtown, or its big new replacement on Spring and First. All the paperwork filed on time. The murder books tidy. The reports typed instead of written in longhand. She sighed.

Every desk had to be skimmed off at the end of every shift. She'd read the memo but hadn't really believed he was serious. She had real work to do.

"Glor, don't you know that pinhead graduated from the Solid Waste Management School of Penology?" Lt. Parks had whispered to her when she'd found the "Come see me" note, right on top of the foot-high mound of archeologically filed paper work on her desk.

She tried not to replay the meeting again, or reformulate her answers. It would only make her angrier.

She took the beer out back to give Loco an emergency petting. The emergency was hers. It seemed to do wonders for Maeve and Jack, though she herself was not crazy about dogs and had little faith in the maneuver. Especially dogs that were half coyote by DNA and had those flat yellow eyes that sometimes watched you like they were thinking of gobbling your liver. Of late, though, Loco had been a lot sweeter to her, even nestling up when she dropped off to sleep in her TV chair.

But the dog was nowhere to be found.

"Loco!" she called. "Front and center. I demand some attention."

Her hearing had always been remarkably acute. It was an almost subliminal scuffing noise—back among the dormant tea roses. Normally in Boyle Heights that meant an opossum or a wild raccoon, but she sighed and headed for the sound. Once a cop, always a meddler, she thought.

"Loco!" She gasped when she saw the dog lying flat on his side on the earth, his chest heaving in a labored rise and fall. Why me? she thought, envisioning the long wait at the local veterinarian, surrounded by enraged pit bulls and mewling cats clawing at cardboard boxes.

# 3

# THE SO BITTER GUYS

"I WON'T TALK ABOUT HERBAVIGOR IF YOU DON'T TALK ABOUT MY PROCE-
DURE," MAEVE OFFERED.

Imogen Mendez was a bit overweight with puffy cheeks and too-
round arms but Maeve had always thought of her as some sort of
dark Central European Madonna.

"Deal. I guess we both ate it pretty big for our enthusiasm."

"That's one way of putting it."

They were sitting at the picnic table in her backyard, munch-
ing on Doritos and Mrs. Mendez's tuna sandwiches—in honor of
something, Maeve was making an extremely rare exception to her
vegetarianism. Probably because she'd somehow internalized good
manners that in cases like this made it easier to go with the flow. She
guessed that Mrs. Mendez had probably never quite absorbed what
she had suggested several times about the horribleness of meat, possibly seeing her protestation as mere preference rather then princi-
pled exclusion. The woman was from Hungary and her English was
still imperfect at best.

"But are you really feeling okay, Maevie? You don't have to talk
about it," her friend added quickly.

"I'll always be okay."

"That's the spirit." She touched Maeve's hand lightly. "There was a lot of phoney-baloney, but I took one good thing away from HerbaVigor: *You can accomplish whatever you visualize.* I guess it just means be strong and confident."

"Gennie, I got some heeby-jeebies here!"

It was a slightly panicky voice from the kitchen window. The two girls looked at one another as if they'd been expecting something of the sort.

"It'll be an insect," Imogen said. "I'd better go deal with it. Mental moms."

"But they're the ones we've got." They grinned.

Imogen hurried inside. When she'd gone, Maeve discreetly poked the fibrous beige tuna out of her sandwich into a planter and pushed it down into the loose earth. Immediately she thought better of how it would start reeking eventually, but it was too late to retrieve it.

"*Jebo te bog! Zdaj se boš pa še opravičeval!*" The wondrous phrases looped out the open window, in a kind of laughing rage.

Soon Imogen came out, straight-arming well ahead of her a jam jar with a magazine atop it. As she walked it carefully past the picnic bench, Maeve could see that a yellow jacket appeared to be furiously attempting flight inside. Imogen released the angry insect over the back fence.

She watched it go, then sat back down with a sigh. "Karma still intact. You can chill."

"What was that wonderful curse your mom let out?"

"It's pretty idiomatic, hard to translate. 'God fuck you. And *now* you're trying to apologize?' It's actually pretty funny, addressed to a bug. It's Serbian. Everybody in Central Europe swears in Serbian so they won't anger their own gods."

Maeve smiled. "Like making the Mexicans do all our heavy lifting."

"You know I'm always taken for one. It's so unfair."

"Why?"

"Well, a lot of these soches expect Mexican girls to put out at the drop of a hat for any white guy that asks. I get felt up all the time by some Porsche-head who doesn't know me from his mom's cleaning girl."

All at once Maeve found she'd lost interest in the topic, in fact, lost interest in Imogen. It was as if a big cartoon anvil had fallen through from another world and clonked down in front of her—probably from the world babies came from.

Rather than get too gloomy, she came up with an idea for restarting their friendship. "Gen, have you ever met my mom's friend, Helen Hostetler? She lives up in Palos Verdes and looks kind of like Mrs. Darmuller."

"All the times I been over at your place, I don't remember."

"Her daughter's disappeared, I heard my mom talking to her mom about it. The girl's name is Blaine. Just our age."

"Jeeze, I don't know a Blaine. Do you think there might be *foul play?*"

"Might be anything."

Imogen brightened. "You need a distraction, don't you? A mission. Oh, girl, I'm so *there.*"

**Maricruz Olivares**
**Behind Aztec Market**
**Huépac, Sonora**

Dear Maricruz,

> *I haven't sent you any of these letters yet, but maybe I can take the risk. When I first came to* El Norte *I stayed with five others in*

a part of South Los called Hawthorne. We took turns on the bed and sofa. I got my first job from the mosca outside a Home Depot.

—Who speaks English? said the young gabacho with a ponytail who drove up and stared out the window of his pickup.

—Me here, boss.

—I spik good. You take me.

—No problema, boss.

I had the secret weapon, of course.

—I'm the man you want, sir. There won't be any misunderstandings with me.

He shoved two others out of the way and looked straight at me.

—What's your name, kid?

—Jamey. Oh, Mari, I admit it, I said it with that hard English J. Easy to remember, easy to pronounce, I told him.

—Can you do fieldstone? It's heavy work and I want them fitted properly, real crofting. Twelve dollars an hour for good work. Less if you're sloppy or slow.

—Sure, I can do it.

There was no argument from the other jornaleros. They know they have to accept the patron's decision gracefully.

—I'm Mike, he said. He didn't offer his hand. We got us a great contract, Jamey. Lady even brings us lemonade and sandwiches. Let's not F it up. Last of you guys didn't know his left from his right.

—Left, I said, holding up my left hand. Right. I was afraid he would hear the mockery, but if he did, it didn't bother him.

We drove for a while toward Palos Verdes. And all that drive, watching the crucifix the guy had swaying from his mirror, I thought of Don Ignacio's face when I hit him hard with the rock and the way his eyes rolled up to whites. It wasn't as satisfying as I thought it would be. I haven't confessed it yet and I *still wonder if I will. What North American priest would understand? So then.*

*—It's really Jaime, ain't it? Mike pronounced it almost right, very close, hi-me.*

*—It goes either way.*

*—Know why you guys will never run out of names? he says. You know why? After Jose, you always got Hose-B, Hose-C, Hose-D, like forever.*

*I smiled the best I could. After Mike, I thought, you've got Spike, Bike, and Dyke. But I needed the money. That's real funny, man, I told him.*

*—We'll get along fine. I like a guy who's not sensitive as a toilet seat.*


*I think he took our fieldstone illegally. We drove around the back way to a closed quarry where someone had broken the lock on a gate. It surprised me to see that Mike did his share of lifting the heavy stones into the truck. Then we drove to a very large white house set back from the cliffs over the ocean. There are so many houses like that here, and all of them so big and clean and carefully maintained. Even now I don't really understand. I guess it's complicated why there's so much money here and so little at home with us.*

*Mike backed up a driveway and then onto the lawn at the side of the house. We were building a retaining wall behind the house to hold back a really steep slope. I hoped Mike knew what he was doing because there's a lot of force pushing at a wall like that. I saw them build that rock-fill dam outside Huépac and how wide it had to be at the bottom.*

*First was the pick-and-shovel work to cut into the slope, and I could see that would be mostly my job. That first day, the lady seemed to forget all about the lemonade and sandwiches and at one o'clock Mike said angrily, Burger and Coke okay with you? He didn't wait for an answer before driving off.*

*I wondered if I should keep working but I was exhausted and I walked out front of the big clean house and then across the road and along a path to the edge of the cliff where there was a nice cool breeze to dry the sweat off me. It was so beautiful, Mari. Below me, a dozen surf riders were bobbing on their surfboards waiting for good waves. I watched as one paddled fast ahead of a wave and then came up to his feet on his short surfboard. The boy balanced with great skill as he scooted along just ahead of where the wave turned to foam. I had heard of surfboarding, of course, but never seen it before. It was truly amazing, Mari. Just wonderful.*

*Then Mike showed up with a McDonald's bag.*

*—I'll take $4.70 off your pay, Mike said.*

*We sat on the cliff edge to eat, 30 meters above the green water. Tomorrow, if there was a tomorrow with Mike, I would bring something cheaper of my own to eat.*

*—Little surf shitheads, Mike said as he ate.*

*I realized then that everybody hates somebody else.*

*—I bet the prick kid that lives in our house is down there and never offers to help his parents fix anything.*

*—Do the rich ever work here? I said.*

*—Hah. You got it, amigo. How come your English is so good?*

*—I read a lot of books.*

*—Good for fucking you. Then he lost interest in me completely.*

*Don't you forget me, Mari. Please! I will mail this one. I promise. As soon as I feel safe.*


Jack Liffey could still hear every nuance of reproach and entreaty in the voice on the other end of the phone call he'd just completed.

"Jack—you know, every single day I think I made the biggest damn mistake of my life letting you go."

"I'm sorry, Beck. But it's probably for the best. We're from different worlds, and mine would only impinge on yours again."

Rebecca Plumkill was an old girlfriend, and he hadn't seen her in a couple of years. One of his jobs had unleashed a terrible destructive vengeance on her upmarket craftsman house where he'd moved in with her—everything inside the place had been spray-painted fire engine red, including a Kandinsky, a Goya sketch, and a lot of fancy furniture. She was headmistress of the snootiest girl's school in L.A.—Taunton in Hancock Park—and he'd just called to see if she could give him an introduction to whoever was in charge at Prestwick, Blaine's school in P.V. Perhaps the whole idea had been a mistake.

"Oh, Jack. You made me laugh so. *No*, Madge, I'll take care of it later!"

In the background a door slammed. He could hear her sniffling and felt terrible.

"Couldn't you come for dinner sometime, please?"

"Can I bring Gloria?"

"You're still with her?" The disdain in her voice was her only weapon. "No, you can't. We need to talk about us."

"Gloria and I are 'us' now. I'm sorry."

Even after this, he'd somehow pushed on with it, asking for an introduction to D'Artagnon Brooke-Rose, the headmaster of Prestwick. (Couldn't just one of these people have an ordinary name?) Which Rebecca had agreed to give him only if he contracted to come to dinner by himself sometime. Bald blackmail. He traded her back the kind of lie that such a proposal deserved.

Now he was parked on a bit of shoulder off Harvard Road,

overwhelmed by the scent of eucalyptus trees that seemed to grow everywhere up here. White fences marked out an empty bridle path beside the road. Across rolling grassy hills with scattered trees, white frame buildings clustered together for moral support. It might have been a fancy winery or even a prosperous Dutch dairy, but it was neither. He hopped the fences and headed cross-country toward the buildings. There was a regular access road to the school for cars, of course, strewn with redwood chips and graded very flat between rows of feathery pepper trees, but he felt that this unorthodox approach evened something up between him and the place, he wasn't sure what.

He noticed a boy hunkering behind an outlying shed, ineffectually hiding a cigarette.

"Yarg. Cripes," he said as Jack Liffey approached.

"I'm not a snitch."

"I'm just a walking disaster in search of actuation." He looked about sixteen, acne-scarred and possibly anorexic.

"We all are, with a sufficiently kindly outlook. My name's Jack."

"I'm Harry Potter." The boy stood and they shook hands.

"Sure you are, and this is Hogwarts. Or some other warts. Go ahead and smoke it. I've been there." The kid had been about to crush it out behind him.

The boy sighed. "I'm Donnie Marevich. You think I hate it here but I don't. I'm just not really at home anywhere in the world." He sucked hard on the remains of his filterless cigarette, burning it down to a pinch of what used to be called a roach. Jack Liffey had no idea if the term still survived.

"Are we talking philosophy or just posturing?"

Donnie used his last inhale to blow a perfect ring and grinned. "Chill, man. Can you pretend I don't exist?"

"That depends on whether you know Blue Hostetler."

That brought his eyes up and seemed to inspire a couple of fleeting emotions, a kind of alarm that gave way to wariness.

"It's a small school, man. Like living in a one-Audi town. Everybody knows everybody and everybody's business."

"Then you know she's missing. Do you have any idea where she might be?"

"Ah, you're a cop."

"No. I just find missing kids."

"A real private dick. Amazing. I didn't know they existed any more."

"Was Blue a friend of yours?"

"I'm a lowly junior. She's a senior."

Apparently he was incapable of giving a straight answer to any question. "At the end of the day, do you give a shit about her?"

"Do you lose a lot of them, Mr. Detective?"

"No. I always find them." Jack Liffey was getting irritated, but he tried not to let it show. "Does she have any enemies here?"

The boy shredded the remains of the butt onto the ground and took some care covering it up. "From the outside, you'd think I'm super-superprivileged, wouldn't you? Private school. Rich parents. My roads are all wide open, all the lights are green-for-go and my choice of futures is almost infinite. Why, I could read the canon at Yale, do law at Harvard, go straight ahead and shine my money light on Wall Street, or else maybe make my altruistic way to the starving villages in Africa. I can see you thinking, so why is this little shit so cynical? He's too young for that. I guess I need to escape to the Tibetan mountains and meditate."

He looked up at Jack Liffey, his expression now unreadable. Then he laughed. "Go for the bucks, they say these days. They're probably right." He pressed his palms together in benediction.

Jack Liffey handed him a five, hoping it wasn't wasted. The amount might well be meaningless, even insulting, to a kid going to school here. But Donnie took the bill quickly enough.

"Maybe it's the money, but you can't be sure. Maybe I actually have a heart." He pointed to his chest as if Jack Liffey needed the anatomy lesson. "Blue's a nice girl, a brushcutter. On weekends, she'd go off on these outings, pulling out weeds like mustard and Scotch broom to restore the natural environment for the butterflies. What you've got to know is that she was pretty self-righteous about it all. It's weird, man, but there are some people that that attitude really really pisses off, maybe not even for any logical reason.

"Eat a spotted owl. Pour your old motor oil into the bay. Bury a tree hugger. Eat a dolphin. I know them well. They call themselves hard-headed realists. Or maybe they don't call themselves anything, I don't know. Maybe they don't think about life in terms more intelligent than a snail. What they do think about is how bitter they are at the world, or the school, or their parents, or—as Marlon Brando said in *The Wild One*—What have you got? They lash out at anything sincere. There're lots of them up on The Hill, though not so much in this school. Here we specialize in goody-goodies. Maybe she ran into one of them, though, outside, and he sent her to meet the dolphins."

"Anybody in particular you have in mind?"

"Not for five bucks. It's just kind of a plague we live with. Do you think it comes automatically with money?"

"You're the guy who took the five."

The boy smiled. "That's about eight seconds at my dad's billable rate. Watch out for the bitter guys, Mr. Dick. And remember I said so."

**Dear Dad,**

*So Im over at Condors dumb house whipping his ass at "Grand Theft Auto: Shred the Hos." I gotta get out a quarter to challenge him on who runs over the next one and I feel this envelope in my pocket thats gone completely outta the brainbin. I dont know why but it gave me this chill.*

*So I punch his shoulder and go pause it bra.*

*He goes hey Im creaming you.*

*Pause dipshit. Or Ill have to pound your ass.*

*I finger open the envelope and its not from a lawyer or anything like that. Its some official gobble I cant make out. The seal at the bottom looks hella official so I try again to read it. Nancy Reid the thing talks about. Im not sure I remember the name but it might have been the Nancy tinytit chick I hooked up with at Rabbits party.*

*Has named me as a correspondent it says. What the hell does that mean. I dont write letters to nobody except you. Maybe somebody I texted.*

*Nancy has tested positive for HIV. Well shit too bad for her. But if its the one I think I had her blow me and never fucked her that way. Guys dont get the thing that way. Everybody knows its a fag disease and the fags only get it from ass fucking. Or they use old meth needles again like winos. Advisable that you be tested as soon as possible. Highly recommended you get tested for reassurance.*

*Dad! The sound of all the shit around me just stops for a while and I dont hear Condor yakking and its like bugs are running up and down my arms. I mean I know this is bullshit. Why are they trying to scare me like this. Im not a homo. Its got to be a mistake.*

*I look on the envelope and think it must be for somebody else but its my name all right. (Dad I dont think Ill send you this one. Its all gotta be a joke. But I still really really need a address to reach you.)*

A fat man clutched a big green snake in a wire carrier on his lap, and a little yippy dog nearby had frozen in a woman's arms into a comic posture with his eyes distended and his tongue caught in his teeth. All the cats in their carrier-cages were frozen in vigilance, too, by the presence of the dogs. Gloria was not in a good mood. She wondered which pet she might spare if she decided all at once to yank out her Glock and just go high school on every miserable useless animal in the room. She definitely would not spare the teacup dog with the bug eyes. She and Jack shared that antipathy.

"I'd pull the *adiós* myself," the fat man muttered, seemingly talking to his snake, "if I wouldn't go straight to hell. I hate the thought of fire. Sammy, what do you think of it all?" His one-sided conversation was like a bad dream, but one similar enough to those encountered in the daily run of her profession that it didn't bother her much. Loco's semi-inert body had already been gently taken from her and carried inside to see Dr. Solís by a timid young woman who had braces on terrible buck teeth.

The things she did for Jack. She wasn't that crazy about dogs in general, though she'd developed a sneaking affection for this one. She'd even decided to give him extra credit for his half-coyote parentage, thus sharing her own Native American bloodline in some theoretical way. The Trickster, the prankmaster that every Indian loved. She even knew the name in Paiute: *e-tzwa*. Recently, Loco had taken to chumming up to her as soon as she got home, like some pathetic old man rubbing against girls on a bus.

"Mrs. Ramirez . . ." It was the girl with the braces, and Gloria let the "Mrs." lie. Never happen.

"What's up, girl?"

"Dr. Solís wants to keep your dog for a few days. We took some tests, and the results won't be back till then. Can you leave him?"

"*Claro que sí.* But has the vet got a guess?"

The girl winced. "I shouldn't say."

In quick Spanish, Gloria struck hard at the girl's weaknesses and fears. She linked Loco and the girl herself to the concept of ugly ducklings—*patitos feos*—an incredibly powerful concept now that the Argentine soap opera *Yo soy Betty la fea* was playing all over the Spanish-speaking world and was even being mimicked in a sanitized English-language version as *Ugly Betty.* It was ordinary interrogation technique, and Gloria was pretty good at it.

"It might be cancer," the girl caved in quickly.

"What kind?"

"Osteosarcoma. That means the bone."

"And what's the worst case for the dog?"

"A month or two. But we don't know anything yet. It could be something else, or it could be operable."

"Thanks, hon." Gloria didn't want to know any more. Baptized into the inevitability of death, she had no idea what she'd tell Jack and Maeve. Introducing that word into their daily life was not a responsibility that she wanted.

The school's administration building was more ordinary than he expected, and the secretary nodded and waved him on to a doorless office as soon as Jack Liffey gave his name. He knew at once that Rebecca had actually called ahead as promised.

A silver nameplate beside the opening said D'ARTAGNON BROOKE-ROSE: HEADMASTER, and the name irritated him unduly once again. The tall thin man at the desk must have seen Jack Liffey's eyes on his nameplate.

"I answer to Art. Absurd, isn't it?"

"I was wondering where Athos, Porthos, and Aramis have got off to."

"Or Cardinal Richelieu, for that matter. Or Milady. Amazing how few people know anything about Dumas these days, except as some sort of tickle in their cultural memory."

They shook hands.

"It appears Blaine Hostetler was nicknamed for an endangered butterfly. Blue."

"Please have a seat, Mr. Liffey." Standing up, he indicated what had to be an astonishingly expensive corrugated cardboard Frank Gehry chair, and Jack Liffey stared down at it as if afraid that by sitting there he'd soil it or crush it.

"If you're Art, I'd better be Jack. I can't sit on this. It has more net worth than my house." He didn't own a house, but still.

"It's a knockoff, Jack. Yes, she worked hard to establish Blue as her nickname. We thought it might also have referred to her mental state. I tried to get her to see someone."

"She was depressed?"

"So I'm told. You should talk to her peach. It's what the kids here call a counselor."

"Any idea why?" Jack Liffey was curious.

"Please risk sitting down. Many do. It doesn't collapse. The kids tell me the term 'peach' is from some video game."

They both sat, Jack Liffey very gingerly. The convoluted shape was not very comfortable, but it didn't collapse. "You know that her mother has asked me to look for her. I'll be as discreet as I can."

The man waved the offer away. "I really don't care, Jack. If she was into sex or drugs, whatever . . . I just don't find that worrying about the school's reputation carries much weight in the face of a missing child."

"You may be the only headmaster in the Western world to feel that way."

"It's true I'd prefer a shroud of privacy over everything evil. I want the world to note and reward only a state of grace. But I know I can't have what I want." As if to illustrate his preference, over his desk he had a small yellowing print of God reaching down from the heavens with giant compasses to take the measure of something. Jack Liffey guessed it was based on Blake's *Ancient of Days* but that was in color and this was not. It was a copy of some sort.

"Who did that?" he asked. "It's based on Blake, I can see, but it's not Blake."

"It's an etching for an old Masonic text. They love the symbol of the dividers, you know, for obvious reasons. It's by an artist known as Il Guercino who died in Bologna in 1660 just about the time *Vicomte de Bragelonne*, the final volume of the D'Artagnan Romances was being published in Paris."

Jesus, Jack Liffey thought—*way* too much information. "Was Dumas a Mason? I never realized."

The man shrugged. "We're not sure, but the books were anti-clerical. After all, Dumas was black."

"And are you a Mason?" Jack Liffey thought there had been an odd moment in the handshake, a kind of tickling at his palm that might have been some secret sign. He was not particularly opposed to the Masons, since they'd had a fine history of supporting revolutions back in the eighteenth century. Latterly, though, they'd seemed more inclined to recruit the police and the rulers. In any case, it might help to know.

"You don't ask that, Jack."

"I wish I had a large sum of money for every forbidden question I've asked. Maybe it's just a matter of semiotics."

"Not on my watch." The headmaster suddenly looked like he'd smelled something bad.

"Hey," Jack Liffey said. "It was you who uttered the word Masons. Now the word is vibrating out there, all around us."

The man in front of him seemed to grow more grotesque. "I. Am. Not. A. Mason." It was one of the weirdest lies Jack Liffey had ever heard out loud, about as valid as an old lover denying that the relationship had ever had any emotional meaning.

"I really don't care," Jack Liffey said. "God can be a Mason for all I care. Forget the higher bullshit. I just want to know what you know about Blue and what you're right now not telling me. I'm a child finder, and I don't have an Ivy League degree or a classy name. I just know when a guy's tap dancing around his answers."

The man looked past Jack Liffey as if he wished he had an office door to shut. "Madison, would you get us some coffee, pretty please."

"Milk?"

"Black," Jack Liffey said. "Strong."

The men watched each other for a while as the secretary walked pigeon-toed away. "Ah, a secret," Jack Liffey said finally.

His host shrugged. "I have a lovely house on campus here. A beautiful wife, kids well educated and already moved away from home. I'm respected. I teach one class of art history on a subject that I truly love—Mannerism and the winding-down of the Renaissance. The job has many other perks. I'm not a cruel or vindictive man."

"Have you got any daughters?"

"Two, grown."

"How do you think they'd feel about this?"

"Blue was not very stable. I can say that much. She was an older sister, with the father gone and the mom a bit ragged, so she thought she had to hold what there was of a family together by her fingernails—maybe the whole planet. She was responsible for every exotic mustard plant that invaded and interfered with the P.V. Blue's habitat. Have you *seen* how much wild mustard there is?"

He waited for an answer but didn't get it.

"Okay, do you know how attractive some men find that sense of galloping earnestness in a student?"

"You?"

"Oh, heavens, no. This isn't a confession. A couple of my guys, though. They looked on Blue as a kind of saint, or somebody to send out into the world remembering them as a Great Mentor. It didn't hurt that she was cute as a button. The English teacher and the Life Sciences teacher. I'm absolutely, truly, certain that they didn't harm her or ever touch her, but sooner or later someone will point them out with an ugly fable. Talk to them, but, please, keep a sense of proportion."

"Proportion is my middle name," Jack Liffey said. "Oh, wait, I forgot. Belligerent-asshole is my middle name."


It looked like a great day for the surf-inclined, with mammoth waves, some approaching ten feet high, rolling in and breaking toward the left in perfect tubes. A couple of dozen guys were out braving the ride, decorously taking turns and hot-dogging when they caught a good one.

"Wow, this is the best surf I've ever seen outside movies," Maeve said.

She and Imogen sat on the rim of the hundred-foot cliffs above Lunada Bay, a semicircle of a cove maybe a half mile wide with water green as seaweed. Even up there they could feel the retreat of each breaker as a faint rumble under their rumps. "Awesome, girlfriend," Imogen said. "It looks like that famous place in Hawaii. What's it? Some coast."

"We're not dressed for the beach, but let's go down and see if anybody knows Blaine." There were several separate groups of obvious girlfriends sitting on towels. They seemed to have segregated themselves into distinct areas on the sand with no-woman's-lands between them. There was only one girl out surfing, waiting her turn in the lineup like anyone else, but the apparent division into show-off surfers and eyelash-batting babes annoyed Maeve no end.

"You just want to meet some dreamy surfers," Imogen said.

"I've had my fill of guys in general for right now."

"Sorry, Maevie, I forgot."

They started to pick their way carefully down a well-used diagonal path.

# 4

# We Make the Road by Walking

MAEVE ASSUMED THAT THE CLUSTERED GROUP OF VICTORIA'S SECRET–
TYPE GIRLS TOPPED THE PECKING ORDER, SO SHE HEADED FOR THEIR
TOWEL ENCAMPMENT FIRST. All but one were blonde and thin and each
one wore a skimpy solid-color bikini. The likeness was remarkable,
she thought, as if some factory had stamped them all out of a Barbie
mold. Their towels were laid out around an odd hot-dog maker, like
a toaster, that was wired to an auto battery, and an ice chest of beer.

"Excuse me," Maeve said. She could see now that the one with
bright red hair was smoking a joint, which she switched adroitly into
a cupped palm.

"Troll?" one of them said, as if trying to identify a rare species.

"Vals for sure. I bet this one reads books. *Cares* deeply."

Imogen plucked at the back of Maeve's blouse as a kind of warning.

"Do any of you know Blaine Hostetler?" Maeve pressed on
quickly. She had half a mind to throw them the Greenwood gang
sign and promise a terrible vengeance.

No one met her eyes, but three or four of them reacted to the name.

"How do these riffraff get down here?"

"America is a democracy, after all," said the first girl.

"I heard it *isn't* any more."

Another one laughed.

Imogen tugged harder and Maeve gave up. "*Vete a la chingada,*" she said. A parting shot.

A blonde with a barbed-wire circle tattooed around her bicep glanced threateningly for an instant. "Was that something about fucking, cunt?"

"Not really. Talk to me again when you know how to speak the language of the city you live in."

The next clique on the sand were all Asians; they kept their eyes downcast as Maeve and Imogen strode away. Near them was an even smaller bunch, and Maeve made a snap judgment based on the appearance of two of the three. They were Jewish or maybe the intellectuals. The ones who would be scorned as "brains."

A girl with thick dark curly hair, just as drop-dead gorgeous as the Victoria's Secret girls, smiled knowingly for an instant and handed Maeve a slip of paper as she stalked past. She took it automatically and stuck it into her jeans pocket without thinking. They were still no wiser than they'd been when they arrived.

"I tried to warn you," Imogen said as they retreated up the path.

"What disgusts me," Maeve said, "is that every one of those stuck-up *putas* knew the name Blaine."

**Maricruz Olivares**
**Behind Aztec Market**
**Huépac, Sonora**

Dear Maricruz,

*I miss you and the family. It's like a knife in my breast that I must endure.*

*When I first came to* El Norte *our cousin Tizoc from Los Hoyos got me into a one-bedroom apartment on 135th Street in Hawthorne with five* compas. *I wrote you about this but I never sent that letter. There were holes in the plaster and the toilet was always overflowing and the manager was an old Greek who wouldn't fix anything but we did our best. Izek was the official renter for the Greek and we each promised to pay him $134 a month and so that was money I couldn't mail to you and* mamá *and the family.*

*—Muévese, I'd say when it was my turn for the mattress but I could never budge Victor who was always exhausted from stripping wallpaper or plastering overhead. We also kicked in money if we needed to borrow Izek's 1963 Oldsmobile, which was a real smoker, to get to a special job.*

*—Compa, Izek said one day to me. Hang out with me Sunday. You're an educated man.*

*—You going to an opera?*

*—Just the Hawthorne mall. We can watch girls and look at stuff.*

*Mari, it's like looking at the rich man's world through three panes of bulletproof glass. But I didn't say it. I liked Izek, and the mall would be a change. Maybe I could talk him into making a run through the Dumpsters behind the mall. I'd already learned you can get wonderful stuff that way.* Gabachos *throw away anything, the most amazing valuable things, if the things displease them.*

He was told that Mr. Nicholson—Don Nicholson—was away from school with his crew, whatever that meant. At least the Life Sciences teacher had the advantage of a perfectly ordinary name that didn't make him sound like a slave owner from Georgia. A stringy-looking kid with the knot of his school tie pulled down gave him complicated directions to the Lillian Hoffman Land Preserve, which wasn't too far off P.V. Drive North—the road that made a rough square surrounding the whole peninsula, changing only its surname with the compass.

He followed the Little League sign off the road, as instructed, and then took a hard left down a dirt road, bouncing harshly on the springs of his old pickup. He parked beside a stubby yellow bus at an open gate that led into a remarkable sight for these days on the hill: a large open field of completely wild land. As a boy Jack Liffey had hiked all over these hills when maybe three-quarters, or even more, of the land area had been undeveloped. The flatter spots had been tilled as bean fields by Japanese farmers, only provisional tenants now on land that they had worked for generations before being interned at Manzanar during the war.

Today the Palos Verdes Hills were 95 percent house. He had a nutty tendency to think of all change as tragic, but he knew you had to set aside some of your capacity for anguish, so you'd have a little left when the time came for the real losses.

He could see a middle-aged man bent double beside a low outcrop of rocks, plucking at weeds alongside a scattered group of a dozen or so young people. Jack Liffey made his way down a ragged trail toward them. He froze for a moment, almost gasped, as a small silver-blue butterfly fluttered up and then went right past his face. Like a greeting from another world. Then he went on.

"Mr. Nicholson, I presume."

"Yes." The man grinned. "So I was thought to be lost out here."

"My newspaper has spent a small fortune financing this overland expedition," Jack Liffey said, for no particular reason other than encouraging the clumsy cheer of this man, who already seemed likable.

Several of the kids looked over curiously.

"Enough," Nicholson said. "Would that I had the courage for a real expedition to somewhere challenging."

Something about the teacher's appearance put Jack Liffey a little on edge—a geeky softness combined with being in charge of a lot of young people suggested trouble.

"My name is Jack Liffey, and I've been hired to try to find Blue Hostetler." That got the attention of the nearest kids again as the two men shook hands. "Hired by her mother." He could have sworn there was an odd tickle in the handshake, not unlike the headmaster's. He would have to find out somehow what the Masonic grip was supposed to be. It could open a lot of doors for him in the future.

"I don't want you to think I'm in charge here," Nicholson said. "The Native Plant Restoration Project is being run out of UCLA. We're just a volunteer team. Today we're clearing horseweed."

He demonstrated by using a forklike device to lift out a stalk about two feet tall with individual fingerlike leaves below tiny white flowers.

"*Conyza canadensis*. Just another urban weed that's choking the native coastal sage habitat. Inoffensive looking, I admit, but a significant foot soldier in the exotic plant contamination army. Not as bad as mustard, but more prevalent than Bermuda grass or the castor bean." He inserted the plant very gently into a black plastic trash bag, presumably so as not to jog loose any seeds or pollen.

He beckoned and Jack Liffey followed him across the wild field past where the students were all going back to their weeding. "Blue loved this work," he said. "Beyond love somehow. She was obsessed with doing good, but she had that kind of personality. Save the butterfly. Save the world."

"I thought I saw a P.V. Blue when I was walking in," Jack Liffey said.

He nodded. "Not impossible. We've got about thirty of them here now. On this particular twenty-eight acres. The main problem is that the preserves are so small and separated."

They stopped at a tall chain-link fence. Beyond it was a park and several baseball fields, empty now except for a single boy plucking baseballs out of a bucket and shagging flies out to left field.

The teacher pointed. "In 1982, that was the last known habitat of Mr. and Mrs. P.V. Blue. The EPA told the city not to build the baseball fields, but they went ahead and built them. The feds sued but it was all dismissed. The theory is you cannot hold a city liable. I'm not sure why. The naturalists all went apoplectic. They thought the Blue was gone, extinct, until years later somebody rediscovered a few of them flying around in a navy fuel depot down on Western."

"The old navy tank farm?" Jack Liffey said.

"You know it?"

"I know San Pedro." It was time to get back to the human Blue he cared about. He wasn't that interested in the reclamation project or the butterfly. "So the girl was one of your volunteers here?"

"Habitat restoration is a bit more than weed pulling, Mr. Liffey. We get the exotics out, but there's a lot of other amelioration to do. Humans can make quite a mess, and some of this area was a bean field for a long time. Blue was definitely enthusiastic about it all."

Jack Liffey watched him for any telltale twitches at the mention of her name. It was a pretty useless tactic, really, but you had to try. He saw nothing beyond the usual thoughtful concern you'd expect from a somewhat intense teacher talking about a missing student.

"She even came out here in her spare time and did what she could. She'd ask for the gate key before weekends."

"And you'd give it?"

"Sure."

"Did she work on other sites, too?"

"I don't think so. This one's nearest the school."

"And after she'd get the key from you, she'd come alone?"

"As far as I know. And I never heard of any wild parties or buried treasure up here."

Jack Liffey stared hard at him. "You're joking about her as if you expected her to wander in from Vegas any minute."

The man went crestfallen all at once. "I'm really so sorry. But I can't make myself believe she's hurt. Something so splendid should be invulnerable." He was staring down at his shoes—strange orthopedic clogs.

"Tell me about your medications," Jack Liffey said.

Nicholson glanced up quickly. "How'd you know?"

It had, in fact, been a wild guess, but in addition to his other mannerisms, the man appeared distracted, as if watching for things that would materialize suddenly and nobody else would see. And almost everybody was on something, these days. "Antidepressants?"

"I'm okay. Really. Just controlled and dull, to myself and others, the curse of the wonderful world of chemistry. I'm like a Bengal tiger hit over and over with big Thorazine darts. And, yes, I'm gay, but I'm not a pedophile. Are you going to tell the school? I know I should have been more open."

"I wouldn't dream of it. I imagine most everyone knows. And with the meds, your sexual urges are pretty much nullified."

He grimaced. "They're not even in the picture, Mr. Liffey. I'm trusting you with my life here. I've known I was gay since I was twelve, but I can't perform. And I'm too scared of everything even to think about it. Even if you came on to me right now. My last partner left me eighteen years ago."

"Mr. Nicholson, is this a good guy or a bad guy?" a girl with long straight hair yelled, pointing down at a knee-high growth of dusty green leaves.

"Oh, lordy," he said.

"Just stay here now," Jack Liffey ordered softly.

"If in doubt, yank it out!" the teacher yelled back. "I'll be over in a few minutes!"

"What is it you aren't telling me about Blue?"

The man nodded, but hesitated. It took him awhile to get around to an answer. He gave the impression he was checking all points of the compass first, in some ordained system ranging from near to far. "I know Blue brought food here, quite a lot of it."

"Keg parties?"

He shook his head. "Common food. Bread. Big Costco cans of things. Not chips or beer. I think beans."

"Yes?"

"That's it, sir. I never checked up on her. It's not a crime to stash food, I think. Maybe she was a survivalist or preparing for the End Times. I really should get back to the students, Mr. Liffey. I promise you I have not touched anyone at all with unseemly intent, including Blue, and I don't know anything more about her."

Jack Liffey gave him one of his old business cards, with the defunct phone number crossed out and his new 323 number in East L.A. scribbled in. "Mr. Nicholson—Don. You've been a real help to me. Your secrets are safe with me, and if you need my assistance in any way, please give me a call. I mean it." He touched the man's shoulder for a moment affectionately. Real losers always held a kind of sway over his emotions.

The teacher stared hard at the card, as if it might have a hidden danger imbedded in the tiny print. "Gosh." A loud buzzer went off somewhere, and the teacher started back toward his pupils.

Jack Liffey set out to make a search of the field. It appeared to him to be about the size of three large city blocks, though so irregular, with the land rolling up and down, that it felt a lot bigger. He took a footpath that appeared to lead to the far corner of the field, cleanly trod through the weeds. The hard meandery path reminded him of the half-forgotten title of a book he'd read many years ago, *We Make the Road By Walking,* an expression that seemed wonderfully appealing, though he wasn't quite sure why.

Hearing a beckoning call in the distance, he looked up and saw the kids assembling to return to school. He figured he could climb the fence if he got locked in, despite the fact he was no longer as spry as he'd once been.

The path ran irregularly downhill, avoiding outcrops and the larger shrubs, to follow the line of least resistance. It branched off here and there, but he stuck to what was obviously the most used choice. It'd be a good start on a thorough search if the path took him to the farthest point of the lot, and he had a hunch that might be all he needed. He'd expected to see a few more P.V. Blues fluttering up along the way, but none appeared. In the distance behind him, the minibus started up.

*A line of poetry by Antonio Machado, but better known as the title of a book that was a record of a long political conversation between the radical Brazilian author, Paulo Freire, writer of* The Pedagogy of the Oppressed, *and the legendary American organizer, godfather of the civil rights movement, Myles Horton.*

The path turned aside at the lip of a steep gully, but he could tell not everyone on it had turned aside. Dislodged dirt along a faint trail suggested that there had been a regular amount of foot traffic down the ten feet or so into the bottom of the ravine. On the far side of the ravine was the chain-link fence that bordered the preserve, with a tall clipped hedge beyond that, crying out its role in civilization. He knew that the gully below him would be dry 99 percent of the year, but the wet season was almost upon them. The arroyo took a right turn ahead where dense chaparral plants made it into a hidey-hole at what must have been the eastern margin of the fallow land. The gulley probably passed under the fence to somewhere out there, but he could not see past the shrubbery.

Jack Liffey stepped cautiously over the rim of the gulley, his toes hunting for roots and stones to help give him purchase as he descended. One rock broke loose under his shoe and sent him into a panicky high-step down the bottom of the slope. He caught himself against a small invasive eucalyptus at the bottom that the native plant-lovers hadn't gotten around to chopping down.

Past the tree, past more shrubs that he saw now had just been piled up as a barrier, were the remains of an encampment. Cardboard hovels, black plastic lean-tos, a firepit, and random detritus. He stooped and fingered an empty can of refried beans that was just beginning to rust, and it was hard to tell how long it had been abandoned. How many dews did it take for a dented can to begin to oxidize in a dry climate? Sherlock Holmes would have known to the hour. There were no possessions here, so the camp had clearly been abandoned for some time.

But he knew what he needed to know. A dozen or so domestic

servants from the homes hereabouts had been living here, probably unable to afford anything to rent within miles, though it wasn't too far to Walteria, Lomita, or Harbor City, which had become far northern suburbs of Sonora and Chihuahua. Still, he knew the rents in those areas probably approached $700 a month or even more for a one-bedroom apartment. Even sharing, five to a room, would eat up a pool boy's wages fast. And he guessed that Blue Hostetler hadn't just been championing the cause of threatened butterflies.

He wondered if any of those who owned the big comfortable homes nearby had realized that their yard boys and maybe even their maids had been living rough in makeshift hovels not so far away. Probably not. They weren't utterly heartless. Though they rarely even knew their servants' surnames.

A rough trail led up the opposite slope and some dirt had obviously been dug away under the fence, as if a big dog had been desperate to get out. He fought his way up the slope, flattened himself reluctantly to the ground in order to wriggle under the fence. He then pushed up and out through a burrow torn out of a hedge. His head emerged from that green-frog's-eye world into a grass borderland between two large houses that stood only a few feet from a tidy street without sidewalks.

He fought his way out from under the hedge onto the turning circle of a short dead end and walked past several outsized ranch homes to where the cul-de-sac met another road just so he could read the street sign: Silver Bridle Lane. Just for reference.

Now he knew he had to look into the world of Latino day laborers—and probably their nemeses, too, which added up to an awful lot of people.

**Dear Dad,**

 *I pretended I wasnt scared but its not true so I went to a doc. I just want you to give me the damn test I go really loud.*

 *He goes calm down son. Is there any reason you want to be tested? Do you have any risk factors?*

 *None of your business I go.*

 *Dont worry son he goes. Its all completely confidential. The law requires that I keep it that way.*

 *So I go just stick me then. Jesus how many ways can I tell you to stop treating me like a pussy. I dont suck dicks I dont use no needles for drugs. I just want the damn test.*

 *Will do he goes finally. Ill get it myself so the nurse doesnt have to know. Happy? You PV kids pretty much get things the way you want dont you?*

 *You said it doc.*

 *He was starting to piss me off badly. Mom is still giving me the name of your lawyer when I ask for a address. You got to send me a address dad. Please! You can even send it to the guy named Ledge at the Chevron station you used to use.*

Jack Liffey looked down from the cliff at the greenish sea but there seemed only ordinary waves. All his life he'd heard how good the surfing was at Lunada. It must have been good earlier in the day because a dozen boards were lying there, and twenty young people were eating a late picnic among them. Most of the girls were blond and thin, of course, wearing sweatshirts or boy's shirts against the afternoon chill. The guys were all toughing it out bare-chested. It was a good hundred-foot descent to the beach and he thought twice about going down there since his heart had begun to thump back at him these days whenever he made serious demands on it, and he definitely didn't want to have to go to a doctor and check it out.

Jack Liffey sighed and started down. His heart could just tough it out. The boys were passing around unmistakable tall clear bottles of Corona and eating hot dogs. All we need, he thought, is Norman Rockwell painting away off to one side. California Picnic. Children of the Waves. But he had no faith at all in the innocence of appearance, especially among kids as far up the social scale as these. P.V. Blue, indeed. He'd seen plenty of innocent-seeming butterflies at the corner of his vision snap over into wasps when he focused.

One of the girls, noticing him approaching, gave a warning. Many eyes came around.

When he got close, Jack Liffey flashed his badge wallet. For many years he'd carried a plastic mail-order badge from New Jersey, but the silvering had finally begun to wear off the edges to show orange plastic underneath and now he'd bought a much better replica FBI badge and ID from Japan. If you looked close, though, the ID card said Special Agent Fox Mulder with a fuzzy photo of David Duchovny. But nobody ever looked.

"Special Agent Liffey," he said.

"Fuck you, Liffey," a crewcut boy said. "Any of you feds *super-duper* special agents, or just *normal* agents?"

Jack Liffey did his best not to smile as he squatted to put himself at their level. He'd said just about the same thing himself several times so he could hardly complain, but he kept himself grim. "*We* ask the questions. I want to speak to Duke Manning and I will speak to him. If we all have to go downtown to sort it out, we will. You don't want to be on my bad side, believe me. Duke can just raise a hand and save his friends a lot of aggravation."

A square-jawed eighteen-year-old with a long scar on the side of his chest handed off a beer bottle to a friend. "I'm Duke." The voice was lazy and impudent.

"Fine. Let's have a brief chat over there, and then you can get right back to your picnic."

"Don't go, Dukester," a girl put in. "He just wants to bust your balls. Or lick them."

"And you're the sensitive type," a boy called and stifled a laugh.

Without looking back, Jack Liffey walked confidently to a rock outcropping at the foot of the bluff that would be out of their earshot. He could see it would quickly devolve into a dick-waving contest if he wasn't careful. He sat on the outcropping and saw Duke swagger toward him, working hard to build up an attitude for himself. He had to do something to put the boy off-balance right away.

Duke stopped a few feet away and Jack Liffey looked over at the others, watching them for so long that his prey began to fidget.

Finally, after a long enough silence to unnerve the boy, Liffey started talking between clenched lips. He did his best to channel Bogart.

"I promise if you don't talk to me right now, you'll find yourself hanging upside down over a water tank on the sixth floor of the Federal Building in Westwood with a big rubber hose shoved up your ass. Eventually you might get to like it. Tell me about Blue Hostetler."

"Huh! There's no Blue here."

"You two hooked up at a party. Start there."

Duke tried not to look surprised. "Shit, man. The bitch stalked *me*. She's from another galaxy. We weren't an item or anything. She wanted to be Bayboy pussy, that's all—she was all the time going on about us. Sure I made it with her, in the head, but she said she'd do anything I wanted if I'd pretend she was my girlfriend, and she could come down here and watch." He grinned unpleasantly. "After she blew me I told her to fuck off and die. I hate groupies."

The late-afternoon light was reddening as the sun slumped gradually into a bank of smog that Santa Ana winds had pushed offshore. Gulls swooped and squawked, going pink in the dying sun. It was a radioactive world.

"Did you see her after that? Don't lie. I know."

"Just when she, like, followed my car. She even had binoculars on me. I shoulda called the cops on her—maybe even you, Special Agent Shitty."

Neither of them said a word for a while, mad-dogging each other. Silhouetted against the dying red sunlight, the boy's face was contorted in some way Jack Liffey couldn't make out, and then abruptly the boy craned his neck and howled softly up at the sky.

"Sometimes I just wish everybody in the world would die." Duke seemed to have turned a little more serious. "I get so fucked-up-feeling inside I could scream. That cunt was a hundred percent goof, man—the way she *cared* about everything. Butterflies. Trees. Mexes. Why's any of it her business?"

"You tell me," Jack Liffey said.

"It's never going to be like it used to be," the boy burst out with an emotion that sounded almost like real anguish, then turned on his heel.

It never had been that way, Jack Liffey thought.

A big bird dived eerily across the bloodred sun approaching the ocean surface, a pelican that didn't stop until it splashed into the rusty water. The surfer group made a place for him as their champion returned.

Jesus Christ, Jack Liffey thought. Where did such privileged kids come up with so much resentment?

The climb back up the cliff, even trudged out in carefully allocated portions, really winded him, and he wondered if the smoking he'd done in years gone by had left his lungs more damaged than he knew. Then again, he'd had a collapsed lung for a while, too, and that undoubtedly contributed. He could hardly complain. No matter how much you hoped for a special dispensation out of life, you were really only an accumulation of the indulgences you'd let happen. Bending elbow and chasing skirt, for example, both of which he had banished from his life now. If only to prove he had the willpower.

He took a minute or so to recover his breath at the top of the cliff. He found the pickup where he'd left it, but not *as* he'd left it.

A deep scratch in the white paint on the curb side traveled all the way along its original paint job, from just behind the headlight rim to the tailgate. He might have ignored that, but from the same taillight forward someone had scratched in large letters, **FUCK OFF OR D**

The **D** bothered him more than the rest. He wondered if he'd interrupted the artist at his work.

Gloria was several sheets to the wind when he got home, he could tell, even though she held it well.

"I figured out what life is all about today," she said with a strange smile. "It's about making the beer taste better. I mean—*sorry*, doing the right thing and all that stuff. Being part of something bigger. Peps up your satisfaction." She didn't look very satisfied.

"Sure," he said warily. "I used to want to feel part of something bigger, too. I think there's a lot of people out there feel like that, but they don't find each other much. But that was all then for me."

"You trying to say something?" Gloria said, annoyed. "About me?"

"Not in the way you're thinking. Just because I don't drink doesn't mean you can't. You have plenty of good karma, that's a fact."

She thought that over, but wasn't really focusing.

"Actually, I'd like to talk to you about some day laborers. Down in Palos Verdes."

She frowned at him, then sucked down the last of her beer and sighed. "Hold off your poor *jornaleros*, please. This is still my turn. Siddown, Jackie."

He didn't like the sound of that, but he perched obediently at the edge of the threadbare sofa. "Ten-four," he said.

"No jokes. No police codes. Not even a smile, okay?"

Now he was getting worried.

"I'm sorry, Jack . . . Loco's really really sick. *Really really* sick. Maybe a kind of cancer, the vet says."

After whatever his overactive imagination had been concocting—Maeve's sudden death by auto or a diagnosis of the big C for Gloria herself—he was ashamed to be a little relieved. And then his affection for the dog hit him like a big stone from very high. Loco had been with him almost ten years, through thick and thin. Always tugged by the call of the wild, the dog had never fled or betrayed him when it'd had the chance. And Loco and Maeve adored one another.

"*Cancer?* Aw, fucking shit."

# 5

# Tough Hombres

A BAD NIGHT. Did he need to define it any further than that? Weren't all bad nights the same, and each good night good in its own way? Indigestion, restlessness, long periods of insomnia, then nightmares. Gloria was doing her three days on, four off schedule, like most of the LAPD, which meant mind-numbing twelve-hour shifts, and she was long gone when he got up, her silvery nightgown flung over the chair. After they'd fought a bit the night before, they'd tried to make love, but the jangly emotions they'd unleashed had gotten in the way, and she'd rolled away from him finally.

It hadn't been much like real sleep, and toward morning he'd dreamed about Loco, the poor dog gone radioactive and whining for help. Jack Liffey felt absolutely wrung out with the afterburn of the nightmare and he sat down with coffee and the *Times* to try to reclaim the day. Redesigned for the fourteenth time to try to interest teenagers, the paper now looked like a gigantic ransom note with subheads dribbling off subheads in the most amazing fonts.

The front pages were depressing so he started halfway in, and on page A14 a small item caught his attention. A charred body had been found in the ashes of a small brushfire in Palos Verdes. They were having trouble with identification but a county fire department spokesman said they thought it was probably an illegal immigrant who'd been camping in a ravine, and he might have touched off the dry brush himself with an illegal campfire. He got out his Thomas Bros. mapbook, but the fire had been on the south slope of the peninsula, nowhere near either Lunada Bay to the west or the butterfly park to the north. He sat up straight, all at once imagining a desperate flight from fire and then a charred body and the pain and fear involved. He'd been singed himself, running from a rampaging Malibu wildfire, and he could feel for the poor guy, in deadly jeopardy so far from home.

Jack Liffey wondered how many of them—houseboys and gardeners and pool boys—were camping out in those hills. He'd seen South Africa briefly during his long-way-'round return home from Vietnam in 1969, and at least there they'd provided little hovels behind the big opulent houses for the help. He tried to imagine living rough in a black plastic lean-to in a ravine (a ravine that would run with muddy water in the winter, a season that was coming fast) and then cleaning up somehow every morning to walk to a sumptuous ranch house and make a cheerful appearance before mopping the red tile floors or trimming the hedges. He couldn't quite picture the mechanics of that life. He made a mental note of the fire department spokesman, a guy with the unlikely name of Dick Friend. Ricardo Amigo.

When he couldn't put it off any longer, he set out for the vet's.

"Liffey? Hold that thought." She was a slatternly looking woman in a blood-spattered white coat and a cigarette in the corner of her mouth that dribbled ash down the coat. Dr. Griffin. A mythical beast for sure.

She went into some back room and then returned. "Loco is that yellow part-coyote?"

"That's the lad."

"We did a biopsy, then had to sedate your pal a second time to get him into the recovery pen. He doesn't take to enclosures, does he?"

"He does trend toward panic."

"He's sleeping it off right now. This is my night on, if you want to come back about eight. We'll know more then. Frankly, you should prepare yourself for baddish news."

Fuck you, he thought. He was offended by just about everything about her, but he'd been told she was good at her job. You couldn't have given me one more day of false hope, could you? he thought.

Outside, he sat down for a moment on the window ledge. Loco had been with him through a lot, several homes, several women he'd loved. He thought of a couple of times, after tragedies of his own, how he'd taken Loco for a walk and, hugging the dog to him, had felt that rapid heartbeat. He'd wondered if that's what it was about dogs that used time up so much faster for them. Seven times faster, they said. A calm-looking woman nodded to him as she got out of a black SUV carrying a cat in a box, and he had to look away to hide his tears.

Maeve had alerted her mother to the fact that she'd emerged at last from seclusion and mourning, and that flat foods would no longer be required. She was just glad her mom had never resorted to prosciutto. She was trying to come up with a way to help her dad penetrate the secrets of the surfers, which she knew he'd never be able to do on his own.

She and Kathy had a civilized breakfast—no recriminations—

and talked about college choices. For some reason Kathy wanted her to go to Cornell or Brown. Maeve was fixated on Reed, UCLA, or the local El Camino Community College.

"You need to pump up your ambition, hon. Harvard or Yale, if you wanted, meet some of the best minds of your generation."

"I don't want the same things as everybody else."

"Don't tell me El Camino has a private-eye major?" Kathy asked suspiciously.

Maeve laughed. "I'm sure they have law enforcement, but that's a fish of another color, or something. If any Ivy League offer comes in, I'll definitely throw an *I Ching* on it, don't worry."

"Don't you dare."

"I'll give it *serious* thought." With everyone prodding at her she'd gone through weeks of hell to write up forty-two college applications, and it had cost her parents almost a thousand bucks in fees. She couldn't even remember today why Ohio State had been on the list. Relatives of her mother? She'd kill herself with a hatpin before going to a football school.

All her friends were in the same fix, only some had it down to a half dozen schools, while a few were focused on one or two, and a couple even had early admission. She had some of those, too, but nothing she wanted. It all made Maeve a little sick to her stomach. Her dad had promised to get her into the East Orange, New Jersey, school of bail bonds and divinity. He said he'd kept the matchbook cover with the offer. But that was for laughs. His real alma mater had been Long Beach State, or as they preferred now, Cal State Long Beach.

"What are you thinking of these days?" Kathy asked.

"Honest, mom. I don't have a clue. There're good people everywhere."

"There're better people some places," her mother insisted.

"Look who didn't go at all," Maeve said, in a spasm of mischief. "Hemingway. Mark Twain."

"I hope you're not planning that. I'll blame your dad and strangle him."

Maeve laughed. "Or kick the dog. He's a bad influence, too."

**Maricruz Olivares**
**Behind Aztec Market**
**Huépac, Sonora**

Dear Maricruz,

> *I want to tell you about a time when I was still living with Izek in the apartment in Hawthorne and he took me to the mall. We sat on a bench eating things they called tacos that weren't what you and I call tacos. They were some strange hard U-shaped sandwich wrapped in big sheets of wax paper. The ingredients had no flavor at all and the dry shell kept snapping and letting the food fall out. Izek emptied many packets of what was called Super-Mex salsa over his to give it some flavor.*

> *—Sorry, Jaime. I made you get the Superama Taco as a joke. I knew it was* mierda.

> *I wrapped the paper over twice and pounded the whole mess on the bench. Then I scooped up edible-looking food with pieces of the shell.*

> *—Next time we'll get the burrito. It's almost acceptable.*

> *—Claro, compa.*

> *—Hey, eyes up.*

> *Two little Mexicanas in short shorts wriggled past us and one glanced over at us with a sly look.*

> *—Qué transas, chicas?*

> *The girls laughed dismissively.*

—*Come back and see us, one said in English, when you've got the cowshit off your boots. They both thought that was hilarious.*

—*I'm not wearing boots, I called. But I can kick your impolite little asses.*

*They giggled and hurried away.*

—*I'd like to do something else to those asses, Izek said.*

—*They can tell we're new here, is it? I asked.*

—Claro que sí. *So what? Their* pocho *Spanish really sucks when they even try to use it. El churcho. El trucko. Huacho out!*

*We dumped the remains of our meals into a barrel and walked through the mall. I had been attracted for some time by a long storefront in the distance that said Surf City. As we got close, I could hear the sound of water and squeals. Dark windows along the side of the hallway allowed us to look into a long narrow pool of water. There was something like a paddle wheel to make waves. Two boys in baggy shorts waited in the water on short surfboards until a bell rang and then they started paddling hard. The machine chugged and slowly came to life and the paddle swung around to send a big wave after them. One boy fell off but the other got to his feet and rode along for about two-thirds the length of the pool. Before he, too, fell off, he threw out his arms and howled.*

—¡Ay, que padre! *I want to do that, I said.*

—*You see any* carnales *in there, friend?*

*I didn't answer him.*

—*Let's go, man, Izek said. This is* gabacho *stuff. Maybe I'll get a new shirt at the Macy.*

*On the way home, I had Izek stop the car in the alley behind Surf City and I saw it right away, poking out of the big* basura. *I lifted the lid and tugged it out and saw that part of the back end had snapped off. It was as if a giant knife had carved away some of the*

*surfboard from the middle to the rear. Beneath the shiny hard white*
*skin, it was like some weird fruit, all foamy and rough.*
*—Come on, man. That's all* desmadre. *It's no good no more.*
*I ignored him and climbed up on the Dumpster and dug through*
*the cardboard and rotting food. Like a miracle, after I crossed myself,*
*I found the broken piece. A small shape was missing, but it almost fit.*
*—Mi plancha de* surf, *I said. I will be your doctor.*
*Mari, I don't know why I am telling you so much and I never*
*send these letters. Some day I will or we will visit again. I know that.*

Jack Liffey found that the county fire department offices were only
a couple of miles east of Gloria's house, up a hill in City Terrace. So,
because he hated to conduct business on the telephone for a whole
variety of reasons—not the least being that he couldn't see the other
party's face and judge the effect any necessary lies were having—he
drove over to the aging headquarters to see if he could talk to Dick
Friend. But the public relations chief was apparently out on location
with an arson investigator, down in Palos Verdes. The dead illegal had
turned into one of those five o'clock TV news topics, repository of the
short-memory outrage of the city, and so PR was needed on-site.

When Jack Liffey got to the blackened hillside off Crenshaw just
after noon, a Channel 9 truck was pulling down its big cherry-picker
microwave antenna. They insisted on doing at least one report live
these days, even if the news was a day old. He guessed it proved to
the public that the prettier reporters weren't just tarted up cheerlead-
ers but were actually working. Several men were wandering across
the scorched hill inside a yellow keep-out tape. They were wearing
full yellow fire department slickers and helmets that said ARSON.
One of the reporters and her cameraman were lugging equipment

back across the seared land to an SUV with the KCAL 9 logo on its door. He parked uphill of a red fire department Chevy Suburban and walked discreetly around the outside of the tape, sidestepping down carefully into a shallow canyon, until he could hail the fire hats who were farther down the ravine.

"Gentlemen! Is Dick Friend there?"

One of them looked up and appraised him. At that range he looked far too small inside all the gear he had on. Jack Liffey must have passed muster, for the man began to trudge uphill. When he got close, Jack Liffey could see that he wore civvies under the unfastened slicker, and his fire helmet said PIO. Public Information Officer.

Friend shook his hand in a distracted way and let Jack Liffey explain about the missing girl and the butterflies and the attempts to restore natural habitat in areas just like this all around the hill.

"Do you think this was one of the . . . what'd you call it? . . . exotic-plant contaminated zones?" Friend asked. He looked around at the charred hill. "Hard to tell now."

"Well, take those two," Jack Liffey said, pointing. Just outside the burn area there was a large bushy elephant-ear plant that was unmistakably castor bean, and a skinny green seven-footer with little white trumpet flowers. "I grew up in Pedro and hiked up here, and my mom warned me in no uncertain terms about those. Castor bean and tree tobacco. They're both poison. I heard they only grow on what the naturalists call disturbed ground."

"I guess you could consider this ground pretty disturbed." The man looked sadly at the burn area. A few stumps remained, but the rest was soot-coated dirt with a few stone outcrops. "I really hate fire, I mean it. I used to be a reporter, and after covering the things for years, I decided I wanted to work for the good guys."

"Everybody likes firemen."

"Fire fighters," he corrected.

"Not to mention that civil service benefits are a whole lot better than those on a newspaper," Jack Liffey suggested.

"You said it. Do you have any reason to think the girl you're looking for is connected to this site?"

"Can you tell me why you think it's arson?"

"I'm sorry, I can't. That information is confidential."

Jack Liffey shrugged. "My wife's a cop. I can find out what I need to know without getting you in trouble. Are you sure the body found here was an illegal?"

"It's hard to know for sure, but the stature and the bad dentistry and the buckle of a cheap plastic belt from a ninety-nine-cent store suggest it. Does that matter to you?"

"I have an intuition. If it helps you any, I think the girl I'm looking for was bringing food and other supplies to the encampments in these hills. Are there any official guesses how many houseboys and laborers might be living up here?"

Dick Friend watched him for a few moments. "There's not much empty land left, except down the ravines where you couldn't possibly build a house. And the landslide areas where they've cleared the homes out. I've heard people say there might be two hundred illegals here, maybe more. They camp in pretty primitive conditions."

"I had no idea they were here."

Friend blew out a long breath. "You know what it reminds me of? It was a long time ago, but not that much has changed in immigration. In 1928 when Mulholland's Saint Francis dam north of the city collapsed, and all that water took off down the Santa Clarita River bed, something like five hundred people died in the small towns along the river, like Santa Paula. But they've been finding remains as late as 2002. We know hundreds of farmworkers were camping along the riverbed. Mostly their bodies were swept out to sea."

"Jesus. Do you know Woody Guthrie's song, 'All They Will Call You Will Be Deportees'?"

"No."

"Never mind. Do you think anybody tries to hunt these guys down to bring them any services? County people, school people?"

"I doubt it. If you owned one of those houses, would you care very much where your gardener lived?" They both looked around at the ridgeline where he'd pointed. The big homes crowded the edge, their guest houses and pool houses and garden sheds all having great views of their own.

Jack Liffey didn't know how to answer him.

"Listen, we aren't a very nice people anymore in this country. It's what I learned working on a paper. And it's why I'm at the fire department now. They're mostly pretty good guys."

"I want better of the rest of us, too," Jack Liffey said. "Something went wrong, I'm sorry. I don't know what. If I were still young, I'd probably be full of cries of wrath. What was the name of that Woody Guthrie song?"



He waited in his pickup on a road called Crestview Avenue. It was the winding road he'd discovered intersecting with Silver Bridle Lane after wriggling under the hedge from the butterfly field. From here he had a good view of where a similar dead-end street named Spinning Spur turned off a little farther on. Short of renting a helicopter, he thought watching these stub streets was his best bet when it came to finding one of the encampments. He figured that at least some of the help got off about four, since they probably had to start the day pretty early. It was winter and Daylight Saving Time was over, so twilight was already gathering at four o'clock.

Sure enough, a short, squat Latino carrying a threadbare TWA flight bag soon emerged from the side of a house, heading toward Spinning Spur. But just as Jack Liffey's heart began to thump with anticipation, the Latino walked right past and on down Crestview toward the flatlands a few miles away, the great low basin of the city where the white working class had once lived. It was the part of the complex social geography of L.A. that a British social critic had once called the Plains of the Id*—the place where things are done to people who have no choice about it. These days even the Plains of the Id were gentrifying, and the working poor had to settle for going farther and farther inland or a half dozen sharing a single dilapidated apartment at $1,500 a month.


A Latina emerged from the front door of another house and wearily followed the same course downhill. He began to wonder if he was on the right track after all. Another woman in an ill-fitting print dress came out of a house with a big canvas handbag and waited at the street. A gorgeous redhead backed down the driveway in an Audi and picked her up. He noted that the maid actually rode in front with her boss. It wasn't such a stretch. Even the South Africans he'd talked to years ago had thought of their servants as acquaintances, sometimes even friends. It was ridiculous, of course. How could you not realize the gulf in power and status that made friendship impossible? *But everyone everywhere wanted to be thought of as virtuous.*

*Reyner Banham, The Architecture of Four Ecologies.

Then a thin man walked past the truck, coming from higher up the hill. He turned down Spinning Spur, a road without outlet, so unless he lived in one of the houses there, worth $5 million or so, or had a beater parked down there, he was probably off through the bush. Okay, *amigo,* Jack Liffey thought. I'm on it.

He let his pickup drift slowly out into the mouth of Spinning Spur but already the man was gone. He swung the wheel and gunned down the lane to the end to park with a jolt where the fence over a culvert had obviously been slit halfway up. Through the fence in an instant, he began sidestepping carefully down the slope, noting where the underbrush was disturbed. A police siren whooped in the distance, but nearby there was only wind and crickets and his own footsteps tearing downward through the weeds.

His universe now was a tangle of wild shrubs, trees, and shadows that could have been anything in the gathering darkness. Jack Liffey wondered if they ever played poker down here by the moonlight— perhaps at the faint glow he saw ahead of him. There had to be some way of eking out the long dark nights, and he doubted that they sang Mexican campfire songs. Perhaps they just complained about the assholes they worked for and compared notes on the insults they'd endured. He wished he had Maeve's command of *norteño* idiom. But his very bad Spanish would have to do.

A voice broke the silence, calling up at him softly. He had no idea what it said.

"*Soy amigo,*" he said. "*No soy jura.*" I'm not the fuzz, that much he knew.

He came down very slowly into a faint ring of light from an old kerosene lantern where a half dozen squatting Latinos eyed him with the deepest suspicion. The smallest of them held a Buck knife, point straight up as if it were a votive candle, not exactly threatening him, but reminding him of possibilities.

"*No cuchillo, señor,*" Jack Liffey said. "*Por favor. Soy carnal.*"

"*Hombre,* you can't be saying you're our *carnal* if you're not a Mexican." The English was very good. It was a young man wearing a button-down blue shirt and chinos frayed at the cuffs, like a war refugee from Harvard.

"In my own way," Jack Liffey said with a smile. "*Alviáname. Soy pobrecito.*" Give me a break, I'm nothing. He wouldn't plead special favors just because his daughter had been knocked up by Beto, and that he'd gone far out of his way to rescue a Mexican-American gangbanger once himself. "I want to help you. Do any of you know the *chica de mariposas? Una güerita.* She brought food out here." He was taking a flyer: the butterfly girl. A blonde. "Did any of you stay over by Silver Bridle before the fire?"

"Yes, I did, *hombre,*" the blue shirt said.

Little by little, the men relaxed and retreated to what he could see now were makeshift shelters out at the edge of the weak light, largely cardboard and black plastic.

"*Me llamo* Jack Liffey."

The young man gestured to join him.

"Jaime Olivares," he said, and they shook hands. The young man's hand was limper, less assertive, than an American eighteen-year-old's would have been. He pushed over a small wooden crate for Jack Liffey. It was more stable than the folding beach chair, restrung with rope, that the boy was using. Jack Liffey sat and looked around. Here he was, he thought, in one of the richest suburbs in the United States—maybe *the* richest—in a rude campground with some of the poorest workers in the country. A little cognitive dissonance was always good for you.

"*Señorita* Blue was a *santa, hombre.* She came to many of the camps and brought us food and also soap and disinfectant and medicine. And picture books to learn English. I know English, but others still need to learn. Why are there so few like her?"

"If I knew the answer to that, *Señor* Olivares, I could make a better world tomorrow. This world is full of the wrong people."

The young man laughed. "As I say, I speak English well, Mr. Liffey. Because I've read books all my life."

"Then I need to ask you some questions."

A ship hooted out in San Pedro harbor as it was leaving port, a deep comforting sound that carried Jack Liffey all the way back to his childhood. Walking downhill to school. Playing hide-and-seek in the park. A sound that could erupt at any time in a port town and eventually became a comforting white noise, like a train whistle heard on the prairie.

"Tell me about *Señorita* Blue."

Two other men, squatting on their heels, were talking softly on the far side of the lantern. It was as peaceful here as anywhere in Los Angeles, he thought. Next time he'd bring a bottle of tequila and some food.

"*Amable. Generosa.* She worked without a net."

"*What?*" Jack Liffey said with amazement.

The boy looked sheepish. "I don't really know what it means but it sounds good. Like in a circus? She said it about herself."

"Do you know what danger she was talking about when she said it?"

"I think she knew the police wouldn't like her bringing us food. And many of her neighbors, too. And some really bad men who ride motorcycles. They are all dangerous to those who would help us."

"Do you blame them?" Jack Liffey said. "You have to piss and shit in the streambed, I suppose. And that lamp can tip over and start a fire."

"We dig holes for our wastes. And we are very careful with the lamp."

"Apparently not careful enough."

"Oh, no, Mr. Liffey. We didn't start that fire. It started downhill from where we were. I heard it eating bushes like a lion. David cried out to warn us all, and when we were almost safe, he went back to get something he said was precious."

"Do you know what?"

"Probably his dollars to mail home. A hole with a glass jar in it is the only bank we have."

"What started the fire?"

"I don't know, *señor*, but there are young people here who really hate us. They come at night and yell things and throw firecrackers and sometimes they shoot guns near where we sleep. I think it is a sport for them."

"Have you seen them?"

The boy asked around the lantern, if anyone had seen the *cabron-azos alborotadores*. The Spanish was way past Jack Liffey's abilities, but he made a mental note to ask Maeve later. The gist was clear: bad guys.

"Ramon says he saw some of them once, throwing rocks from a road. They were blonds. Young and tall. Dressed like everyone here."

High school assholes, Jack Liffey thought. Jocks. Probably surfers. Like the kids who'd tormented the Goths at Columbine. But they were Blue's own people. He doubted they'd hurt one of their own. He and Jaime talked a bit longer as the other workers brought out a couple of Sterno cans and began to heat a big tin of *frijoles*. Just as an afterthought, Jack Liffey asked the boy, "If this place caught fire, what would you run back for?"

The boy smiled shyly. He ducked into his low shelter of cardboard and came out with a broken shorty surfboard, which he held up proudly for display. Yellow and red flames had once billowed along both sides, but about one-third of a side had been snapped off. He had that piece, too, but it would never be adequately repaired. Two of the three skegs on the underside had been snapped off.

"You want to fix that?"

"Of course." The boy pointed west. "It is about eight kilometers to the beach with some of the best surfing in California. I work there every day building a wall."

"Jesus Christ, you mean Lunada Bay? The Bayboys would kill you if you went down there."

"I watch them and swim sometimes and they yell names at me. I just ask them which boy wants to die first."

"Well, son, you've got balls." He shook his head, "Listen, that thing will never be much good, but if you want to fix it," Jack Liffey said, "I'll get you some lag bolts and some resin."

**Dad,**

*I come home and guess what moms doing in the dining room with all the old photo albums. Her eyes are puffy. Shes peeling up the plastic pages and taking the photos out one by one. And shes cutting you out of every picture. Theres a whole bunch of little yous on the floor. Shes not too careful and some of the pictures that she puts back still have your foot or your elbow. Its weird.*

*Your the man of the house now Brandon she goes. Shes the only one left except the principal who calls me that horrible name. The gym coach and most of the teachers use last names.*

*And mom goes you got to take care of me now. And all I can think of is the damn test.*

*Brandon would you fix me your special mac and cheese mom goes. You do it so good.*

*I just heard one of the peacocks scream. You know. The curse of PV. It gives you chills just like a baby crying. But you always said you liked them because they validated your revulsion. Have I got it right? What does that mean?*

*Mom I went just now. You got to get it together. What if Im not here one day?*

*Are you going to run away from me? I can see the panic on her face.*

*Of course not. I love you and Ill always protect you. But I might die or something. You got to be able to take care of yourself.*

*Well start a new life soon she goes. Itll be okay. Just sleep in my room tonight. Please Brand. I get so lonesome. Dad are you maybe still in Southern California? Have you got another woman? I know she knows but she wont tell me.*


"I was raised fundy Protestant," the veterinarian said, lighting a new cigarette. "We were told to speak the truth."

She had brought Loco out. He was on a leash, an indignity that Jack Liffey had never visited upon him, and he seemed to be enduring it though he was tugging in a kind of implacable voiceless desperation toward his master.

"I'll remember that." Jack Liffey took the leash from her and let Loco slam flat against his leg.

"With no treatment," she said, "he has a month or two to live.

But he's in pain and it will get worse. Loco has osteosarcoma, a fancy word for bone cancer. It's in his throwing arm if he throws right. A surgical resection can remove the tumor and much of the pain with it, but he'll still have only a month or two to live. It's metastasizing. That mean's it's spreading."

Jack Liffey knelt and pressed his hand to Loco's shoulder. He thought he felt a tiny recoil which might have been from the pain. The dog still made no noise. A wild animal who knew he was stalked by much wilder predators out there in the dark, he dared not reveal weakness.

"If we follow up with chemotherapy to get what we can of the cells that have metastasized, the prognosis is much better. The one-year survival rate is about fifty percent. Not too bad. And the chemo isn't quite like what you know of human chemo. He won't lose his hair and there's much less nausea, which can be partially controlled without having to teach him to smoke marijuana." She smiled, but he wasn't in a mood for jokes.

"The gold standard of chemo for this cancer is a medication called carboplatin. I should say it's the platinum standard, which it actually contains in some quantity so it's quite expensive. This is roughly what you can expect to pay, all in." She handed him a sheet of paper with the prices written out per procedure. It had enough zeroes on it to make him swallow hard.

"The alternative is we can put him down tonight and end his pain."

"Aw, *Jesus.*"

"Would you rather I lie to you?"

"Of course I would. I want you to say everything will be all right."

"Poor man." She patted Jack Liffey's cheek. "Take him home tonight and think about it. I'll give you some pain killer to give him. I've grown to like his spirit. You've got a tough *hombre* here."

"I never knew just how much I liked his spirit, too, until right now."

# 6

# The Jewish Columbus

"I'M THE PERSON YOU HANDED THE NOTE TO," MAEVE SAID INTO THE CELL PHONE HER MOM HAD GIVEN HER THAT EVERY SINGLE TIME SHE LOOKED AT IT, SHE WISHED WEREN'T BARBIE DOLL PINK. "You know, at the beach. With your phone number."

"You were looking for Blue Hostetler and you weren't having a lot of luck talking to the towel girls."

Maeve noted that she knew Blue's last name. "My name's Maeve Liffey. My dad's a detective, and I'm helping him look for her. Would you tell me your name?"

"I'd rather not."

"You know, it's nothing to use a reverse directory. I can find out."

"Ruth. Is that good enough?"

"No. Come on, Ruth. I'm not going to hurt you."

"Ruthie Loew. It just means lion in Yiddish. To most of those boys it just means I'm a Jewgirl."

"So, why hang with them?"

"They're my friends and classmates. Who else do I have?"

"Hey, can we meet and have a girl talk face-to-face? You gave me your number for some reason."

After a long pause she said, "I'm not sure why I did."

"Well, I am," Maeve said. "I think you know things that you feel you have to tell someone."

"If I did, I wouldn't pick a wannabe Nancy Drew."

"I've actually helped my dad a lot," Maeve boasted, and she had. "I could tell you about some of the cases we worked on. Just give me a time and place."

"I don't think so."

"Come on, haven't you ever wanted to be Nancy Drew with her runabout?"

Ruthie laughed. "Who hasn't? But then I realized a lot the stories were written by men and I quit reading them. I don't read men any more."

"Why's that?"

"Because all at once I got this feeling that men don't really have emotions, and I'm tired of wondering what's going on inside them."

"Wow," Maeve said. "You're hardcore. We've got to meet. You need a friend."

Gloria could see Maeve as she pulled up the driveway in her little Echo. For some time now Sunday breakfast had been a ritual no matter where Jack's daughter was spending her nights.

"She's here. You want me to be scarce?"

"No. We're a family. Okay?"

"Stay inside or go out?" Gloria asked.

"Do you mind cooking today?"

"Not a bit. I got all it takes for breakfast burritos and it's nice and quiet out back." It was. *Ranchera* music was still thumping away a few doors down, and a dozen or so crows were going strident in the big sycamore in front, but it was quiet out back. Jack Liffey quickly took himself off to the back yard.

"Dad! Glor!" Maeve came in the front. "Are we breaking fast today or are we not? Hi, Gloria."

"*Buenos, mija.* Jack wants us to eat in this morning. Is that okay with you?"

"Sublime." She hugged Gloria from behind as she fussed with a teakettle.

"Feeling better, are we?"

"Everything's a bit delicate, like I'm made out of crystal, but I'm out of hiding."

Uh-oh, Gloria thought. This would be Jack's call. "Your dad's outside. I'll bring the food in a few minutes."

"I'll help you."

Gloria turned and squeezed her arm. "Go talk to him, hon. Please." She could see the light dim in Maeve's face, like a cloud sliding in abruptly to darken a cabin out on the plain. Maeve inquired with her eyes but Gloria only shook her head and gave her a little push toward the back door.


On the cracked flagstone patio her father was drinking coffee with the disordered heap of the Sunday *Times* scattered on the old iron table. He seemed deep into some article in *Parade*.

"Dad." She kissed his head. "Love you. But *Parade*! Really."

"I always read what the Smartest Woman in the World has to say. I learn something every week."

Maeve noticed Loco lying at her father's feet and hardly moving. "Loco looks like he's run the four-minute mile. Have you been exercising him?"

Jack Liffey put down the *Parade*. "Loco is sedated, hon. Please sit down."

She never liked it when somebody told her to sit down. The last few times it had happened, her father was either at gunpoint or out cold. Gloria appeared with green tea at just this moment. Maeve knew it was too hot to sip yet.

"Thanks, Glor."

Gloria practically ran back into the house. She had the big flour tortillas set out, and some frijoles, a half dozen eggs to scramble, some chorizo, onion, green pepper, tomato, cheese and salsa. She felt relieved by the sizzle as she began to sauté everything but the eggs and cheese. Maybe she wouldn't hear too much. Before anything else could go in the frying pan, though, there was a hopeless wail from the patio, skirling higher and higher until it broke off.

Gloria stood with her head bowed over the fire for a while and then turned it off and went out to find Maeve collapsed over the dog and Jack on his knees trying to hold his daughter. The surgical price list was open on the patio table.

"We'll find the money. We'll get it," Jack Liffey was saying.

"You can have my car!" Maeve bawled.

"That won't be necessary."

Gloria knelt and rested a hand on each of them. "I've got a piece of property in Owens," she said. She'd been dreading this. "We'll see what it's worth."

"Not necessary. I'll find it," Jack Liffey insisted.

It was early Sunday afternoon, and the do-it-yourselfers were swarming Home Depot, dodging one another's plywood sheets on wobblewheel carts and backed up six deep and demanding at the paint mixers. Jack Liffey was still shaken from the scene at home, but, hidden away in the lightly attended hardware section, he was considering his options. In the end he picked out three ten-inch lag bolts and then found a quart of resin, a little squeeze bottle of MEKP catalyst, and some glass fabric tape. He didn't know much about using it all, but he knew enough. He had his fully charged drill out in the car, plus a selection of hand tools.

A half hour later he was parked on Spinning Spur and cramming everything into a canvas carry bag to get it through the fence and down to the encampment. It was an adventurous descent with the heavy bag held over his shoulder so he didn't topple forward. Occasionally he had to remind himself that he was sixty now, and all the Superman illusions at last fled to cower somewhere else, perhaps another world where there were no swollen prostates or arthritic joints. Down in the camp he found half a dozen men, none English speakers, chatting in the shade. He learned that Jaime was gone somewhere, but, when they realized why he was there, several of them offered to help him get started on the board. One man who wore a strange white scarf like a World War I ace watched very carefully as if he would be tested on the procedures.

Jack Liffey drilled holes longitudinally through the broken fragment of the board and into the core of the shorty surfboard itself. The drill was long but nowhere near fat enough for the big lag bolts, and they took turns widening the holes out with a tiny rat-tail file. He used a countersink and rasp to make much bigger holes for the bolt-heads. Then he mixed up a bit of resin and hardener and dribbled it down the holes. He buttered up the joint surface and cranked the bolts home with a socket set. They put the board aside for the resin to set, and they all laughed and joked about something, probably a lot of it at Jack Liffey's expense.

He hadn't forgot the tequila, and they were very appreciative as he brought it out of the canvas bag and mixed it into plastic glasses of flat Coke that they poured from one of those big plastic cylinders. He excused himself as best he could with talk of *el doctor* and drank the warm Coke straight.

In his miserable Spanish, he asked them the easy stuff, where they were from and about their families. *¿De dónde, señor? Y usted.* It turned out that only two villages were represented, though they were a long way apart, something in the *cientos* of kilometers. Huépac, Sonora, he thought he remembered as the boy's hometown, and two more of them were from there, also. Four others were brothers and cousins—if *primo* meant cousin—from La Perla in Chihuahua. No work. No land. No farm. Many children. Wives. It wasn't surprising, but it humanized the whole story. He wondered if he'd have the courage himself to cross an international border illegally into a hostile land where he didn't speak the language. Maybe he would, if Maeve were going hungry. And if a lot of others had blazed the trail for him.

Luckily, Jaime soon came strolling into the camp with two shopping bags of groceries. They'd probably made him their official shopper because he spoke English so well.

"Mr. Liffey, is something wrong?"

All around, the men competed with small secret grins to hide and then tell the remarkable tale about the surfboard that was under repair, and then the one with the scarf fetched it from the fork of a bush where they had left it to set up. The boy understood and looked at Jack Liffey with a kind of surprise.

"You did this?"

"We all did the work. I brought the tools."

He stared at Jack Liffey for a moment as if the man had two noses. "I never thought I'd see kindness like this from a *gabacho*. I'm sorry, that is not the word to use for a friend. North American? How do you say it?"

"I guess we call ourselves Anglos." His father wouldn't have, though, only two generations from the auld sod.

"Ang-los. I have bad dreams about Anglos beating me and locking me up in a jail," the boy said. "But maybe you will cure my dreams." They shook hands with two hands. "Thank you very much for fixing my surfboard."

The men began to distribute the foodstuffs with a kind of practiced certainty of what belonged to whom. There was no arguing or reference to lists.

The boy looked over the resined joint in his surfboard and tested the tackiness with a finger. "Is this finished?"

"Not yet. I'll leave you the materials to do the finish work. When it's hard as a rock, the joint should be sanded and then covered with another layer of resin and glass cloth and then sanded again. Do you know how to mix resin?"

He shook his head and spoke to the man in the white scarf who seemed to reply in the positive.

"Miguel Angel knows how, thank you. Can I do something for you?"

"I guess you can tell me the name of the man who died in the fire at Silver Bridle Lane," Jack Liffey said. He wanted to talk to his new friend Friend again. "I'll tell the people who need to know, and they'll notify his family."

"He was named David Puigcerver Luz." He sighed. "I did not know him well. He crossed himself often, but he told me he was proud also to be a Hidden Jew from Guadalajara. I will write his name for you.

"He said there are many hidden Jews in Mexico and in your state of New Mexico, too, from centuries ago when they were running away from the Inquisition. He said many of them have forgotten completely their history. In his family the only remaining evidence was a toy that he was given from his mother's family. A spinning toy."

"Yes, I know it. A dreidel."

"I don't know very much. I'm from a small village. We have no Jews, but I met one once and he told me that on the exact day Columbus departed on his journey to the new world, Queen Isabella said that all Jews in Spain had to convert to become Catholics or die." He smiled. "And he told me it was a Jew on the ship, Rodrigo, who was sitting up the mast and was the very first to see the New World."

"Ah," Jack Liffey said, smiling. "The Jewish Columbus. That's great."

"Yes, and someday maybe I want to be the Mexican surf champion."


**Hey Dad,**

*So today Mavis goes you were really shredding Twitch.*

*We were all of us shredding and I go pretty cold. But what I dont tell her but I really remember is fucking up and dropping in too fast and screaming into the wind as I almost wipe out.*

*There was a storm ocean all day. The water is that funny thing. Its thicker and heavier than usual and then all at once it gets icy. The surge is strong and quick and perfect for carving and riding fancy if your ready for it. It lifts you up just like good dope.*

*And were on the beach and Rabbit tells the girls how I had to key some more Val cars on Paseo. I hear this from Rabbit like from far away but I dont see it. Know what I see? I see some bigtooth germ with an evil look on its face swimming in my bloodstream. Then all I got is a lonely silence. You know being by myself. People around me are talking and happy but I dont hear them.*

*After a while somebody shouts hooray for Twitch!*

*Our savior keeps us safe from all the dickheads.*

*You can spot a Val anywhere Rabbit goes and then they all start putting in at once.*

*Hes got neon trunks*

*Colored wetsuit*

*Mullet haircut*

*Rusty old car*

*With bumper stickers!*

*Rabbit hits my shoulder and goes they ride with a wimpy bungee cord safety line on their ankle.*

*We all groan and whimper and eek and roll around in the sand.*

*You dont show off goes Ledge real serious all of a sudden.*

*You ride well somebody else continues.*

*And two girls finish the whole truth—*

*And you dont fall off.*

*Pops why have you gone so far away. Are you far away? Im only 16 and Im scared.*


The theme of the overpriced coffee place was cows and it was called—using one of the most cringeworthy possibilities—Udderly Latte. It was in a block of storefronts in Manhattan Beach, decorated with stuffed cows, wall murals of farms, blotchy black-and-white tablecloths, and baristas in Farmer Johns. Maeve wasn't really in the mood after hearing about Loco, but she could handle it. She put in her order at the counter and went out on the street at a high round disk of a table.

"You smell good," a male voice said only a moment after she'd gotten her tea. "May I join you and bask in it?"

A handsome dark-haired boy maybe a year older than Maeve stood there almost radioactive with that sense of rich-boy entitlement that never failed to infuriate her. He wore all the right clothes and was clearly about to take even a no answer for yes when she said, as politely as she could, "I'm waiting for somebody. Sorry. And I'm not wearing perfume. You must be mistaking me for somebody who walked by."

He leaned close to sniff her neck, confident and audacious. "I think it's just a natural wholesomeness you surround yourself with. You're a soap-and-water woman."

She had an urge to shock him. Or maybe just get up and punch him. "*¡Váyase a matar chinches a otras partes!* That means go away, man, now."

"You said a little more than that, I think, Miss Soap-and-Water."

"I said, Go kill your bedbugs somewhere else. I mean it, jerk-off, leave me alone."

He bowed slightly. "I guess I can take a hint. *Cunt.*"

She glared him down the street as he went on his way cockily. Ruthie Loew arrived a few moments later, having held back to watch, smiling now like the Cheshire Cat.

"Bravo. Tight. Direct. Effective."

Ruthie plopped herself down. Maeve remembered the dark wavy hair from the beach, but she didn't quite remember how drop-dead gorgeous the girl was. She wondered if she'd ever tried modeling.

"Hi, Nancy Drew," Ruthie said. "Who was that?"

"I'm sure he answers to Asshole."

"Guys." She shook her head. "Sometimes they're just bored with themselves, you know, and trying to seem interesting."

"Well, I've known gangbangers. Interesting like that I don't need. You can make yourself really sick with feelings you didn't even know you had."

"Whoa, too much information."

"Sorry." Maeve waited for Ruthie to go get an order of coffee, leaving Maeve to ruminate once again on the abortion, and the empty feelings she'd been left with. That time was gone now. Would she ever let herself be that daring again? *I hope you've learned your lesson, Maeve Mary.* She carried her mother's voice around with her for special use.

Ruthie came back with some complex foamy drink in a tall cup. She held out an open paper bag. "Scones. Coconut-raspberry, lemon zest–chocolate, and cinnamon-walnut. You first."

Maeve took the cinnamon-walnut.

"What grade are you in?"

"Eleven," Ruthie said. "I can't escape this hell for another year. So let's talk secrets. But not *those* secrets. What have you got?" Ruthie bit delicately into the lemon zest–chocolate.

A shiny pickup truck came to a stop and idled in the street beside them, its gigantic speaker system thumping away with some rap tirade, like an artillery bombardment. She spoke a little louder: "I'm more interested in Blue . . ."

"We'll get to her. First, I want to hear about you right now. I'm off boys, and what's great about girls is that they aren't boys." She stared at Maeve, with the hint of a smile.

Oh, God, Maeve thought. She's coming on to me. What is this place? What do they put in the drinks?

"Why do you think I gave you my number?" Ruthie tossed her hair out of her eyes.

"Because you care about what might have happened to a girl who's not that different from us," Maeve said.

"Wrong. I saw you coming toward us on the beach and thought you looked smart . . . and maybe hot."

Maeve could see she needed to play this right, or she'd lose her for good. "I'm flattered. I'm kind of down on guys myself right now, but enough about me. What about Blue?"

"Not yet. Let's try double-dare. I tell a secret and then you. I just got Hoovered."

"You mean an abortion? I'm so sorry." She was amazed that it didn't seem to affect the girl at all.

Ruthie shrugged. "My second. How stupid can a girl get, right? Your turn."

Maeve had an urge to own up to her own procedure, but all of a sudden she couldn't.

"Okay, I slept with a guy in a gang and he made me get a tattoo on my breast."

Ruthie grinned. "You've got to show me."

"Someday. I played your game. Please tell me about Blue."

"Okay, I knew her. She was always totally on a mission of some kind. Maybe she found the perfect guy and they rode off to Wyoming together. Or the perfect girl. I tried with her, but she was too focused and intense. Don't get me wrong. I respect all that stuff that attracted her. But can you imagine trying to live with Mother Teresa?"

Maeve smiled inwardly. Ruthie should meet her dad and see if she could handle the intensity he carried around with him. "Would you help me try to find her?" Maeve asked.

"Not interested. I gotta bounce soon."

"Can you give me anything? Information."

"If you talk to people about Blue, they're going to say she fucked Duke Manning. It's true but it didn't mean a thing. I think you should be looking for a guy called Twitch Dedrick."

"Who's he?"

"Just a surfer, one of the Bayboys." Ruthie took Maeve's hand in both of hers and stood up. Maeve rose, too, feeling slightly hypnotized. Ruthie hadn't told her much, but she'd swamped her with feelings, and she had a lead or two. Abruptly Ruthie came around the tiny table and put one arm around her without saying anything and kissed her *hard* on the lips. Surprised, every atom in Maeve vibrated in a way that she hadn't expected. When she felt a tongue probing her lips, however, she refused to open her mouth.

"Don't count it out," Ruthie said with a grin, pulling away.

Maeve was so embarrassed she could only laugh. "You're, like, one of the most beautiful men I've ever met," Maeve said.

**Maricruz Olivares**
**Behind Aztec Market**
**Huépac, Sonora**

Dear Maricruz,

 *I got to tell you about this guy, an old* gabacho *named Jack Liffey. Out of nowhere, he helped me fix my board.*

 *After the man had left our camp, I asked the others what they thought of him.*

 —*Be careful,* amigo. *Nobody is a friend outside* la raza, *Jesus said.*

 —*That* gabacho's *got other* tortas *to fry, Erubiel said.*

 —*I don't know,* hombre, *I said. He didn't have to do all this.*

*I got the board and held it up. I could feel that a drop of the resin on the surface was as hard as a little pebble. Even my thumbnail didn't dent it.*

*—It's strong, I insisted, and I showed Miguel Angel by trying to bend it.*

*Together we sanded it down so the edges would smooth over, but I sanded right through the strong outer surface to some softer stuff inside.*

*—I don't know, Miguel Angel said. It all looks like* mierda.

*—How many times have you played football on the dirt in your old* poblado *with a tied-up ball of rags? It's the player's skill that matters.*

*He showed me how to put down some more resin, then some of the glass tape that Señor Liffey had left us. I guess I was smiling and Miguel Angel said:* No le busques cinco patas a la fregado gato. [Don't go looking for five paws on the crappy cat. —ML.]

*It was true but not very helpful. I knew I almost had a surfboard now, Mari, no matter how imperfect it was. I swear to God, it's all amazing. I wish you could come with me to the ocean.*

Jack Liffey was parked in the upscale shopping retreat of Malaga Cove on the edge of P.V., a fantasy of Spanish-Italian colonnades capped with a garish Neptune fountain. He knew he did this to himself again and again because he refused to buy a cell phone. He seemed to spend half his life haunting convenience stores and gas stations to track down pay phones, and by now he was the greatest living expert on L.A.'s minimall culture. This one had to be the fanciest he'd ever seen, with nary a doughnut shop anywhere—all designer jewelers and pet boutiques and upscale restaurants.

He'd found the phone in the back of a French café so snooty he had to outstare the annoyed waiter after asking if they could do him a nice French hamburger of some kind. Finally he got through to Helen Hostetler. He was calling because he'd neglected to get a phone number for her ex-husband, with whom the Goth daughter Beatrice—Blue's little sister—was living these days. He wondered if his memory was starting to lose it. That was pretty rudimentary information to gather in the first pass, even if he was pretty much still an amateur at the game. (Could you still be an amateur after ten years at it?)

Apparently Blue's dad had had to find a way to outclass Rancho Palos Verdes when he left his wife. They lived in Rolling Hills, the gated city up at the very top of the peninsula's food chain, the richest of them all and the place that, growing up down in San Pedro, he and his friends had made the semimythical seat of all privilege.

When he got there, the guard at the gate looked dubiously at his old pickup, but Jack Liffey had already called through to Sloan Hostetler, who'd been guardedly polite, so his name was on the guard's clipboard. The old man took his time writing out a pass that was meant to rest gently on his dash. This was just the kind of stuff Jack Liffey loved to abominate so he crumpled it and tossed it ostentatiously over the seat into the alluvial accumulation at the back of the cab.

"Wiseguy," the guard said sadly, but the striped barrier-gate went up—if only partway, *just* enough—and he drove under.

You crossed some pretty weird frontiers if you spent your days looking for people in L.A.—driving along Wilshire, for example, and passing from neon-lit high-tech Korea into teeming Central America within a few blocks. But this was like dropping into another dimension. Country lanes that followed the swell of rolling hills. Real goddamn orchards. An honest-to-god *vineyard*. The farmhouses and ranches here were set a long way apart and well back from the road. It wasn't some overcute mimic of a rural landscape, jammed into too little acreage and fleshed out with movie flats. It *was* a rural landscape. Astonishing, he thought. The only thing he missed was a peasant on a bicycle with a baguette under his arm. But a pair of young girls wearing English riding caps cantered blithely alongside the road on magnificent Arabians as if to nail the travel-poster version of the scene to his retina for good.

# 7

# Life Is More Complicated
# Than Any Theory

THE MINUTE MAEVE GOT HOME, HER HEAD STILL SPINNING FROM RUTHIE, SHE GOOGLED AN ESSAY RUTHIE HAD TOLD HER SHE HAD WRITTEN FOR AN ONLINE PHILOSOPHY AND LITERARY MAGAZINE. And there it was. Sampling articles, she could tell that a lot of the magazine was way over her head. Then she sucked up her envy and went straight to Ruthie's piece. It was about fakery and sentimentality—which she defined as "tears of compassion directed at ourselves, for the banality of what we feel." Written by a girl a year younger than herself, and it had been *published* in what seemed a reputable magazine. Maeve bet they didn't know their author was only a junior in high school. Online, nobody knows you're a dog.

Maeve's lips still burned, and she ached to speak to Ruthie again.

"Your first time visiting Rolling Hills, Mr. Liffey?" The man smiled, a handsome forty-something-year-old in the crisp gentleman's jeans that only Europeans usually managed. "I grew up in San Pedro,"

Jack Liffey said. "We hated this place up here, and I guess we didn't even know why."

"What do you think of it now?"

"I think I'm in the Twilight Zone." He pointed to the grapevines, an utterly improbable vineyard of several acres. "Or maybe Sonoma County." Sloan Hostetler had his viticulture stretching out behind an impressive farmhouse that was itself really three farmhouses gabled end to end. Several Mexican laborers were working amongst the vines, prodding and snipping.

"I'll bet I know where your workers live," Jack Liffey said.

"Where? Lomita?"

"Actually, there's tent encampments down some of the *barancas* out there in the hills. Cardboard slums, really."

"I doubt if my men have to resort to that. I pay eighteen-fifty an hour, Mr. Liffey. It's not really a living wage for you or me, but it's damn generous for them."

"What are you growing?"

"Pinot noir. There's a microclimate here that's pretty good for it. We've got chalk in the soil which is good, too, but it's a rebel grape. Often the offspring of a vine will be nothing like the parent, no matter what you do. We'll never match the hills of Bourgogne. Like they said in that movie *Sideways*, 'Only somebody who really takes the time to understand pinot can coax it to its best.'"

"And you have the time now."

He shrugged. "I made my pile so I can kick back, yes. A parasite on the system, as my ex-wife says. I never produced a tangible good, but I never hurt anyone, either. I wasn't an arms dealer or a white slaver. Freight expediting is a useful and fairly benign occupation."

"I don't even know what it is."

"It's about lending large sums of money to tide importers over while we're shepherding their goods through customs. And we got our drop or two of blood when the goods came out the other end. Much of the business was word of honor. Once in a great while we got stuck with a hundred thousand fluorescent T-shirts with the picture of a recently discredited celebrity on them. While some Syrian or Israeli was disappearing into the sunset. It's not what I saw myself doing when I was twelve, but I imagine you didn't picture yourself a private detective, either."

"I'm not really a detective," Jack Liffey demurred. "My practice is limited to looking for missing children. I feel pretty good about it on long dark nights, and it pays slightly better than delivering pizzas."

Sloan Hostetler laughed once, probably not taking him literally. "I don't actually believe my Blaine is in trouble, Mr. Liffey. She's headstrong, like her mother and her sister. The distaff Hostetlers tend to light out for parts unknown in order to declare their freedom, but in the end we all lead charmed lives. In a year, she'll be at Stanford, studying to put an end to all disease. Or whatever."

No one is charmed, Jack Liffey thought, but he saw why someone who had a twenty-million-dollar house and no special skills might think he was, and his family, as well. And from what he'd seen and heard of the wife, "lighting out for parts unknown" was hardly a description of the bitter divorce that this man had reportedly initiated.

"I hope you're right. My own daughter is her age, and I know the troubles that lurk around every corner for girls."

The man nodded as they approached a big solarium that contained a side entrance to the house. "You can speak to Beatrice about her. Unlike her sister, she's right now into the deepest, most intense meaningfulness for what seems to be its own sake. Maybe it's just drama without content. Or maybe it's real. If you figure it out for sure, please let me know."

Jack Liffey thought about Maeve. This guy probably was on the right track about his daughter: in the end, it takes other people to see your children clearly.

"Bea!" the man called into the plant-filled glasshouse. "Come meet the man your mother has hired to find your sister." He cleared his throat as if about to shout louder, but a girl rose up between potting tables not thirty feet away, with dark soil inexplicably marring the tip of her nose.

"No need to shout, Dad." She wore all black—sweatpants and sweatshirt and oversized black Chuck Taylor tennies. "I'm probably a little mad, but it's okay."

Jack Liffey remembered the photo of the drowning Ophelia he'd seen in her bedroom in her mother's house.

"I saw your Ophelia."

He couldn't read her expression. "I put that up a long time ago. I suppose Mom has kept the room as a shrine of the child I was."

"Could we talk?"

"I doubt it. A noble mind is here o'erthrown."

That was *Hamlet*, too. "Yes, this guy's mildly literate," Jack Liffey said. He glanced at her father, a mute request to leave them alone, and, without seeming to mind, Sloan Hostetler just continued on in his confident, prosperous way into the house.

"Sister Blue goes sadly missing," the girl said with an air of false melancholy. "Obviously, you want to talk about the good sister. The bright one. The saintly one. The well-loved sister."

"No. I want to talk about the sister who may be in real danger. Can we take a walk outside?" He pointed at her nose and brushed his own, rather than presume to touch her, and she squirreled away at her nose with both hands and seemed to relax a little as she brushed off the soil. She followed him outside, moping a little.

"Don't you find this an incredibly bizarro world up here?" she said. "I mean, a whole vineyard, for *Chrissake.*"

"Sure. But it can't be unpleasant for the residents."

"Everybody thinks living rich completely obliterates all your worries. Believe me, it doesn't."

"I'm from San Pedro," Jack Liffey said. "What I don't understand is why so many of the kids up here apparently have such a deep grievance against the world. Some of them even seem to be taking it out on the poor. They can't all have cold-hearted dads or evil stepmothers."

She finally smiled. "What was *your* big problem?" she asked. "You know, you probably got over a lot of stuff. You're old. You can look back and say, Whew, I'm glad I'm past *that.* But I still go to school, and I don't know that a whole lot of the shit I worry about isn't going to happen to me. It's all pretty scary. Handsome boys ignore me every day in class. Bad boys try to feel me up—and those are the ones I'm attracted to, unfortunately. I'm scared of being dissed by the popular girls. I'm still the outsider from downhill. My dad's rich, but I'm lonely. Is that so weird?"

She was brighter than he'd anticipated, and it made him wonder about the other sister. They were walking across a patch of overtidy lawn, like a golf green, and she seemed intent on leading him straight ahead into the shoulder-high vines where the crew was at work.

"Could you tell me about your sister?"

"Ah. If I wanted to."

"Do you think she's more innocent than the other girls your age—or less?" Jack Liffey said.

"Ooooh. A loaded question. You probably know that us Goths aren't so worshipful of the idea of innocence. What we yearn for is experience."

"I like the Goths I've met. You seem to be the heirs of the Beats I admired as a boy. Especially Ferlinghetti."

"Some of us do poetry. And some of us just wear black for the fuck of it. All the way down." She turned her back and yanked up her loose sweatshirt for a moment to flash him a frilly black bra on an impossibly shapely bosom. At least one of the farmworkers noticed and kept watching her as they left the lawn and passed into the grapevines.

"That isn't my weakness," he said dryly.

"What is?"

"First tell me yours."

"I already told you, sir. Fear. Fear and loneliness."

"Everyone has those. What have you got special?"

"What am I supposed to tell you—I do Thai stick, black-tar heroin? I do snort a little at parties. I don't inject. Giving blow jobs? *Yawn.* It's all over with, you know, these days—the righteous indignation, the shock. There's nothing left in our tight little world that's considered revolting any more. Somebody you know does *that*, too."

"I can think of some things," Jack Liffey said. "Racism is revolting. Cruelty to the weak. Inflicting pain for your own pleasure."

She looked back thoughtfully at the workers, their brown heads rising and falling rhythmically among the shoulder-high vines.

"Showing off to guys like those who are miles away from their wives," she suggested.

"As if they weren't even there. Nonentities. That's a start."

She stopped as if to study a big grape leaf, but really she was thinking about what he'd said. "You sound like Blue, you know. But I'm not as bad as all that. I guess I'm thoughtless sometimes, but I don't really diss the Mexes or shoot at them."

"Is that standard procedure up here?"

"Some boys brag about it. Mexicans are your standard issue *Other* up here. The blacks are way too cool, you know? The boys brag about what they call 'target practice,' and other stuff."

"What's other stuff?" He was thinking about fire.

"Calling them names to their faces. Sneaking up on where they're working and stealing their cheap radios playing that horrible music. A bunch of guys will walk along in a tight group and force them off the sidewalk and laugh. Mostly they just tell Mexican jokes for hours. 'You know why Mexicans don't barbecue? The beans would all fall through the grill.'" She laughed, but it was a phony laugh and that, Jack Liffey understood, was the point. Still, he had to ask, even if he knew the answer.

"That wasn't Blue's style?"

"God, no." Bea gave a little hop of excess energy and began touching the taut galvanized wire that ran between the stakes to support the grapevines. "I mean, hardly a discouraging word. . . . She was PC from her pussy all the way up. Save the butterflies, save the dolphins, save the Beaners. Oops, sorry."

"Do you think that's a bad way to be?"

Her mocking manner abruptly erased itself, startling him. "I'm so sorry I wasn't born her." Then she turned, and he expected a smirk, not quite trusting any of this. He could see tears in her confused eyes, and then, astonishingly, she ran against him, and he held her as she cried. Drama did run in the family. He did his best to make what could be seen above the vines appear as avuncular as possible.

"I'll find your sister if you'll help me."

She nodded against his shoulder but was too stricken to speak.

"I need to know any trouble she's gotten into. Any kind at all, and the names of any friends who might be holding grudges, or anything you know about local kids ganging up on Mexicans. Trust me. That could be important."

She yanked her head back and stared into his eyes. "Do I *have* to tell you everything?"

"Not really," he said. "But it'll help me, and it might make you feel better."

She led him to the end of the row where a weathered gray bench looked out across the property line to somebody else's orchard, maybe peaches, on a rolling hill. Another imitation Provençal farmhouse was off to the west.

They sat on the bench, and she talked to him for a while but little of it turned out to be confessional—most of it recounted the manifest pains of being the *younger* Hostetler. Oh, you're Blaine's little sister, of course, I see the resemblance, she heard over and over. She's so bright and so very thoughtful. You're *so* lucky to have her as a mentor.

Tales of trying to follow in her footsteps but getting no credit at all for treading up the broken ground. Of course, you start resenting what you really like about her, and you start keeping score. (Blaine never kept score, of course.) And nothing you do in life will ever matter enough to yourself. When you get mad at her, she's gracious about it, and you're brought right down.

Jack Liffey found Bea a pretty shrewd but wary girl, just as he'd surmised after seeing her room. Despite seeming to come clean, she was actually offering a version of their relationship that was fundamentally devoid of any self-blame whatever. When she ran finally down, he said, "It's okay to feel you want to destroy everything about Blue, you know. Deep inside. It's what Cain-and-Abel was about. It's human."

She turned and glared at him.

"When families break up there's always a stormy period," he said. "When mine hit the skids, it was the same. Honest. And when kids try to hold the marriage together, they can get caught up in a terrible emotional spiral. Sometimes it spins off into drugs or self-destructive behavior—or something else extreme. Then there are kids who just learn to hide inside themselves, to watch and survive."

"No question which I am," she said resignedly. "You know, drugs and sex are like a huge Santana that's been roaring through all my friends for years and sweeping away the unprotected."

"Why did Blue stay with your mother and you with your father?"

"I should think that would be obvious. You're a dad. They don't ask very much, and they don't see very much."

"Touché." He nodded. "You suggested you wanted to tell me everything. There's something more."

"What makes you think there's something wicked to tell?"

"Some people are good at confining hurt deep inside in a lockbox they manufacture. You're trying, but I don't think you're strong enough or selfish enough."

She looked at her hands and then out across the fields. "Sometimes I think I am. I look a lot like Blue, you know? Early this year I wanted Duke Manning. He's a Bayboy. I wanted him bad. I got this idea I might have a better chance with him if I was *her*. So I dressed like her and went places where he was. I actually stalked him."

A small helicopter came in low across the orchard and he wondered if this was the way someone around here commuted.

"What does dressing like her mean?"

"Crunchy and organic. Jeans, men's T-shirts. Like I know what composting is. Okay?"

"Then what?"

"I came on to him a couple of times, and he was too stupid to see I wasn't really my sister. He really is a jerk-off. I've heard she crossed his path at a party and he practically raped her once." She sighed. "But I've also heard she had her own reasons for trying to get close to him. I'd like to believe that, because it relieves me of some of the guilt."

"You think *he* made her disappear?"

She gave a shrug. "The timing is right. He hurt her, I'm sure."

"Who would know? Who's her best friend?"

She shook her head. "We weren't close. Not any more. It's all very complicated."

"Life is always more complicated than any theory," he said.

Jack Liffey was sure this was a moment to pull back. Bea Hostetler couldn't tell if she felt sorrier for her sister or herself right then. She reminded him a little of Maeve, brash and sensitive at the same time.

He gave her his card. "Stay in touch, please.

"That big dorky-looking teacher out there is Mr. Nelson from Prestwick. Everybody but the parents knows he's gay and pretty whacked out, too. They say he's harmless as long as he's on his meds. I bet a public school would have canned him long ago or put him in the attendance office counting paperclips."

Two days after their meeting at Udderly Latte—and the kiss that still managed to worry her quite a lot—Maeve had gotten together with Ruthie once again, picked her up at Ruthie's house on the northern slope of the Palos Verdes hills, and driven them to a spot overlooking a slope where a group of teenagers were pulling up plants and sticking in their place small shrubs wrapped in paper cones. Ruthie had promised to show her Blue's haunts.

# LABORATORY REPORT  Confidential

| Req No | | DOB | Fast | Supv | | |
|---|---|---|---|---|---|---|
| NA | | 11/16/92 | | | | |
| Date Col | Draw | Chart ID | Reprd | Spec No | | |
| 11/20 | OK | | | | | |
| Pat Name | | Age | Sex | Provider | Received | Reported |
| Brandon Dedrick | | 16 | M | Dr. M. Girard | 11/22/08 | 11/28/08 |

| Test Name | Result | Out of Rnge | Ref | Loc |
|---|---|---|---|---|
| HIV-1 AB, Elisa | Reactive | | | |

Note: This is a positive test, indicating the presence of antibodies to HIV in your blood. There are a small percentage of false positives. We recommend a retest as soon as possible, using an alternative method.

"It's not my thing, but it was Blue's, for sure."

"Look!" Ruthie said, pointing at the windshield.

"Yikes!" There on the windshield of the Echo, a delicate violet butterfly had landed unobtrusively on a wiper blade, its ghostly white veins glowing in the sunlight on trembly wings.

They both put their heads up to the glass. The wings folded closed, opened, jittered once. There was a perfect double border at the outer edge of the wings, a white rim, then black. It flapped once, then evaporated out of the world.

Ruthie took her hand and held on. Maeve tried half-heartedly to pull free, but Ruthie held tight. "Don't get all bunched. We can be friends. Let the idea seep in."

"Thanks. You know, I read your essay. It was really smart. I have to read it again to say anything."

"Don't bother. Just be you."

Ruthie let her hand go all at once. "I'll call you when I hear a good surf's up. Come get me and we can go to Lunada Bay. I'll show you Twitch's house. And if he's surfing, we can try to talk to him."

"Where does that name come from?"

"From video games. They call all those shoot-the-monster games twitch-games because you're just flicking your thumbs as fast as you can. Or, who knows, maybe he was a spastic."

"You won't believe it," Dick Friend said enthusiastically. "I actually found a Woody Guthrie CD with 'Deportees' on it. But the song's really called 'Plane Wreck at Los Gatos.'"*

*Alas, he couldn't have. To the everlasting shame of the American recording industry, and to the best of my knowledge, Woody Guthrie's only version of this song, on 12-inch vinyl, is no longer available in any form whatsoever, except used.

Jack Liffey had tracked Dick Friend down at his county fire department office in City Terrace, where he was at his desk keying away madly.

"'*Goodbye to my Juan, goodbye, Rosalita,*'" Friend warbled for a moment over the flat-screen monitor. "It's very touching."

"If you let it touch you."

"I spend my days witnessing, when I should be comforting the afflicted. Those big overcrowded apartments burn down and leave the poorest of the poor standing in empty lots clutching a doll and a few rags. I tag along while better men than me put out fires and apprehend the culpable. I'm just the Big Rubberneck at the calamity of others. But that's okay. It's good to let yourself feel for others."

"Many believe otherwise these days. I'll trade you real information for real information."

"Okay, why not?" Dick Friend looked expectantly at Jack Liffey.

"That's not the way it works. I have the name and hometown of your dead man from P.V."

"It's going to get expensive. That's what you're telling me?"

"I just want to know about the arson. Why your guys think it was arson, and who they think might have done it."

"Okay, it'll be out soon enough. We found a road flare at the point of ignition and evidence of an accelerant."

"What accelerant?"

"Uh-uh. There's half. Now you give me half."

Jack Liffey took out the note he'd jotted down and tore it down the middle so it read:

David Pui

Gua


"It's for real," Jack Liffey said. "As far as I can determine."

Friend studied the scrap of paper as if an intense enough scan might reveal the rest of the information. "Okay, man, you win. The accelerant was 2-butanone. I hope that helps you."

"Any suspects?"

Dick Friend shrugged. "We all know the kids up there harass the illegals who're camping out in the hills. A lot of it's just your basic freelance nastiness, or at least so we once thought." He held out his hand and Jack Liffey nodded and handed him:


gcerver Luz

dalajara


"I got it right up there in one of the camps, from one of the illegals. I can't take you to them, but I believe them when they swear they didn't see anything. They suspect rich kids, too, surf punks. They all have stories of getting hassled."

Dick Friend held the two halves of the note together and looked at it thoughtfully. "We'll try to contact the relatives through the *judiciales* down south. Thanks, Liffey."

"What's 2-butanone? It's easy enough to look up."

"Methyl ethyl ketone. MEK. It's an industrial solvent used for cleaning lots of stuff, and it burns like a sonofabitch. The investigator figures about a pint, no more."

It was also the hardener for fiberglass resin, Jack Liffey thought. Surfers. Indeed.

"'You won't have your names when you ride the big airplane,'" Jack Liffey said. He really liked this guy.

"'All they will call you will be "deportees."'"

They'd walked all the way up Greenwood in the dusk to the big car-surrounded Mexican family restaurant where all the cops ate during the day. He'd taken Loco, and then Loco had obediently followed him on the way back down, a bit confused since they rarely went for walks any more, and the dog was probably a bit woozed up, too, given that he was still on the pain pills.

"You know, pal, I've always had nothing but scorn for those old ladies who mortgage their summer homes and sell all their GM stock to get some sawbones to ream out the prostates of their teacup dogs."

Jack Liffey looked around to make sure nobody was lurking in the shadows to hear this one-sided chat. Kids were skateboarding along a cross street and somewhere music was thumping away in polka rhythm. But there was no one nearby but Loco, padding along good-naturedly.

"In a world of sufficient human tragedy, it's obscene to spend large sums of money on a pet. We've both always known this moment might come upon us, haven't we? Well, I guess I better not really speak for you. I don't know much about coyote consciousness at all, and you've become a bit more dog than coyote recently. For which I have to say I'm grateful."

He stooped and hugged Loco's warm flank for a moment.

"You've got to start thinking about turning in your lunch pail, kiddo." The dog leaned hard against him, and Jack Liffey's whole being filled with dread and guilt. He felt heat on his cheeks.

"Yeah, yeah, yeah, tug at my heartstrings. There's just no way, kid. I'm sorry. I'm giving you a walk for old times' sake."

A pop-popping motorcycle with an antique sidecar came down the hill past them, and he thought how great Loco would look perked up in the sidecar and trailing a long Snoopy muffler into the wind.

"We've got a little drive to make now, and I'll let you stick your head out the window the whole way if you want. Don't go begging and pleading, though. I'm hard as nails on this. *Que será será*. You know, I think that might have been Doris Day. She was before your time."

The pickup was waiting at the bottom of the hill, and he only had to pat the seat to invite Loco inside—offered rides had been infrequent enough recently. He cranked the window down, and the whole the way there, the dog thrust his nose and open mouth into the wind, enjoying the ride unself-consciously, the way dogs did everything. Though, as the truck parked, Loco let out one small howl of complaint, as if he knew where he was and what was coming. As luck would have it, it was the slovenly woman vet who came out into the waiting room and looked them both over coolly.

"Hello, Loco," she said. "Strange, but I can't remember your boss's name."

Jack Liffey was weeping too hard to answer. He didn't even recognize his voice when he said, "Fix him."

# 8

# Every Boat Is Looking for a Place to Sink

LOCO HAD COME HOME WITH HIS HEAD VELCRO'D INTO ONE OF THOSE PLASTIC LAMPSHADES THAT WAS MEANT TO KEEP HIM FROM GNAWING AT THE FRESH STITCHES AT THE TOP OF HIS RIGHT FORELEG. Before the surgery, they'd said at worst case he might have to lose the whole leg, but he was fortunate enough to have kept it and to be able to hobble slowly around the house on it. The dog's main problem seemed to be the sudden involuntary stops. Taking his accustomed random route, he would try to brush past a door or a chair, and the collar—thrust forward wider than he was—would catch suddenly on the doorframe or the chair leg and snap him to a surprise halt.

Still, he took it pretty well, turning to eye the obstruction with something vaguely like a canine sigh—just another indignity of his life these days. The chemotherapy, which he knew nothing about, was yet to come.

"How are you going to pay for this?" Gloria asked, watching Loco's erratic progress out of the living room.

"The old condo has gone up so much in value I can refinance and take out some cash."

"And you won't just sell the condo because. . . ."

"Because you won't marry me. I need to keep a safe house in case you start shooting that Glock at me during some dark night of the soul."

She nodded. "Makes sense."

He'd hoped for a different answer, almost any different answer, but he didn't push it.

His bad joke must have given her ideas. She was sitting within reach of the service pistol in its little clip-on skirt holster. She picked it up and popped the magazine out into her lap, then yanked the receiver to eject the live round. The receiver stayed locked back, showing a couple of inches of naked barrel. Ugly but decidedly safe. She released the receiver manually, letting it snap home with a decisive sound that he didn't really like very much. The pistol no longer looked so safe now.

She knew better than to aim at a living thing, despite knowing for sure it was unloaded, even as a random gloomy reverie. She picked out the dark television set, using the palm-on-fist two-hand Weaver grip that she'd been taught at the Police Academy.

"*Boo*-yah," she said.


It was almost a week before the surfcast announced a good six-foot run at Lunada, said to be hitting maximum at a nice convenient 3:30 in the afternoon. Maeve picked up Ruthie at three, having skipped only one class. They parked, following Ruthie's directions, on the coast a half mile north of the bay.

"You can bet the Bayboys will be out in force. I'll get us down to the beach in secret, from right here, and we can creep up on them and make like spies. But if I go to all this trouble, you have to do something for me, too."

"What?"

"Nothing terrible. We can talk about it later."

Maeve was a little dubious, but she really wanted this stealthy peephole into the surfer world. All her life she'd been on the outside, or at best the outer edges, of a number of local subcultures—the soches at Redondo High, the science brains, the readers, and poets. Her last attempt to belong has involved an intense dip into the Greenwood gang in Latino East L.A. She'd never been close to the surf culture, and was only as familiar with it as any Southern Californian. Gnarly, dude. Anyway, since the whole adventure was in assistance of her dad, it was worth the risk.

Just before they set out, Ruthie let her hand brush over the fine hairs on Maeve's forearm, setting off a chill. "I believe in alchemy," she said. "I believe in making ordinary things into gold."

Maeve didn't want to ask her what she meant. Bending forward, Ruthie eyed Maeve's footwear.

"I'm glad you've come prepared," she said. Maeve had recently taken to wearing oafish walking shoes, on some kind of Always Be Prepared theory. (She was also probably trying to be as unattractive as possible, scaling her appeal back to match her flagging libido.) "We have to hike a ways along the rocks. It's like walking on a field of bowling balls. Though some of the bowling balls are the size of Buicks."

"I'm game." They headed across a path to the cliff edge and then along the rim about thirty yards until Ruthie found the descent she was looking for. It wasn't much of a trail, more a six-inch pathway worn into the slope. Within a few yards they had to turn flat to the cliff and inch along, clinging to the weeds and uneven face to get past a largely fallen-away section of the path. Maeve found her heart thumping but wouldn't admit to the fear.

"Are you a Buddhist?" Ruthie asked.

"I don't think so. Are you?"

"I'm trying to be. I try to keep my mind calm and respect all life."

"Isn't there a little more to it than that?"

"Sure, a lot I think, but the great thing is you don't need any gods or dogmas. I think the Tibetans are really cool."

Maeve considered this. "I don't know very much about it. I read some Zen stuff once."

A gull swooped close and shrilled at them, as if they were about to disturb her nest.

"We mean you no harm," Ruthie called out calmly, and the serene appeasement seemed to send the gull flying straight out to sea.

"Good job," Maeve said. She was glad Ruthie was watching her footing and couldn't see the brief grin Maeve couldn't control. She wondered if magical thinking was just a game to Ruthie.


**Maricruz Olivares**
**Behind Aztec Market**
**Huépac, Sonora**

Dear Maricruz,

 *Mister Liffey came back to our hill camp on Sunday as he promised me and he drove me and my surfboard to Manhattan Beach in his truck. He tries to speak a little Spanish but it is halting and the accent is terrible.* [No kidding. —ML.] *He asked about my family. Of course I can't tell him why I left Huépac.*

*He took me and my board to a part of the beach where there*
*were surfers and said he would come back before dark. Right away*
*the blond surfers started making fun of my cutoff jeans and laughing*
*at the repaired surfboard and then a group of them came and yelled*
*insults at me.*

*—Mexicans go over by the pier, they yelled.*

*—No wetbacks allowed here, Pancho.*

*And much worse. I didn't want trouble so I walked about a*
*kilometer up the beach and hoped Mr. Liffey would not miss me*
*when he comes back.*

*At first it was very hard to learn what to do, and I fell off again*
*and again. This was the Mexican area. There were even a few*
*Mexican surfers near the pier and some families on the beach. None*
*of them had the long baggy bathing suits that the* norteamericanos
*wear. In fact most of the men with their families wore T-shirts and*
*regular shorts and some even wore their* calzoncillos *so I felt better*
*here. The ones in the water seemed to be* Californios, *or maybe*
*they have been here for a long time, I could hear it in their voices.*
*They gave me advice and were friendly. I learned how to stay in*
*my proper place waiting until it was my turn to ride a wave. And*
*how to get up on my knees at first. I could see right away that a*
*normal surfboard has two or three of the little fins on the bottom that*
*they call skegs. Mine has only one and it is not in the center. That's*
*something else that must have broken at the mall.*

*I had to start teaching myself to make up for the missing fins by*
*trying to keep my weight to one side. It was a long day with some*
*big waves and a thousand falls. I got very tired swimming out again*
*and again and I thought I might never learn this sport. But near*
*the end of the day I had two long rides with the sun low on my back.*
*One of the* gabacho *surfers nearby even smiled at me and nodded.*

*Mari, I discovered a cheap copying machine in a drugstore near here. I am going to copy this letter twice and try to send it to you through Cousin Eufemia in Sinoquipe and to Lupe also. I will tell them that secrecy is most important and they must not tell one soul other than you.*

**Your loving brother, Jaime**

The rocks were worse than Ruthie had indicated, worn down to every size from house cat to house. You had to pick your way very slowly along, trying to keep from wrenching your ankles, and sometimes they had to boost one another up a real cliff of stones. Maeve wasn't sure but she seemed to notice that when Ruthie needed to touch her, she did it a little more intimately than was necessary.

After a half hour they found a rusting hunk of iron about the size of a desk that looked like it'd been a part of some grotesque machine.

"What's that?" Maeve asked.

"You'll see in a minute."

And, sure enough, they came up onto a high mesa of stones and just beyond, there was a large rusted form on the rocks, as big as a two-car garage. It had rows of rivets on the side so rusty they looked like they were each slowly exploding from within. What should have been the roof of the garage was pried up like a giant sardine can. From their vantage point, they could see beyond this piece of wreckage to others, all made of the same flaking, rusting iron, all catching the low sun in a thousand autumn shades of red-orange.

"Back in the 'sixties, long before we were born, a Greek freighter called *The Dominator* got stuck on the rocks out there. Rocky Point." She pointed to a spit of rock that ran offshore into the ocean. "I hear they tugged at it for days but they couldn't get it off the rocks and had to abandon it. Over the years, the ship broke up and rusted and pieces got pushed ashore."

"It's creepy," Maeve said. "But kind of pretty, too." She could imagine close-up photographs of the rust and how lovely and mysterious they would look. She had a sudden vivid image of herself as a celebrated photographer, traveling the world to all the interesting places with three cameras dangling around her neck, pursued through hotel bars by tall, interesting journalists who would later become famous novelists. She could document the plight of orphaned children in Mexico City. Poor African villages where they didn't even have fresh water. Tribes fleeing wars across deserts. It was definitely a concept of an ambition. She'd have to dig out the old 35mm camera her dad had given her and see if she had any aptitude.

"Let's keep our voices down now," Ruthie said softly. "Lunada Bay is just around that point. We can stay against the cliff and then behind some bushes."

There was no way to know yet how many surfers had congregated in the bay, but they could see that the waves coming in weren't at all as promised. Mostly they were mushy-looking and as foamy as Spray Whip. A strong gusty wind was coming off the shore now. The sun was a strange bloodred sinking into a band of air pollution over the ocean. Maeve understood it all at once—a mild Santa Ana had come up to wreck the surf and blow the normal smog offshore.

Resting on one prominent rock out at sea was the magnificent silhouette of a cormorant, swiveling its head on its long neck.

"Weird light," Maeve said softly, looking at her hand and then the red tinge gathering on everything.

"Earthquake weather, I've heard people say," Ruthie whispered.

"I'll bet in Florida they call it hurricane weather," Maeve said.

"And in the plains it's tornado weather." Ruthie grinned. "I like it. That's my transgressive urge."

"That doesn't sound very Buddhist."

"Ah, true. We're all full of contradictions."

Maeve followed Ruthie as they hiked cautiously down off the irregular rocks and along a narrow path that led around the point and along the cliff face. Overhead, gulls shrieked at them, as if trying to warn that they were coming.


"Let me buy you dinner," Jack Liffey said. The boy had already told him excitedly the highlights of his day surfing—or doing his best to teach himself surfing while negotiating the social challenges of a California beach. Jaime hadn't been hard to find by the pier once all the surfers had given up and come in. The cutoffs and broken board.

"You don't have to."

"I want to. Would you prefer a *taquería* or something more adventurous?"

"You choose. I'm the *recién llegado*."

"Recent . . . comer," Jack Liffey tried out and laughed. "It's literal. How do you feel about Italian?"

"Sir, please don't make fun of me. I will try anything."

"I swear to you, Jaime, I had no intention of mocking you. I just don't want to make you uncomfortable. You realize that you're a different person now. You go much farther down the American path and you can probably never go back to your village."

For a moment the boy had looked shocked and frightened, and then a steel curtain of self-protection came down. "Maybe."

Jack Liffey realized there was something here he didn't know. "I just mean that you're a *norteamericano* surfer now. Part of you, anyway. How can you talk about hanging ten with your old friends?"

The boy took his time replying, and it was clear to Jack Liffey that for reasons he couldn't yet understand, some of the sense of trust they'd developed had been affected.

Suddenly, Jack Liffey had to hit the brakes hard at a light, coming to rest in the crosswalk. A dozen very small men dressed as leprechauns, green top hats and all, walked in single file across the street, glaring in at him as they were forced to detour around his front end. He figured they meant nothing to the boy—how would you ever recognize oddity in a strange land?—but Jack Liffey struggled to guess at a reason for the strange parade and finally gave up. It was nowhere near St. Paddy's Day.

"You know, I've driven only one time, in my uncle's big *camión*. It was very hard to shift the gears. There were eighteen."

"If we find a quiet street in the hills, I'll let you practice on this heap of junk, if you want. I only have four gears."

Jaime watched him with sudden suspicion. "Why are you being so kind to me?"

Why was he? Jack Liffey wondered. He already had a daughter who kept his life full of apprehension. Then all at once he realized that even in a rural village, Jaime'd probably been warned not to get into cars with men who offered you candy. "But why help me?" Amazingly, he seemed on the verge of tears, but, Jack Liffey guessed, for some reason he couldn't fathom. "No other Anglo even talks to me here, except to give me orders. Mostly they look right through me as if I was made out of glass."

"Maybe that's why I do it. You helped me when you could, remember. Now I can help you a little. Human kindness can spread outward from the two of us all over the world."

The boy looked at him now as if he might be crazy. "Do you think that's true?"

"No. I don't. But it's a nice idea."

He pulled in and parked behind Luigi's Pizza.

"This is the place? It's very elegant," Jaime said.

Jack Liffey smiled. "In this town, Italian is almost never elegant, *amigo*." The car engine dieseled a bit before stopping, and he wondered if his heap of junk would soon need serious work. "What does your father do? I never asked."

There was another long pause from Jaime as they got out. It might not have been, Jack Liffey realized, the best question.

"He died in the Arizona desert, Mr. Liffey. The police told me he hurt his ankle bad, and the coyote who was bringing his group across left him in the sun. It was very bad luck. He had a regular job making plastic boxes up here, and he came home every year for the *Día de los Santos Reyes*. That's our Christmas."

"Shit. That's terrible. When was this?"

"Two years ago."

A flashy couple were laughing as they came out the back door of the restaurant. They held the sprung door for a moment, as if for no reason at all. Jack Liffey and the boy entered a narrow hallway between toilet and kitchen. The kitchen staff were all Latinos except the boss, like every other restaurant in the city, no matter what the nationality of the food.

"My younger brother says I have no soul," Jaime said unexpectedly.

"Why does he say that?"

"He thinks I sold it to a rich farmer near our village for a job in his fields. I think maybe I did rent my soul for a time—but I took it back."

"Now you're being mysterious," Jack Liffey said.

The boy nodded. "The man was a pig. Disgusting. He was, we say, a fucking *pendejo*. Without respect. He was a powerful man who took what he wanted. Even in such a small village in the middle of no place at all, that is a bad thing."

"You use the past tense about him. Is that why I shouldn't ask?"

"English verb tenses confuse me."

"No, they don't. Spanish verbs are a lot harder. Here he is."

A waiter greeted Jack Liffey and seated them in a booth for four and offered wine.

"Just water," he said, and the waiter left menus and walked away.

"Did you see?" Jaime pointed out. "The *mesero* didn't look at me at all. I'll bet if I am with another Mexican and come in here, I don't get a big comfortable table like this. You think?"

"Yes, I know. Should we kill everyone who does that?"

"No. But we should look straight at it and not refuse to see it."

Jack Liffey was learning to have a lot of respect for this plucky boy from a small village in the middle of noplace at all. "You can have wine or beer if you want. It's fine. I don't drink."

Jaime waved the offer away. "Why don't you drink, sir?"

He shrugged. "To prove to myself I don't have to. I used to like it too much, and long ago it made a mess of my life."

"I like one or two *cervezas* sometimes. After that I become confused and that is not a good thing. I bet I made a bigger mess of my life than you did."

"You don't have to fill me in if you don't want to. Let's look at the menu and order, and then you can tell me whatever you want about the past. Or else nothing."

They both studied the menu but he could see that figuring out the Italian dishes was difficult for Jaime.

"Why don't we split a big pizza," Jack Liffey said. "That's what

I feel like." He figured pizza would be something familiar to anyone from anywhere.

"That's a good idea, *señor*."

"Do you think you could call me Jack, please?"

"Yes . . . Jack, sir. *Jack*. That's what we call *tutear*, you know— using the familiar form of *you* with someone who is a friend, and the *nombre de pila*, the first name. Life is so much easier when everything is understood by both of you."

"You came to *El Norte*, Jaime. I'm sorry. Nothing is ever going to be easy like that again, for most of your life here. And there are people who'll always look down on you. It's shit and it's wrong, but there it is."

The waiter came back, and Jack Liffey could see Jaime shut down like a robot who'd been unplugged.

"We'll have your large pepperoni pizza and two beers," Jack Liffey said. "Mexican beer, if you have any."

"Modelo?"

The boy nodded faintly across the table and so did Jack Liffey. "*He'll* be paying," Jack Liffey said, pointing at the boy, and the *mesero* actually glanced at him for the first time.

It was becoming so gloomy it was hard to find their footing, and Maeve began to worry about the trek back.

"How are we going to get out of here?" Maeve whispered.

"Don't worry. We can go straight up right here on an easy trail. Shh."

They'd come to a break in the bushes and caught a glimpse of the Bayboys sitting in a circle around a big ice chest, drinking longneck beers. The surf in the crescent bay had collapsed completely and the boys were all ashore, inside a Stonehenge of their boards. No girls were in sight.

Maeve and Ruthie got as close as they could, lying low behind a plot of iceplant, but the offshore wind was blowing away most of the boys' talk.

" . . . long legs, man."

" . . . hate that avocado."

Whenever a mushy wave rolled up the tideline, the rote of water-on-sand washed the voices out completely for a few moments. Then a *wisssh* as the sheet of water withdrew and they had another few moments of snatched pointless fragments.

"Twitch, pay attention here. Don't fucking sulk."

Ruthie touched Maeve's shoulder lightly and Maeve nodded. She saw a head rise in silhouette. Whoever it was had been lying down.

" . . . I want to kick some beaner ass!"

" . . . hate the way they go djoo mad-dray."

A bigger wave covered the rest of the exchange. The girls listened for probably three-quarters of an hour as the wind grew chillier and the deep red sky turned to brown and then purple-black. Some of the talk was of Mexican interlopers, but they never picked up enough of it to know if the macho threats were just boasting or for real. Then, as the session was breaking up and the surfers began to filter past them toward the uphill trail, boards under their arms, they heard:

"What's your problem, Twitch? You ain't been no swingin' dick for days now."

"Shut up, ass-hat. I got my own worries."

"I wanna be your friend, man."

"Eat me, Ledge."

Neither girl spoke until they saw the last of the surfers trudge up the cliff in nothing but the ambient city light off the sky.

"I wonder," Maeve said. "You think any of those threats were real? Or were they just jerking off?"

"How should I know?"

"Hey!" Maeve just realized something. "This is where I met you. You were one of the hanger-ons."

"I was bored. Those guys are nothing to me except a long slow decline in expectations. I used to think there might be something special about them—you know, the knights of the surf and all that crapola. It took me way too long to find out they're just assholes with a little physical skill. White guys with little dicks and big boards. I hate the entire sucky troll population of Palos Verdes, especially the boys."

Maeve felt Ruthie's hand on her arm.

"You promised to do something for me."

"It depends."

"It's dark now. Nobody can see us."

"I'm freezing. We have to go up."

"Soon. I'm cold, too. I want you to take your bra off and let me feel your breasts. I promise, that's all."

Maeve stiffened, but then began to wonder whom it would hurt. It was so dark, Ruthie wouldn't see the embarrassing Old English 𝕰 tattoo the Greenwoods had put on her left breast. She knew if she rebuffed her new friend straight up, she'd seem like a wimp and hurt Ruthie's feelings at the same time. Besides, she was a little curious if it would feel different from a boy touching her. She could stop it any time.


Jack Liffey slipped Jaime two twenties so he could get the bill. During the meal he'd slid his beer across to the boy, too, and concentrated on the ice water.

"As I say, my father is dead, it's two years," the boy said morosely.

"Someone has to make money for the family. Everybody has to make money. My mother, my sisters, too. This rich *pendejo* there gives us all bad luck. I think he's a *demonio* of bad luck."

"Bad luck, uh-huh. That's why your little brother says you have no soul."

"I refuse to go to church. I won't confess what is not a sin. Why should I?"

"I won't argue. If God exists, he doesn't need our help. But it sounds like you have unfinished business with your conscience."

"I think conscience is for *norteamericanos* and Protestants."

Jack Liffey laughed. "You'd be surprised how *Señor* Freud gets into the mind of people who think life is simple."

"*Señor* Freud?"

"Just another name for your conscience, my friend. You go ahead and do what you think is right. Don't budge an inch. I like that. I'm guessing you've got a pretty well-developed sense of ethics. In my world, I figure I've got the right to offend anybody who has the power to hurt me. That's what keeps me above some moral waterline in life, you know? Like the spot in your toilet the water always comes back to."

"Did you tell someone about David Puigcerver?" Jaime asked.

"Yes, I did. A man I know in the fire department here. He said he'll contact the family. I'm sure they'll ship the body home. It was good for him to have the information, thank you."

"I was only knowing him a few days."

"And the butterfly girl?"

"I heard about her. I never met her. Maybe she was *Señorita* Freud."

Jack Liffey smiled. He had a feeling Jaime actually hadn't met her, but he still had a share of secrets of some kind.

Taking Jaime back to The Hill, Jack Liffey stopped at a Ralphs. There they selected a few bags' worth of food for the encampment—beans, coffee, tortillas, boiled tomatoes. Jack Liffey threw in some chocolate. Jaime didn't protest too much. Jack Liffey wasn't going to get into making regular food runs like Blue, but he was in an expansive mood, and he figured a few bucks would go a lot farther for them than for him.

Once they got the handle-bags under the chain-link fence, the boy could tuck his surfboard under one arm and balance himself with the bags in the other, without help. Jack Liffey had little interest in schlepping down and then up the hillside again in the dark. He watched Jaime disappear into the murk of shrubbery.

The warm glow of satisfaction he was feeling lasted about thirty seconds, just until he'd wriggled under the shrubbery and stepped back out onto the dimly lit street. Something amazingly hard walloped him then in the left kidney. His entire innards seized up so he couldn't breathe. Several other blows rained onto him.

"Just go down, fuckhead," a gravelly voice said, and a big shove ensured that he did.

He was kicked twice, yelping involuntarily the second time. They didn't seem to be going for mortal wounds, just methodical punishment, and he tried to curl up into a ball to protect himself. Then a wooden instrument, probably a baseball bat, walloped his forearm and something seemed to snap.

"Prickface, don't be helping the Mexes. This is a love tap from Special Ops."

A few more kicks and then they were gone, no more than receding footfalls. He lay listening to the wind, a little distant traffic from P.V. Drive and some electrical crackle that might have been the ballast from a streetlight starting to go, or it might have been the fizzing inside his own throbbing head.

Finally he sat up and felt his arm with a wince. He'd be good and bruised, but whatever the snap had been, he didn't think it had been him.

There's an aphorism for this, he thought. Later he realized that what he'd probably been thinking of was "No good deed goes unpunished." But all his addled brain could come up with at that moment was something a San Pedro fisherman had told him long ago: "Every boat is always looking for a place to sink."

# 9

# Special Ops

IT WAS NEARLY PITCH DARK WHEN THE GIRLS STARTED UP THE CLIFF
TRAIL, BUT THE FOOTING WAS MUCH BETTER HERE, AND THERE WAS
SO MUCH ORANGY SCATTERED CITY LIGHT SUFFUSING THE SKY THAT IT
GUIDED THEM UP FAIRLY EASILY. Which was good because Maeve was
too agitated to pay much attention. She was basically unfastened at
every hook and button, outer and inner. Totally disassembled.

Ruthie took her hand confidently. "Hey. You're changed forever—
for about a week. Longer if you want, or not at all, if you don't. You
were great, you know."

Of course it hadn't stopped with Ruthie caressing her breasts—
heavenly sensation!—or even leaning forward to bite softly on her
nipples. It hadn't stopped until they were both naked in the cold
sand and shivering with the chill and the emotion, crying out to each
other and doing everything they could imagine, or had ever imagined. At one point a gull that had been perching on a rock jutting
from the cliff above them had flapped free and shrieked twice, and
Maeve knew she'd remember that startling bird cry all her life.

"It was mind-blowing. I can't think. I'm really confused,
Ruthie."

"Of course you are. You're wondering if you're a permanent Lebanese now. It's not written down anywhere, you know—not for us. Some people are probably fated, but we're way beyond that. You're whatever you want to be. Don't pick at it so much."

Maeve managed an uncertain chuckle. "I'm a carpet eater," she said. Only a month after she'd had an abortion because she'd completely lost her head to a Latino lover. Jeez Louise, she thought. Didn't that make her bad in some way? Fickle?

"Words have no sting, girl. We were lezbos tonight. Dykes. Fairy ladies. We licked each other's pussies and we loved it. Let it sleep inside you."

"Thanks for everything, Ruthie. You're a big sweetie."

Her new lover stopped on the path and turned back and kissed her hard with lots of tongue.

**Daddy,**

> *This morning the surf was stormy gray like fresh cement and way too crappy for putting on a wetsuit and even Rabbit wasnt there. Just me fussing. You always said I cant hardly keep my thoughts on one thing for more than a few seconds.*
>
> *I saw some tearjerk flick once about a guy with cancer and back then I tried to imagine somebody who tells me your going to die and if I had to face it I felt Id want to do everything I ever wanted to do* real *fast before it was too late. Id want to fly to Hawaii and see the big surf at the North Shore at Sunset and Waimea and even South Africa and Jeffreys Bay or Madison Bay in the Eastern Cape. Id treat my friends too. Drop my face into a big pile of blow like Al Pacino in Scarface.*
>
> *But you said I was all wrong.*
>
> *Nows the bad time for real and I dont want nothing at all. The*

world is all boring and gray like the water. Hey if theres no real next week then its all just shit isnt it. Theres no future. Why would I want to do anything at all.

I havent told anybody about the stupid blood test. Not mom who gets hysterical about goddam ants in the kitchen. And I just couldnt tell you when you finally made your "weekly" call. I mean maybe you do call every week but as you know mom doesnt put me on very much.

The doctor talked to me and wanted me to take some bunch of killer drugs that I know are going to make me sick and feel like shit. And then Id have to admit I have the fag disease. I cant do that. When the time comes Ill go out quick as a goddam wink. I got your old gun you left in that box in the closet or I can use too much drugs or just jump off the cliff. But I got to be honest now. I cant even imagine that. All my mind can wrap around is just nothing but nothing. Just gray empty unhappy shit.

I was sitting there dad and feeling like that and I barely heard a car stop behind me on Paseo del Mar. I did hear the footsteps but I didnt give a shit. I figured it was one of the Bayboys with more need to surf than common sense on a day like this. It might be Rabbit or Flea or even Ledge. At least it could be somebody to make me forget for a few minutes.

I looked up and !!!cazart!!! there was this skinny Mex in cutoff jeans carrying one of the ugliest broken surfboards Ive ever seen under his arm. He was ten feet down the cliff trail before I woke up.

Hey man I go real loud. Where the fuck you think your going.

He just stares back at me like Clint Eastwood in some big eye to eye moment.

I go you know you dont belong here. Go home and surf in TJ.

We stared at each other for a long long time and I thought I ought to get up and kick his ass.

*Then out of nowhere he goes Ive been working on the wall in your own backyard for almost a month gringo.*

*I tried to make sense out of that and slowly I recognized the guy for chrissakes. He had his shirt off a lot and whaled away with a pick on moms big stupid project. He worked like a machine in the sun all day like all Mexicans.*

*Okay your that Mexican I go. Hot tamale. Mexicans dont surf.*

*I surf he goes real quiet and cold.*

*Then I dont know Fuck it I go to this fuckin guy who cares. Theres no surf anyway.*

*Dad did I do wrong to let him go down there.*

*Your son. This is Twitch. Please call me.*


It took two days for him to stop gobbling Vicodin like an addict and to be able to unclench his limbs and lever himself out of bed in the morning without crying out in pain.

Amazingly, Gloria was so estranged from him these days she didn't even notice, and—to be fair, working her twelve on, twelve off, it was probably hard to notice anything that didn't slap you right in the face. He had plenty of bruises but he kept them covered. He wasn't sure why he hadn't told her about the beating. Maybe just not to worry her. Maybe to keep her from riding to his rescue, which he couldn't really handle just then. There was some kind of privacy urge at work, some demand of the gods of the self-contained man that he didn't quite understand. Too, he was well aware that there were other problems in the universe. Loco's, for example.

"This is one strange dog," the vet said across the counter. She handed Jack Liffey a conked-out Loco in a big stiff cardboard box and then put out her cigarette in a cat-food tin on the counter.

"Yeah," he said. "Does the coyote part explain it?"

"Sure, I know that. A lot of people say that about their dogs, but I think you might actually got one there. Technically we call them coydogs, and the only thing of any value I know is they tend to breed in February."

"This one tends to eat anything that was once made of meat and chew anything else that wasn't, just for the hell of it."

"He won't be eating a lot of your slippers for a while, I promise you. He's had carboplatin and adriamycin. That's strong stuff. He might wake up and need to hurl a bit later today. If he does puke, give him some Pepto-Bismol. That'll soothe him down. Let me get the door."

"Thanks. I'll never get him to drink Pepto-Bismol."

"Get the pills and put them in some cheese. You know how to massage it down his throat?" She demonstrated with a finger on her own throat. "Just think of performing this nursing care as a kind of step in your own evolution. We don't know what his ancestors did to try to heal, but he trusts you now, Mr. Liffey. You're his tribe."

"Does that mean I've got to start sniffing women's butts?"

She roared with laughter and slapped his bruised shoulder so hard he yelped and almost stumbled down the steps, and he had to cling to the cardboard hard. She was back inside the clinic and gone, the screen door whapping, before he could say anything else.

"Let's go home, boy. You get through this, and I promise you no more of that cheap dry shit that Gloria's been buying at Costco. Ground sirloin from the human meat counter."

One yellow eye slitted open but there was no recognition in it, and the morning light seemed to make the dog recoil and shut down again.

Maricruz Olivares
Behind Aztec Market
Huépac, Sonora


Dear Maricruz,

*I don't know if you got the letter I finally sent, two ways. I started learning how to surf with my new board and Sunday I went by myself to the place where I been working where everybody says the waves are so good.*

*I started to walk down the hill and the boy who lives there yelled at me. That very angry* gabacho *boy is a little crazy for some reason, I think. I was afraid he was going to try to jump up and hit me, and I'd have to punch him down. I must be careful tomorrow when I'm working on the wall at his house.*

*After we spoke angry words, my heart pounded the way it did when I confronted Don Ignacio. I have control of myself again and I decided to think of Mr. Liffey and the fact that Anglos are not all like this* loco. *I turned and carried my surfboard down the path. What a nothing it was on the* playa! *The boy was right. There was almost no surf at all.*

*But I went to all the trouble to walk 7 or 8 kilometers from the camp carrying my board so I decided to wait. I sat on the smaller rocks where I used to see the surfers' girls wait. If the surfers come I will stand my ground, I thought. I have rights. This new anger made me think of Don Ignacio again and how he seemed so amazed that I would stand up to him. What emotions I felt, Mari! Anger and guilt and determination. I know I can hit someone if have to. But I have decided it is a sin when you want to hurt someone that bad.*

*One day I must find a church where they do not know me and confess. I wonder how I am remembered in Huépac. Maybe somebody like Pando has written a* corrido *about me: The poor man who fought back! My little brother Esteban may even be proud of me.*

*I know my mother is angry. How about you, Mari? I know that Don Ignacio always had many enemies. Maybe people will think he deserved it. If you can write me, have Eufemia or Lupe send the letter to Izak Beltrán at the address I have written below. Please tell me if the* judiciales *are hunting me. Then I will know if I can come home again some day.*

*Today I waited for a long time on the* playa *even though the waves were very bad. After a while, all these bouncing thoughts were interrupted by a strange noise from the ocean. It was a long rumbling sound and an even longer splash. I saw that a big wave had come ashore. It chased away the gulls and a pelican that was sitting on the safe rocks, and one seal on a small rock had to slip into the water. Before long, on the horizon there was a gray line. I could almost see that the whole ocean was rising up. I wondered if it was my imagination. In a minute the swell reached the mouth of the bay and it made a perfect tube almost two meters high. I was astonished. There was white foam where it crashed down and the place where it was crashing moved slowly from north to south like a picture in one of the surf magazines I take out of the trash. I have never seen such a wave before and quickly I took off my shoes. I picked up the board and ran for the water.*

*It was amazing, Mari. I can only guess there was a secret storm far out on the ocean that nobody knew about. Once every three or four minutes, a swell came toward me from far away until I guess it reached at the rocks deep under the water where I floated. Then it rose and threw me forward like an angry hand. Every time, the big wave ran along for thirty meters or fifty meters or more and then it made a perfect round tunnel rolling into the bay. I think they call it a "curl" or a "tube."* [These two words were in English. —ML.] *It was amazing, there was boiling water at my heels, and I could feel my riding was getting better and better. Nobody has ever had practice like this, I was thinking. It's a miracle. I pushed forward out of the tunnel and then let myself go back inside and I rode up and down the tall wave. One time I felt so glued to my board that I walked forward on it, as I have read about, almost hanging my toes off the front. Next time for sure I will, I thought.*

*Late in the afternoon, I was getting very tired and I was falling off badly. I had to swim fast to catch my surfboard being pushed toward the rocky beach. When I caught it I looked upward to the cliff and saw the shape of that* loco gabacho *boy standing there. He did not wave to me or anything.*

*But what a day it was, Mari!*

**Your Jaime**

It's a daytime soap opera, that's all it is, Maeve thought with chagrin—maybe *As the Clitoris Turns.* Being with a girl was no big deal in America any more. Why was she so agitated about it? She tried to do her calculus homework, but the symbols wriggled under her eyes and she slapped the book closed on a pencil. She couldn't forget the magic of that pale blue butterfly she had seen. It was no wonder Blue Hostetler had been so anxious to take part in saving it. But it wasn't really the butterfly that was affecting her, of course. It was Ruthie's voice as she talked about the butterfly.

If I don't study, my final grades will collapse and all the colleges will reject me, Maeve thought. But then, of course, she could stay home and make love to Ruthie all day long.

Stop it!

She probably needed to talk to her mom, but her mom was getting her hair cut and then going to her own therapist up in Hermosa Beach. Whatever it was that old moms had to talk out—or this particular old mom. *I'm not getting any, anymore. Feeling passed by.*

*Having a neck that's turning into a wattle.* (You pitiless girl!) *Having an ungrateful daughter.* Or maybe, still being a bit in love with an ex-husband who was long gone, living with someone else. Pointless guesses.

*What a wicked person I am,* Maeve thought. *I promise to be more sympathetic to her.* She realized that when she used to judge her dad so harshly—at his old, straying worst—he was at least trying to stay loyal to someone, to Marlena or that conceited rich headmistress Rebecca or even that dried-up, so-very-over movie star Maeve had never liked. *I can't even figure out who I'm supposed to stay loyal to. Certainly not Beto over in Boyle Heights. Boys in general? The person I am inside? Well, who am I?* She felt a wave of nausea and had to put her head between her knees. Soon it passed.

How could she change her character so quickly? If she was a lesbian all at once, did she even have a character? She felt maybe she had no inner essence at all. She was so fickle she might wake up some morning as a different species entirely, like Gregor Samsa the cockroach that they'd read in English. What would define her in a year, ten years? Would she be able to look back and recognize herself as the same person? Would her friends look back and say, That *Maeve,* she was always *so . . .* so what?

*I'll just make up my mind to be good, I have the willpower.* So—what is good? She kept seeing Ruthie's confident grin, a jut of her chin, and she imagined Ruthie's stiff breasts against her fingers as she caressed the nipples, and she could feel that she was tingly and wet already thinking about it.


Twitch glared down at the two pills in his hand, one a gold capsule with a blue stripe and the name of the manufacturer and another big ugly pink tablet. He was safe because he could hear his mother in the living room, the squeaking of her fat felt pen going at it on the whiteboard like crazy. She was writing up another of her unbearable lists.

*10 cerise lipsticks*
*potato chips (thick hard kind)*
*make Allan pay a lot more*
*Brandon's fav. steak*
*forget blanced meals*
*lots cookies*

He downed the pills with a big glass of water, fighting one of them past the lump in his throat, just as the *Aa-oo-gah* horn went off in the driveway.

"Who's that, *Bran*-don?"

She didn't even know Ledge's car, and his friend had come by for him a thousand times. "Mr. Henderson, mom. He's taking me to my violin lessons."

"I thought they were Saturday?"

"Not any more." He heard the potato chips go crunch and crunch again, and he knew he needn't even bother to get the violin case. As he passed through the living room, he didn't glance around. The whole room was an obstacle course of catalogue and on-line purchases bought with his dad's credit cards, boxes that hadn't even been opened yet, some so huge that they could only have contained a stuffed chair or a big flat TV.

"Don't be late, honey. Please." There was a terrible entreaty in her voice, but he was out the door fast. He hurried to the maroon 1949 Mercury woodie with the bumper sticker reading: MY OTHER RIDE IS YOUR DAUGHTER.

"Hey, dude. Let's get the fuck goin'."

"Mom stuff?"

"Yeah. 'Course. You know, if you're ever *really* hard up, you can probably fuck her brains out if you want."

"No offense, Twitch, but your mom's kinda hard to look at these days." The car exhaust crackled as he backed down the drive and then sputtered away. Ledge did most of his own car work at the Chevron station where he worked, and he was no genius at it.

Twitch looked out the windshield and didn't answer. It had been a stupid idea, pimping his mom. He had no idea why he'd said it, other than the general crappiness he was feeling.

The windshield was split in the middle by a chrome divider, and the divider had been weirdly echoed by a chrome accent piece on a big maroon visor that extended the width of the roof over the windshield, like a single droopy eyelid. He was amazed that he was so preoccupied these days that even the car's remarkable cool abandoned him within moments to dark thoughts.

"You ready to really roll, brah?" Ledge asked. "These guys are the real deal."

"I'm all tubes."


He'd settled Loco onto an old blanket on the service porch in back, and the dog had almost immediately thrown up all over it. So he got out the generic Pepto he'd bought—PINK BISMUTH, it said weirdly on its foil packaging—and pushed one pill into a small chunk of cheddar, the strong kind Loco usually liked. He stroked it down the dog's throat the way the vet had shown him, waited, and another bout of heaves brought it right back up in a pool of yellow and beige.

"Well, hello, *Ralph*," Jack Liffey said glumly.

He cleaned up and left a shallow bowl of water, and then gave the poor animal his privacy to nurse his own complaints in doggie peace.

Gloria had the oven door open and was sliding in a big hunk of *carnitas*, which he loved.

"Some occasion?"

"It's Thanksgiving, a day early."

"My god, I completely forgot. How can you forget men with buckles on their shoes?"

"It was never a big deal for me, Jackie, but Maeve says she wants to be with her mom tomorrow so it's our turn to have her tonight. Also she seems to want to talk to you about something. I know she won't eat the meat, but I've got some veggie tamales, too." She nodded at a tray of corn-husked oblongs on the counter.

He hugged her. "Thanks, Glor."

She sighed, but he could tell she was pleased. However stiffly she was holding herself, she at least softened a bit. For a minute or so, anyway.

"Listen," he said, changing the subject. "Have you ever heard of a group called Special Ops?"

She took a swallow of beer as she thought about his question. "I think they've been mentioned at roll call. Your dad's kind of people."

That meant racists. "Anything else you know?"

Her eyes narrowed, and, for a moment she was on the job—or maybe just constipated. "Is there anything I should know here?"

"They might be a lead to the girl I'm looking for, that's all."

"Or is it about those bruises you been hiding from me?" she said.

"I thought you hadn't noticed." The deep hostile scratch and graffiti on his pickup truck was on the far side, too, the way he'd

been parking it, and he figured she hadn't seen that either. He realized he could be wrong.

"I am a cop," she said.

"It happened outside your jurisdiction. I was beat up three nights
ago. Not very seriously. Just being warned off."

"You're a stubborn bub, Jackie. What am I supposed to do—let
them kill you next time? Haven't we been here before?"

"You seem to have enough problems of your own these days."

"Well, a dead boyfriend wouldn't solve any of them, would it?"
Her voice got harder. "Or maybe it would. I'll ask around about these
guys if you'll promise to stay out of their way."

"Sure. I don't need any more bruises. Is there something else serious eating you?"

She folded her arms. "If I could, Jack, I would just puff up and
squirt out all the black inside me like a squid. It would either blind
everybody near me in the whole damn city or else empty out that
blackness."

"That's past serious, I think."

She turned her back to tend something on the stove. When
he got it together, he was going to suggest again that she see a
shrink or therapist, some kind of mind-healer, and maybe try an
antidepressant—but off the books, an outsider, since he knew she
was terrified of what it would do to her career if her superiors found
out. But he didn't want the further aggravation of suggesting such a
thing just then. He didn't even try to hug her because he was afraid
she might respond by accidentally elbowing one of his bruises, which
would set him whimpering.

"Loco says hello," he said. "Actually he said something a bit more
eloquent. *'Ralph!'*"

"Yeah, I heard him barfing. I hope you did the right thing not putting him down."

"That's still a possibility. If you get angry enough at whatever, you could just go out and strangle him with your bare hands."

She turned and glared at him, like a predator, studying something she might soon eat.

"Just ask," she said, and he had no idea how serious she was. "Him *or* you."

But later when Loco started to howl and moan—sounds the dog had never made before—she was all comfort and motherly consolation. The dog's whimpers—on and off at random—were eerie, as if it knew something terrible had changed forever in its life, something that could never be undone.

"This is my man, Twitch." Ledge grasped the back of Twitch's neck as he ushered him into the funky cottage, and Twitch wished he wouldn't do that. "Connie, Big Bob, Bibleman, Hoke, and that's Kurt the Condom."

"*Fuck* you, Ledge."

It was a little frame bungalow in a back street of Hawthorne, an area just south of the flight path of LAX, and three or four miles from the ocean. Hawthorne was a town that had once, long ago, been working-class white and had given rise to the Beach Boys. It was now more than half Latino and another third black, the apartments and little houses deteriorating by the hour, and the white families mostly gone—leaving a rump of embittered older whites with no way out.

"Have a beer, Twitch. You're welcome with us. We hear you keeping the beaners off your turf." That was the guy introduced as

Connie, a thickset man with a sandy-colored Marine haircut and what looked like a death's head worked in gold in his front tooth when he grinned, which he did only briefly.

Twitch was handed a cold can of Budweiser.

"American beer," Big Bob reminded them. "It's got no piss in it." He was even bigger than Connie, and his nose and cheekbone had been broken at some point in his life, never quite healing right. "Sit over there. We'll come to order."

Twitch and Ledge took worn-out ottomans that filled a gap in the rough circle made up of the kitchen chairs and the sofa. The guy called Bibleman actually had a Bible open on the coffee table in front of him. It was much underlined in many colors, and he intoned: "The invocation. Exodus 13:43. The Lord said to Moses and Aaron, 'These are the regulations for the Passover: No *foreigner* is to eat of it.'"

"Amen, brother." Big Bob seemed to be in charge of the proceedings. "Proposed, seconded, and passed, by me and all, that there will be no piss or shit breaks for twenty minutes. There will also be no whining about any insults that take place."

Guffaws filled the room.

"This meeting of Special Ops is hereby convened." Big Bob belched for emphasis.

"Mine the fucking borders!"

"Mine the fucking boners!" somebody seconded.

"Out of order. Any old business?" he demanded, wiping his mouth.

"How about donations for those guys from San Diego? You know, the guys that said they were gonna stick ipecac in the water jugs that all the bleeding hearts are putting out on the wetback trails over the border."

"Out of order! We already decided that border crew was just a bunch of rip-off artists. Minuteman Central was clear on that. You musta been asleep, dipshit. New business."

"I want us to officially recognize the positive contributions of Twitch Dedrick to the holy struggle against the brown invasion," Ledge said, raising Twitch's arm like a boxing referee. "He's been driving outsiders off Lunada Bay for years, specially Mexes, and I know he's one of us in his heart of hearts."

"Kid, did you light up those wetbacks who were camping up there?" said Hoke, who was more conservatively dressed in wool slacks and an alligator shirt. He had hard, unconfiding eyes behind tinted glasses.

"That wasn't me," Twitch said. "But a couple of us did shoot at one of their camps up there with my dad's old .38."

"Hey!" Big Bob said. "I bet that set off a Mexican fire drill!"

"Think you hit anything?" Hoke wanted to know.

"We weren't really trying to," Twitch said. "I've got enough trouble with Deputy Dawg and kinda need to stay off his radar."

"Just thought you might be ready for the big time," Hoke said. "Sometimes you gotta teach people a object lesson."

"Cool it, Hoke," Big Bob snapped. "Anybody'd think you're a damn agent provocateur."

"Fuck is *that*? Voc-a-tour? I just want us all to know this is serious business—it's not no Church Sunday sit-in and Monday back-to-work. We're doing all the shit our own government ain't got the balls to do. If they'd only take it seriously with some firepower, they could clean up the border in a week. We know they got the means. They got infrared, they got mines, all kinds of shit. They got the gear, man, they got the manpower—they just don't got the will."

"Oooh, sorry guys, I gotta use the head." Twitch ran to the bathroom, its location thankfully obvious because the door was standing open. He closed the door and ran water in the sink hard and flushed, but they could probably still hear him puking. Fuck the doctors and their lies about easy-to-take medicine. It's what the fates are giving the homos for their sins, he thought. But why me?

Eventually emerging sheepishly, he made an excuse about the flu, astonished to realize that they were discussing inducting him.

"We need some blood," Big Bob said.

"I hope you're a true patriot, kid," another said. "We got our shit together and this is all slick now."

Twitch could hardly think about what was going on around him, he was so distracted by thoughts of what was happening in his bloodstream, in his vital organs, in the marrow of his bones. The cramping and rumbling continued in his guts along with a new ache deep inside his head.

"We all know," Big Bob went on, "that the bad shit going on is condoned by our crappy politicians—like when they let the limp-dicks and nigras assault law-abiding patriots when we get together." He indignantly cleared his throat.

Twitch's world contracted into a tight cone directly in front of his eyes. What the fuck was he doing here? Somebody was rattling on about wetback labor and how they were too stupid to change a lightbulb. These guys were bigger assholes than any Mexican he'd ever met. Then he was far away, his body shrinking into a dot, soaring over the clouds like a bird.

"Damn it, Twitch, say *yes*, right *now*," Ledge prompted.

"Sure."

And then he had his right hand tugged into the air, his left placed on Bibleman's marked-up Scriptures, and he found himself repeating, phrase by phrase, "I shall be prepared . . . to set aside my livelihood . . . my comfort and my personal interests . . . to answer the call . . . to protect the sovereignty . . . of the great United States of America . . . against all predators and mud people . . . from within or from without our shores."

# 10

# The Gift of Giving

MIRACULOUSLY, LOCO PERKED UP WHEN MAEVE ARRIVED FOR DINNER. He even managed a wag or two. Maeve had that effect on everybody, Jack Liffey thought, even Gloria wagged a bit. But, wagging aside, he could tell something was bothering both women.

"You two go away and let me fuss in here," Gloria said.

Subtle, he thought. Go have your father-daughter talk. It was balmy enough in late November to sit out on the splintery glide on the front porch that had always looked to him like something that had plummeted down from a Michigan daydream. Michigan—except for the angular graffiti someone had tagged it with, the bougainvillea strangling the fence, the mariachi music that was always chugging away up the road, and the Onate brothers under the hood of their old Chevy across the street.

Loco followed them out and was enough like himself that Maeve didn't even ask about his health. He could tell she was deeply preoccupied.

"School?" he asked.

"'S okay."

"Colleges?"

"Same. For now."

"Your mom?"

"She's fine. Lonely, the usual. You know—just Mom."

"Boyfriend trouble?" He was running out of plug-in interrogation topics.

"Not exactly."

A police siren interrupted things, as they often did in this neighborhood. Then it cut off so abruptly it was like a shot animal.

"Somehow, it's the terms of the heart we're fretting over," he suggested.

"Dad, don't be snide. I'm not that innocent any more. Remember, I'm in emotional recovery from a lot. You can't pretend I haven't had sex. I have a past now. I'm owed a little gravitas." She almost laughed at her own manner, then she hugged him to suppress it. Finally she pulled back, but had to catch her lips between her teeth to smother another upwelling of mirth.

"Gravitas," he said. "Isn't that a kind of apple?"

She made a face, then blurted: "Do you think of me as somebody with a lot of inner resources?"

"There's a funny question." And a well-prepared one, he thought, starting to worry more than a little bit about the direction it was all going. But she probably wasn't pregnant again. He might as well let her get it out, whatever it was. "Yes, I think I do. You've been through a lot, and a good deal of it was set off by trying to help me. Recently, you seem to be exploring life's more perilous niches."

That seemed to choke off her carefully organized line of attack.

"Dad, be *quiet*. I'm so nervous I'm ready to cry at my own nervousness." She grimaced.

He nodded assent, his heart aching with love and worry for this strange and wonderful being he'd helped produce. There was a metallic clang and some cursing in Spanish across the road, but neither of them looked over.

"Will you love me no matter what I say next?"

"If you just joined the American Nazi Party, I'll turn you over and spank you right here, I promise."

"Dad!"

"Okay, hon. An angry god couldn't make me stop loving you." She was so transparent, he could see her switch gears and decide not to tell him something after all, something that she had carefully set on the agenda.

"What if I didn't go to college right away?"

"I suppose I'd be disappointed. Do you have other plans?" He did his best not to press. This was not the news she'd been building up to. But he knew the rules: he'd get it only when she was ready.

"I'm just toying with the idea of going to Europe for a while. Broaden myself, or whatever it is."

"Then you'd better work a bit first. I'm not sure how much money I can send with you."

Maeve burst into tears, for some reason, and then both she and Loco tried to climb into his lap at once.


Twitch skipped school Monday, which would have been the startup day after Thanksgiving. He told his mom he felt feverish and she proved a soft touch, as usual.

He really did feel lousy, and when she left to go shopping, he tried to hole up in his room playing "Grand Theft Auto—Hooker on a Stick," but the scraping of the cement-mixing trough outside kept putting him off his game. So he took a Quaalude and found himself nodding off for a while.

After he woke up and brooded for a bit, he found himself wiping away big 'lude tears of self-pity, and finally he peeked out the side window to watch the ongoing work. Apparently they'd dug far enough back into the hill now because the excavation part was over, and both guys were working with the rocks, the Mexican mixing the cement and carting rocks over to the ragged end of about thirty feet of wall where the white guy was on his knees cementing more rocks into place.

Twitch poured out a glass of lemonade and waited for the brawny white guy to go off to the port-a-potty they'd put up on the edge of the yard so the workmen didn't have to troop through the house, though the big guy had done quite a bit of clomping in and out recently whenever his mom was home. He took the glass out to where the other one, the Mexican, was loading fieldstone into a wheelbarrow.

"Man, when you was surfing, you really sucked at first, but I watched you at the end and you were getting awesome. Really. Here."

The Mexican did nothing to take the glass from him.

"I've never seen tubes come in so sudden like. You were shredding them, man. You got natural talent. Don't you want the lemonade?"

"Get him one, too, or I have trouble." The wannabe surfer nodded toward the port-a-potty.

"He's fucking my mom. That's plenty of goodies for him."

"That's not my problem."

They exchanged stony looks for a while and then they heard the flimsy door creak and slam. The Mexican took the glass and walked to Mike with it. "The woman sends you this."

"About fucking time." The big guy glanced once at Twitch and then ignored him, and his helper walked to the rockpile some distance away.

Twitch waited and met him on the way back. "Are you afraid of him?" Twitch asked.

"He owns the job. That's the way it is. I'm not *afraid* of anyone."

"Good for you, brah. Do you know you're surfing goofy-foot? Try it with your left in front sometime. It's better that way, and you'll really get to be primo."

He nodded a thank-you.

"Knock on the back door before you go." Twitch turned away quickly with tears in his eyes.

That's one unstable kid, Jaime thought. He was already trying to imagine riding with his left foot forward and how that would feel.

This is so primal, Maeve thought, obsessing like crazy about Ruthie. She knew sooner or later she had to tell her dad she was a lesbian, and she hoped he'd take it well. She'd worry about her mom later. That was a different kettle of cats.

She was hardly listening in her final-year meaningless-elective International Relations class as Mr. Pistani droned on about the St. Petersburg G8 summit (and Kenny Smiley spoke up in his showoff way to tell everyone that the administrative district of St. Petersburg was still called, by popular vote, the Leningrad Oblast.) She and Ruthie had spoken a million times already by cell, and they planned to meet after school at the Udderly Latte, if Ruthie could borrow her mom's car to get there. If not, Maeve would come get her.

Ruthie had been strangely unavailable for several days now and kept saying on the phone that maybe it was a good idea to let up on the throttle a little and allow their inflamed emotions to ratchet down a notch. But that was not the way Maeve was feeling at all, and the very mention of backing off terrified her.

I do hope this has a happy ending, Maeve thought. It was funny she was already thinking thoughts like that, but the prospect of college was now hovering like a cosmic punctuation mark over her life; a semicolon, maybe, that would mark the end of the long clause of her childhood and—totally outside any act of her will—mark out the first act of whatever it was adulthood would bring. Actually, she could imagine she was riding a giant semicolon in midair right now, a bit tippy on it. She saw some kind of safety in that, as if this last school year and the coming summer didn't really count. The abortion, the attraction to Ruthie, both were still as real and painful as could be, it wasn't that, but they might just belong to a phase of her life that she'd be moving on from.

You had to let life take its course, she thought, with an intimation of a terrible dark freedom awaiting her up ahead.

"Ms. Liffey, at which of the yearly G8 summits did the United Kingdom invite the European Union to attend as an active observer?"


**Dear Daddy,**

> *They always talk so boring about the gift of giving well they took it away from me. I cant give myself to a girl no more because of this fag disease and hey I cant even give my good shit away either. There's this Mex working here. He came to the back door like I asked and I offered him my old surfboard thats still pretty good that I was going to give him to show I was an okay guy but he just backed up like it was on fire. Well fuck him. The guys I met with Ledge woodnt approve thats for sure. Theyre old dudes and mean as mako sharks. Fuck them too.*

*Everything I gots spoiled and wrecked. Whatever. Tonight was your call and as you know mom gave it to me finally but I still couldnt find a way to tell you Im a leper and I know you probably dont want to know anyway. Do you know you just talk right over all the things I try to say to you. And then you go dont be so sullen Brandon.*

*You go as of Friday Ill be in Osaka for three weeks. Ill try to call. And I go dont bother if its a big deal.*

*You go its no big deal. Just theyll be running me ragged making presentations.*

*You have fun with the Japs dad. Maybe next time you can give me a address to write to.*

**Not Brandon but Twitch**

There she was walking out to the school parking lot, utterly gripped by thoughts of Ruthie and of their imminent get-together, and abruptly from deep within that cloistered funhouse that was trapping her, she heard somebody honk and then yell, "Maeve!" It was Imogen leaning out of her big Nissan Armada. There was nothing she could do to slip away. She gritted her teeth and got into the beast to hear Imogen's breathless gabble about her important news. Maeve simply could not come all the way back to Imogen's reality in an instant.

This is what being an HerbaVigor pyramid seller buys you, Maeve thought, looking at the giant SUV—at least until some ugly evidence turns up and your bosses are carted off by the D.A. Maeve's idea of a high school job was flipping burgers at $6.50 an hour, or folding and stuffing mail ads at piecework rates for the fulfillment agency over in Hawthorne. Not for the first time she had the thought that there was just far too much money in

America. It would be good for everybody's soul to have a lot less money around.

"Wetback . . . ," she heard, and finally she clambered all the way out of her well of solitude. She made herself listen to what Imogen was trying to tell her and caught up fast. The girl had heard insistent rumors of a game of "wetback baseball" that was going to go down soon. "You know, the way the Mexicans all wait for jobs outside the Home Depot? Tomorrow morning before school a bunch of jocks are going to drive up on them and teach them a lesson."

"What lesson is that?"

"Oh, Maeve, don't blame me."

It's called a *mosca*—Maeve thought, though she had no idea why the makeshift labor market was called a "fly." It was a shape-up, the place where the laborers gathered to be chosen by local contractors. *Jornaleros*— day laborers, most of them with few skills other than their brute strength. She knew most of the workers were only recently up from the northern states of Mexico—where they'd been thrown off small plots of farmland by agribusiness, much of it American-owned, ironically—and willing to take just about any jobs to support their families.

"I don't know which Home Depot yet. Maybe the Torrance one over on Crenshaw or the one in Hawthorne. Or even Gardena. I thought you'd want to check it out to see if the guy you're looking for is one of the baseball team."

She'd seen Twitch twice now, and thought she could pick him out. "Shouldn't we try to stop it?"

"Who's going to believe us? It's just a rumor. And I'm sure not going to rat somebody out for passing me a rumor."

For a while they discussed whether there was anything at all they could do, triangulating the ethics like the crassest city hall hacks, Maeve thought.

*Your compass is broken, Maeve Mary, even to be arguing this.* She knew perfectly well she had to do something to stop it.

Imogen pretended to disapprove of violence, but she'd obviously worked herself into a kind of edgy anticipation, and Maeve guessed she was secretly looking forward to the excitement.

She wondered about all the displaced anger and insecurity that led kids to demonize these sad hardworking men. The *jornaleros* were taking no jobs the Anglo boys would ever consider, and the boys blew far more on lattes and music downloads than the *jornaleros* earned for whole families. But she'd heard that despising tone of voice so often. *Mexes. Wetbacks. Beaners.* It was as if these stocky brown men were personally offensive to them in some way. She wondered if there was any way to fix it all. The jocks were human, too. They couldn't be irredeemable.

She still had the meeting with Ruthie Loew. A date, really. But what you need now, girl, Maeve thought, is some way to restore your own balance. Less craziness in your life.

No, that wasn't what she wanted. She wanted *more* craziness, real sexual abandon.

**Maricruz Olivares**
**Behind Aztec Market**
**Huépac, Sonora**

Dearest sister Maricruz,

> *Please do not worry, I am well. How are you and everyone in the family? Did you get the dollars I sent through Eufemia? Please send a letter to Izak as I told you. He says he hasn't got any letters yet. Is anybody in Huépac still looking for me? The judiciales from Hermosillo? Up in El Norte we don't have to worry so much about what type of police it is, except la migra of course. They are mostly*

*all just* la jura. [Cops. —ML.] *The Spanish of here is different sometimes, full of new words and English words and they completely forget some verb tenses and talk like five-year-olds. On the TV you hear Cuban Spanish very much and have to strain to understand it.*

*I still have my job building a rock wall that will last another month or more. The* gabacho *I work with is a riddle. He is big and strong, a* pendejo *sometimes and sometimes kind but I don't care. He pays me honestly in cash every day. We are in a very rich area and you would love to see the horse-riding trails. Mostly it is young girls who ride here and often they ride on those* maricón [here it only means "sissy" —ML.] *English saddles and they bounce up and down like ducks on horseback. Yesterday I saw a big pure white stallion. Just like that* corrido *you listened to so much it made me mad,* El Caballo Blanco.

*I have become a surfer, can you believe it? Your own brother Jaime. I had help to fix a broken surfboard and taught myself to ride the waves just like some* gabacho *named "Lance." They try to keep Mexicans in the worst places near piers but I ride wherever I want and one boy who is a real surfer says I am very good. "Awesome," is the word he used in English. It is all exciting. I know I can be great, truly, with practice.*

*Please, Maricruz, write to me and send me news. I miss you all so much and especially Mami.*

**Your Jaime**

As it turned out, she was early for the date, after putting it off a half hour by cell because she'd been held up with Imogen. She parked two blocks north of the coffee bar and sat for a long time in the car, oblivious to the street traffic, fighting off imaginary images of grappling on a big comfortable bed with a naked Ruthie. In the daydreams Ruthie was always the reluctant one, the one with doubts, backpedaling subtly. Was it revisionist history? Maeve would construct a satisfactory reverie up to some critical point, and then Ruthie would say softly, "No, not that," or "No thanks, girl." There had to be a psychological truth to it, some disinclination that Maeve intuited.

Three surf punks with DayGlo hair glared toward her window with impersonal menace. They made faces, big eyes, waggled their tongues lasciviously. What had she ever done to them? Suddenly she wanted to kill them. They laughed and moved on. Four shop fronts in a row had been dolled up from an older baroque building—silent-movie Spanish, her father called its whipped cream plasterwork. The stores there sold jewelry, microbikinis and skimpy Ts, hemp clothing and other paraphernalia and a hundred different kinds of sandals. The whole enchilada for beach people.

She got out and walked the three blocks down to the sand to watch the breakers roll partway up a broad stretch of beach. It was getting dark, and the foam turned almost fluorescent where it boiled off the waves. She remembered the red tide her father had shown her years earlier. An invasion of phytoplankton. You could stand in the water, though it had reeked of sea death and catpiss and rotting vegetation, and you could actually write your name in the calmer sea, the trail of your finger glowing green-white. Waves had been bloodred during the day and winked on like lights at night.

It was an evocative memory because they'd all still been together at Mom's then, unscorched by so much change. Dad still commuted home from the aircraft plant every day. And he wrote whatever it was he'd been writing in the widow's watch in the attic. He'd never told her about it, but she'd always guessed it was poetry, though it could as easily have been a thriller about international diamond smugglers, or a tell-all about his days in Thailand for the army. His writing evenings had mostly left her active memory long ago, but one day she would have to make him tell.

A gull came over low, almost as if targeting her, and it shrieked twice. The smell of fast food took over the walkway that was just above the beach, and she figured that was what'd drawn the gull. Burgers, cheesesteak, fries. It was a wonder they hadn't evolved to have Styrofoam beaks.

"Hi, Maevie." Startled, she was gently clasped from behind, with hands she felt discreetly avoiding her breasts. It was Ruthie's voice. "Don't turn, please. I like holding you like this."

"I like it, too. It's comforting. I'm so crazy about you I'm going nuts."

"Ssssh. Don't be plastic. Your hair smells so good."

"Vanilla in the shampoo."

"No. It's your smell. A little like the patchouli smell of your secret place."

"Ooooh. My knees just went wobbly."

Out on the darkening gusty beach, they couldn't help seeing a boy chase a girl across the sand. The girl glanced back and let him catch up.

"Go for it," Ruthie said softly. "Last one down on the sand is a chickenshit. I used to work in a food stand here, and it's amazing how many seductions are brought about by patches of open skin available to caress." She kissed the back of Maeve's neck, and Maeve tried to turn to kiss her back but Ruthie held her too hard.

The couple running across the sand shrieked happily and the boy lunged forward and tripped the girl.

"You have trouble accepting love, don't you?" Ruthie said. "It's got to be giving for you."

"Ruthie, please. I can't keep up with you. Are you stoned?"

"A hit or two."

"Do you have to get stoned to see me?"

"It helps, sweetie." Ruthie slackened her grip and Maeve turned around. To her own surprise, she gave her only a chaste peck

"You're more scared than me," Maeve noted. "I thought this wasn't your first time."

They held hands and walked out toward the dark surf, angling away from the couple that was laughing and grappling in the sand. "In a few months you're off to college," Ruthie said. "And then I'm Kleenex. Stuck in the twelfth grade."

"That's not true. We've got six months and a summer, too, to work something out."

They sat down side by side on the concrete abutment of an old wooden piling under the pier. Waves washed toward them but flopped back only a few yards away. Maeve was apprehensive, but it seemed to her there was some mellow place they could get to if they only knew how. "Have you still got the J?"

The other girl took the half-smoked joint out of her shirt pocket and started it up with a kitchen match, cupped carefully against the breeze. She inhaled and handed it to Maeve.

Maeve drew in a big hit and was instantly a little woozy. Medications, even the illegal ones, had always overboosted her.

"What was the delay you called about?" Ruthie now asked. It was meant to seem quite casual.

"Is that the trouble? You've been parsing that all evening as some-body else, haven't you? Oh, God. It was nothing at all." She grabbed Ruthie's hand, then carefully returned the last of the joint to her. "A friend named Imogen told me the jocks are going to go beat up some poor day laborers, probably tomorrow morning. It's too awful." She had an inspiration. "Any way you could help?"

"You mean fly down like Wonder Woman?" Ruthie inhaled deeply and held her breath.

"I'm sure we could find a way to stop it as mortals." Maeve had to wait until Ruthie was ready to exhale. Some small ratlike creature scuttled away under the pilings. Laughter trailed along the walk behind them, and a distant car alarm started up and cycled through its annoying repertoire of sounds.

"I'm not even sure I want to help," Ruthie said at last. "Why get involved? You'll make a lot of cool guys mad at you. Maybe even at your own school."

"But it's wrong."

Ruthie looked at her in an odd way. "Haven't you ever heard anyone say the word nigger?"

"Not without letting then know what I think of it," Maeve said emphatically.

"Uh-huh. That's the difference between us. I figure I've got to live with assholes every day. And some of them are cute and funny."

"Cute?"

"I've gone both ways, like you."

Maeve found herself with the joint again, almost gone now. She felt suddenly very lonely, as if Ruthie had slapped her and walked away. "This stuff's important to me, it's all part of real life," Maeve said. She took an ineffectual drag, and had to fingernail it carefully to give it back.

"I'm not big on political enthusiasm, Maeve."

"I guess that's okay. Everybody's different. Do you want to make love?"

Ruthie made an expansive gesture that meant, Where?

"Your house no good?"

She shook her head, then spit out the smoke. "Mom would kill me. She's sharp."

"I don't care. My car." Maeve had been hoping she wasn't losing her love for Ruthie and the marijuana helped smooth things out. They kissed hungrily on the pier, with desire starting to make her feel whole again.

"Mike, what can you tell me about a group that call themselves Special Ops," he asked on the phone. Mike Lewis was an old friend of Jack Liffey's, an L.A. social historian who'd recently come down with some dire immune system disorder that had made him semi-retire from full-time teaching. He was holed up now with a loving wife in a rural redoubt down in northern San Diego County, trying to get better. They'd already worked their way through the pleasantries about Maeve and polite inquiries about Mike's kids. Mike knew pretty much everything there was to know about outsiders and insiders both.

"You probably aren't talking about the official army commando teams of that name."

"That would be a safe bet. Nor any roving carloads of plastic surgeons looking for big noses."

"Jesus, that's reaching, Jack."

"Sorry."

"You're probably talking about a group of extremists who were tossed out of the Minutemen. It was the middle oughts, or whatever we've decided to call 2000 to 2010, and these dumdums were doing their best to seem respectable—just good patriots shining their headlights at the border and talking earnestly on their walkie-talkies to Immigration. Then David Duke showed up with his Dixie flag, followed by a lot of other strange folk who didn't look so respectable on TV. It's hard to know what line in the sand these Special Ops guys crossed to get themselves banished. I heard a rumor about some freelance work with dynamite."

Jack Liffey thought about this.

"They're mostly from the South Bay—Torrance, Redondo, Hermosa," Mike Lewis said.

"Tell me something I *don't* know."

Mike Lewis laughed once. "I think they wanted to call themselves Quantrill's Raiders, but none of them could spell it."

# 11

# A Sense of Honor

MAEVE'S NEED TO FACE UP TO HER MORAL DILEMMA—THAT IS, NOT TO SHIRK—WAS PUT OFF INDEFINITELY AT ELEVEN THAT NIGHT BY THE THUNDEROUS ARRIVAL OF THE YEAR'S RAINS THAT FORCED THE SUSPENSION OF ALMOST ALL ACTIVITY AT THE MOSCAS, ALONG WITH MUCH ELSE. A kind of hysteria grips L.A. with the arrival of real weather, chasing away the climate. The downpour caught even the weather service off guard because an unusual anticyclone in the desert had propelled ice cold air out of the Great Basin in Nevada and Utah, pushing it contrary to the customary eastward march of weather on the Pacific Coast.

This backward current dragged sleety rain in off the deserts and into the San Gabriel Mountains above L.A., where the front ran unexpectedly into an onshore stream of warmer and wetter air so that all hell broke loose overhead as this convergence stalled out over the city. The local TV weathercasters, former models and Rose Queens, who were normally confined to hyping baby changes in the climate, now babbled excitedly about cataclysm, about deluge, about the Colorado Express riding up and over a Pineapple Flow.

Smallish L.A.-size tornadoes spun off into trailer parks, freak hailstones—the size of pea gravel, no, golf balls, no, baseballs—tore through brand-new convertible tops, and ferocious winds shredded the brittle jacarandas. Power went out, came back, went out again and stayed out on the East Side where the poor lived, drivers on the slicked freeways immediately accelerated their cars into one another, into bridge abutments, anything, and grown men, for no known reason, were seen on TV swept down the suddenly overflowing concrete rivers, with valiant firemen dangling from ropes and grabbing for them road bridge after road bridge. More than five inches of rain fell the first day, and another three the next.

Jack Liffey braved the deluge to take Loco to the vet for his second chemo and had to wrangle him inside the clinic's door inch by inch with all four brakes set.

Gloria clambered down a clay path to what was called Sunken City at the foot of the cliffs below Point Fermin in San Pedro to investigate the bodies of a young bride and groom who had left a joint suicide note in their shiny Miata above. The bodies had come to rest on graffiti-covered slabs that were all that remained of the 600 block of Paseo Del Mar that had begun sliding down the 100-foot sandstone cliff eleven inches a day back in 1929, stopped, then slid again in 1943 and seemed to have stalled out about three-quarters of the way down, much the worse for the trip.

Blue Hostetler's mother accepted Jack Liffey's first report on the state of the search for her daughter with sad equanimity and without making another pass at him, though she did offer him home-made chocolate chip cookies. He told her about her daughter's good deeds, the food and supplies delivered to the laborers, but not about the dead body at the burned encampment. There was no particular connection between the two, but he knew a worried mother's uneasy imagination might draw one.

"There are sharks out there, Jack," she said. "Guys with fancy cars and wicked promises. I've run into them. It scares me."

"I understand, Helen. I don't think random fate is necessarily any crueler than some folks' idea of Providence. We can still hope Blue's a runaway. She may even have taken off with some basically decent boy. She was a smart girl. Unfortunately there's a lot we don't know about our kids. Maeve surprises me all the time."

"Do you think she surprises Kathy?"

"I know she does. Mothers don't always get special access."

"The nights are so bad," she complained.

"I'm sorry. I know they are. I had my share of self-medication in the old days."

At school Imogen just shrugged across the classroom to Maeve about her lack of information concerning any impending attacks on the *jornaleros,* and Ruthie told her she felt like a wet chicken and was staying home alone and to call her back in a day or two. Maeve couldn't help wondering if Ruthie was pulling back, having found somebody else.

Jaime waited in vain for Mike the first rainy morning at Hawthorne Boulevard and Silver Spur where he'd been picking him up every day for work, and then trudged back to the camp in his black trash-bag poncho to help the others trench around the tents and lean-tos to divert the rivulets of muddy water. A mile away, unseen, a crack was gradually opening high on the hillside above the old encampment where the fire, in addition to killing David Puigcerver Luz, had denuded the hill of its retaining wild plants to leave it particularly vulnerable to erosion. The waterlogged earth slumped almost a foot before tearing loose just after sunset. A mudslide roared down the unoccupied hill to sweep away what remained of the charred weeds and leave a long naked scar of fresh clay.

Twitch stood in a soaked T-shirt looking out over Lunada Bay as rain pelted the surf to nothing, turning the kelp deep green, and winds swirled unpredictably against the cliff. His mother called from the porch from time to time, and he knew he was wet to the skin but he decided he might have something to prove to himself about his ability to endure hardship. At the Chevron station on Pacific Coast Highway, Ledge took a collect phone call from Pelican Bay, California's supermax prison ten miles south of the Oregon border, in fact from the SHU within Pelican Bay, the Secure Housing Unit where the heads of California's prison gangs were sequestered from one another and from the general population.

Ledge was told by a high-up shot-caller of the Aryan White Brotherhood to take a little trip and tell a man's mother that it was raining hard up north and her son loved the birthday present. Nothing more and nothing less. It actually was raining up north, and the son certainly might have loved a birthday present. Ledge didn't want anything more to do with the Aryan Brotherhood after his release, but they'd protected him while he was inside, and disobedience now could easily mean death.


"Your dad didn't call."

"Mom, don't be so lame. I *heard* you on the phone. You even said something about Japan." The kitchen reeked of fast food— grease from some kind of cheap meat and melted cheese. It was making him sick. Rain pattered and then thundered and then pattered again on the roof like an angry God who kept changing his mind.

"Did you hang up on him, Mom?"

"He didn't want to talk to you. He said he was too busy."

"That's not true."

"He doesn't love us anymore, Brandon. We've got to face it together. He's got another girlfriend. I know it."

"He doesn't love *you*, you mean."

"Don't be mean, please, Brandon. You're all I've got left."

"Why can't you just be *normal*?" Twitch cried out with an unfocused defiance and fled the room. He slammed the door to his bedroom and set the hook that he'd just screwed in so she couldn't bust in on him anymore. He crossed to the tiny half bath attached to the room and dry heaved into the toilet. He was due for more pills, Combivir or whatever it was, but he didn't even reach down the big foot powder canister where he was hiding them. The medication was no go. He had a spasm of rage, and his jaw trembled. The pills worked for Magic Johnson. Why was life so damn unfair? First a mom turning herself into a freakshow, then catching the damn homo disease, and now he couldn't even keep down the medicine he'd secretly sold his T-bonds to buy.

He felt under his mattress until he found the crucifix he'd picked out at a creepy store in the Mexican area of Lomita. It had a tortured-looking Jesus on it, writhing against the nails. He set it up on his desk chair and knelt before it, trying to figure out how to pray in some flowery way that might make God notice him. He knew very little about church stuff and up until now that had been fine with him.

"Brandon!" his mother called through the door. He heard his hook rattle. "What's going on in there?"

Maeve figured that she was probably looking for consolation of some sort, or maybe validation, or maybe just a little more information.

Her consciousness was aboil with conflicting emotions, and her heart beat furiously as she carried the armload of books toward the checkout of the Redondo Beach library. They'd just called closing time, and the lights had flickered once, like at a theater. So it was now or never. A peal of thunder precisely announced Maeve's arrival at the checkout, and she nearly dropped all the books.

Does nothing ever work out calmly? she thought.

For in among the half dozen innocuous titles, she had secreted *The Well of Loneliness*, *The Price of Salt*, and a couple of Colette's Claudine novels. She wasn't sure which one had the hot parts.

Ruthie walked through the all-blue living room as her mom was doing a crossword, legs tucked up at her favorite end of the overstuffed sofa. "Eight letters for redundancy, starts with P-L."

"Pleonasm," Ruthie said.

"No way."

"Way."

Suzanne Loew laughed and sipped at an iced tea. She never drank before five—*the sun is over the yardarm*, she always announced at five or very soon after.

Impulsively Ruthie turned back and sat down opposite her mother. Some days she really did her best to enjoy the woman. "Don't you think we'd all be happier on the Westside?"

"What brought this on?"

"I hear about foreign movies secondhand. String quartets. Talks by people who write books. They'd all be close by. P.V. is like a cultural Sahara."

The woman considered. "Are you sick of all those blond surfer boys at your school?"

If you only knew, mom. "I can last another year for college. But what about you? You gave up New York for this."

Ruthie realized that this was probably the first time in her life she had considered her mother as an ordinary human being.

"The weather's nice," she said dryly.

"But you said once that you hate a place where the leaves stay the same and the air changes color."

Mrs. Loew laughed. "Did I? I was quoting somebody, I'm sure. I'm not that witty."

Outside a peacock cried, so shrill it yanked on their spines. Feral peacocks were the plague of P.V. Neither even mentioned it.

"You know, you always undersell yourself, Mom. You're a brilliant woman."

"What's this about?" Her mother's tone held a note of concern.

Ruthie wondered herself, but she had no real answer.

"Maybe I was a half generation out," her mother offered. "Too soon for feminism. No, too late. The eighties were a terrible time. Bad music. Bad books. No crusades to sign on for. It all sucked."

She'd never heard her mother use that word. It almost caused her to offer a share of her stash. But she thought better of it. She also decided against broaching the subject of affairs—if her mother had ever. . . No, not that.

They were silent a moment and then Ruthie pushed on.

"So why did you major in education? That's so—you know. You should have done philosophy or the history of ideas or critical theory."

Her mother laughed. "Why do we take the easy road, the one right in front of us that they tell us to take? Do you think a different degree would have made that much of a change?"

"Who knows? Maybe you'd have ended up in Paris, meeting everybody and shtupping Sartre."

"Sartre looked like a garden gnome. Could I have Camus, please?"

"You could have had the world, Mom. You're my hero."

Suzanne Loew shook her head. "Thank you, sweetie. That's the nicest thing you've ever said to me."


"You been looking peakéd for weeks, dude. I thought you could use a little field trip." Ledge gunned the old woodie though an intersection, extremely late on the yellow, freezing an old couple with a big umbrella.

Twitch wasn't sure why he'd come along, but he was surely getting nowhere stewing in his room and letting his upset stomach take him off into more dry heaves. The car radio was playing an old Beach Boys set for some anniversary or other.

> *Time will not wait for me*
> *Time is my destiny*
> *Why change the part of me that has to be free*
> *The love that passed me by*
> *I found no reason why.*


"You got to get a new girlfriend, man. You want I should keep an eye out? Plenty of women'd love to do a handsome kid like you." He punched Twitch's shoulder, a little harder than he should have. "Just say the word."

Twitch shook his head. He toyed with the idea of telling Ledge why he couldn't score anymore, no matter what age they were. Impossible. Ridiculous. You couldn't talk to Ledge about anything that mattered. He was such a goof, he'd probably think he'd catch the queer plague by sharing a joint with him.

The car pulled off into the Chevron station where Ledge worked. Ledge waved halfheartedly to Dugan, the overweight young man in the office, and he drove the woodie two-thirds of the way into the lube bay. No mechanics were on after six, but it appeared Dugan had been too lazy to pull down the doors. Ledge revved hard once as he shut down. Draining the old four-barrel, he liked to explain, way too often.

Dugan's body filled the interior doorway from the office, a Hitchcock silhouette against the light, as Ledge climbed out of the car. Twitch turned off the radio because it just made him sicker.

"'Sup, Surfman?"

"Eat me, Doog. You don't look so bushy-tailed, old buddy."

"I'm okay, man."

"You're fat as Crisco, bubba, and you're getting worse by the day. You waddle like Donald Duck."

"Fuck you. I can lose weight anytime. I got special powers from L. Ron Hubbard."

Ledge laughed, throwing his head back, as he walked toward a battered red tool chest that stood shoulder high at the rear of the lube bay. "Put on your Spandex and fly away, Mr. Special Powers. I've got to pick up some tools."

"I don't mean things like flying. I can see into things, I can change things."

"Then change your butt far away, man. I'm sick of you."

The shape disappeared from the doorway, and Twitch watched as Ledge pulled the heavy chest out at an angle and stooped down to a shallow wooden crate on the floor behind it. He put something from the crate into a small carryall bag he kept there and pushed the tool chest back. The wobbly casters resisted and he had to lean into it.

Dugan reappeared in the office doorway. "You oughtn't to be so mean, Ledge. I never did nothing to you. Today's my birthday."

"Birthdays ain't what they used to be, lardass. Get you some self-control."

"Whatever you say that's mean comes back on you ten times more," Dugan retorted. "I believe that to be a true fact."

"Go eat turds." Ledge tossed his bag in the backseat and climbed in. "God, that fatso gets on my nerves. I shouldn't let him rile me up. It ruins my whole night. Okay, Twitch, let's have us a little fun."

Jack Liffey was sitting morosely on the back screen porch, watching Loco's chest heave from time to time as he slept through fitful paw tremors. "You damn well make it through this, old buddy," he said aloud. "I'm not going to be happy refinancing my condo just to bury a big furry sack of disobedient bones."

Gloria was still out on patrol somewhere. He didn't see how anyone could do a demanding job like that for twelve hours straight, and, like everyone else in L.A., he suspected them of finding ways to dog it a bit for the last few hours of every shift. Unfortunate expression, he thought.

The phone started ringing inside, and he thought twice about it before heaving himself up.

"Dad, oh, I'm *sooo* sorry. I don't know how I got so self-absorbed. It's really disgusting."

"Calm down. Hello, Dad," he suggested. "Good evening. How are you tonight?"

There was a long pause. "Hi, Dad. Good evening. How are you tonight? But how's *Loco*? I can't believe I actually came over and didn't ask. I'm such a mess these days."

He thought he could detect a whole new level of turmoil careering around underneath her normal turmoil. The thing was, she'd have to work this one through without much help from him. All he could do was hold fast in neutral, trying hard not to say any of the wrong things. "Loco's about as good as can be expected. He had his second chemo today and is conked out now. He doesn't seem to want to eat, even his favorites. I should probably get him to smoke a joint to boost his appetite."

"Seriously?"

"No, hon, not seriously. Mother Nature will have to tell him to eat when she's ready. How are you doing?"

She fell silent a while, and he heard the rain suddenly beat more heavily on Gloria's old roof. An odd sound, both comforting and mildly disquieting.

"I guess I'm at a place where I experience things I never knew about," she said. "I've got to go with it."

He wondered what was up now, but she didn't seem ready to tell him. "You think you can handle it?"

"I hope so."

"If it ever gets too heavy, just come on over and cry in my arms. I'm here for you, in any state whatever. No judgments."

"I think I know that, Dad. Thanks a lot. And, listen, there's something I need to tell you. Not about me."

"Okay, sure." Something *else*? She'd witnessed an assassination attempt? Kathy was joining a messianic sect?

"Right before the rains began, I heard a rumor that a bunch of P.V. jocks were going to go over some morning and beat up the poor Mexican guys waiting for work outside Home Depot. I don't even know which one. It's complicated because I kind of promised I wouldn't say who I heard it from."

"Manual labor's not for sissies. Those guys are tough enough so I sure wouldn't want to jump them."

"Think baseball bats, Dad. And, you know how these jerks figure the odds—they only make a move when it's three to one."

"Okay, you did your duty, hon. I'll take it over from here."

"Thanks—that's a big load off my mind. I've been worrying it might actually happen, and I'd feel responsible."

"You can't protect every falling sparrow. Use some of that virtuous energy on yourself." Easier to preach than practice.

"I've never failed you, Dad, have I?"

"Stop right there. That sounds like something you'd say in a suicide note."

"I just mean I think I've always done my best. But my whole life is made up of 'I thinks.' I think I think way too much."

There was a burst of static on the line and then a crash and a tingling in his hand, as if lightning had hit a pole not very far away. "I'd better get off," he said into what he realized was a dead line. There was no dial tone when he rattled the buttons. At least he hoped the lightning was somewhere near *his* end. He wondered what he would have answered her. He rather liked the concept of her thinking too much.

Ledge parked the maroon woodie on Skyline, right where the char of one of the P.V. wildfires had stopped. The steady rains had dissolved away much of the gray ash that had darkened the land but new rivulets ran off the road, merged into muddy streamlets and then real cascades pouring down the freshly denuded slope. The water was already carving new gullies into the unanchored soil. In Southern California, mudflows were the inescapable camp followers of the fall brushfires.

Only one of the wipers cleaned well, on the driver's side, and Twitch angled his head over there to get a better look out.

"The taco benders came scurrying back here after I burned them out," Ledge said. "They're like locusts. Just ask anyone over in south L.A. They swarm in and take over everything. They've even pushed the niggers out of Watts so it's like Tijuana now. Somebody's got to plant the flag."

"A guy was killed," Twitch said.

"Not my doing if some Mex can't run faster than a little brush-fire. Jesus. Survival of the fittest, I guess." He looked worried. "You're not going to go all bleeding-heart on me, are you, buddy? I went and vouched for you."

"I'm fine with everything." And he was, in a going-for-the curl, ride-the-thing-in kind of way. Now and then, though, a flash of insight told him it was all some kind of demented lower-class bullshit his dad would have scorned. Just look at those dumbhead low-lifes Ledge hung with! But what was the point of worrying like that when his own death was grinning at him, the horrible viral gremlin in his blood, spreading around its evil sores and yeast infections and cancers and all the other shit. He already had one of the revolting purple blotches on his shoulder.

"That's my man." Ledge held out his palm and Twitch slapped it softly. "Ready to get wet?"

Ledge stepped out into the rain, dragging his bag out of the backseat—which Twitch could now see said Tunic-Semba Construction on it. It sounded familiar, and Twitch realized he'd seen it on sawhorses and construction barriers all over town. Then Ledge went to the trunk and got out a posthole digger.

"You gonna help or just rubberneck?" He tossed the long tool to Twitch and beckoned. They walked a few yards up the road and stepped off the pavement carefully onto a mud shoulder to work their way a few yards out the slippery incline, stopping just before the cliff there fell off much more steeply.

Twitch had no idea how to use the digger, so he just rested the clamshell tip on his shoe as he waited beside the older man. Beneath them were runnels of water excavating their way downhill between blackened stumps that had once been bushes.

"Fuck 'em," Ledge said. "Fuckin' *Pedros* and *Jesus*es."

Twitch, seeing the look of intensity on his companion's face, wondered if this implacable hatred of Mexicans might be the only real idea Ledge had ever had. He knew almost nothing about him, which all at once seemed very strange. Why had he never asked?

"This'll just about do the nut," Ledge said.

He scuffed a small area clear with his shoe and knelt to open his bag. "Hold this, dude."

Twitch found himself clinging to a waxy red tube that looked a bit like a highway flare. There was no pull-off starter cap, though, just paper folded inward in a fan to seal the end. Beads of what felt like hardened maple syrup had sweated out of the tube, and with a shudder Twitch guessed all at once what it was.

"Cowabunga, man!"

"They ain't gonna be no fingerprints left, so cool the worry."

"I heard they can trace this stuff. With chemical markers and shit."

"This is thirty years old, from when I was working construction. Back in the day, before the A-rabs started blowing things up. We're okay with it."

It was thirty years old. Twitch thought he'd seen an old movie about dynamite becoming unstable over time, and he stared down at the beads of syrup exuding from the waxy tube. Was that pure nitroglycerine? Jesus. If the rain hadn't been pelting down, he figured he'd be sweating, too.

Ledge took out a coil of what must have been fuse cord, and a little metal tube and a crimping tool. He went into a strange half squat, with the crimpers behind him as he squeezed hard at the tube and cord.

It was the first time he'd seen Ledge smile all day. "Not dignified, I admit, but they taught us it's better to take a little blasting cap accident in the butt than in the family jewels."

Twitch was shaken, barely able to pay attention, as he handed over the dynamite and Ledge waggled a hole in the stick with the awl of his pocket knife.

"Easy as pie," he said, as he pressed the blasting cap into the hole in the dynamite. For some reason he dug another hole right through the tube and fed the cord through it until the fuse was snugged tight.

"Watch and learn, dude."

But, later, Twitch could remember little of what he'd seen. The clamshell digger burrowing into the mud, then carrying the dynamite down the hole it made. Twirling the fuse cord so it didn't kink. Ledge taking off his flannel shirt as he dug, and the sinews in the man's thin wet arms flexing. Ledge slapped the handles of the digger up and extracted the tool from the earth. Left with five feet of fuse protruding, Ledge packed mud down into the hole forcefully with his heel.

"Radical," Ledge said. He chuckled. "That's how it's done."

Something in Twitch's gut was beginning to hurt sharply. He was unable to tell anymore if a cramp was indigestion or an early greeting from something far worse.

"One more time."

About fifty feet away they planted a second stick of dynamite, and this time, Twitch watched even more haphazardly. He just wanted to be home, back the way home used to be. He wanted to be safe and clean and dry.

"Got a lighter?"

Twitch nodded.

"This shit's forty seconds to a foot, so I'd say two and a half minutes. When I signal, light it up and we'll book it to somewhere we can watch safely. Okay?"

"I guess."

"Don't hassle it. You done good. Just go back and fire up that other one when I say."

Twitch returned to the first stick they'd buried and edged himself carefully out along the mud shelf. He had a lighter he used for weed and hash, and it would be no problem in the rain as long as he shielded it. Sheet lightning lit the whole world for a moment, like the gods taking a peek: What's up down there? Then a rumbling walked all around them, who could tell where?

What a kick if lightning struck right here, he thought, while they were standing there on top of the dynamite like prize assholes, and everything went up in a blast that would end all his problems. Bring it on! I'm *ready*. But God didn't bring it on. Oh, well. Another time. Nothing was easy.

He hunkered down over the fuse cord and picked up the end with a fresh curiosity. It was a rough-woven orange cotton wrapping over something like cookie dough a quarter inch in diameter. Strange stuff.

He watched Ledge fifty feet away, the scene's details etched into the curtain of rain by the streetlights. Ledge held one fist dramatically straight over his head. "Fire in the hole!" he yelled as loud as he could.

Twitch lit his lighter, shielding it from the rain, and watched the wind tear at the weak flame in its little perforated shield. The storm had brought out the smells of sagebrush and charred brush, cloying smells.

Ledge hollered "Go!" and pumped his arm down like a tennis player celebrating an ace. As bad luck would have it, a swirling gust of wind chose that moment to blow out Twitch's lighter. He flicked and flicked and was just about to panic when the flame finally lit. He held it to the fuse, expecting nothing at all to happen. But it started spitting out sparks and smoke. His foot slipped a little as he tried to stand and run, and he had to catch himself by a hand that sank into the icky mud, causing him to lose his lighter in the muck.

"Come on, dude!" Ledge yelled.

Twitch saw the car as he ran, and then he was inside and scooted down in the seat, wiping his hand surreptitiously on the Naugahyde down low. Ledge started up on the first crank.

"Gnarly night for some," he said mockingly as he pulled away.

They circled along Skyline and before long parked the woodie again, engine still running, at an outside elbow of the road that looked straight across to where they had been. Twitch had been glancing at his wristwatch off and on.

"Two minutes," Twitch said.

"Left?"

"No. *Gone.*"

"Come on, come on, baby."

"Fifteen. Ten. Five."

Almost at his zero call, they felt a sharp tremor, and a large cone of mud shot straight upward from where Ledge had been standing. It mushroomed outward and broke up in the insistent rain. Nothing happened to the cliff.

"Well, *shit.*"

The second burst was deeper, with a rumble to it like the lightning. "There!" Ledge cried.

A crack had formed exactly where Twitch had been standing and then a big scallop of waterlogged cliff dirt started to slump. It hesitated as if it had forgotten its mission and then skidded straight down, pushing half the hill ahead of it. An arc of the asphalt road tore away, too, and followed the mud down the slope, skating on the surface before breaking into a hundred chunks that began to tumble erratically. The streetlights all flared up for an instant and then went out. Within a minute it was all over, and the hillside was a raw wound in the starlight, without evidence of vegetable life. An unbroken six-inch iron pipe emerged from the mud and ran straight as an arrow across the inner arc of the missing cliff to tunnel back in again.

It was hard to see much down below with the lights out, only a jumble of darkness.

"It's all good, Mexes," Ledge announced. "See if you mud people can live on mud."

Twitch, feeling only anticlimax and disappointment now, realized that the man's obsession was less a hatred than an addiction. Ledge was almost drunk with it, and he'd be utterly lost without it.

# 12

# The Green Fairy

## 4 DEAD IN P.V. SLIDE

AS HE WAITED FOR HIS COFFEE TO COOL A LITTLE, JACK LIFFEY TURNED THE TRAGIC HEADLINE OVER IN HIS HEAD A FEW TIMES. The *L.A. Times* had recently gone to a really ugly all-caps sans-serif font for its hootier headlines, and the look undercut the intent in some way, like a dull neighbor shouting in your ear. The words on the page became mere sounds, and then there were a number of disquieting metaphysical questions about the use of "DEAD" instead of the more active "DIE." There were even ambiguities in the word "SLIDE." Before long, though, reality took over from all the pre-coffee philology, and he realized he should be worrying about Jaime.

According to the paper, the slide had let go late in the evening on a rainsoaked cliffside that had recently burned, the mud flooding over an improvised campground where perhaps a dozen illegal immigrants had been living. It sounded to him like the same site where David Puigcerver Luz had lost his life, but that camp had been evacuated. There had, after all, been other small brushfires up there this dry autumn, their locations scattered widely. But it was possible some of the workers had moved back, or others had arrived, or it was another camp altogether. He pored over a vague map on the jump page that was too small and too imprecise to help much.

What a horrible way to die, he thought. Breathing mud. It gave his dormant claustrophobia a tweak. As a child he'd fallen down a well and held on to a slight ledge, treading water for fourteen terrible hours, with only a tiny circle of sky showing above. Once in a while, something evocative would bring that dreadful panic back to him, all in a rush. Enough, enough.

Gloria had already left for work. He'd told her about Maeve's vague warning of a threat to attack undocumented workers at one of the South Bay's Home Depots, and she said she'd do what she could to put out a warning. Unfortunately, quite a few other police jurisdictions were involved. One of the worst impediments to getting anything done in L.A. was the hotchpotch of separate cities—and even the patchwork of unincorporated county areas—you had to contact just to get everybody's attention. And there was often one civic entity so jealous of its own autonomy that it refused to listen.

He got up and walked quietly out onto the back verandah. Loco lay almost lifeless on a big foam pad they'd found for him in the garage. Jack Liffey knelt and rested a hand on the dog's warm haunch, which was barely rising. He had rarely been at such close quarters with a living being that was so suspended between life and death, and that fact held a terrible dread for him.

The dog snuffled and yipped once in his sleep, and Jack Liffey resisted the impulse to believe all this pain and this struggle had to mean something important because it hurt so much. What it meant was that he cared for the dog in the here and now, he told himself. There was no supernatural manna, no dog ghost that would float upward and get to romp in the clouds.

"I hope you make it, boy," he said, smoothing the bristly hairs on the dog's flanks. "There's no visiting after hours."

The firemen were wheeling odd devices across the flattish area at the foot of the mudslide where the flow had run out of steam and settled into a lumpy moonscape, maybe 100 yards wide. Jaime sat disconsolately on a blue rubber mat a fireman had laid down for him, watching. The firemen all wore transparent plastic oversuits against the drizzle, and he clutched a tarp they'd given him, tucked over his head. The devices they were pushing around looked like furniture dollies with beeping TV sets strapped to them. In addition, three big dogs led policemen on leashes, sniffing the earth, and from time to time the cops drove thin poles carefully into the soil. The forward edge of the mud flow had gathered up lighter items like a sofa cushion, a worn tire, a lawn chair, and, ironically, his own surfboard, with the last skeg snapped off now and the repair ripped away. Occasionally, over the morning, there was a cry, and then a team of shovelers moved in.

Eight men had been in the camp the previous evening when they'd heard two sharp detonations and then the roar of mud and debris coming toward them. Several who'd survived had fled immediately, terrified of *la migra*. Four bodies had been found pretty quickly, shallowly covered, but Jaime was certain there was one more, an older man named Plato he hadn't seen anywhere after the slide. He'd liked him. A man with a grizzled gray beard and a wonderful sense of humor, but getting fairly creaky and slow for a gardener.

After Jaime had dozed for a while on the mat, he'd been handed off to a new *jura*, in the beige uniform of a *rurale*—at least that's what it would have meant in Mexico. This one was wearing an open yellow slicker over his unform. He expected such authority figures to be corrupt, but he wasn't sure. This man spoke good Spanish and even looked Mexican. Jaime had gone over the story again and again and met with the same skepticism about hearing definite explosions.

"I heard what I heard, sir," he insisted.

"Okay. The name of the last illegal who died?"

He didn't like the word illegal, but he wasn't going to argue. "Plato. That's all I know. We were staying two hills over that way until Monday." He pointed south. "We came here because it's closer to the big road and that Country Market."

"You know this is private land right here?" the deputy said.

Jaime shrugged. "Isn't all of it everywhere?"

"Yeah, most of the world, son," the deputy said sympathetically, and then told him firmly not to move an inch.


At about ten, one of the county's ground radars, on expensive tryout from a company called Ground Effect Systems, found a horizontal man-sized disturbance of the mud density about four feet down. Within a half hour, they had Plato's body out of the gelid mess of the mudslide. The man was clutching a big-bead rosary and looked pretty unhappy, which wasn't surprising since he was thoroughly dead.


Later Jaime could see a whole team wearing beige uniforms and carrying umbrellas tromping around at the top of the slide. A black woman brought him a paper cup of coffee and a cheese sandwich on floppy white bread that he had to extricate from clingy plastic.

The deputy with the good Spanish finally came back. "I'm sorry, Mr. Olivares, there are still some questions about the cause of the mudslide and the identity of the victims, and since you have no fixed residence, we're going to have to hold you as a material witness. Understand, that's *not* a crime. How old are you?"

He tried to decide quickly whether being a minor would be to his benefit or not. "Seventeen."

"Good," the deputy continued in Spanish. "You'll be given a bed in a juvenile facility."

Jaime shrugged. What could he do?

"You do realize that you're *not* under arrest and you're *not* being charged with any crime. We only need to make certain you'll be available for further questions."

"And *la migra?*"

"Ah. That's a gray area, son. The Los Angeles County Sheriff's Department doesn't enforce immigration laws, but we don't ignore them, either. My advice is to go on being very cooperative, the way you are now, and you'll probably luck out."

"You'll let me go?"

"It's not going to be in my hands. But I'll tell them in no uncertain terms that we need you right here."

"Will you do me a favor, sir?"

"That depends."

Jaime handed him a business card. "Will you call this man and tell him what is happening. He's my friend."

The deputy looked over the card skeptically. "Strange friend."

Jaime shrugged. "It's the truth. I speak the truth."

The deputy tucked the card under his raincoat and into a jacket pocket. "I believe you, but I'll have to think about it."

"And what happens to my surfboard?"

The deputy glanced at the board jutting out of the mud twenty feet away, and then back at the boy. "Hey. You surf?"

"Yes, sir. I can carve it." The words felt silly in his mouth.

The deputy grinned at this, but Jaime didn't think he sensed anything cruel in the laughter. He knew the fact of his surfing was unusual.

"*Buena suerte, mijo. Mi surfisto!* I'm afraid your *plancha* is evidence right now. But maybe later."

**Dear Dad,**

> *I dont really feel anything. Maybe I shoud. I didnt even know those dum Mexicans were down there so it isnt really my fault. Blame Ledge if you want to blame somebody. And look at me dying here at 16. I think four Mexicans more or less and nobodys even going to notice. Who will care? But thats not right. Theyve got mommies and families and things.*
>
> *But fuck em anyway. I didnt even get a car out of this crappy life. Everybody white gets a car.*
>
> *I started smoking Marlboros today. Im really terrified of lung cancer ha ha ha. I got to find a bunch of other stuff that kills you real slow and feels good.*
>
> *Hey I coulda been a real jock. I kissed Bambi Morton in the closet when I was seven. I got a blow job from a college girl when I was 11. I had lots of grownups and they all loved it. Im a shredder. Im Twitch the Great. Im Bayboy forever. How do I get out of this goddam gnarly life without pain? Dad just call me please please.*

> **Twitch**

The tiled storefront was called Heavenly Surf Tacos. It wasn't the standard Cal-Mex place with taco-enchilada-beans-rice combination dinners, but modeled more after one of the open stalls the surfers all saw along Mexico 1, the stretch of runaway development between

Tijuana and Rosarito. Fish tacos our speciality. Extra "fresh." He ordered a plain coffee. The long tiled counter was fragrant with grease and cilantro.

Jimmy Hyde, whom he was meeting, wrote for the local alternative weekly in the South Bay, which covered everything from Venice Beach to P.V. The man had been mildly famous once for winning a big lawsuit back East after being fired from a city daily for reporting that a peevish black city councilwoman had banned all whites from addressing her human relations committee. Life hadn't been particularly kind to him since, but he had clung to working the types of muckraking stories that the mainstream reporters generally considered unsound.

Jack Liffey sat on a stool at a high table. Embalmed in resin on the tabletop, small as it was, were newspaper articles about surf heroes, and he read for a moment about George Freeth, the guy who'd come over from Hawaii in 1907 and started it all with planks nailed together and was now in the Surfrider Hall of Fame. He wondered if there was a Hapless Child Finder Hall of Fame somewhere. Probably not.

When he looked up, a slim and smiling Jimmy Hyde was coming in the door, leading a parade of the homeless, meaning grizzled geezers in plaid shirts and too many outer garments. Six of them, at his count.

"Fourteen fish tacos," Jimmy announced at the counter. "And seven giant Cokes."

The Anglo behind the counter gave them all the fish-eye, and then shrugged and went to work on the grill.

One of the men straggling in behind their benefactor wore a greasy overcoat and another sported duct-taped loafers. Two others, weirdly, were sharing an extra-large blue parka shoulder to shoulder like Siamese twins.

"Hi, Jack. You said you wanted information, so you're buying."

Jack Liffey stayed at the manageable edge of annoyance. "I wasn't expecting the whole team."

"I kept it simple. You won't have any rare Kobe beef filets to worry about."

"I sure hope you promised your pals a good long soak in your own bathtub and a place to crash at your house tonight. It's getting nasty out."

"I've evolved past the marshmallow intellect we all had as hippies," Jimmy Hyde said. The tacos started coming and Jimmy distributed them among his entourage. The sad old men spread out in ones and twos through the establishment, hoarding their dinners, as if they didn't much like one another's aroma either.

"He'll pay," Jimmy told the skeptical counterman, and Jack Liffey nodded to acknowledge it.

"Fifty-one eighty," the man said.

Finally, the reporter joined him at the tiny table, with his own tacos and his Coke, which took up just about all the space. "Good to see you again, Jack. Did you find the Watson boy? I knew his folks."

It took Jack Liffey a moment to recollect a Watson boy. It was almost three years back. "The kid was on a complex cycle of drugs and rehab." In fact, the boy had been alternating blow, downers, and acid with various forms of military school and the posher rehab academies. "I caught him on the very bottom step, on black-tar heroin, and he could barely remember his own name. His parents finally found a boot camp up in northern Manitoba, and I haven't heard since. He's probably still there, high on reindeer dung."

Jimmy laughed once. "I wondered where the Watsons'd gone. They were neighbors." He began working at his fish taco. Across the room, one old man was shooting spitwads at his compatriots

"How's work?" Jack Liffey asked.

"The yuppies are on a tear to 'upgrade' all the beach towns. They want to price out the handful of retirees that're left. The economics of the push have to do with burying all the power lines underground, like they do in the fancy towns in south Orange County. While it all sounds green, it's a lot more complex and involves pricing out the poor. Unfortunately, it's too byzantine to make the right kind of sexy story for the big papers. Who are you after?"

"Do you know a group called Special Ops?"

"Do I? They're the neo-Nazi junior varsity. They're coming out of the woodwork now that the Republicans have made all that Nazi mojo respectable."

"Facts first. Editorials later."

"This group is mostly from the South Bay, as far as I know, probably Redondo in the main. Louts. Guys who wear Redwing boots. Smalltimers, but they don't know it. These're the guys who give rednecks a bad name. But they can be serious as a heart attack."

There was an outcry from a young couple at a table nearby who'd caught an errant spitwad. The man in the overcoat was now hugely overacting innocence.

"I've heard most of this, already," Jack Liffey said. "Weren't they kicked out of the Minutemen for going too far? What about some names?"

"I wouldn't mess with these guys, Jack. Even morons can hurt you. Where I grew up, if you fell into the hog pen and passed out, the porkers'd damn well eat you."

"I don't think I want to know where you grew up. Just a name or two of the Special Ops."

"How about Big Bob Lowndes? He used to be well-known on

the cage-fight circuit. I don't 'spect you spent a lot of time keeping up with that. It's a subset of full-contact martial arts, with head butts and elbow gouges and all the trimmings. Though I don't think they call it 'the cage' anymore. It's 'The Octagon,' all tidied up for cable. The whole sport is what happens when the macho gene gets fucked up early on. I'd leave them be."

"I'll be careful."

"I know these guys. They say, 'Aw, shucks, we're just messin' with you, man,' and then belly-laugh as they tear your arm off."

"I'll keep that in mind."

"Jack, Jack, we all used to believe that the world of human decency was indestructible. Bless you and keep you, it really really ain't. Have you watched TV recently?"

Jack Liffey laughed. "Not much. Okay, things are pretty bad."

"Uh-huh. The cable channels are just about up to paying people to chop their own body parts off. Every generation says, Well, *hell,* it can't get any worse than *this,* and then it just falls through the floor another level toward hell."

Two of the homeless men were spitwadding back at the first attacker now.

"Before you get to proceed with your grievances about crack-heads on TV ruling the world, how about coming up with one more Special Ops name for me?" Jack Liffey said. "Pretty please."

"Ledge. Percival 'Ledge' Choate. He's an ex-con from San Q and Pelican Bay, probably still has to do what the Aryans tell him. From what I hear, he likes to blow things up."

"The Aryans?"

"Wonderful name, AWB. Aryan White Brotherhood—as if there was, maybe, an Aryan *Chinese* brotherhood, too."

"You know how to get in touch with these guys?"

Jimmy shook his head. "Would you rather be beaten to death with a tire iron or a bike chain?"

"I'll watch my step."

The original spitwadder sprinted out of the cafe, bellowing. Jack Liffey figured he'd missed a nuclear counterstrike.

"Last colleague I set up to do a piece on one of these crazy groups promised he was gonna take it easy, too," Jimmy said. "He vanished for a while and then fell off a bridge."

"Killed?"

"I sure hope so. The whole staff of the paper went out to pay our respects when he was buried. That was back East, though. Haven't lost anyone out here yet."

Jack Liffey made an impatient gesture, beckoning for more information.

"Big Bob owns a bowling trophy shop in Culver City. On Sepulveda, I think. It's called Big Bob's, so that ought to help a bit. Ledge works in a Chevron on PCH in Redondo. Look for the guy with the blurry yardbird tattoos."

"Now that didn't hurt a bit, did it?"

"Come back and tell me how it all comes out, Jack, that is, if you're not on life support at County. I'm rooting for you."


Jaime sat on a long padded bench at Los Padrinos Juvenile Hall in Downey, a few miles north of Long Beach. They'd left him in the room they'd called "processing." It was cleaner than any official office he'd ever seen in Sonora, as if tended by a whole squad of janitors and repairmen. Except that the windows had heavy metal wire over them and the doors looked especially strong. There were several posters that had uplifting messages in English and Spanish, like WE'RE IN THIS TOGETHER/*Estamos en esto junto*, and THE BEST AUTHORITY IS INTERNAL/*La mejor autoridad es interna*. Each had some variation on a multicultural photo of rough-looking young men of different races walking arm-in-arm, or helping each other scale a barrier.

The only other person in the room was a barrel-chested man in a casual blue shirt and a big moustache, pecking away at a computer like someone who'd rarely seen one. A male voice out of sight was crooning names, one after another.

"Excuse me, sir, have you called Mr. Liffey?" Jaime asked yet again. He'd been trying it on everyone since the deputy had dropped him at the first sheriff's station. From there, they'd sent him to this building in a van with three other teens—Anglos who had been fiercely intent on staring one another down.

But the man just ignored him and went on typing. When the computer beeped twice, he sat back as if challenged. "Kid, do you ever pick your feet in Poughkeepsie?"

Jaime had no idea what he meant. "No, sir."

"Pity. The world needs more people who pick their feet in Poughkeepsie. You like landslides?"

"No, sir."

"Not even to try to steal your pals' money?" The man now swiveled in the chair to stare hard at Jaime.

It was so strange, the guilt that crept up on him like a wolf, reminding him of the sensation of that stone in his hand and the feeling of Don Ignacio's temple bones cracking. "*No.*"

"If you look deep enough, we're all guilty of something, wouldn't you say, kid?"

"And you, too?"

The man laughed. "I guess if you look back, I didn't study for my math finals in the eleventh grade, so in the big lottery I ended up stuck here."

"I didn't do a crime, sir. They said I'm a witness. Can I make a phone call?" He now knew Jack Liffey's number by heart.

"What's it worth to you?"

"They took everything I have at the first station. You can have my surfboard."

"Do I look like I fucking want a *surfboard*? What has to come next comes next, kid. Don't sweat it so much."

Another man opened the door and looked in, glanced briefly at the typist and then pointed straight at Jaime. "*You*, come."

"How's it hanging, Ted?" the typer said.

"Don't even talk to me."

Jaime walked to a low railing with a gate in it and waited.

"It's not locked. We're a facility that offers you great trust."

He said the last sentence with a peculiar twist that made Jaime doubt its truth. He followed the man out and across the street, through a gate in a high wall that the man had to unlock, and then along a covered walkway past row after row of identical barracks.

"Can I make a phone call?"

The man frowned at him and turned away without a word. Suddenly, the man halted on what seemed a whim. "You from East Los?"

"No, sir."

"Good."

He pushed Jaime in the door of what he called the *Casa Azul*, where a dozen young Latinos were playing cards or standing on things to try to peer out the high windows or just lying bored on bunks. The deputy left. But as soon as the others had asked him,

"Where you from, *ese?*" and found out he was a "real Mexican" and had no *barrio* and no *klika*, they lost interest.

One guy with a lot of tattoos and big muscles tried to talk to him in terrible Spanish, *inglesito*, full of mispronounced English words and howlingly misused verb tenses, but Jaime did his best to remain polite. It must be a pity, he thought, not to speak even one language well. How would clear thinking ever be possible?

An hour later the deputy was back. As he hauled Jaime out of the barracks, he said, "My mistake. I make one a year."

The building three more barracks along was called *Casa Aztec*, and Jaime could tell right away that the occupants were Mexico-born. Even though they didn't talk to him for a long time. A few of the boys were from deep rural areas and had that countrified timidity, eyes down and arms limp, but the brasher ones he eventually learned were *chilangos*—from Mexico City—or *tapatios*—from Guadalajara—or *tijuas*—from Tijuana. There was still something common to all of them that marked them out as Mexicans.

Two were from Sonora, but neither had lived within fifty kilometers of Huépac.

"*Compa*," he asked the boy next to him who had a swollen black eye and looked unthreatening. "What happens to us?"

"Don't you know?" He waited for the answer. "Tomorrow we ride a bus to the San Ysidro crossing and then the *migra* hands us over to the *tijua* cops. They'll shout at us and punch us a while and look for any dollars we got hid, and then they'll turn us loose on the *Avenida Revolution*."

"*Mierda*. What kind of papers have you got?"

With a kind of hopeless disdain, the boy showed him a clump of paperwork from his shirt pocket, some of the cards and papers more tattered than others. The name was Gabriel Sanchez. He did have a very good-looking California driver's license. "Sanchez isn't a Sonora name."

"You got it, *amigo*. I found it on the tombstone of a dead baby near Culver where I was working, same year born as me. I made a letter mailed to this dead baby and then used that to get his birth certificate downtown. From there you just keep applying for papers and buying papers and you forget you got a real name. Call me Javier."

Jaime looked close at the driver's license. "Is this real?"

"It cost me four hundred dollars. There's a guy in MacArthur Park." The boy was in the grip of some particular self-contempt. "He made me a fool. No, it's not no good."

He took his papers back. "He made it on a copier and then put the plastic over it. There's something missing."

"What?"

"I really don't know."

Another boy wandered over and Jaime asked him, "Will the police at the border be *judiciales?*"

"No, man. Just *placas*. Mexico forever."

"I don't have any ID at all," Jaime told them.

"Who does? They'll just shout at you for a while. Stop worrying, man. When I get back up here, I want to get a rich friend. The whole world kisses their balls, and they can get you anything you want. Green card. Consulate card. Blue Cross pharmacy."

"Do you think anybody will let me make a phone call?" Jaime asked.

The new boy, without cracking a smile, said in English, "No way, José."

Maeve settled with trepidation among all the blue: the carpet, the overstuffed sofa, even the walls.

"Okay, girl, here it comes." Ruthie appeared in her living room with a silver tray held aloft bearing a small pitcher of some light green liquid, a larger pitcher of icewater, and two ornate glasses that were bulbous at the bottom. "*La fée verte.*"

She set the tray down and sat so close to Maeve on the divan that their hips touched, making Maeve ache all over with desire.

"They say it's dangerous," Maeve said. "Wood alcohol or something."

"That's just an old myth. It may make you amorous, though."

"In that case, it's unnecessary." Maeve tried to kiss her, but her friend pulled back coyly.

"Calm down and enjoy. Absinthe makes the heart grow fonder. Okay, shoot me for that. The green fairy. My father brings it back from Switzerland on his business trips." Ruthie poured the green liquid into Maeve's odd tumbler until it filled the bulb and then laid an ornate flattened spoon with slots across the top of the glass. She placed a sugar cube on the spoon and poured icewater over it until the liquid reached the top of the etchings in the glass. The transparent green had turned abruptly to milk and smelled powerfully of licorice. Maeve leaned forward to sniff more closely. Flowers and wild sage, too.

"That milky liquid's called the *louche*," Ruthie said, winking. She was acting a bit cocky for being a year younger, but Maeve didn't mind.

When Ruthie's was ready, they clinked glasses and interlinked their elbows to sip it. It tasted just like it smelled. "Whoa!" Maeve said. "Pretty weird stuff. But I know it'll make me wasted." She smacked her lips.

"You were born to be wasted, Irish."

No one had ever called her that. She decided that Ruthie had that kind of restless imagination that was always nicknaming, then changing the nicknames.

"I'm feeling dull, dull, dull," Maeve said quickly.

Ruthie pressed her palms gently on either side of Maeve's cheeks and kissed her chastely. "Don't fall in love with me, sweetie. We're just fucking and all the other stuff. That's how it works."

It was as if a horse had kicked Maeve in the stomach. "I can dig it," she lied.

"Drink up. You look a bit hangdog."

"I'm feeling a little sat-on to be honest, R. I was pretty fond of you."

"You still are. I'm fond of you, too. Has anybody ever told you how wildly passionate you are? It can be really terrifying."

"I'm sorry. Go for broke—that's me," Maeve said.

"It's who you are. I can deal with it."

They sloshed down the absinthe and got to kissing.

"Upstairs!" Ruthie barked. "*Now*. I'm going to show you my etchings. No, keep that on until we get there."

# 13

# All Is Illusion

JACK LIFFEY PARKED ON A METER ON SEPULVEDA NOT FAR SOUTH OF VENICE BLVD. He knew the area well because his old condo was nearby. It was his fallback in case the women in his life ever threw him out, as they were wont to do, and it held the accumulated junk of a lifetime that he had no interest in transporting now to the eastside. From time to time, he actually checked in there to do some quiet thinking or napping or hiding.

As he was fighting one of the new digital meters that kept flashing red and spitting back his quarter, a black man in a faded Statue of Liberty suit walked toward him, plinking along in shiny shoes with taps. He/she carried a hand-painted sign that said YOUR AD HERE FOOL with a phone number. Jack Liffey wondered if such a getup could possibly sell anything. It was just too ragged, but so was life. The man did a stutter-step as if to get in tip-tap time with a song that was only in his head. His eyes looked a bit wasted.

"Hey, send me your tired, your poor, your huddled masses," Jack Liffey said in a friendly way.

The Statue of Liberty turned slowly to frown at him. "Take a walk, friend."

"Anything you say."

"Want any dilaudid? Dacron?

"*Dacron?*"

"I mean Vicodin."

"No thanks."

"Peace out." The man made a zero with his free hand, whatever that meant, and tappety-tapped on.

Big Bob's Trophy's, as it was spelled on the glass window, displayed a lot of plastic signs and plaques, plus tier after tier of silvered cups, actual "trophy's," presumably waiting in vain for their claimants like forgotten umbrellas at a library. The great number of prizes gave the odd suggestion that doling out awards had become a minor obsession in America, and he stopped for a moment to read the fine print on a few of them. *Best Real Estate Campaign for a Single Residence over $799,000. Best On-Time East-West Metro Driver. Fastest Drummer at Skyliners Summer Retreat, Big Bear, 2006.*

Many of the dusty cups in the window were accompanied by tiny batters or bowlers or golfers. All this frenzied intent-to-honor created a strange and contrary impression. He pictured a black cloud of insecurity hanging over the suburbs, growing with every stray moment of doubt, the inhabitants *needing* all this recognition somehow. He wondered if this was where the famous strut of American Exceptionalism had taken us all—not into empire but into exceptional dread.

He had half a mind to buy the abandoned World's Biggest Fussbudget cup for Maeve but decided against it.

A sizeable and suspicious man with a ponytail was reclining in an old barrel chair behind a glass display case. This had to be Big Bob, he figured, or the world had become unreliable. The man didn't budge, but his eyes, planted just above a broken nose, came around as Jack Liffey entered.

"Hi," Jack Liffey said. "You've sure got some swell trophies."

"Um-hmm."

"I notice none of them are in Spanish."

"None of them are in fucking Zulu, neither. This is an American store."

"Good. That's what I'm looking for. I only do business with real Americans." Jack Liffey offered a couple of gratuitous slurs about Mexicans—which he almost choked on—but Big Bob only yawned.

"I'm a security consultant, you might say, and a couple of families up in P.V. have brought me in on a little exterminator-type job. They're tired of putting up with the Mexicans getting all cozy in the canyons below their homes. Fire risk's bad enough, but then there's the smell of refried beans."

The big man still didn't seem to be biting, and Jack Liffey wondered if he was laying it on a little too thick.

"And you've come in here because . . . ?"

"I heard you *know* people, the kind of people I need to hire. The money's good."

"Little rough stuff what you're after?"

"Nothing that'll draw too much attention. Just go in and discourage the campers. Tell them to move along. Convincingly. Efficiently."

"Who told you I knew people?"

"A guy at the *Times*. Not someone you hang with."

"Try." The big man stirred now, and as he shifted to attention, Jack Liffey could see the tattoos on his forearms, solid blue and green designs so intricate they'd take a close inspection to decipher.

He named a city desk *Times* man at random. "He said he was working on a story about the people guarding the border."

"So you're just a guy likes to chase off Mexicans."

"It's a job."

Jack Liffey didn't actually see the movement, but a powerful hand suddenly locked down hard on his wrist. The sudden grip made his legs tremble a little, and he lost breath. The man tugged him a few inches closer and off balance. Jack Liffey felt awkward and weak—and he recognized this was exactly the way you felt just before you got really hurt.

"The fuck you say," Big Bob said. "What else you want?"

Jack Liffey realized he hadn't anticipated anything properly. If only he'd had real combat training in 'Nam instead of going to electronics school, maybe he'd have sensed it coming. He had none of the right instincts.

There was a steady stream of low-intensity cursing from Big Bob now, like someone reading a malevolent litany. "You're too stupid to live, asshole. You're that motherfucker we caught bringing food to the wetbacks."

All the hairs on Jack Liffey's neck stood to attention. He didn't recognize Big Bob, but he knew now that the man was deep into the violence he had so naively hoped to learn about.

"Why don't I call the cops," Big Bob growled, "and say I saw you there right before the fire that killed those Mexicans?"

"Go for it. I'll tell them about you and your pals and a girl called Blue Hostetler. You know, the *white* girl you guys killed. Cops may not care much about Mexican corpses, but dead rich girls are something else."

The hand squeezed a little harder for a moment, hurting him quite a lot.

"Time to let go, man," Jack Liffey said.

"I think we've come to what they call a Mexican standoff." There was a snort, and the vise grip released all at once. "I'm not a worrier, jerk-off. But I want you out of my face."

Jack Liffey had learned all he'd needed to: Big Bob was one of the thugs who'd beat him up. "All the shit that used to make me mad, you know, it just makes me sick to my stomach now," Jack Liffey said.

For the first time, Big Bob looked a little confused, and Jack Liffey realized that perplexing the man might be putting him at his most dangerous. "See you in church, Big. I'm in the wind."

**Dad,**

> *I cant take much more of this. Mom is always like Dont you have a new girlfriend. I just want to become a monk or something. I tried praying and it just seemed stupid.*

> *I cut my hair back to a jarhead so I dont have to worry about how good I look. If you dont look spiff here people talk and I dont want talk. I hate talk. Why are people so stupid. Mom is always going on about getting money out of you now and how you always had girlfriends and what a mean shit you were. I know shes starting to go crazy I mean for real and I wonder whats eating away inside her. I used to like her. Please come take me away. I dont like my new friends that Special Ops stuff is for shit but their all I got. Surf is dead for months and the Bayboys dont come around much. Help me dad.*

> **Twitch**

"What we got here is a CFNF," Ruthie said. She sat crosslegged on her bed in baggie sweats with the late morning sun streaming in and burning at Maeve's eyes like a laser. Absinthe *does* kill you, she thought.

Her head throbbed, and she realized she was absolutely naked and Ruthie was eying the big blurry ✆ tattoo on her left breast.

"That's a gnarly one," Ruthie said. "Looks like a jailhouse tat."

"What were those letters you said?"

"Don't you ever browse around in porn? That's clothed female with naked female."

Maeve waved even the thought away. She didn't see her clothes anywhere in the scattered sheets and duvet. "Can I have my clothes back?"

"Not yet. I like having you at my mercy. It seems to calm you way down. You were screaming for more until I took charge."

"You're making this up."

"Not much. But it's lucky mom never came home last night. You probably don't even remember that she called. She was off with some new boyfriend, I think, a screenwriter. I met him once. A real schmuck who talks about 'jumping the shark' and all that inside TV crap. Then you started chugging the absinthe bottle without even diluting it."

"Oh, god, I'm sorry."

Ruthie laughed. "Forget it. I don't even like it that much. It's more that it's a keepsake from the old man, still on the road."

"I'm sooo sorry."

"I said, forget it. Tell me about that G on your tit."

She really didn't want to, it was too great a collision of worlds.

"Truth or dare," Ruthie said.

"Okay, what's the dare?"

"You have to walk naked as a baby, just like you are, three blocks down the street to P.V. Drive, press the cross button as all the gawkers and whistlers drive past, wait for Walk, and go to the Silver Spur Market and buy me a pack of Marlboros."

"Isn't that a little over the top?" Maeve was rubbing her throbbing forehead. "Have you got some ibuprofen?"

That, too—the entirety of Maeve's well-being seemingly dependent on Ruthie's goodwill—was withheld. So she gave in and went for truth. She told her a little of the Greenwood gang who controlled the barrio around Gloria's house, and then even some about Beto, the thirty-year-old she'd fallen for, and being jumped painfully into the gang. But what she knew now was she was probably never more than an honorary mascot from the Anglo universe. The tattoo had been the lesser of the souvenirs of her emotional thrall to Beto, but she was definitely going to leave out the aborted fetus.

"Holy Virgin of Guadalupe," Ruthie said. "You're more interesting than I thought."

"Ibuprofen, please."

Magically, several orange pills appeared, along with a glass of water, and she took them all in one gulp.

"So are you still in a Mexican gang?"

"Technically, the answer is probably yes, but I was a minor, and Beto didn't want trouble with the cops. I guess I'm sort of in exile to them."

"I'd give anything to experience all that."

"No, you wouldn't. Wise up, Ruthie. You already think I'm too intense for you. Real life *eats* people like us."

"I want you to tell me what you know. Tell me what's in your heart, right under that big blurry G."

"Goodness. You actually want my heart?"

"I want to know what's in it," Ruthie insisted. "You're a powerhouse, and I've always felt second-rate. I couldn't even read *Ulysses*."

"The Greek one or the Irish one?" Maeve said.

Ruthie laughed. "It's like I get frustrated too quick when

something's difficult. I get angry at it and just give up. That's a pretty lousy sign when it comes to somebody's character, isn't it?"

"Sometimes you just have to push forward. On faith."

"I feel like I'm only walking through all this . . . what? I don't know . . . *information* about the world," Ruthie said in a deeply serious voice that seemed a bit new to Maeve. "But you're living deeply in the real world. I want you to teach me things."

"Then you have to love me," Maeve demanded.

"Your love scares me, Irish. Is that supposed to be the stick or the carrot?"

"I want a big kiss and I want my clothes."

"Pretend we're slaves." She extracted Maeve's clothes from a pillowcase. "I'll tell you something I meant to tell you last night before lust and liquor walloped us off our feet. This is a public service."

Maeve got her kiss, which turned out to be rather sexless. She nodded to Ruthie to go on as she started dressing.

"There's this guy at school who's starting to go nutty, acting all out of character. He's not quite schizo enough to call the padded wagon and, anyway, they've got no guts for that, the counselors. But he's crying one minute, then pretending he isn't, and a few seconds later he's got the thousand-yard stare. He's a Bayboy surfer—I mentioned him to you before and I think we saw him on the beach. He used to know Blue pretty well."

Maeve stopped buttoning.

"The other day he went into a tirade against Mexicans, and he's never been like that. Never before. Just an ordinary guy, sexist as all of them are, but you expect that. Nobody I know's called Mexicans taco benders for years. It's like he's got a brand-new gang of brainless racist friends from back in the day that he's trying to copy. That's my guess."

"He knew Blue well?"

"Pretty. I don't think he dated her, but she came down with us sometimes at the bay. She said she wanted to know *him.*"

"Okay, my slave," Maeve said. "You're going to get me to meet this guy. What's his real name?"

"Brandon. A real soap opera name. We specialize in names like that up here. Tiffany. Cade. Drake. Oh, yeah, *Devon*—probably every British county is represented."

"Tomorrow. You find Brandon and tell him I'm really a hot slut— or whatever it takes."

"Don't go overboard, Irish."


He had the window seat on the bus and figured he might as well enjoy it. The angry guy next to him wasn't talking and looked like he'd rather gnaw off Jaime's leg than acknowledge him. The old fender bus didn't look like much, painted a drab khaki, and it kept up a harsh bounce all the way down the freeway. Dead shock absorber, Jaime was pretty sure. All the deportees were handcuffed to the seat rail ahead of them.

"Fuck *gringolándia*," his seatmate said finally.

"*Sí, compa.*"

"*Haz patria, mata a todos.*" Be patriotic, kill them all.

"I met a good one," Jaime said. "Not stuck up. Not cruel. He bought me food."

"Fuck him, too."

Jaime watched the small factories and the glossy suburbs roll past the wide and clean freeway until they merged with an even bigger freeway and finally passed into an area of undeveloped scrub. They bounced and rumbled past two giant concrete breasts that he guessed were a nuclear plant, and soon he knew exactly where they were. On the opposite side of the freeway, the traffic was backed up at the famous "surprise" *migra* checkpoint 100 kilometers north of the border, the one everybody in Mexico knew about. They were in the middle of the U.S. Marine Corps Base at Camp Pendleton.

In a few minutes they passed a long wall along the ocean with the ugly boast: No Beach Beyond Reach. He remembered his political friends getting indignant about the Marine anthem that bragged about seizing the Halls of Montezuma.

An hour or so later the handcuffs were coming off in a parking bay just over the border, and they were being turned over to a Tijuana city *placa* who didn't seem to care a bit about them.

As they waited, Jaime squatted beside a guy from the bus who looked sympathetic. His name was Chuey. "What happens now, *amigo*?"

"Nothing, *amigo*. They take our names and hassle us a little and then push us out into the great sea of humanity. This town was built by the devil and all his henchmen, and it'll probably take us a few days to get back across to *El Norte*."

"I hope so. I'm broke."

"You're lucky. The guys hiding a little money are the ones get killed right away in this hellhole."


Deputy Ross was still simmering down from the monumental tantrum he'd directed at the warder he'd reached at Los Padrinos Juvie. He lit an American Eagle cigarette, illegal inside the sheriff's station, and stepped outside before anybody could start bitching at him. You couldn't smoke anywhere but up your own ass these days. He'd sent Jaime Olivares out on the jail bus to go to juvenile hall and be held for a few days as a material witness and, like something out of Laurel and Hardy, they'd immediately put him on an express bus for Mexico. The jails were run by raw sheriff's recruits—it was still the traditional first posting out of the academy—and stuff like that was always happening.

Ross supposed the kid was lucky they didn't lose him in the system for six months or confine him to a room with some junior gladiator from White Fence or Eighteenth Street who wanted his ass. But that was the last he'd ever see of Jaime Olivares, and the kid had been remarkably cooperative, even spoke good English. Now he had to explain to Lt. Stanley Lake at the Career Offender Detail that their probable witness on the Special Ops bozos had just gone south, literally.

Dynamite seemed to be the signature of these particular baddoers. Old-style dynamite, no chemical tracers, not C-4 or some ANFO fertilizer mixture. Rain-soaked land or not, everybody who saw those clean scallops cut into the hill up on P.V. found them downright suspicious. Scientific Services was still looking for chemical tracers in the mud, but he was 90 percent sure that the stuff would turn out to be pre-2004, which was when they'd started adding traceable glass microspheres to all explosives.

Then, like an inspiration from the heavens, he remembered the business card. He slapped his breast pocket as if that would magically make it appear, then realized he'd taped it into the crime book he'd opened on the suspicious deaths below Crestridge Avenue. He flicked the cigarette away, only half smoked, far out into the ivy bed at the Lomita Station and hurried inside.

"This is Sheriff's Deputy Dennis Ross. May I speak to Mr. Jack Liffey, please?"

"May I tell him why you're calling?" a male voice said warily

"It's about his friend Jaime Olivares. The boy needs his help."

There was a long wait.

"Uh-huh. I understand. Can I tell Mr. Liffey a little more?"

"Look, Liffey, knock it off. I'm his friend, too. He's just been deported, by a horrible bureaucratic accident, by some zealous asshole at the juvie. I need him to identify two more bodies we found from the mudslide, and I'd like to talk to him. Could you tell me how you came to know him?"

"Sure. I found his camp in the hills by accident and helped him fix a broken surfboard that he must have pulled out of the garbage. He seemed a promising young man."

"And you gave him your business card . . . ?"

"I gave it to him so he could call me if he needed help. I guess he didn't get a chance."

"With minors it's not like on TV. The call, the lawyer—all that shit. Usually they're better off, though. Could we talk face-to-face?"

"One condition."

"Enlighten me."

"I'd like to know what you people know about the disappearance of a girl named Blaine Hostetler, from P.V. About a month ago. Her nickname is Blue."

"Not my department, but I could look into it for you. Do you think it's connected?"

"It would be a long shot, wouldn't it?"

"So's finding one decent kid somewhere in Mexico."

**Maricruz Olivares**
**Behind Aztec Market**
**Huépac, Sonora**


Dear Maricruz,

    *What a week! We had a terrible mudslide that fell down on our camp and killed four men who I knew a little, and I think the* norteamericano *cops think somebody caused the mudslide. They wanted me to stay around, but something went wrong and I got deported instead! It's like that in* El Norte. *You never know what's next. I was scared to death there might be* judiciales *at the border or they'd have my picture in some computer, but I just gave a bored* jura *a phony name and nobody cared. I used the name Pedro Moraida, isn't that delicious. He was such a righteous little altar boy.*

    *So now I'm stuck in Tijuana for a while but a nice guy named* Chuey [This is the nickname for Jesus. —ML.] *who I met on the bus is letting me stay in the back part of his family's house. It isn't really a house as you and I know it. If you can imagine the families who live down the* barranca *in* cartolandia ["cardboard box-land" —ML.] *and multiply it by maybe a million. People here do their best. They plant geraniums in old tires and the children are usually dressed pretty well, but they are all very poor, and it almost makes you ashamed to be Mexican to see it. Why why? Why can't we lift ourselves? We all work so hard.*

    *So this Chuey tells me a group is going to cross the border tomorrow. None of us have any money so we won't be relying on coyotes but just our own initiative. Wish me well. I had a good job and maybe I can get it back if I make it to Los Angeles. There is a man up there who may help me if I can reach him.*

    Remember me. Your very loving brother, Jaime

"Maeve, you're not going to believe this." It was Ruthie on the phone, and Maeve's heart lifted to hear the voice with its confident throaty ripple.

"Ruthie, you have no idea what I can believe. I can believe people long ago voted for their best interests."

Her caller snorted. "Don't talk politics. It makes me sick. All is illusion, girl. Only you and I exist."

"And the guy Twitch."

"Okay. And he's not into girls at all. I swear I tried. I told him you saw him surf and liked him and that you did tricks—which is code for kneepad blow jobs—but he just wasn't interested. It was like some door slammed inside him when sex came up."

"So you think he's gay?"

"I didn't get the vibe. It's something else. You know, in another twenty years this whole hill is going to be inhabited by defectives. The children of those who live here now. But Twitch: I know he used to fuck everything that moved. They say he'd have fucked an open wound if he could."

"I need to get close to him. Try another in. Say I'm a reporter writing about the Bayboys."

"They hate publicity."

"Well, then, girl, get creative," Maeve said. "Lie your little head off. Say I'm a garbage dealer in whatever garbage he wants. I don't care. Are you with me or not?"

"If the time comes and this all blows up, Maeve, my dear sex slave, I won't be here at all," Ruthie said.

"Where will you be?"

"A hell of a long ways away, fucking some guy who owns the film rights."

# 14

# Your Soul Shrinks

Now he sat on a bus bench watching the commo-
tion on *Calle 20 de noviembre*, a business street that for some reason
seemed to be made up principally of shoe stores. He counted ten
within his vision, at least four of them owned by a shoe cartel he
knew well, Dos Hermanos.

He'd lost track of Chuey now, and everyone else from the bus.
For years, travelers returning to Huépac had offered tales that filled
him with fear of this legendary lawless megacity crowding the border, with rip-offs at every streetcorner and hard-luck pleas coming at
you from all directions, but he had so far experienced nothing at all
to mistrust. Only hundreds of working people shopping or waiting to
get home on the old overcrowded buses.

Fresh from North America, it was hard to ignore the bright colors and the extra energy here, but also the crumbling streets and
cracked buildings, the dilapidation of just about everything, as if
some critical 10 percent of extra effort and material had been left

out of everything, maybe stolen by a thieving contractor or just lost through incompetence. And there was the smell, too—compounded of dust, diesel fumes, and a strong suggestion of rotting garbage.

He knew north by the sunset, and eventually he strolled in that direction toward what he knew would be the border wall. He could tell he was passing near the airport by the takeoffs thundering overhead. And then there the *frontera* was. He shinnied up a telephone pole to look across the forbidding metal barrier into the no-man's-land guarding *Norteamerica* from the poor. He saw cleared red earth, additional barrier walls fifty meters away, and dirt roads criss-crossing the denuded hills. At intervals, the green-and-white American *migra* trucks roared now and then out of hidden parking spots, like angry beasts prodded by sticks. He watched four forlorn-looking men who'd scaled the nearby wall get caught almost immediately by one of the beast-trucks. He wondered why they even tried it here.

"Jaime, *amigo!*"

Miraculously, in a city of so many millions, it was Chuey. He let his distrust simmer quietly in a back corner of his mind rather than shut this new and only friend out. Who could live in a world of total suspicion?

"*Amigo,*" Jaime said.

"*Orale.* Good we meet again. I'm recruiting a football team."

Jaime was one of the best footballers within many kilometers of Huépac, but for some reason he didn't think Chuey was talking about football as he knew it. "I have no time for games."

Chuey laughed. "Come down from the pole, *compa.* It's not what you think. The man with a little money down here, the man who wants to be . . . over there, hires an experienced *pollero* to lead him across the border, and half the time the *pollero* turns out to be a *ratero* and the man is ripped off. Now, the good man like you, with no money at all but in a hurry, he joins a football team. You will see."

Jaime shinnied back down the pole and walked guardedly alongside the swaggering Chuey to the end of a street called *Padre Kino* and through a backyard to where they could see thirty lanes of shiny American cars creeping stop-and-go toward the border guards of the main border crossing. Scores of hawkers strolled between them with armloads of flocked dogs, ceramic Bart Simpsons, and serapes over their arms. Chuey whistled, and maybe twenty sad-looking people materialized out of the dusk on *Padre Kino*. They looked like the poorest of the poor, a few even wearing the baggy white cotton trousers that were the uniform of peasant-farmers in Mexico. All of them carried plastic trash bags or frayed bookbags as their luggage.

"Follow me," Chuey whispered. "These *bobos* will screw it up, but we'll be all right."

Chuey instructed his football team very patiently to find something, anything, among their possessions that could look like they were selling it to the gringos in the stalled cars, and make their way separately and unobtrusively between the lanes toward gate number 19. He insisted: Go slow. Never, never antagonize the real vendors who were going to hate the disruption that a "football game" brought down on them but who would still never betray a countryman unless badly provoked.

"*Siga!*" Chuey cried, and the would-be border busters set out down the alley and then slowly through the massive field of traffic. There was a momentary swell of honking and catcalls as they filtered out among the cars, but it died away, and Jaime followed Chuey out into the sea of creeping automobiles. Surprisingly, he and Chuey weren't heading for gate 19 at all but taking a roundabout route past a Coca-Cola pushcart and a sad-faced barefoot Indio girl of about seven who had nothing to sell but a cardboard tray of Chiclets. He could tell the vendors knew what was happening but only glanced up at the "footballers" momentarily and then looked away with scowls of disdain and nuisance.

Before long three *pollos* reached the Chevy Suburban at the front of lane 19, right at the border gate, and they panicked at a shout and bolted around the guard shack to the American side, as whistles and a hooting siren went off. Jaime was distracted for a moment, and Chuey plucked his sleeve and led him toward gate 5. When the biggest mass of hopefuls converged on gate 19, Jaime and Chuey went through gate 5 with the *migra* inside his booth shouting at them.

"Run, *amigo!*"

They sprinted along the lane markers as the wide roadway narrowed and narrowed and cars around them began to accelerate and merge. Chuey waved and led them toward the central divider where there was a meter-high cement wall. Police sirens started up behind them, but running was what Jaime was good at and apparently Chuey, too. As the other *pollos* thinned out, and a dozen *migras* appeared out of nowhere to grab them roughly off the road, Chuey and Jaime ran hard past. One persistent *migra* truck was right behind them, gunning its engine just to chivvy them, and Chuey shouted, "Jump, *amigo!*"

The *migra* SUV roared on past as they went over the center divider and then ran back toward a small minimall near the border.

"He has to go two miles to turn around," Chuey gloated.

Now they bolted and dodged across the lanes of cars heading *into* Mexico, enduring the glares of *norteamericano* tourists, and then they both slowed to a stroll as they came off the highway and pushed into the McDonald's. Chuey snatched some discarded bags out of a trash bin.

"*Calma,*" he said, and they sat at a red plastic table with two old paper cups and a box out of the trash. A few Latinos stared at them, but most went about their business.

"We just have to wait it out," Chuey said.

"You're a genius," Jaime said.

"Of course."

But then the *migras* in their khaki uniforms swarmed into the restaurant, and an Anglo manager behind the counter pointed them out immediately.

"Where were you born?" a *migra* with a bushy mustache challenged.

"East L.A., man," Jaime said. "On Greenwood Street. I went to Roosevelt High."

"Yeah, and *I'm* Franklin Roosevelt. Let's see some I.D."

"We left it home," Chuey said. "You can't arrest Americans in America."

"Wanna bet, Panchito?"


"He hasn't called me," Jack Liffey said.

"Too bad. I have a real passion about identifying unknowns. Nobody should die unknown, nobody. Not in a war, not in a dark alley, and not in a landslide in the richest place on earth."

Two aggressive seagulls vied for some old french fries at their feet, and the cop watched them for a moment, then shooed them off when they started getting too importunate.

"Think of that blind guy in New York who died in front of his TV and was found mummified after thirteen months," Jack Liffey said. "Watching TV alone, dying alone."

Deputy Dennis Ross grunted. They sat at the outside tables of an eatery called Utro's at the top of the diagonal slip where the San

Pedro fishing boats now tied up. Jack Liffey hadn't been down here in ages and he was the one who'd suggested it. He loved the tarry, salty smells, the fishing boat masts swaying gently, and the piles of nets up on the dock being mended by old Croatians and Sicilians, even though tuna fishing had been dead for thirty years now, done in by the Japanese long-line boats and low-wage canneries in American Samoa.

"Look, *I* could turn in my lunch bucket just that way," Ross said. "After my wife left me, I don't know who'd look into the apartment while I'm watching HBO."

"Nah, you got a job. Your boss would send somebody to check, man. You gotta go out of your way to die off the grid unless you're very old or very poor."

"I don't know, Jack. Cities are pretty impersonal these days. Sometimes I've checked out complaints of bad smells, and I find a guy who's been eating nothing but sardines and throwing the heads in the sink for months. Or old ladies with cat shit everywhere. Loneliness—it's like a whole city of nothing. You can be as wise as Solomon, and you can't cure it."

It was occurring to Jack Liffey that this was one of the more sympathetic cops he'd ever met. "Funny, I imagine it about the same—a room of flat black walls all around somebody with no family left," he said. "But enough gloom and doom. Did you find out anything about Blaine Hofstetler, aka Blue?"

"Word on the street . . . Funny expression, isn't it? Like there's some omniscient kid out there chalking all the truest rumors on the sidewalk. They say she sleeps with the fishes. Somewhere off the cliffs at Lunada Bay. They say she was warned to stop helping the Mexicans who camp out in the hills, and she didn't listen. I think she went up hard against a bunch of assholes known as Special Ops. They're bikers and maybe a few surfers who seem to've made it their business to try to drive Mexicans out of P.V."

"I know about them," Jack Liffey said. "That's a whole other species of lost loner."

"Why do you say that?" Dennis Ross said. "They've all got enough money to live a normal life."

"I don't know—it seems guys are always coming to big forks in the road. Over and over, people get to choose between staying in touch with the human race and hating it. And it's amazing who goes down the hate path, you just can't tell. Worse, they always end up hating the wrong people." It was his dad he was thinking about. "Think of the pure hostility of a snapping turtle."

Ross smiled. "Spend a day in cop shoes, Jack. It'll give you a new appreciation for snapping turtles."

"I think that's what my girlfriend Gloria's usually trying to tell me. But somewhere inside she doesn't think I'll ever get it. It's the cop credo, isn't it? Civilians are from Mars."

A noisy party of short, squat fishermen speaking an oddly inflected Spanish came out of the building and took up a table nearby.

Ross ignored them and looked Jack Liffey over thoughtfully. "In a way, you *are* from Mars, Jack. I imagine Mars as a place where only occasional people lie to you, not everybody. There you can walk into a party and four people won't shout, '*I didn't do it!*' It's like Iraq vets coming back to their wives, you know. Half of you wants her to understand what it's been like to live under fire, everything every day a matter of life and death, and the other half knows it just can't be described. You end up resenting everybody close to you for what you know deep inside and you're certain they can't."

"So you don't even try to tell them," Jack Liffey said. "Because what they don't know won't hurt them. I've got a nodding acquaintance with that theory, but it's a really lousy one. You talk long enough to people you love, they understand."

"Nah. I been there. Believe me, they don't wanna know. They want a tidy little scrap of your experience that they can tuck away somewhere safe and get on with whatever they think is normal."

"*El mar es el enemigo de cada peruano!*" one of the small brown men declaimed loudly. He and his companions chinked beer bottles, and nobody showed the slightest levity.

"That's who the Slav captains hire now," Ross said softly, with a nod toward the long table. "Peruvians. They know boats, and they're tough as nails."

"And cheap. Wait'll the government starts finding a cheap source of cops overseas. In our race to the bottom, we'll end up with our streets patrolled by gorillas on steroids."

Ross smiled for the first time, but not for long. "They're welcome to it. I can't wait to finish my eighteen and get out of here to the Eastern Sierra. I've already got a cabin above Independence Creek."

"No shit. I know that place. It's glorious."

"It's away from people. That's the best we can probably ask. You'll let me know if this Jaime character calls you?"

Jack Liffey took his time, on purpose, as the Peruvians raised another toast, and one of them finally laughed, a strange high giggle.

"Do you think it will help a single human being to identify these dead bodies of yours?" Jack Liffey asked.

"No."

Onshore gusts of wind sent chilly billows through the wild chaparral on the untended crescent of land between the road and the Lunada

Bay cliff, right above where she and Ruthie had first— Never mind about that, Maeve thought. Across the brush she saw a small male figure in a gray hoodie sitting on the edge of the cliff, slumped forward as if utterly disconsolate. She watched him for a while, trying to work out a plan, but nothing would come. She remembered her father telling her once that if you wanted to rope in a reluctant informant, the fail-safe approach was almost always to tweak his or her vanity hard and then keep them mystified.

Act a bit loony if you have to, he'd said. Everybody in L.A. believes everything they hear, so you can get away with the worst sort of craziness.

In effect, to follow her dad's system, she would have to write a chunk of fiction in her head very fast, tailored to the ego of this sad gray ghost. Yet she knew so little about the elusive Twitch—if this was indeed him sitting there. But this was where he'd reluctantly told Ruthie he would meet her mystery friend.

Maeve left her car and pressed through the knee-high weeds. As she got close, an unforeseen muse descended on her, and she found herself saying softly, "Twitch, I'm here for you."

His head rose slowly, and red disturbed eyes stared at her out of the darkness of his Sand People hood. "If you're just a little surf gremmie, you can fuck off now. I don't surf anymore."

She resisted looking out over the cliff at the waves she could hear rolling in far below.

"I'm not a gremmie, Twitch. I'm your dream gog." Where had that ridiculous word come from?

"My dream god?"

She smiled as serenely as she could. "You don't know about dream gogs?"

"Oh, shit," he said. "Who cares?" He yanked off the hood but turned away from her to watch out to sea. She peeked, too, and saw that the waves were tubing over perfectly like an endless-summer movie, with twenty or thrity surfers lining up their boards to take their turn. One lanky figure was riding the nose at that moment.

"In everybody's life there's a time called a calamitope," Maeve heard herself say. Oh, lord, she wished she'd come up with better words. "It only comes once and it's like a crisis that brings you right to the edge of disaster—but even bigger. You're there now, Twitch, and you know it. Every person has a gog—it's g-o-g. It's the one person in the world who can help you when you're entering a calamitope."

"Are you from County Health?" he complained.

That told her a lot, all by itself. "No. I'm from your own guardian consciousness. I only learned this week that you're my dream swaddo—that's the opposite of a gog. I didn't choose to come here. My dreams told me to. They sent me to help you get through this."

"What asshole told you all this shit?"

She squatted down, though back a foot, as if she needed the extra angle in case he reached over to try to swat her off the cliff. "Take your meds and I'll show you how to get over."

That got his attention. "Who the fuck are you, cunt?"

"You don't really mean all that hostility, do you?"

Surprisingly, he just shrugged and said, "Honk, honk, honk. It's my dad who's going to come help me."

"It was a man in my dream who sent me," Maeve said. "He said he couldn't come right now. Maybe this is all he can do right now." What if she'd gotten the cues wrong and was blowing it badly? Christ, girl—*gog* and *swaddo*?

Now he did stare hard at her. "I swear to god, if you're fucking with me . . ."

"No, Twitch." She set her hand very softly on his shoulder. "I'm here to help. I promise."

"Then you'll let me *fuck* you, won't you," he said with a cruel twist in his voice.

"No. You know we can't do that."

His bravado collapsed at that, and he seemed to shrink physically. She waited a while until he said: "Can I call you something? Not some stupid word. Like a *name*."

It's actually working, she thought with astonishment. "You can call me any name you want. My real name is Maeve. I promise to be here for you and help you all the way through your calamitope."

He frowned at the word, as if she was trying to put something past him. "You can keep the damn calama-calliope-thing. What's your school?"

"Redondo Union," she said. "My last year."

"Got a college yet?"

"No. How about you?"

"I'll never get there. Who cares? I'm a dead man walking."

Go for it, she thought. "No. I can see your life-course, Twitch. It stretches out in front of you. I see it perfectly, and there's no place nearby where it stops. I mean, we all die eventually, but you aren't going to be early."

"You can see that?"

"I swear to God." She crossed her heart, amazed that the gesture could add the tiniest bit to anybody's belief.

It didn't seem to convince him, but it calmed him. "What was your name?"

"Maeve. It's Irish."

"Well, I didn't think it was Chink." For no apparent reason, he began to rotate his trunk back and forth, making robotic whirrs and clicking as he did.

She decided to call his bluff and mimic him. She made her own robot movements, along with a higher pitched whine, like something from a bad sci-fi TV show. She added a few chirps and twitters from the Star Wars droids. Finally he smiled at it all.

"When I was little I used to pretend I had a robot friend," he said. "I mean, when I was really little. He was awesome. He could do anything. Crush big Cadillacs. He could jump all the way to Catalina." The west end of the island was just visible thirty miles away through the sea mist.

"I had an alien friend, too," Maeve said. "My friend was from Mars and I had to explain everything to her. Even how to swing your legs when you walk. I guess it gave me somebody so I could be an older sister."

He seemed to think about that. "You're a strange girl."

"You're a strange boy. Why do you think you wanted an omnipotent robot friend?"

"What's 'nip-a-tent'?"

"Like Superman. Your robot friend could do anything he wanted, right? But you shouldn't have needed a friend like that. You're supposed to be one of the greatest surfers ever, and everybody around here knows who you are. They respect you. Your family is rich, you're famous."

Seagulls passed overhead, shrieking as if trying to send a warning. But to whom?

"You're no shrink," he said accusingly.

"Have you been to a shrink? I have." She hadn't, or not exactly, but she wanted to stay on his level.

"I had to go to a therapist for a while, but it was only a friend of my mom's that was crazier than batshit. This horrible woman wanted me to keep lists of all my 'unpleasant' thoughts. Shit. To do that I'd have to start writing before I woke up." He did another whirring robot rotation, away, then toward her.

Maeve laughed. "I like you, Twitch. You're smart."

He whirred and clicked around to look hard at her. "Nobody's ever said that."

"That's *their* problem. You're smart, all right, but you drew a lousy hand when they passed out families."

"No *shit*. Why are you being so nice? What's in it for you?" He was abruptly suspicious again, almost enraged.

"I think that's just the way I grew up. Were you so angry—I mean, before you got the HIV?"

He glared and then a shoulder twitched as if he was about to punch her, but she didn't budge. She wondered if that involuntary twitch of anger had anything to do with his nickname. "Okay, my mom's a whale, she's a selfish bitch, like one of those dorks from a reality show. I love my dad, but he's somewhere far away where he can't call me very much. And school sucks, big time. I've always hated it because I read too slow. And just today I decided I can't stand any of my friends. They're all pricks or biters, or just assholes."

"Calm, Twitch. It's okay." Anger was always the worst thing, she thought. Nothing could fix it.

She rested her hand on his shoulder again, and she wasn't sure but there was a shudder as if he was crying. They both squirmed around so he could hold her and then he began to keen at the top of his lungs.

"Let it out. When you're forced to be alone too long, your soul just shrinks up like a raisin."

The wailing intensified until it choked off in breathless spasms.

She had never seen anyone let himself go quite like this, as if years of pain had been impacted inside him, and she'd inadvertently pulled the plug. The responsibility of what she'd done in befriending this lost boy came over her now, but she would do whatever she had to.

Out on the screen porch, he mopped up the orange puddle of dog vomit without looking at it too closely. Loco lay with his head flat down between his forelegs but with his paws tucked under, as if to protect fresh nail polish, a cat-like posture he'd never seen a dog take up. The yellow eyes were open and staring at him, and Jack Liffey was trying his best to avoid anthropomorphizing. Still, his best was useless. The eyes seemed to be accusing, or maybe they were just expressing a world of weariness and grief. How could you tell with those depthless coyote headlights?

The porch seemed to tremble under his own knees. Maybe he just wanted the old, pre-cancer, status quo too much.

"There's no permanency in life, is there, Loco? Something is always tipping us downhill. But you're being a tough old guy, the best you can."

He rested a hand on the dog's warm flank, which was slowly filling and exhaling. The tenderness and intimacy seemed real to him, even if he had no idea whether it was real to the dog. He felt helpless against the animal's mute suffering. As it must be, he thought. He resisted offering a treat, knowing it would be more to salve his own discomfort than the dog's. The last thing Loco needed right then was to ingest another strong-tasting scrap of ground animal.

"You don't have to take it beyond what you can stand," Jack Liffey said sadly.

He remembered that Kafka had written of a mouse that was

caught between a deadly trap and a ravenous cat. "Alas," the mouse had said, "the world is growing narrower every day."

"If it gets too narrow, boy, let go. You have my permission to depart. But I'd like you to stay around if you can. Find out who wins the pennant."

He laughed because he knew nothing of baseball; didn't even know if they still talked about winning the pennant. His laugh was interrupted by the telephone, and it took him a couple of rings for his eyes to unglaze and then to realize where he was. There was a phone in the kitchen now, a cordless Gloria had insisted on buying. He hated the way cordless phones squawked and hissed in your ear, taunting you with their imperfection. Give me an old black wired telephone with a dial.

"Hello."

"Mr. Liffey?"

"That's either me or my father. I'm Jack." He'd heard the accent and had a strange feeling he knew who it was—but Gloria got a lot of calls offering variations of that wonderful Mexican lilt.

"You said to call you if I was in trouble."

"*Jaime?!*" For just an instant, he wondered if Deputy Ross might be tapping his phone, but that was way over the top for such an unimportant case.

"Yes, sir. The police deported me to Tijuana. I tried to come back once but I got caught. Can you help me?"

Ross could probably get the kid back up to ID the bodies, but they'd likely hold him in some jail and then just deport him again. Jack Liffey was certain it was a pretty dodgy felony of some kind to bring an alien across illegally, and not particularly easy to do in these post-9/11 days of rancid hysterias.

"Yeah, I'll help you, Jaime."

Maeve lay in her bedroom in her mom's house listening to the pounding rain. It had rained so much already that even the profound skeptics at school were taking about the onset of global warming, or as the Machine of Euphemism liked to call it now, climate change. The rain was crashing down so hard the drops seemed to bounce, creating a sound like somebody dragging a thousand tin cans along her Redondo street.

She liked the sound of it, and left out the silicone earplugs she often used to shelter herself from random scary noises in the house, including the occasional boisterous lovemaking of her mom.

Against the steady drumbeat of the rain, she heard an unmistakably sharper rap at her window, like a tossed pebble. She'd never had a boyfriend—or girlfriend—call her out like that. The tiny noise came against the glass again—*tak*. Her spine prickled, and very slowly she got out of bed in her long T-shirt. *Tak-tak*. She spread the curtains an inch, expecting Ruthie, but whoever it was was probably hiding behind the laurel bush in the yard. It was almost an electric shock that hit her as a shadow scurried toward the house where she couldn't see. It was so quick that she wasn't sure whether she had only imagined a skinny fifty-year-old guy. For her mom?

"Girl," a voice called softly but unmistakably. She was determined not to let in one of her mom's beaux. "I saw the light coming out of your room."

She slid the window open a foot. "Go away. I've got a gun."

"No, you don't. Don't be a jerk."

*"Oye, Paco, entre aquí con su cuete!"* she called out.

"Cut that out, girl. They ain't no Paco in there, and I don't speak Mex anyway."

What a ridiculous spot to be in, she thought. They were separated by a few inches of wall, a few feet of altitude, and the imma-
nence of male threat. And she had no idea at all who he was. What
would her father have done?

"I know who you are," she said.

He laughed. "Leave the boy alone. He belongs to me."

"Are you gay?"

"Fuck you, bitch. He's mine to use, and it ain't got nothing to do
with being queer. You just back away from this wall real fast and get
out of there if you know what's good for you."

She saw a thin shape running off into the rain and decided to take
him seriously—in case he turned back and shot some stupid macho
gun at the house. She'd been shot once, and they'd had to cut a section
of her colon out, and she didn't want to go through that again.

She was just moving across the room to get behind her bed when
an invisible hand, as big as God's, slapped right through the wall and
hit her so hard that it sent her sailing backward off her feet. She had
no memory of coming down.

# 15

# A Sickness in People
# Who Migrate toward Money

AS USUAL, THE BORDER CROSSING ON I-5 WASN'T BACKED UP AT ALL ON THE NORTHERN SIDE, BUT HEADING INTO MEXICO AT NORMAL CITY SPEED, THOUGH OFF TO THE LEFT HE COULD SEE THIRTY SOLID LANES OF CARS INCHING NORTHWARD ON THE MEXICAN SIDE, THE BIGGEST PERMANENT TRAFFIC JAM ON EARTH. The disparities made him feel uncomfortable, the way abject poverty always did when it was thrust at you as the only frame of reference.

The Mexican border guards didn't even stop him for a perfunctory question or two going in. The border wasn't built to do that. Emerging into the glary carnival world reminded him unpleasantly of his first trip here back in high school. He'd tagged along with a group of boys to see the infamous Blue Fox Club, and one of the guys had joked as they'd parked the lumbering old Buick on a rutted street just off *Avenida Revolución*, "You know what's the matter with Mexico?" and after three or four facetious but not very funny impromptu replies, the boy had answered his own question: "Too many Mexicans."

It had begun the process of spoiling the trip right there, but the

Blue Fox managed to do that quite thoroughly not much later, leaving his adolescent heart pounding hard and his head awooze with trans-gression. He wanted to comfort every woman involved in those duti-ful and automatic live acts and then meet every man responsible for bringing the club into existence and dropping them off a long pier.

He was a bit more sophisticated now and a bit more in command of his own sexuality. It was no longer a sin to him to *learn* about sin, even outrageous sin, and he knew now that all you could really do in life was try to do your best at the moment.

In his phone call, Jaime hadn't known TJ geography at all, and he'd asked Jack Liffey to suggest a meeting place. The only thing he could remember that was probably still around was the big Sanborns near the jai alai *fronton*. Sanborns was a grand old Mexican tradition— sort of a cross between Denny's and Sears, except Jack Liffey remem-bered seeing a photo of Zapata and his central command plopped down to eat at the Sanborns soda counter in Mexico City, rifles and crossed ammo belts and all, and the idea warmed his heart. He knew the boy had no money, but he could easily loiter in the music section of the huge store or the clothing or even wait on the street outside. The tightly pruned ficus trees lining the block-long pink façade sur-prised him, but somebody seemed to have cleaned up the street quite a bit since his last visit, forty years ago. At least in the stretch up here by *Calle 8*.

As he walked toward the big emporium, a squat brown man got in his face. "You want to see the donkey show, *señor*?"

Jesus. It was the exact come-on that he'd heard a dozen times during that trip of his youth, not to mention the repeats much later in Saigon. "You want me to shove a donkey up your ass, *señor*?"

"Maybe you could stay a little longer, *rulacho*, and learn to truly love the donkey."

Never try to outpoint a professional pitch man. Pushing him aside, he let himself into the sanctuary of the upper middle class, all his angry instincts working overtime. Come on, Jaime, hurry up, this is going to be unpleasant enough.

He knew English would work just fine in here, and he sat at the long counter and ordered a Coke Lite. He looked around, and with his instincts for depravity still ticking over hard, nothing seemed innocent. The old *abuela* by the greeting cards had bags of drugs up her voluminous skirt, the two teen boys were thinking of ways to steal something, and the little girl by the door was a lookout. Cool it, he told himself. It's just another too-big city of several million people, poorer and a lot angrier for being slapped hard up against the U.S., but normal in its own terms. You're here to pick up a young man and take him north. You don't want to fuck this up with any unwarranted surges of indignation.

And then, miraculously, he saw Jaime push open the glass doors with a profoundly lost look on his face. Jack Liffey left three U.S. dollars beside the Coke to cover any absurd contingency and walked toward the boy.

A short old shill cut the boy off immediately, like a bird of prey, and they conversed a moment in a Spanish that was way beyond his poor powers.

"Jaime," Jack Liffey announced, trying to head off trouble. "*Mi primo.*"

As Jaime heard the voice, his face bloomed into the happiest smile Jack Liffey'd seen in a long time, and the small man slunk off.

"What did he want?"

"To rip me off. I don't know. I must broadcast that I am vulnerable."

"This is a town for buzzards, Jaime. Border towns are like that. You want something to eat? You're safe now with me."

"I want away from Mexicans. I never thought I'd say that."

"You can't judge anything at all by TJ. Come on, eat."

"There's a real sickness in people who migrate toward money, I think."

"You did it, too, *compa*, in your way."

"In desperation, yes." The boy looked at Jack Liffey, as if considering the man's character and finally deciding, maybe, to trust. "Thank you for coming so far to help me. I have to tell you, Mr. Liffey, I am running away from old trouble in Sinaloa. A man who hurt my mother. If they learn my name, it could be big trouble for you here, too."

Jack Liffey smiled. "You have no idea how much trouble I've seen in Mexico," Jack Liffey said. A few years earlier he'd had to cross the border illegally, climbing right over the metal wall, with only a Persian boy as his guide, and with the *federales* and the army right behind him. The whole escape had been so dodgy as to be laughable now.

In the end he reclaimed his three dollars at the counter and his Coke Lite before anybody got there, and the boy had a Coke, too, and a big *Papi Hamburguesa con papas fritas*, which he devoured as if he hadn't eaten for days.

"Want a second one? It's okay, really. Have three."

Jaime smiled. "Maybe it's best for me to stay light on my feet."

Jack Liffey laughed. "Your English is very good, you know."

"Since I was small, I have read many books."

"Who's your favorite writer in English?"

"Mr. Hemingway."

Like every Spanish-speaker—at least every male, he thought.

"I like Raimondo Chandler, too. And Robert Stone."

"Do you know Kent Anderson?"

"No. Who is he?"

"I'll give you one of his books. Your English is good enough that with the right clothes, we might be able to drive straight across, and you could pretend to be my grandson. What do you think?"

"I got across yesterday, and I was sitting in a McDonald's, and I talked about Roosevelt High School, and still the *migra* heard something in my voice that was wrong and knew I was Mexican. These guys are smart."

"Well, let's go for a drive, then. I want to get out of TJ, just like you." He had a vague hunch that if he kept driving east, the ugly steel wall, the wall of hate, would end somewhere. Probably naïve, he thought, but it was better than hiding the poor kid under a tarp in his truck bed.

Gloria fought open the lock on her front door, always balky in the rain. She was already in a foul mood after a run-in with another cop who'd been temporarily assigned as her partner, a blockhead who'd said right off that he was willing, for the day, to forgive her for being a girl. Without a trace of irony. Shooting him right then would have felt good, but she carried him the whole shift through a string of macho blunders and idiotic snap judgments. She'd only come close to losing it at the end when he'd wanted to wade into a family dispute on the side of an overbearing husband who was an obvious abuser. She'd taken over as graciously as she could to calm it all down.

She sighed and did her home duty, checking the answering machine, then the fridge for any notes, then checking on poor Loco, who was passed out deeply on the screen porch. He still had a strong pulse in his neck. She wondered how Jack was thinking of paying for the chemo. She was weakening about it herself and had decided to contribute, but he'd still have to come up with a big chunk of change.

She'd just opened a can of Tecate and sunk into collapse mode on the crumbling Morris chair facing the TV when the phone shrilled at her.

"Hello," she nearly snapped. It was bound to be one of those calls from a boiler room, offering mortgage reduction or a new credit card or an extended car warranty. "Gloria, is Jack around? I have to speak to him." It was his ex-wife Kathy, who sounded pretty upset—which was mainly the way Gloria knew her.

These maternal frenzies of Kathy's usually had something to do with Maeve. Since Gloria, too, felt protective of Jack's girl, she dealt with her mother as gently as she could.

"He seems to be out, Kathy. Could you tell me what's wrong?" In fact, there'd been a long note on the fridge that she'd intended to read after she caught her breath.

"I want to know what the fuck he's working on that's put Maeve at risk again. Life'd be a lot simpler if he were a librarian or a house-painter is all I can say."

"You married a technical writer. You can't help what became of him. Tell me about the 'at risk,' please." She had her professional manner on now and was prepared to listen carefully.

"Somebody blew up the whole front of our house last night! Gloria, I mean it! Blew it right up like *fucking* Baghdad! It threw Maeve against the wall so hard a pushpin on a poster penetrated her shoulder."

"How is she?" It was so like Kathy not to get to the central issue right away. Maybe only cops knew how to do that.

"She's going to be all right. She's home now, but she's pretty shaken up, and she has a lot of glass cuts. She won't talk about it at all."

"I understand. Let me call the Redondo cops and see what they know, and I'll get back to you." She didn't want to deal with this level of emotion any more than she had to.

"Everything to do with Jack goes so fucking *bad.*"

"Listen, Kathy, I'll call you within an hour. I promise."


*Maquiladoras,* the mid-size factories emblazoned with all the familiar Japanese and Korean names, straggled out for miles on the east side of Tijuana, long flat boxes of concrete that crowded along the beat-up pavement of Highway 2 and then crouched up on the long mesa that rose between the road and the border. Eventually, the factories fell behind, and then the last lights of any kind, leaving a spooky darkness. Every few miles they drove through a dusty *poblado* containing a Pemex station, a couple of bars, racks and racks of home-cured olives along the road and a small cluster of adobe dwellings.

He tried a few rutty dirt side roads to the north, but he turned the pickup back each time when he spotted the ugly steel curtain at the border blocking the way.

"Well, shit. They've been building eastward."

"Is it like this on the Canadian border?" the boy asked innocently.

Jack Liffey smiled. "You *are* kidding, aren't you? There's no fence at all. Nowhere. And as I remember, all those 9/11 pilot-students came across from Canada."

"So why do you hate us? I don't mean *you.*"

He thought about his countrymen's enmity toward Mexicans. "Some hate you because you're different. You don't assimilate the way the Irish and the Polish did. You wave Mexican flags a lot—even at soccer games, which is a game that most Americans hate with a special passion unless it's their own little girls playing. You're brown. You have accents. You work cheaply at jobs we don't want. And most of all, you push things out of the shape we're used to. But there's one more big thing."

That got the boy's interest. "What's that?"

Overcast hid the moon as he drove, which might help them get across, but maybe not. Jack Liffey tested another northbound track, but soon saw the seemingly endless ribbed steel wall and gave up again.

"What?" Jaime repeated.

"Your very presence in America questions our purity of motives. Like the Indians."

"I don't understand."

"I don't really, either. There's nothing either of us can do about it. Let's worry right now about how we're going to sneak back into the land of the free and the brave."

Thirty miles out of TJ, they came to a track that was quite a bit worse than any of the earlier ones, little more than a place where a car or two had once gone off the highway. It didn't even seem to carry on very far ahead, but he turned onto it, anyway, and headed northward, for luck. He just didn't know if he'd ever been very lucky.

Brush scraped the pan underneath the engine, and he drove very slowly because the broken land began to heave the truck at angles.

"I hope you've got good tires," the boy said.

"Good enough. What's that ahead?"

In his headlights there were low rocky hills, really little more than mounds, but first a wide lighter-colored zone crossed their path. It was a landscape wiped free of vegetable life, rocks and topsoil, like one of those ancient Peruvian Nazca lines that could only be landing strips for the gods. The cleared swath followed a logic of its own, ignoring the rise and fall of geography, presumably to cut an arrow-straight path. Then a blinding portable light unit snapped on, and Jack Liffey saw four bright beams up on a stalk, aimed along the bull-dozed swath. An automatic motion trip, he thought, which probably meant an automatic signal to someone, too.

At least there was no metal wall here. He'd seen the no-man's-land they'd built on the U.S. side of the wall nearer Tijuana, and it was much like this. He guessed that somewhere ahead, not very far, there would be green-and-white Immigration trucks parked in ambush in sheltering brush, or lurking behind dirt berms, though he'd bet not so many this far out of town. There would probably be more high-tech sensors, too, and eventually, helicopters, and guys with night-vision binoculars. Sooner or later, if the country kept get-ting angrier, they'd get around to installing automated machine guns like the old East Berlin.

"Get down," Jack Liffey said.

The boy folded himself small and lowered himself uncomfort-ably under the dashboard. "I'm not scared," he offered.

"You, they'll just send back. I'm probably committing a felony as a human-smuggler."

"Oh."

Unaccountably, no interception arrived as he crossed the bare ter-rain. He emerged onto rough chaparral now into the low hills, rising, steering around small thorny trees and bushes. Another lit-up swath of bulldozed land lay ahead. The overkill was almost insane.

"Here we go, Jaime. Another dead zone. I have a bad feeling." He couldn't see over the crest of another range of the low hills.

"Whatever happens, I thank you with all my heart, *mi amigo*."

Jack Liffey kept his eyes on the shaved yellow earth he was just entering. Four more glary lights off to the left flared on and lit him up all too well. Maybe he really was lucky, he thought. Maybe the *migra* . . . what did they call them now? . . . the men from ICE— Immigration and Customs Enforcement—maybe they were all off eating dinner at IHOP or snoggled out on red wine. Or maybe not.

He tried to look away from the dazzle as he crossed the cleared strip, waiting for a klaxon or a helicopter or even a sudden eruption of gunfire across his bow. At least the ride smoothed out. He glanced around quickly as he speeded up to take advantage of the graded earth. There were no obvious *migra* trucks or ATVs hiding in blinds, but he was certain they were coming.

"When I give you the signal, I'll slow down," Jack Liffey said. "I want you to open the door and jump out fast and hide wherever you can. I'll go another half mile due north and wait with my lights off. You'll have to do your best to find me."

"Yes. I understand."

"I think we're well across now, but I'm being careful."

Gloria sat glaring at the phone for a while. Another utterly disagreeable evening due to Jack, or related to Jack, or just carrying some of Jack's innate DNA. Each catastrophe worse than the one before. She wasn't sure she shouldn't end this odd liaison with the guy before it managed to kill her. He fucked okay and all that, and as often as she wanted, and he was kind enough, and he really listened to her whenever he was around. But he got himself into fixes, and when you added the whole complicated math problem together, it always seemed to come out very high on aggravation. For her.

"Hello, Kathy. This is Gloria. I talked to the Redondo P.D. at length, and they say they have a pretty good idea who your bomber might be. The M.O. matches another explosion that caused a landslide that killed some illegals up in P.V. last week. Did you hear about that?"

"Of course. It was all over the paper."

"Jack's been working on something to do with that case, I'm just not sure exactly what. The sheriff's department's is primary on it, and the guy in charge isn't reachable tonight. Even for me. But Jack certainly didn't involve Maeve in that. Not in any way that I'm aware of. Do you think she's playing Nancy Drew again—trying to help?"

"Can I talk to Jack?"

"He's left me a note saying he might be away for a couple of days. You should talk to your daughter—that's the end where you've got some control—and maybe she should speak to the cops over there, too. The man handling the case in Redondo is Detective Sergeant Irving Mosher." She gave his direct number. "If it's down to Maeve, she's got to put a stop to this adventuring, Kathy. I love her dearly, but she's got no sense of responsibility for her own safety."

"Don't I know it." Kathy seemed to choke softly for a moment. "Thanks a whole lot, Gloria. Honestly. You've been a good friend to us, I know that."

"Jack is a piece of work," Gloria said. "When you're with him, it's always a matter of adapting to the circumstances on some Mars mission, one that's just about to go totally out of control."

"I lived with him for fifteen years. You don't have to tell me."

"Well, two and a half years is starting to seem like too much. Talk to your daughter. I bet she's the key to this. Jack may not even know anything directly."

"I'll do my best. Bless you."

And the horse I rode in on, Gloria thought.


Out in the driveway, Ledge's old woodie cycled through a complicated honking tune involving horns of at least four notes. The honking annoyed Twitch, since he retained that much sense of rudimentary courtesy. Friends came to the door. Twitch could hear his mom banging around hard in the bedroom, in some sort of panic he just didn't care about any more.

He tried to think of his dad, his dad flying to the rescue, as he'd convinced himself for almost a year was ultimately going to happen. The trouble was, after the last two uphill phone calls, the rescue had become a lot less imaginable. Nobody was really on his side at all—except maybe that strange freckled girl. What was her name? "Maver" or something odd.

Ledge finally got out of his car and gave his rappety-rap-rap knock on the door.

"I'll get it, Brandon," his mom called.

At the top of the stairs, it occurred to him all of a sudden that his mother had never really paid him her undivided attention, not in many years. Like a flash, he realized she was too needy herself, and in a strange moment of time, as if suspended between what he thought he was and something else, he decided he should do his best to try to forgive her. Still, it wasn't the best moment, and he put the thought off. He knew he had to protect himself first. Maybe this Maver girl could actually help him.

"Bran, can you come down?" his mother called.

He remained on the upper landing, still unable to get off the dime. The whole idea of Ledge and his friends was beginning to make him uncomfortable for some reason.

"Twitch, I need to see you," Ledge shouted.

One step after another, he thought, as he headed down ponderously. Guys like Ledge always had bad timing, he thought. This was a night for lying facedown on the bed and trying to figure things out, not for drives with dunces.

"Twitch, I need to see you," Ledge reiterated, trying to ignore his mother, who was looking upset.

"I'm here."

"Twitch, come on. I need to get some things in order."

Twitch could see his mother draw back. Something in the man's tone was worrying her.

"Let's book," Twitch said.

"Don't leave," his mother said, but they were already hurrying down the porch.

Jack Liffey was jouncing along slowly in near darkness, hoping to come upon a road, when an amplified voice filled the air.

"White pickup, stop where you are! You're in a restricted area!"

"Get out *now!*" Jack Liffey yelled at the boy, and he reached up quickly to cover the dome light with his hand. He slowed and the boy popped the door in the dark and rolled out into the weeds.

He drove on another hundred yards to get clear of the boy and then stopped. Bright lights approached him from two sides. The nearest appeared to be a high-riding four-wheel truck with a light bar over the cab, the lamps blazing away.

That dreadful amplified voice again: "Show your hands!"

The green-and-white Immigration truck skidded to a stop and a quadrunner approached from the other side.

"Stay there!" a second amplified voice called.

Jack Liffey showed both of his empty hands out the window, and two swivel lights came around on him. "No worries, officer," he called.

"What are you running? Coke? Black tar?"

"I'm looking for these guys I'm meeting up with. The Minutemen are supposed to set up a post around here to help you guys watch for wetbacks. The other Minutemen got all my gear."

"We don't need your fucking help, mister. Come out of the truck slow."

Jack Liffey carefully extricated himself. An agent in a beige uniform stepped out of the truck and held a long-barrel revolver on him.

"Hey, I'm on your side, pal."

The quadrunner finally arrived up a small hillock, giving the strange vehicle a few feet of height advantage for its own spotlights.

"Any Minuteman stuff going on around here tonight?" the first agent shouted.

"Not a thing. I keep up on that shit. Got another story, Bubba?""

"All's I know is Bobby said we was all to meet near here at eight o'clock."

"Get down! On your face. Now!"

Can't all this harassment keep? Jack Liffey thought, but he knelt, keeping his hands in plain sight, and then went prone gently between the chaparral plants, smelling the powerful aroma of sage and clay dust.

He did his best to switch his mind off for a few minutes as the two agents went into power-trip mode, the truckdriver uttering random insults as he searched Jack Liffey's car, the other one keeping up a steady stream of taunts.

"How come you got no Minuteman radios and stuff in your piece-of-shit truck, asshole? No litterchur, no night goggles, no by-nocs."

"I told you, Bobby's got all my stuff for tonight."

"Bet there ain't no Bobby."

"Listen," the first one snapped. "And listen good. You been around the block twice and think you got rights. Forget all that." He touched the side of his nose in a gesture that was supposed to mean something, but Jack Liffey had no idea what.

"We're not out here selling Avon, doof. It ain't our business to get taken off by guys with egg-salad sandwiches going green in the back of the cab." He hurled something off into the night for the coyotes.

"You got the key to the camper shell?"

Great investigative powers, he thought. "It's not locked."

"What's the matter with you guys? I came all the way down here to help, and all you do is give me grief."

"Amateurs are nothing but heartburn," the quadrunner-driver said.

It was hard to keep pretending he was a bigot idiot, so Jack Liffey clammed up and let them carry on. Except for a moldy egg salad sandwich they threw to the coyotes, there was nothing incriminating in the truck. They kept at it, however, until an urgent radio message called them away to some other hotspot.

"Man, are you lucky tonight," Andy said. "Go home, Jack." He'd seen the I.D. "Whatever you're up to out here, you're not cut out for it. *Adiós*, okay?"

Jack Liffey watched their lights disappear over the horizon before he turned his parking lights on. Before long Jaime appeared out of the brush.

"I think I'm a little sick," the boy said. "It's probably just anxiousness."

"Tilt the seat back and try and relax, and I'll get you home. All we've got now is that stupid 'surprise' inspection on the freeway 50 miles north of the border. And it's shut a lot of the time."

# 16

# We Used to Like the Underdog

ON THE WAY OVER THERE'D BEEN A NEAR THING WITH A BIG BLACK
HUMMER, BUT THEY BOTH IGNORED IT. Ledge had parked on the cliff
above Abalone Cove in Portuguese Bend, and he reached in back
to hand Twitch a beer out of a cheap foam cooler. They cracked the
windows to let a cold breeze leak through and carry off the smoke as
Twitch smoked a Marlboro.

Twitch didn't feel like a beer, but he realized he should make the
effort. A crescent moon had just risen and was catching phosphores-
cence in the foam of the long blown-off unsurfable breakers down
below that were rolling up onto the rocks. Just before leaving, Twitch
had scarfed an old upper he'd found in his room, and he could feel his
pulse marking off the seconds.

"Twitch, you been initiated now. You know shit and seen me do
shit that's not safe if you're not cool with the shit."

"I'm no snitch."

"Why you messing with that skinny girl? I seen you. She's been
sticking her nose where it don't belong and you know it. There's an
old guy nosing around, too. Me and the boys had to cool him out
when he was helping the taco benders."

He didn't have a clue what Ledge was talking about. Or, maybe, he *did* have a clue about the girl, but he didn't really connect all the dots, and he didn't want to. He was so self-consumed these days that he didn't want anything to be required of him. "What skinny girl?"

"The one with the freckles and big tits. You were talking with her for a coon's age up on the cliff."

"She's just some gremmie from the flatland." Normally he wouldn't have challenged an old-school guy like Ledge, but he could feel that his normal and reasonable switch had shut down in the face of the speed he was taking. And he was consumed with worry about death and too much lonely fear. He just didn't give a fuck anymore. "When did you become my babysitter?"

Ledge drained his Corona bottle.

"Don't take it wrong, boyo. We all like you and want you around. You've always been the best of this generation of Bayboys. You just got to get off the stick and make some effort to fit in."

What was this shit all about? Twitch wondered. But he knew, deep down, that Ledge was seeing into him in a way he wasn't fully able to compute. The older man could probably see he wasn't really on board.

"I'm going to take me a ciggie break," Ledge announced. He got out of the car and lit a cigarette with a paper match bent back on the matchbook. Twitch stayed inside, the windows open to the cold air, while Ledge blew plumes up at the moon. It was lighting up a few lumpy clouds that Twitch thought looked strangely like brains.

Twitch almost felt sorry for Ledge, but he had his own problems. He began to feel their whole relationship had been based on some kind of misunderstanding.

The cigarette arced away off the cliff, and Ledge stuck his head into the car. "We got business to take care of. And you listen to me, you're part of Ops now. Stay away from that skinny cunt. She's poison."

"I hear you," Twitch said. But he wasn't, in fact, listening.


"Maeve, goddamit! Open up! I'm not room service." It was the spare room in back now, as Maeve's old bedroom in the front of the house was uninhabitable, a classic scene of violation with orange tape across the missing wall, like one of those news photos of an air strike or an earthquake with the private contents of a life exposed to the world—a dress laid out on the bed, ugly art on the wall, a toilet hanging in space.

He'd only been home in Boyle Heights three and a half minutes before he'd got enough of the gist of the story about Maeve's dynamited bedroom to head straight out the door again to Redondo, leaving Jaime behind to make his own peace with Gloria.

"Dad, let me be. I'm so spooked."

"Be spooked, honey. Come on, talk to me. You know it'll be okay." He heard a sob.

"When have I ever beat you up over a mistake?" he said.

The hook on the door clacked audibly, and the door came open on his daughter, with several small bandages on her face, and her left arm tucked into an efficient-looking black sling. "Oh, Dad."

She hugged him as best she could with one arm, and he felt her trembling a little against him.

"We'll work it out, hon. But I'd really like to know what you've been up to. No blame. Whenever you're ready."

"Do you think maybe you came to the wrong address?" she asked him.

That was his Maeve. He smiled. "Could be. I've got hapless daughters all over this fancy beach town."

She bit her lower lip but still sobbed a laugh at herself. "Oh, God. I've always been a trial for you, haven't I? And I'm not even counting the pregnancy."

"We don't have to unpack everything at once. Unless you want to." He knew there was something hanging fire.

"No no no no."

He sat down on the stiff old hand-me-down chair that had been forgotten in Kathy's back room for years, maybe decades, and she sat down on the edge of the swayback single bed.

"In your own time, at your own pace."

"Dad . . ."

Time stretched out. "Uh-huh. Here."

"What if I told you I was a lesbian?"

Jesus, it *was* going to be a rough discussion after all. "This is a little sudden, isn't it?"

"Things happen faster than you want sometimes. I fell in love. With a female person."

This is all the adjustment period you're going to get for this news, Jack Liffey told himself. She's right, things happen faster than you want sometimes. Adjust *now*. Sure, why not? It might even be temporary, the way Beto had been. He'd never had any problems with gays, even the deeply closeted Robert Toma in his radar trailer in the army. Bobby'd had great taste in books and a wonderful sense of humor. "That's fine, hon. If you're happy, I won't have any trouble loving the both of you."

"It's not as sudden as it may seem. I've been thinking about it for a while. Or feeling about it."

"I'm okay with it, really. But that's not what got you blown up, is it?"

He could see her thoughtful look gather itself again, trying to decide what to admit to good ol' Dad. "I told Gloria and I told the police what I saw. The guy was thin and he was old, maybe fifty. It was dark and I only got a peek."

"This didn't have something to do with Blue Hostetler, did it?"

She seemed to collapse into dejection all at once, as if she'd been clinging hard to her first line of defense, and he had just blown straight through her second and third. "Dad, how'd you figure it out?"

"Hon, you always try to help me. I don't have to be Sherlock. Maybe you want to tell me about it."

"If I do, will you tell me all about the case?"

He thought for an instant about the missing girl what might have become of her. He'd have to abridge things a bit for her safety— though that seemed out the window already.

"Don't bargain with me about putting you in danger, hon. I'll tell you what I can." She leaned over to hug him again with the good arm, and the sling flopped against him.

"How bad is your arm?" he asked.

"Not terrible, but there's a bruise the size of Kansas on the back of my shoulder. I was thrown into the wall. It hurts when I flex."

"Don't flex, then."

"Sure. Listen, I'm sorry. I asked around school and some other places about Blue, and I guess it must have made somebody angry."

"Somebody, huh?" There was more, but he wondered if he was going to get it.

"I'll stop," she said. "I promise."

"That's all?"

"Does cross my heart help?"

He wondered if there was any way he could send her to Paris or Tokyo for a month. But all the money he didn't have was promised to Loco, anyway. It was sad to realize the were reaching that point in their lives when she wouldn't be confiding in him very much any more.

Once he was satisfied there was nothing more he was going to find out, he decided to show the proper respect for this new relationship that was consuming her. He asked about her girlfriend.

"Oh, dad, it's . . . like finding boys for the first time. Her name is Ruthie, and she's smart and beautiful. I really love her. But, wait a minute, you were going to tell me about the case."

"People don't always do what they promise, do they?"


"Why, Jack, what a surprise!" Gloria said with mock astonishment.

"I missed you, your warm and welcoming heart," he said, grabbing her for a hug. Right away he'd seen that she was more than a bit lubricated, so it seemed the right tactic.

She laughed and kissed him hard, pressing against him. "The heart is not the organ at issue."

"Whatever's going. I like all your organs."

"I'm still too mean to flatter," she declared and gave him a playful slap that was just slightly too firm.

"How're you and the boy doing?"

"He's out back whispering to the dog."

"Pardon?"

"Go on, check outside."

Things seemed to be okay for the moment and he relaxed a little. He was always worried about accidentally transgressing one of the many invisible fault lines in their relationship.

He saw Jaime sitting on the grass, having a very gentle tug-of-war with Loco over a rubber ball. Loco never played with balls and hadn't even stood upright in some time, but he was upright now. Jack Liffey watched for a while from the screen porch as the boy spoke softly to the dog in Spanish, and he remembered that Loco had spent his first year or two in a Latino household.

Jaime set the ball a few inches in front of Loco and tapped it twice. Loco looked up at the boy, as if for permission. Jaime said a few words. Still pretty shaky on his forelegs, the dog wobbled forward and took the ball very gently into his mouth.

Jesus Christ, Jack Liffey thought. The boy was somehow working exclusively with the genetic half that wasn't coyote, and that half was eating out of his hand. The beast had taken years to warm enough to Jack Liffey or even Maeve to show them any doggie affection.

He opened the screen door quietly and stepped down into the back yard. Mariachi and norteño music was going all around the compass, and the moon, peeking out of a few fluffy clouds, was bathing the yard with silver. Loco glanced up immediately at the sound of his steps.

"I'm impressed," Jack Liffey said. "He's a very independent soul."

"It's just being very gentle," Jaime said.

"I think it's a real quality some people have. Inspiring trust in animals." He'd often wondered if the ones who possessed it transmitted it unwittingly. All he knew was that, whatever it was, animals and small children, too, seemed to pick up its presence by radar.

Jaime stroked the dog's ears back. "He's a very unusual dog."

Jack Liffey laughed softly and knelt down with them. "Did Gloria tell you he's half coyote?"

"No. *¡Carajo!* Of course, I see it now."

"He's been my loyal *compadre* through a lot. And like an idiot, I guess, I'm selling my only real asset on earth to pay for his doctoring. They say all it'll buy him is another year, maybe."

Saying that aloud, Jack Liffey sensed something deep inside that he hadn't felt in a long time. It was almost like that one day in 'Nam when he'd committed himself to stay with a fallen buddy no matter what. He'd only experienced the sensation that once, the one time he'd been in real combat—as the Tet offensive swallowed up his R-and-R in Saigon, trapping him for several hours behind a whitewashed stone wall with three combat pros, also on leave, who'd fast become his best buddies—Samuel, Jim, and Marcus. He felt at the time he'd have died for them, with them, gladly. An experience like that stamped a pattern on you that never went away, he thought, though he'd never seen those three grunts again and didn't even know if they'd survived the war.

Jaime looked up at him as if he didn't quite understand.

"Truly? So expensive here even for dogs?"

"Sure. For all the defenseless. This is a merciless country. You have to have noticed that, living in that camp of yours. Back in the 'fifties, all Americans used to like the underdog. I don't know what happened to that, but now we mock the underdog. We only like winners."

Loco seemed to run out of steam, and the dog settled between them on the scraggly lawn. Jack Liffey rested a hand on his warm haunch.

"Are you a winner, Loco?"

"Why do you call him Loco? It's not respectful."

He'd never thought of it that way. "His first owner was a Chicano boy whose mother was killed, and he had to go back to Mexico with a grandmother he'd never met to a town he'd never seen, speaking only broken Spanish. He wasn't a winner, either. That boy named him, and I guess I felt I ought to keep it. Maybe because I was too late to save the mother's life. Anyway, I have a horror of naming anything."

"What do you mean?"

"Too many times people are trying to memorialize someone. It puts a real burden on the one being named—a child or even a pet.

Everybody should have their own identity, a hundred percent. I let my wife pick my daughter's name, and nobody I've ever met has the same name."

The boy seemed surprised. "What's that?"

"Maeve. It's very Irish. One of the Irish names that never really migrated."

The boy stroked the dog gently. "We have so many Mexicans named Plato and Octavian."

"Amazing. A real love of learning."

"In my school we had Omar and Heracles, too. You know that Jaime is James?"

"Yes, I know. I like it better in Spanish."

"Why is that?"

"I don't know," Jack Liffey said. "You know, son, I'm not really an authority on anything. I just pretend I know a lot when I have to. Everything in life gets harder to understand all the time. Like the minds of dogs that are half coyotes."

"You're right," the boy said. "This country is a lot more difficult to understand than I thought it would be."

**Maricruz Olivares**
**Behind Aztec Market**
**Huépac, Sonora**

Dear Maricruz,

*I hope you are getting this. I can send you a new place to write to me now, and it will work I am sure. I am back in L.A. because of that kind man I told you about who helped me fix my surfboard. He is much more of a real man than any man I ever met in Huépac. He drove down to Mexico to meet me and he risked going to* la pinta [slang for jail—ML.] *himself to bring me across the border. I told you in another letter that you can never know what is next in this strange life up here.*

*So now I'm staying with him and his woman, who I cannot believe is a* placa [slang for a cop—ML.] *but she is trying hard to be kind to me. They have a wonderful two-floor house in the Mexican part of town which is the east side away from the ocean that they call East Los.*

*The man wants me to go with him to identify some more men who died in the mud slide where we were staying in the hills. He says he will work it out so they don't deport me again but I am not so sure he can do it. I fear my job is probably lost but I will try to see if Mike will let me back to work on the rock wall. However, the job is a long way from here, as far as from Huépac to Baviácora, if you can believe it, and yet it is all in the same city. This city is a lot like what they say about Chilangolándia* [slang for Mexico City—ML.] *and how it goes on and on until you have worn the foot bones down to your ankles.*

*Remember me to everyone if you can and let me know if it is safe to come home.*

**Don't forget me. Your loving brother, Jaime**


Ledge hated this kind of frustration. The old Ford Torino ran perfectly most of the time, or so said the owner, a skinny old coot thirty years older than the car itself, who told him that every once in a while the engine just stopped on him. Right there on the freeway, he'd complained, or trying to park at the Vons. The trouble was it could be almost anything—an electrical fault, the fuel pump, or the old injection system clogging. They always thought you were a car genius when you worked on cars, but he was only working at the service station because it was what he could get, and basically he hated cars—engines anyway.

All Ledge was good at, and all he really cared about was surfing. In fact, he'd like nothing better than to load this old junker up with dynamite from the box behind his tool chest, take it up to the Paseo cliffs and push it off so it blew itself to hell on the way down, the way cars always did in movies.

Which reminded him that he'd decided to get the dynamite away from the gas station. He'd been a little too free with it lately and he'd heard that the girl had gotten hurt. It was stupid—he'd done it pretty much on impulse that night, except he'd had the stick and a cap along with him so maybe it was a very long impulse.

Where he was keeping it behind the tool chest, one of the other mechanics might stumble on it trying to borrow a tool, despite the hundred pounds of engine parts he had holding the box down. Unfortunately, the pool house where he lived out back of Mrs. Greevy's was even worse. There was nowhere to stash another thing there. The bed and his three surfboards and an old four-drawer Sears chest took up all of the cabana, and Mrs. Greevy was nosy.

He worried about Twitch, too. The kid seemed to be going squir-relly on him. Once he'd been the most reliable of the young Bayboys. He'd seen Twitch scare off Vals and gremmies with the best of them. But now his eyes kept going vacant, and something unpleasant was happening inside his head.

Ledge blew out the fuel line with the air hose and then started up the old Ford with a profound sense of futility. It would run fine now, and when he sent it home, it'd probably gasp and die an hour out of the station. And the owner would blame him, no matter what.

This was in his dreams all the time. A balky car with some elusive problem, a disagreeable customer—and some young gremmie college student, with supervisory power over him, sitting in the office and telling him in his snot voice what to do. Ah, shit. Sometimes he just wanted to blow everything up.

"High-Impact Team—Aliens," the voice on the phone answered, one of the odder official designations he'd ever heard. Like a bureaucracy on Neptune.

"Is Deputy Dennis Ross at this number?"

"May I advise him who's calling?"

"This is Jack Liffey."

"Please hold." While he waited, he was forced to listen to a recorded woman's voice soliciting him to join the Sheriff's Department which kept repeating the absurd motto, Real People, Real Leaders.

"Jack, it's good to hear from you."

"Your unit's got a damn funny name, you know."

"Don't even go there. We try to protect aliens, believe it or not."

"Look, I've heard from the boy, and I may be able to find him. But first I want to hear again what's up and if you can keep him on this side of the border this time."

There was a long pause, which didn't give him a lot of confidence. "You seemed like a stand-up guy when we met, Jack."

What had Gloria told him the night before—she was too mean to flatter? He was too damn skeptical to flatter. "Sure, uh-huh."

"Okay, well, there aren't any more bodies for the kid to identify," Ross said. "He told me that he definitely heard explosions before the mudslide, and I know he's been pushed around by a couple of these Special Ops mokes, and he can probably identify them. I can put a lineup together in a day." Jack Liffey realized he'd seen them, too, but only in masks and balaclavas.

"And for risking his life like this, the kid gets . . . ?"

"A free pass from me. Do not collect two hundred dollars; do not go to Mexico."

"That didn't work out so well the last time, did it? And this time you want to sic a gang of homicidal Nazis on him. Guys that we *know* hate Mexicans."

"It's one-way glass, Jack. Sure—someday the kid may be asked to appear in court, and I know he'll disappear before he does, but I've got to try."

"Okay, I'll explain it to him if find him. It's his choice."

"Jack, he wouldn't be sitting right beside you, would he?"

Jack Liffey glanced up over the phone to where Jaime was eating a bowl of cereal and listening intently to as much of the conversation as he could.

"Word of honor," Jack Liffey said. "But I'll stay in touch."

"You do that."

Jack Liffey set the phone down gently. "We'd best take a ride out of here pretty soon. Just in case they scramble somebody here to look for you. I have to go down to the South Bay. Maybe you can check on your old job."

"That would be great. You mean, I don't have to go back to the sheriff?"

"I'll tell you all about it. I never take people places they don't want to go, even if somebody calls it home. Come on."

# 17

# Honor Is the Rotten Board in the House

LEDGE HAD GONE BACK TO WORKING ON THE BALKY TORINO FOR A SECOND DAY AND WAS HUNTING IN DESPERATION FOR SOMETHING REALLY OBSCURE, LIKE A SHORTING SPARK PLUG CABLE, WHEN THE COPS ARRIVED AT THE CHEVRON STATION. Actually they were sheriff's deputies, which made him take them slightly less seriously for some reason, though he did crane his neck to glance once at the corner of the dynamite box to make sure it hadn't grown a flashing neon sign implicating him. It was still inconspicuous when he ducked down the lube bay.

"Hey, asshole!" the younger deputy said. "I said, Come up out of there."

"Ask nice."

"Come up, please, fuckhead. How do you ever get any decent pussy, stinking of axle grease?"

"Okay, Chris," the older deputy said calmly. "Mr. Choate, would you please come up and talk to us?"

"Why should I?"

"Any more attitude, and I'll tell the judge you fuck babies," the belligerent deputy said.

"*Chris!* Mr. Choate, please. There are some questions we need to ask you."

"Oh, questions. Shit, man, why didn't you say so? That's what you guys *do*. Don't let me step all over what you *do*."

The older deputy came around to help him up the steps if necessary. "I can still walk uphill, man."

"So. Are you the guy known as Legend? Or Ledge?"

"They say there's a little legend in everybody."

"We'd all like to think so. You seem to be the real thing. One of the first generation of Bayboys."

"You surf?"

"No, but I saw *Endless Summer* as a kid, and I loved it all to hell."

"Man, that was the middle of the 'sixties. Long before people in Hollywood decided surfers were all burned-out druggies that looked like Sean Penn. You know, they couldn't even get a normal release for *Endless Summer*. Bruce Brown had to four-wall it."

"What's that?"

"I only know because I helped at the old Warners back then. Bruce went around the world, renting movie theaters on his own money to show it," Ledge said. He didn't usually let himself get so talky around cops, and he began to realize that this older cop was probably playing him.

"I'll bet Bruce Brown did okay on it," the deputy said. "The theater was packed where I saw it."

"I wouldn't know. What's these questions?" The deputy had led him toward the office and then stopped by the diagnostic console, just before the inner office door, maybe so he wouldn't be embarrassed in front of the kid they had running the shop.

"Wouldn't you like to sit down somewhere more comfortable, Mr. Choate?"

"Why? Your own life so crappy you want to fuck up mine?"

"An informant has told us that you're a member of an anti-immigrant group called Special Ops. We need to straighten this out."

"Look, I once rode thirty-foot tubes on the North Shore of the Big Island. Three years after *Endless Summer*, Bruce Brown put me in a film called *Pacific Vibes*. Me. I *am* a legend. What would I care about some Mexicans trying to surf in cutoff jeans?"

"Maybe the Mexicans are getting in the way when you see a primo wave."

Ledge made a dismissive sound. "Nobody gets in my way. I carve across them."

"Nevertheless, someone has set off a series of dynamite charges that have killed four Mexicans and hurt a young Anglo girl. You *will* have to come in and talk to us about it. I'm sorry to disturb your work day, sir. You'd better tell your boss."

"I don't have a boss."

"Fine. Maybe you could just tell that kid holding down the chair in there that you have to take off right now to help us with our investigation."

"Fuck you, deputy. Who can take sheriffs serious? Those beige suits, like Smokey Bears."

"We busted Charlie Manson, creep," the mouthy one said. "You can come along in handcuffs, doing the perp walk half off the ground between us, or you can talk to the kid and step out to our car on your own power, right now."

Jaime saw the truck parked up on the grass, and sure enough the retaining wall was still going up, but not much progress had been made. He'd always felt it didn't extend deep enough back into the cliff. Mike was down on his knees wearing bricklayer's plastic knee pads, setting and pointing and making a new assistant fetch the stones. Jaime watched Mike shout in exasperation, something about size or shape.

"Christ," Jack Liffey said. "This is where you worked? It's the middle of Lunada Bay. You're in the heart of Bayboy territory."

"The boy who lives in that house was nice to me at first. He wanted to give me his old board. I think his mother was having sex with Mike but things started getting in trouble."

"You want to talk to Mike about the job? I can wait."

*"Gracias, mi caballero."*

"Why am I your horseman?" Jack Liffey asked.

The boy laughed. "It's a term of respect. It's like sir or gentleman."

"Come on, son, I'm Jack. Anything more makes me nervous."

The boy walked across the road to the two workmen. He glanced back and saw Jack Liffey get out and take the short path across the chaparral to the edge of the cliff that he knew overlooked the glorious bay below. Just getting out of the truck, Jaime could feel the salty onshore breeze at his back and smell the tar, fish, and kelp. It was wonderful, and not one other person from Huépac would comprehend that smell.

"Well, fuckin-A," Mike said, looking up.

"Hello, Mike. I'm sorry I left the job suddenly, but the cops picked me up and I was deported to Tijuana. I just got back. Is there any chance of work?"

"You want to arm wrestle that guy for the job? You guys can play taco gladiators."

Mike's partner was lugging over a large flat stone, staggering under the weight.

"No. I won't do that."

Mike shrugged. "The guy's for shit, don't worry, but I'm not double-paying for today," he said. "If you want the job, come to the Home Depot tomorrow by seven."

"How about I come right here by seven-thirty?"

"No shit? Can I count on you? I don't want to get here and have to drag my ass all the fuckin' way back to Hawthorne for a replacement on Mexican time."

"I got a place to stay. I won't fail."

"Don't bust my balls, guy. I mean it."

Jaime realized Mike had already forgotten his name. "Jamey will be here."

The other worker arrived and set the stone down with an audible thump next to Mike. "*Buenos.*" Jaime guessed he spoke only Spanish.

"Where you from, *amigo?*" Jaime asked.

"Tapalpa. It's in Jalisco."

"We're both a long way from home." Jaime knew it only as somewhere near Guadalajara, a lot closer to Mexico City than to the U.S.

"No work, no land. *Juro por mi jefecita,* I'm not a bad man."

"I'm not a cop, my cousin. I'm a proud Mexican, too. Be sure you get your cash-money from this *bobo* today. He won't give you a job tomorrow."

"Thanks, friend."

"Don't thank me, it was my job for ten days, and I'm taking it back."

Jaime turned and walked away before the poor man could react.

"Seven-thirty. Don't fuck with me, *Hymie,*" Mike called.

He waved without looking back. If I wanted to fuck with

you, Mike, Jaime thought, you'd have a caved-in skull. Like Don Ignacio.

He crossed the street and found Jack Liffey on a big rock near the edge of the cliff. A half dozen surfers were sitting on their boards below, chatting and joking, but the waves were mostly blown off.

"*Jefe*," the boy said. "I think I got my job back."

"No, no, I'm not your boss either. Call me *amigo* or Jack. How are you going to get here to work?"

"I don't know. Maybe I got to ask you to drop me back at the camp in the hills."

"That makes me sad, and it'll upset Gloria. We'll work something out."

They watched the surfers down below for a while, and nobody in the lineup was making a move with the surf so broken up.

"Bad waves?" Jack Liffey asked.

"Yes, *amigo*. There's no real swell, and wind is blowing it off."

They watched the sea for a while, and Jaime wondered why he found it so comforting. Maybe the sense that it was trying hard to wear everything away, every feature and city, so the earth would eventually be smooth as glass, without human scars.

"You know, you've got yourself right in the middle of a big murder and conspiracy investigation by the sheriff's department. Do you really think you can go back to work over at that house and keep out of it?"

"It's my job. I got to fight for it. You can't let bad luck rule your life."

Jack Liffey turned and looked at him with a curious eye, and Jaime felt a welling of affection for this man.

"Yes, I understand," Jack Liffey said. "But what I've learned is if you try to protect yourself in some absolute way from bad luck, that's when you really get hammered. It'll drag you into the thing you're most afraid of."

"Maybe. What are you most afraid of, *Señor* Jack?"

"Immediately I'm tempted to say what scares me most is harm coming to my daughter. But she's almost in college now, and it's time for me to let her make her own mistakes. I can't ride along behind her forever shooting healing arrows." He laughed for a moment. "If you want the utter truth, I'm probably most afraid of finding out that I've done something really wrong or really stupid and I've hurt somebody innocent. There's nothing much worse than that."

Yes, Jaime thought, he did want to stay close to this man if he could. It was amazing to find someone to admire in this cruel world. Somehow, it made him worried, too, as if this relationship might be taken away in a wink, like so much up here in *El Norte*. The idea of forever, of lasting, taunted him. All Mexicans believed they had tragic souls, and they all knew nothing lasted. He wished the man were Catholic.

"You worry like this about right and wrong and you're not religious?" Jaime said.

"How would that make a difference?" Jack Liffey said. "Do you think God wakes up every morning and makes a new decision on what's right and wrong and then let's all the priests know? Right is right, wrong is wrong. Nobody can change it."

The boy thought about it. It was a strange window to a way he'd never looked at things, and it stretched his thinking.

"You know, a lot of people go to church every Sunday and think that makes them Christians," Jack Liffey said. "It's like standing in a garage and thinking that makes you a car." The man laughed at his own joke, and then looked embarrassed when Jaime wasn't laughing. "Sorry, all I mean is, I think we're stuck trying to figure life out for ourselves. Luckily a lot of the time it's pretty clear. Even God can see what's right pretty quick."

Jaime was thinking about Don Ignacio, but the man didn't know anything about that, and he didn't think he'd tell him. "I'm very strong-headed, Mr. Jack. I think honor can make me do things that aren't nice. But I have to do them."

"Yeah, honor is a tough one," Jack Liffey said. "It's always the rotten board in the house."

"What do you mean?"

That was the one moral fact that even Faulkner had never figured out, Jack Liffey thought, or maybe he'd figured it out but couldn't stop himself clinging to his ideas of honor so fiercely, and excusing it so often among his countrymen. The Old South and Mexico shared that moral warp—passion and pity and pride and sacrifice. Killers, all of them, puffed up emotions that permitted no gray areas. He preferred a kind of jesting at weakness and failure, an acceptance of vulnerability, the half smile of survival.

"No matter what they tell you, the idea of honor is a sickness, Jaime. I've been there. I've stood on a square foot of space, called it *my* space, marking out who I am. And then when I faced something much stronger than me and told myself if I let myself get pushed off that space, I'd never get it back—that was my mistake. It's just so amazingly dumb."

One surfer attempted to take off and wiped out immediately in the weak swell.

"I don't understand."

The other surfers sat up on their boards and gave the one who'd tried an ironic hand of applause as he righted himself and paddled back out. There was something in those shared values down below that the two onlookers up above both understood.

"Nobody understands it. It's impossible. Any time we suffer a loss, we try to find some meaning to make up for the loss. But there isn't any meaning, never ever—there can't be and won't be. Honor is just a furious shout against that fact. We punch out at somebody who seems responsible. It almost always makes things worse. Honor always and forever becomes violence."

Very few people can look that fact in the face, Jack Liffey thought. He knew he was probably overburdening the boy, and at the same time not telling him enough to grasp what he was saying.

"You probably shouldn't listen to me, Jaime. Words don't always clarify our experience. Just keep asking whatever you want to."

"I will, *señor.* I want to stay your *amigo.*"


Jaime wondered what this kindly man sitting beside him was trying to tell him that seemed to go so fiercely against the man's priestlike character. He'd never known anyone remotely like this.


"I waited for you and now you get to wait for me," Jack Liffey said. The man had driven him a mile and parked in front of a big house in yet another row of ultra tidy homes in Palos Verdes. There were so many places like this around here. Once again he wondered where all the wealth came from. Had the people who lived here worked that much harder than the people he knew? It didn't seem very likely.

"No problem," Jaime said.

"This is the woman who started the whole thing. Or maybe her daughter did. You've run into the guys who harass Mexicans up here, right? "Maybe. There are so many." Jack Liffey laughed, recognizing the small joke. "They bumped me and didn't really think I spoke English. They said some stupid thing like, 'This is our country. Love it *and* leave it, wetback.'"

"Wetback. They've never seen the Tijuana River. Just wading through it would have dissolved your legs right up to the knees."

He had seen the foul river in its concrete banks in the *colonia* near the border. Its color was not that of any water he'd ever seen, with a rainbow sheen on the surface suggesting some other chemistry.

Jack Liffey got out. "I'll see you soon, Jaime." He walked across the evenly green lawn that looked like it had been manicured by a whole grounds crew on their knees, using nail clippers. He should have called first, a great failing of his, but she was there at the door. "Jack. I thought maybe you'd fallen down the same black hole as Blaine."

"I've been on the job, Helen, don't worry."

He followed her into the kitchen. He knew he could lie a bit to make Blaine's chances seem better, but, still, he told her a little about the guys who called themselves Special Ops and how her daughter might have rubbed them the wrong way.

Listening to him, she seemed not to be taking it very seriously and it annoyed him and made him want to crank up her level of concern a little, just in case Blue's body was found one of these days.

"These can be rough guys. The sheriff's deputies are looking at them for killing some Mexicans."

She glared at him suddenly. "Don't you think I'm worried enough? Jack, *please*—if I have three breakdowns a day, it isn't going to bring Blaine back any sooner. Heavens, I even went to Mass this week and lit candles for her."

"I didn't know you were Catholic."

"I'd almost forgotten I was. I went to confession, too. The asshole priest wanted details. *Details!* I haven't been to church in twenty-two years, and he wants to know whether I participated in any 'abnormal sex.' I almost asked him if he meant with altar boys."

"You've got a perfect right to be upset, Helen."

"You wouldn't believe it—'abnormal sex,' and 'out of wedlock,' he kept saying. They've got their sins so subdivided it's like the federal sentencing guidelines. Just a blow job. Six decades of the rosary, no parole."

She sat up suddenly and put her face in her hands, and he was sorry he'd felt it necessary to prod her fears.

"I'm sorry. Blaine could have run off. Maybe these creeps threatened her family, and she's gone off somewhere to protect you."

She shook her head. "Blaine wouldn't run away. Never." And then she started to sob and he didn't know what to do. He was afraid if he tried to hold her to comfort her, she'd misinterpret. He settled for putting his hand over her hands that were crushing her eyes closed.

"Listen to me, Helen. You've done nothing wrong. I'm doing everything I can to try to find her." He avoided using a name. This woman was probably the last human being on earth to call the girl Blaine, but names were meaningless. Blaine Hostetler. Blue Hostetler. Palos Verdes Blue. Maybe the girl would be sighted unexpectedly, reappearing in some unlikely place to surprise everyone, like the butterfly.

When he got back to his pickup, the boy was gone. It wasn't as if he had a lot of possessions over in Boyle Heights to abandon. Jack Liffey assumed he'd taken off to find an encampment near his job—knowing with certainty that any Mexicans he found up here would welcome him and take care of him.

Ironic, he thought. These far-from-home men had more feeling of fraternity and security in this country than he did.

"Where have you been?"

"Just busy," Ruthie answered.

"All day and all night?"

"Calm down. I only came over to see you now because you threatened horrible stuff if I didn't. I like you, but this sex stuff is so new to you that you're getting to be out of control."

"I'm sorry, Ruthie. I can't help it. I love you." Maeve was doing her best not to jump on Ruthie and start kissing her, as they sat five feet apart in the back bedroom at home.

"No, you don't. You're rebounding, and you've got your hormones in the spin cycle. Pretty soon you'll settle down and realize that I'm not for you."

"Can I just kiss your ankle?"

"Maeve, be cool. You're an intelligent woman."

Maeve felt like weeping. The rejection was so much like an episode of a TV sitcom that the frustration made her crazy. "Maybe I should know better, but it doesn't feel that way. I realize I went crazy for a gangbanger last year, but this is different. I haven't been able to sleep since we were last together, thinking about you. You're just a super person, Ruthie."

"*Stop it*. Think about it a minute. You're not in love. You're getting suffocating."

"God, I am, aren't I? If it's not love, you tell me what it's all about."

"You've discovered a whole new menu of sexuality, and you want to grab all the goodies you can, all at once. But I'm not an experiment, okay. I'm me. I've got my own agenda."

"Your agenda doesn't include me?"

"Only as a friend, for right now. Can you dig it?"

"Oh. Did you find another woman?"

"You don't ask that, Maeve. Have some dignity."

"It's like another explosion in my face. I want to bite your nipples, but I have to think of discussing Proust instead."

"Yes, you do. Or maybe Joyce Carol Oates."

"Who are you, Ruthie?"

"I'm a nut in my own way, girl. Don't you go worshipping me. I'm too emo. I don't believe a word anybody ever tells me. I don't even believe what I say."

"I promise I'll be your platonic friend—but I hate it to death."

"Keep it real. We don't want any more crossed wires."

Ledge slammed out the door of the Lomita sheriff's station, or at least as much of a slam as he could manage against a heavy glass door with pneumatic buffers. He'd demanded a ride home, since they'd brought him to the station in a patrol car, and the guy at the front desk had flipped a quarter at him contemptuously and said, "Call one of your scumbag friends to get you."

He'd let the quarter arc past him and twirl into a long death spiral under a bench. "We got you a file number now," he'd heard the deputy mutter behind him, as the door wouldn't slam.

Throughout the interrogation, Ledge had kept trying to figure out from the questions if somebody had dropped a dime on him. There were a lot of things they knew that he figured could only have come from Twitch. It was hard to believe, but maybe that explained the boy's odd behavior for the last few weeks. He'd turned snitch on them. Why would anyone ever do that?

He looked back at the sheriff's station as he walked away in the gathering dark and wanted to stash all his dynamite in some basement under that whole lit-up building, making sure it blew to hell. If only he could get more, a lot more, he'd wipe the whole of the South Bay and Palos Verdes off the map.

A steady stream of headlights wound their way up P.V. Drive North toward the reservoir, commuters heading home. He had to go the other way, down into the flatland. Someone in Special Ops had once told him that it was in the flatland where you had no choices: the rich were free to do whatever they wanted to you. It made perfect sense, but he knew he had something most of those rich commuters would never have, and it eased the pain and resentment considerably. He could kneel on his board, readying himself to experience that amazing surge from behind that signaled a launch onto a really gnarlatious wave.

One day in the 'eighties he'd come ashore knowing he'd outridden the gods—one utterly perfect ride on a perfect wave—and he'd loaded his board into his car as if he were sheathing a Samurai sword. He'd looked around then at the citizens driving past him, and all he could think was, You assholes, you went to your little jobs and you don't even know that a miracle happened out there today.


The P.V. Blue flitted toward the road and then back toward the sea, searching, investigating, sniffing, as the last of the daylight was dying out far to the west. Perhaps there were other places to make a home, but there were none for her now. Only alien stalks and fronds, tiny flowers that were quite the wrong color. Fear and night chill, a fight to go on at all. Then she relaxed right down to the veins in her wings and settled gently into the wonderful mothering scent of the single rattleweed growing above the Lunada Bay cliffs. She felt a sense of immense relief as she looked at the fernlike leaves just below the yellow flowerings that she knew would hold the nectar she craved. Here she could eat her fill and lean into the wind and lay her eggs with the assurance, way deep in her instincts, that her offspring would thrive. It was all she sensed that first night, but it soothed the panic she'd been feeling all day that she had wandered too far from where she had been born in search of the sweet nectar, so far that not one other plant she had investigated that day had meant a thing to her needs. And a day was a year, nearly a lifetime, at this heavy stage.

# 18

# A Coded Portrait of His Own Life

WHEN HE SAW THE CAMPFIRE, JAIME HOLA'D SEVERAL TIMES FROM UP ABOVE AND THEN NAMED HIS HOMETOWN AND HOME STATE AND EVEN NAMED OFF SEVERAL BRANDS OF MEXICAN CIGARETTES—"FUMO EMBAJADORES, DOMINOS, Y FAROS"—THAT ONLY A MEXICAN WOULD KNOW. Several voices down in the barranca laughed at his makeshift passwords.

"*Sobres, amigo. ¿Cómo estamos? Venga y visítemos.*"

He scrambled down the hill to visit, knowing he was home here. He was sure Jack Liffey would help him and shelter him and protect him to the best of his ability, but these men knew in their bones who he was.

"Gentlemen, I need a place to stay for a few days. *La migra* caught me right out of my job near here, but I think I can get it back if I stay nearby."

"Of course you can stay. In my shelter over there. *Hermano. Sonoriense.*"

It was a very short older man with wavy hair. Jaime shook his hand politely beside the campfire.

"*¿Usted es de . . . ?*" Jaime asked.

"*Sonora también, hijo. Como usted.* But I am from the big city, Hermosillo, not the stupid little *poblado* of yours."

"It is not stupid, sir. It is utterly useless and rubbish."

Another man said, "You can't go home, can you?"

"*Más vale no meneallo.*" The less tail-wagging the better. The three men he could see by firelight all nodded. They knew with a pang of longing what it could mean to have to let sleeping dogs lie.

"Sit down, son," his host said. "On that chair. Share our *menudo.* Here is an implement to eat from. Oscar over there walked four miles to buy the ingredients."

"Thank you," he said to Oscar, and to his host: "What is your name, sir?"

"I am called No Man from Hermosillo. No Man from Sonora. I am No Man Gardener-for-*Gabachos.*"

Jaime smiled gravely. "I am Jaime Stone-Wall-Builder. I speak English very well, and I have a gringo friend if any of you need help. He is a good man, and I will lend him to you."

"How can you be sure?"

"You can never be sure, of course, but he drove all the way to Tijuana to rescue me. And he risked the police for himself. And he offered me a home, but it's too far away."

"*Muy gente,* but no *gabacho* can be trusted in the end of things," the cook said.

"That is most probably true," Jaime said. "But I trust this man."


The sun hadn't come up yet by at least an hour. False dawn, Ledge had heard it called—a faint aura over the top of the P.V. hills from the east. It was sometimes the hour the surf was the very best.

He had got up several hours earlier still and played a round of *Warcraft III: Tides of Darkness* for luck on his old computer. Then, he had unlocked the grease monkey bays with the key he'd made and moved the engine parts so he could take away his entire crate of dynamite, making absolutely sure no one was paying any attention to the Chevron station, though it was hours before it was set to open. He'd locked up again and driven up here very cautiously—the dynamite was old and he'd seen the beads of nitro sweat on the sticks. He was parked at the big cliff off Via Olivera, a quarter mile directly above Twitch's house. This much explosive, planted properly, would bring down the road, the cliff itself, the long windbreak of eucalyptus trees, the parked SUVs and Mercedeses, the swimming pools, the tennis courts, and just about every house above and below. Nobody down on Paseo Del Mar would know what hit them when a billion tons of Easy Street picked up its skirts and ran downhill.

He dug slowly and carefully into the hillside off the road. No mistakes now. Everything he'd absorbed of sapper training before washing out of the Army Combat Engineer School at Fort Leonard Wood would have to come into play now.

Maeve woke in a funk in the predawn dark, devastated all over again by the realization she'd never make love to Ruthie again. Her mind ran back again and again to tangible details of the lovemaking, irresistibly tormenting herself, like a tongue working at a sore on her gum. In fact, she did have a sore on her gum, and immediately she worried about herpes, or worse. Maeve the hypochondriac, she thought. Next she'd be finding lumps in her breast or feeling twinges in her cervix, punishments from the gods for not being chaste.

Her arm was still sore from the explosion bruises and the wound. She wrapped it in a plastic bag and sealed it with several rubber bands and then propped it up on the side of the tub and soaked in the dark for a while until she felt a little better. As she lay there, she convinced herself she had to talk to her dad. For some reason that she couldn't really put her finger on she hadn't told him about her visit to Brandon "Twitch" Dedrick. It was just so hard to admit that she'd been meddling in his detective business again—and Twitch was probably why that Mysterious Stranger had tried to blow up her bedroom. Weird, but that had seemed to be what she'd heard him calling out to her: *Leave the boy alone.*

Her dad deserved to know everything. She felt terribly guilty every time she kept something from him, even though he'd kept a good deal from her this time. He was so bugs about the truth usually. The trouble was, just about every time she'd withheld something from him, things had gone bad. Very bad. But it could wait another hour or two, until he and Gloria were awake.


Sheriff's Detective Dennis Ross leaned back in the Aeron chair he'd swiped from the captain over a year ago (and then carefully swapped property stickers with his own chair to make it untraceable). He sipped his morning coffee and ran his finger down a list of what the Gang Intervention Team called "known associates" of Percival "Ledge" Choate. Half the names were probably linked to Special Ops, but ne couldn't be sure which. He was hoping for a small chime to go off deep in his memory as he read the names softly to himself.

Bourden "Big Bob" Civetich
Joseph "Bibleman" Kardos
Conrad "Connie" MacNeal
Wallace "Hoke" Murray
Kurt Trendler
What was wrong with Kurt Trendler, he thought, that he didn't

rate his own goofy monicker—"Big Foot," "Butt-sniffer," "Toejam?" He was like some Mafia wannabe who was still known only as Alvin.

George "Rosey" Magidson
Brandon "Twitch" Dedrick

*Ding.*

Oh, yeah. Twitch Dedrick. He'd heard about him, all right, off and on for quite some time, from Luke Gordon on the surfing and Bayboy detail. The guy the kids all called Deputy Dawg.

Twitch had been known to key the cars of outsiders and generally terrorize any interlopers who dared try to surf in their 'hood, but he'd been a bit too clever to be caught in the act. Definitely worth a visit. Talk loud, wave a little dick at him, threaten fingerprints or DNA. Yeah, DNA. Everybody watched *CSI* these days. These guys were so dumb you could convince them they left DNA right through their tennies everywhere they walked.

Slowly she spread her wings to the morning sun, an orange ball just rising over big hill, to let the very first radiant warmth begin to revive her near-suspended animation. This was beginning to feel like the big day. She would lay her eggs. The weight of them was exhausting her, almost to dormancy. The rattleweed seedpods had grown to the size she needed. She only had to nibble a small hole in the pod to lay her eggs within, so her precious larvae could feed as they grew. She could feel in her veins and her tissues that it was time to gather her strength for the last acts of her life.

Loco had taken to digging again, a habit he'd given up years earlier. His pawing was glacially slow now, a scoop with the left paw, pause, then a determined scoop with the right. But it was so encouraging to see him erect and industrious early in the morning that Jack Liffey threw on some pants and a shirt and went out into the back yard to the soft patch of earth where they'd dug out last year's chiles and cilantro, to keep him company.

"Got a bone you want to hide, Loc?"

The dog eyed him, almost furtively, but went on working at dead slow, as Jack Liffey sat down in the grass nearby.

"No sweat, *amigo*. Whatever you need, you can have it. You can eat my slippers. Well, okay, I don't have any slippers. You can have a first-rate sirloin, but it would be a real crime to bury it, I have to say. Anyway, just go on doing whatever you're doing. Any logic in a storm."

It was almost painful to watch, the raking action much more feeble with the left paw, and Jack Liffey was ashamed to realize he didn't remember which side had had the cancer worst, though he was guessing the weaker one.

"I'm afraid your new friend won't be around today, but maybe later. You really liked Jaime, didn't you?"

There was a small hitch in the dog's attention, but whatever he was up to, he was nothing if not singleminded.

Jack Liffey looked up and noticed Gloria in her nightie at the kitchen window. She smiled, and he nodded.

"Your Auntie Gloria's finally taken a shine to you, too. You don't know how lucky you are. Okay. *Sure*, real luck would be not getting the damn bone cancer at all, and not having to go to the v-e-t for the c-h-e-m-o. Right you are."

He heard the back door, and Gloria came out in one of those gauzy robes that didn't hide much, though combined with the nightie, it was probably modest enough for any neighbors who happened to peek out their windows. "Morning, Jackie. I've got some breakfast burrito coming, if you want."

Nearly the last thing he wanted, first thing in the morning, was hearty Mexican fare with a lot of beans and spice in it. "Sounds great."

She came up behind him and rested a hand in his hair, a gesture so uncharacteristically affectionate that it instantly gave him an erection, and he realized he wasn't wearing anything beneath the trousers. "What's Loco up to?" she asked.

"Beats me, my love. Tunneling to China to get away maybe. At the rate he's digging, he'll get there just before the sun goes supernova."

"I'll bet there's something valuable he wants to hide."

"Could be." What Jack Liffey actually thought all of a sudden was, What if the dog was digging his own grave? Jesus Christ. That's a caution, his mom would have said, long ago. Why did he think of his mom then? Then he finally realized that what was disturbing him was the fact that all this slow pointless labor from the old dog seemed a coded portrait of his own life being acted out.


Ledge wasn't sure why he found it suddenly so hard to move, like somebody had given him the Vulcan death grip or something. He'd been immobile on the curb beside his car for almost an hour now. He was directly across the road from the cliffs where he'd dug a small cave and firmly planted the dynamite, and he was looking out to sea, over the foreshortened houses on several streets on the steep slope below him. The homes down there weren't giant braggart mansions like the ones in Beverly Hills or Brentwood, nor did they flaunt vast acreage around themselves. What they were was manicured and gardened beyond reason, not one flake of paint awry, not one geranium leaf going brown, every home down there with a swimming pool crammed into its minimal back yard, as powder blue as washed jeans and utterly free of leaves. It was a world that reeked of being looked after daily, hourly, with unending buckets of money spent upon it to keep any suggestion of time or decay at bay. In his loneliness and his near-subsistence life, his single cramped room of a pool house, surrounded by a world of indifference, he found he resented everything these homes suggested of whole armies of hired help sweeping across them daily and a world that would inevitably cater to their needs. His last foster dad, toward the end of high school, had worked for a rugsteamer franchise, and to Ledge supertidiness meant mainly limitless daily servitude with hoses.

A truth like that had to be passed on to someone else, he thought, but now that he couldn't trust Twitch, he had no one at all, really. Who could tell something that intimate to Hoke, or Big Bob, or even Bibleman? He had a feeling that holding a raw truth like that in your sole consciousness meant you'd already lost some game of life.

An hour and a half ago he'd pried open his cellphone and attached the wires of the ringer to the first of three mercury fulminate percussion caps lashed together and then forced into a hole he had drilled in a stick of dynamite with the awl of his pocket knife. The telephone and all its attachments—forty-three more sticks of dynamite—he had planted in the rain-softened clay of the cliff, enough explosive to bring down a fair-sized bridge if he could trust the truncated training that he'd had. All he had to do was go to any telephone in the world and dial his own cell number—and hope like hell nobody else called him in the meantime. But who ever did? He couldn't remember the last time the cell had rung. Ops always called him at work, figuring all cells were broadcasting straight to the FBI. It would be ironic indeed to have some boiler-room salesman call him just then.

Ledge wondered what he was waiting for, why he didn't simply retreat a safe distance to a pay phone and punch in the number. But he knew he was waiting for something, some sign, maybe an omen of permission. Or maybe he needed a goad to further kindle his anger at Twitch, and the thought that he really wasn't very decisive vaguely depressed him, like a failure of manhood.

He could see the offshore portion of Lunada Bay below him, with flat dead surf creeping in and offering no challenge at all, no opportunity. Far off to the right was part of the ugly marina at Redondo, only a mile from his Chevron station, a mile and a half from his "home." He wondered what other reference points his life offered. Fort Leonard Wood, for example, may as well never have been. In the wind-down of Vietnam, they hadn't even pushed him over into the cannon-fodder hopper, just sent him back where he came from. His high school in Torrance had been a daily torment, crushing him with failure after failure, then his job at U.S. Steel in South Gate, good pay for a few years, a real man's job, but it had shut down with all the other steel plants in L.A., even the huge Kaiser complex out in Fontana.

Then there were all the women he'd lost or offended by being too rough or too clumsy, or just not caring enough about them. Somebody had told him once: it's just like drinking a dog's tears. At least, everything in his life was dead simple now: frozen TV dinners from Ralphs, the dumbass garage, nine or ten or eleven hours' sleep when the surf was down because there was nothing else worth getting up for. Even slapping around Mexicans had lost its attraction. Nobody else seemed to take defending the country seriously.

He wished he had one thing in his life he couldn't forget, one thing too complicated to disregard. He felt spent, empty and old. He thought his heart might just grind to a stop like the hundred-day clock his second foster dad had had in a bell jar, running out the very last nudge of its rotating gold balls. He remembered a priest—his second foster had forced him to go to St. Columbkille—saying that even the hardest work and the saddest life was a form of praise to God. Ledge thought now, *How the fuck could that be? God doesn't have to live in a pool house with only a hotplate and a faulty microwave. God doesn't climb down into the grease pit to change the oil of a fucking Valiant that ought to be in a junkyard. God takes what he wants, and so should I.*

*I rode thirty-footers on the Big Island, and I rode them heroically. I was awesome then. I let myself be sucked back into the magnificent green room, into the tube. I was filmed for history by the great Bruce Brown. I'm Ledge. I'm legend.*

*But I ain't got the knack no more of looking forward to nothing. Shit just happens, I know it. When I go into the supermarket now, women grip their kids and look at me like I'm rubbish. I see their eyes, like I'm some guy that's going to come to his end in an alley. Or be found flotso on the beach.*

He felt a prickling of rain on his neck. *Let it come, he thought—let it rain for forty days and forty nights.* He wondered if he still existed at all in the minds of anyone he'd fucked. He couldn't really believe he did.

"Dad, you've got to meet me at this guy's house. He's the key, I'm sure. To everything. I'm sorry I didn't tell you sooner. I was trying to figure things out on my own. I even channeled you a bit when I was talking to him."

"More."

"Twitch is his nickname. His real name is Brandon. I can tell he's seriously depressed, but he's not really a bad guy. Though he does have a certain assholish quality. It comes out as hostility. He's kind of a famous surfer in the Bayboys, but he's so freaked now about something that I don't think he's been on the water in weeks."

"Do you know why?"

"I might. He thought I was from County Health when I first approached him, and that's not a big jump to HIV, is it? We talked awhile, and I think he was just starting to confide in me. He told me that as a kid he'd had an imaginary friend he had to explain things to. He actually started imitating a robot. It's kind of like a guy where loneliness is driving him nuts."

"Could be. Anything else about him that connects?"

"I was there because I was told Blue Hostetler made a play for him a few months ago. He's coming apart, Dad. It's really No Help City for guys like him up in P.V. And, yeah, I'm sorry, I was trying to play junior detective again. Come to his house and I'll introduce you."

"When?"

"How about ten o'clock?" she suggested.

"Is there a rock wall going up behind it?" he asked. He'd actually nibbled for a while on one of Gloria's breakfast burritos, scrambled egg and bacon plus chopped tomato, beans, and cheese with salsa all over it in one of those flour tortillas the size of a spare tire. Individually the ingredients were unobjectionable, but together, at dawn, they seemed to settle right to the bottom of his stomach and then burn right on through.

"How'd you know that?"

"I think I know the very house, hon."

"Wow. Well, meet me there when you can."

He wished for just once he could worry only about the job at hand. A missing girl. But there were surfers. Mexicans. Bigots. Jaime. And then his daughter. Everything was ripples on ripples, building up and up behind your back when you weren't looking and threatening to wallop you with the seventh wave.

Ledge called in sick, refusing to *sound* sick, knowing this would profoundly irritate the kid who thought of himself as the boss. He hadn't played hooky in a long time, and he bought a nice satisfyingly square bottle of Jack Daniel's at Aldo's Liquor and decided to go home to bed and get undressed and drink himself to bliss—that most satisfying of life's dodges. Because of a sudden downpour, he had to slam out of the car and trot with his bottle to the poolhouse, then wipe his hair down with the old T-shirt that hung on a nail by the door.

He had no land line in the room, but he knew there was a pay phone at the liquor store a few blocks away where he'd bought the hooch, and the old slob who rented to him had a phone in the house up front he could borrow in a pinch. He could go either place and dial his cell any time he felt like bringing down the mountain. What a feeling of power!

He lay back now, wishing for the fiftieth time he'd been only a few years older and had got himself to Vietnam so he'd know what it was like to shoot as many mud people as you could or blow them to smithereens. It was the big lottery reward of his generation, and he'd missed it. He knew, or thought he knew, that outside of surfing, all the really good things happened when you held a weapon. And he tried not to remember his helplessness at eleven, getting whipped with an extension cord, an extendo antenna, a broken fan belt.

Being alone—sometimes it made him feel powerful, self-contained and strong, but eventually a hollow feeling would always come over him and ruin it. It made him think there was something really wrong with him, but he didn't know what it could be. Rain roared all at once on the thin roof, and out the window it was dimpling and roiling the pool. He could see the tongue-and-groove boards above him and knew by the ugly brown stains just where they'd start dripping in a few minutes. He knew he should get the pans and jars ready, but he just didn't give a damn now.

He liked to imagine himself a cowboy on a golden horse (he'd never been near a horse) out on some hilly prairie, the appointed guardian of a group of vulnerable little white boys—determined to keep away all the nastiness of life.

Deputy Dennis Ross pulled over reluctantly at Malaga Park where he saw two gray-haired Vietnam-era leg amputees fighting out in the pouring rain. Each of them apparently had yanked off an artificial leg and kicked their wheelchair away and now they were balancing one-armed against a live oak, walloping one another furiously with the plastic legs. *Thwok—thwok*, he heard as he got out and locked up, tugged a plastic rain cover glumly over his duty cap and headed across the green.

The rain was a lot worse than it had been a few minutes earlier and was threatening to stay that way. The air was dark and ugly and had a cruel tempest feel to it. He'd always hated rain. It was an imposition on his whole concept of living in Southern California—

he'd moved here from Minnesota to get away from weather—and it should only have come at night, or off-duty. The inconvenience added ten percent to everything, making him feel impaired.

He had very little capacity for the soothing blather meant to pacify crazies like this, one of his chief failings as a cop. He always wanted to say, Come on, assholes, just *can* it, but that was never the right thing. Alternately, he wanted to shoot them. Maybe this was the morning he actually would. As he got close, he saw that one of them looked like he'd bought his eyeballs at a joke shop. Black-tar heroin, he guessed.

"Geniuses!" he yelled at them. "What seems to be the problem?"

The one with the eyeballs shouted, "Line!"

It took Ross more than a moment to realize that the man had probably been an actor once, and he was calling out to some imaginary prompter. Shit, he thought, he didn't need that kind of comedian at eight-something of a bad rainy morning.

"Out, out, brief candle," the shorter amputee said.

"Life is nothing but a walking shadow . . ."

"Knock it off! I'm not worth impressing, boneheads," Ross said, though even he recognized *Macbeth*.

Both sat down hard on the wet grass simultaneously, looking like drenched cats.

He could see it was a dispute that had probably been going on ever since the bars had closed at 2 a.m. and was now bottoming out. He tried to set the rules. "Okay, let's shake hands and make up."

Ross wanted nothing more than to walk away right then and drive on to Lunada Bay, but a sixth sense, plus an unenthusiastic feeling of duty, concerning getting these impaired men in out of the rain, held him there just a moment longer.

"Guys—" Ross started in.

"I had to tell somebody about the woman, didn't I?" the smaller one piped up.

"Strictly speaking, *fuck no*, dude. Look, we got a wet-ass cop wanting to bug out on us. Let's be cool."

Out of the blue, the little one took a wide roundhouse swing at his pal, ridiculously ineffective from his sitting position, but he connected, and it counted as a punch, and Ross sighed, knowing it meant paperwork. He reached out to grab the small man's wrist.

Maeve accepted a cup of steaming herbal tea, tasting of anise and citrus and maybe ginger. She'd seen the woman lace her own tea surreptitiously with Triple Sec before sitting down with them at the kitchen table. Twitch sat glumly with a Coke, obviously wanting to be elsewhere. Rain was rat-tatting against the kitchen window. Outside, she had seen two laborers wearing black plastic bags laying out stones for a wall, despite the rain. She wondered how they could possibly mix and use cement when it was so wet.

Twitch had called his mother out of her bedroom because he said he had an announcement, and Maeve dreaded what might be coming. But if he needed to have her there for courage, that could be the gift she gave him.

He let out a huge breath. "I gotta tell you something, Ma."

"Don't say you're leaving me." Her eyes went liquid with dread.

"It's not always about you, you know. Life used to be pretty okay here, and now that Dad's gone, it's gone and got all fucked up."

"Brandon!"

"He won't even write back to me now," the boy continued.

"I bet he's flying around first class," the woman said bitterly. "With some chippie."

Maeve wanted to crawl under the table. Her own parents had broken up with a lot more civility, but it still hadn't been easy. Rain roared against the house all of a sudden.

"Mommy!" he suddenly cried out. "Listen to me! This is about *me*! I've got AIDS—you know what that means. I'm going to die. Horribly . . . It isn't fair. I hate the pills. They make me sick and they don't work." Tears were rolling down his cheeks, and the anguish inside him was so powerful it got Maeve to crying, too. The woman shrieked and covered her face.

"Twitch, listen," Maeve said. "I'll get you to a better doctor. They've got more medicines now. Honest."

"Why bother?"

"Because you're worth it."

# 19

## Dragging Lost Boy Scouts Out of the Snow

JACK LIFFEY HURRIED ACROSS THE LAWN CARRYING A CHEAP COLLAPSIBLE UMBRELLA WITH TWO BROKEN RIBS THAT WAS ABOUT TO FLAP ITSELF TO DEATH UNDER THE DRIVING RAIN. The storm was a steady torrent now, and he'd seen the two workmen sheltering in a big pickup that had worn a muddy two-track path across the lawn to where they had depositing their cairn of stones. One of the workmen was clearly Jaime, but the boy gave no sign of recognition, and Jack Liffey gave him his head, letting him play out whatever hand he thought he had going.

He saw Maeve and a blond boy who might have been about a year younger than she was sitting on kitchen chairs they'd apparently carried out onto the verandah to watch the pounding rain, an occasional L.A. entertainment.

"Dad, come out of the wet. Meet Twitch Dedrick."

The boy stood up abruptly and fled into the house.

Jack Liffey clambered up beside Maeve, shook out the umbrella, and took over the vacated chair. "I sometimes have that effect on people."

She shook her head. "It's not you. He's in a kind of emotional free-fall. He's got AIDS, and he claims the drugs aren't working for him. He's scared out of his mind."

"That's enough to freak anyone. Are you sure he knows something about Blue Hostetler? Or could he be suckering you for sympathy?"

"I'd give it to him anyway, wouldn't I? I am your daughter. I promised you'd help him if you could."

He decided not to go there, not for the moment. "And how are you doing?"

A jacaranda tree in the front yard was whipping crazily in the monsoon. She clasped herself with both arms, as if she needed to hold something in. "I'm confused, Dad. Sexually, I mean. I haven't told mom about Ruthie. How do you think she'll take it?"

He gave it some thought as his eye was taken by a sudden spate of rain so fierce that it actually seemed to be bouncing off the walk. "Every time I thought your mom was going to lose it, she surprised me with her resilience. Don't sell her short."

Maeve gave him the fish eye. "That's Parents Union Local 6 talking, isn't it?"

He smiled. "Not entirely. I married a good woman back in the 'seventies. In the end we weren't right for each other, but I can still respect her."

"Are you and Gloria right for each other? You know I love her, but you're awfully disparate."

"Disparate, wow. Disparate is the spice of life. Let's not get off into dangerous territory so early in the morning." It reminded him of other talks he'd had with her, when she'd always seem to spring vital questions at an inopportune time.

"That's where you live, Dad. Danger man."

"Me and Loco. You'll be happy to know he's revived a bit. He's very slowly digging a hole in the backyard to bury something. We can't figure out what. Maybe just the last couple of weeks."

"Probably what he values the most."

"Then be careful he doesn't come drag you off."

She was about to slap his knee in mock retort when they heard a peculiar keening from within the house.


Ledge had eaten two greasy Breakfast Jacks after a fifty-yard sprint to the Jack-in-the-Box out on PCH, and now he stepped slowly, reluctantly, back into his room, so sleep-deprived he was buzzy with it. The thought that nothing in the room would have changed position since he last left it—hell, since the time before that—oppressed him like something witchy. He believed in witchy powers. He'd met a redheaded woman on the beach once with unkempt white-person dreadlocks and a torn velvet dress who'd promised him great waves if he gave her money for a meal.

Not an hour after that he'd felt the rumble coming and snaked one of the best rides of his life, jumping the lineup ruthlessly to grab the freak wave that had come thundering out of nowhere, the acceleration so sudden it had slapped his hair over his eyes. He'd seen the horizon fall away as he lifted, and when the supernatural ride was over, he'd ridden the leftover foam in a fist-forward crouch all the way to the sand. It had been one of the great rides of his life, rivaling the North Shore of the Big Island.

Afterward, the witch woman had run up to demand her money. "Pay up, surfer man."

He'd just laughed at her and walked away as she cursed him, but he'd never again had a ride half as great. Maybe he was cursed.

Ledge looked around his room. He was sick of his own possessions, shabby and worn and second-rate. But ticking away in his brain was a sense of his power. Just one phone call. Wouldn't that be the antidote to everything that ailed him?

Dennis Ross had finally pacified the two feuding amputees and managed to extricate himself from their scene without having to write it up after all. That was a relief, since the huge storm was aggravating him no end. As the saying was, the only good 10-6—*on scene, investigating*—was one that ended with no paperwork. He always seemed to catch the inconvenient and the odd, but it did keep his life from getting boring.

He drove along Paseo Del Mar toward the address he had for Twitch the Bayboy, resenting the hell out of the whole Palos Verdes hills. He'd grown up in a working-class area of Duluth. Hell, most of Duluth was working class.

He remembered Jack Liffey saying he'd grown up down toward the docks in San Pedro. That had probably been about as working class as you could get back then, too. He'd liked the guy and felt a kinship right off. He'd probably never see him again, though, one of the curses of being a cop. Friends disappeared, wives disappeared, and everybody assumed you were a lot stronger than you really were.

"Your pals just don't seem to know how to express their feelings," his wife, now ex-wife, had once said.

"You're a great kidder," he had said, practicing for his fate.

Hurrying inside the house, Jack Liffey had seen a woman rush past him and slam into a back room. Twitch Dedrick was seated at the kitchen table, feigning indifference and drinking a Coke, but tears were still dripping off his cheeks.

Jack Liffey sat down across from him, and in the corner of his eye he saw Maeve watching them from the living room.

"Your mom?" he asked.

"She ain't my fuckin' sister. Don't get amped. She's okay."

Jack Liffey did his best to offer the boy his help and comfort, and alleviate his sense of doom, but he didn't really feel like beating around the bush. "First you've got to help me. I hear Blue Hostetler liked you. What happened to her? I hear a rumor she's dead."

"Who cares? *I'm* the dead man walking." The boy stared hard at him, and then something seemed to break free inside him and he wilted into the seat. "Oh, hell. Sure."

Twitch had no direct information about what had happened but his friend Ledge had got drunk one night and let slip some hints about catching a girl delivering groceries to some Mexicans. "I think she dissed them and they all just tripped out on her. Then they realized they were lit up real bad if they didn't shut her mouth, and they had to do the thing. Probably the cliff. Everybody knows how to find the rip tide that pulls all kinds of shit out to sea. I'm sorry, man. I didn't have anything against her. Does that mean you won't help me?"

"No, of course not. We'll help."

The boy looked questioningly at Jack Liffey. "You're one of those rescuers I see on the TV news, right—always dragging lost Boy Scouts out of the snow?"

The mildly ludicrous characterization had a strange effect on him. It made Jack Liffey feel trapped suddenly in his own fate, as if he were watching a huge meteor with his name on it plummeting straight toward him.

After all the searching, the idea of Blue Hostetler dead was going to take some getting used to. But, meanwhile, there was a live boy who needed his attention.

The boy dried his eyes surreptitiously. Then they were both startled by a ringing telephone.


"Good morning, gentlemen." Dennis Ross had found two workmen waiting out the rain in a big pickup truck on the side yard of the Dedrick house, near a half-built retaining wall. He'd almost stumbled over some of the flat field stones getting out of his car. He'd rapped on the driver's window, but quickly recognized the young Latino on the far side of the bench seat. Ross's smile broadened. "What an amazingly small world it is, *amigo*. Jack Liffey swore he didn't know where you were. Imagine that. I think it's all going to work out after all."

Mike turned to glare at Jaime. "What's this *about?*"

"Is mistake, *señor*." His command of English had seemingly evaporated.

Dennis Ross shook his head. "If I know anything at all, I know faces. You should trust me, Jaime, and be my friend. Trust me—as if you actually had a choice. Maybe you didn't trust me before," he said wistfully. "I understand. I didn't want them to send you back. But now it's essential that we be friends."

"Any way you want it," Jaime said, resigned in the face of such potent authority. He only hoped that the sheriff had little communication with the Mexican police. He could live with being deported again, but not into the waiting arms of the *judiciales* to be charged with murder.

"Hey, man," the driver said to the deputy. "I just picked this wetback up at the Home Depot. I'm not responsible."

"Shut the *fuck* up before I find something to write you up for. This kid is okay." The rain and the maddening humidity were making Ross's whole attitude go swampy. "You want to argue, or you want to go home?"

"No trouble, sir," Mike said, readjusting his scowl.

Something was gradually working on Ross, and he saw the futility of playing hardass with such a no-account. "Okay. It's get-out-of-jail-free day. Go home and kiss your wife. Tell her you got lucky. And *you*—" pointing at Jaime—"Get out of the car *now*."

Twitch grabbed the phone and listened, his face gradually taking on a shocked look.

"Hey, Ledge . . . No way, man. You drunk? That girl's not in here. You were watching the *house?*"

Twitch listened some more and then broke out angrily, "I'm no snitch . . ." He looked at Jack Liffey, apparently hoping for approval now from this new source. His face clouded, and Jack Liffey could hear a tinny little voice ranting at him.

"You choker! I never did a thing to you." Twitch pulled the phone away from his ear. "If that's what you think, fuck you!" he shouted into it and then ended the call.

The deputy showed his badge because the soaked raincoat was obscuring most of his uniform, and he banged his plastic-wrapped cap against the doorframe to knock the water off. The woman at the door had obviously been crying up a storm, but he didn't want to know about that—he just pushed inside, rather, herded them all in, the Mexican boy and the girl he'd found waiting nervously on the porch. He kept herding them right into the kitchen, where a familiar face was sitting at the table.

"Jack Liffey in the flesh."

Jack Liffey rather liked the deputy. Not counting Gloria, he'd had few enough enjoyable relationships with cops. Yet something was beginning to worry him about the whole morning—he felt curiously impaired at dealing with things. There was a strange sense of doom he'd thought would never catch up to him as long as he stayed a step or two ahead of the game, but doom seemed only an inch away now. There was no logical reason for it, but it was there. There are mysteries everywhere, he thought.

"And I'll bet you're Twitch," Ross said. "Now we can try to clear everything up."

But his pitch was interrupted when Twitch caught a glimpse of Jaime.

"Jaime! You're back!"

He saw the boy's face change. All that fear and rage seemed to ebb away, replaced by a naked small-boy look.

"Hush," Ross said. "There's too many of us. I do the talking for now. Let's start with this: Does anybody here know anything about dynamite?"

Ledge leaned back against the wood mullions and small glass panes in the old crimson British phone box. The Three Bells Pub and Fish Restaurant in Redondo had put it out in front for authenticity of décor.

All Ledge had tried to do was be friendly with a younger Bayboy, he thought, just like tradition called for, and to show him how to stand up for his rights as a patriotic American. Everybody's manhood was at risk if they let the little brown motherfuckers swarm in and take over everything. He thought Twitch had the balls to help fight them. But the rich kids always let you down. Some of them even helped the Mexes, like that goody-two-shoes little cunt with the big mouth. So it got out of hand: shit happens.

His quarters fell into the old phone with that resonant bong-bong. He dialed a number, watching it spin around with its old-fashioned whirr, dialed again—all but the last digit. Then he ran the last digit around and held it at the finger-stop for a long time. You don't work up all this effort and walk away, he reminded himself. Specially with a rich little snitch.

Oops. He'd let up only a little on the pressure, and the insistent spring had yanked the dial off his finger. His eye followed the droning dial around. So it wasn't his doing at all. It was fate and the big spring inside the machine.

He heard one ring and then the sound cut off.


Overhead somewhere there was a deep rumble and then an explosion, as if blasting had vented unexpectedly from a mine shaft, the reverberations billowing over them all and stopping Ross in midword. Still there was the steady hammer of the rain. Jack Liffey wondered if they were testing Navy ordnance.

"Dad, what's that?" Maeve asked.


Twitch was the first to get to the back window of the kitchen. "*Bail!*" he yelped. He sprinted for the hall, grabbing for Jaime on the way.

"Hey! You two stay here!" Ross ordered ineffectually, as the boy's mother suddenly grabbed at him, demanding medical help.

"It sounded like a whole lot of C-4 maybe," Jack Liffey answered Maeve. "They have radar domes up on top, but they're not worth blowing up to any terrorists I can imagine." His heart nearly seized when he looked out the window and saw through a haze of rain a mudslide bigger than anything he could have imagined sledding down the hill, carrying whole eucalyptus trees and half swimming pools with it. Was that a silver Maserati going airborne above the muck?

Mike had seen it coming, too, and overrevved his truck in second with his foot flat to the firewall, cursing himself that he'd been so curious about the weird goings-on here that he'd dawdled a bit. Liquefaction, he thought. As long as it's moving, that whole mudslide is just like water.

Jaime and Twitch, arm in arm, shoulder-bashed their way out the floor-to-ceiling windows in the front room, like Doug Fairbanks and Errol Flynn, shattering glass and carrying Twitch's two boards that they'd grabbed from his room. Twitch clung to the newer one with laser-cut 3-D swirls all over it. Jaime had the one that Twitch had tried to give him a few weeks ago—the one he'd scorned—an older board with a hand-painted design of rat-finks and speed-wheels by somebody named Duke-B. Not new, but perfectly wave-worthy.

"What now?" Jaime yelled.

"We run like hell!"

The nearest person he saw to save was Twitch's mother, so Dennis Ross grabbed her and dragged her toward the front door.

"I can't breathe, I need a doctor."

"I *am* a doctor," Ross cried out in frustration.

With a burst of superhuman strength, he carried her down the steps into the rain. Where the hell was everyone else?

"What do we do, Dad?" She'd seen it coming, too, pressed beside him.

"We're better off inside, I'm sure. This is a well-made house. Let's get in the bathtub and hope they're quick at digging us out."

The boys ran down the lawn and across Paseo Del Mar, hardly aware of the rain, feeling the rumble of the enormous slide gathering speed at their heels and hearing the terrible booming and snapping of a world behind them being torn to pieces.

"Get ready!" Twitch called on instinct, and they both brought their boards around to mount.

They had just got into the tub, and he had yanked a whole armload of towels over them for cushioning when they heard an enraged giant smash through the back of the house. Something tore away the whole second story above them, and then, piece by piece, their ceiling, their front wall, the rest of the bathroom. They clung hard to each other pressing themselves down in the tub as everything in the world bucked and roared and disintegrated around them. Jack Liffey kept one shoulder wedged under the spout, but he knew the whole tub could rip away as easily as anything.

"I love you, Daddy!"

"I love you, too, Maeve Mary!"

"I'll never be disobedient again!"

"I'll remember you said that!"

Mike screamed when he saw the forward edge of the brown slurry, lumpy with palms and debris, just wipe away a big Spanish home and head straight for his truck. His world began to tumble and his head hit something. He was aware of little but disorientation and panic when his truck reached the cliff edge and the bottom dropped out of the world.

Ross dragged a screaming Mrs. Dedrick down behind his substantial Ford Interceptor patrol car but realized all at once how insubstantial it really was when he saw the wave of mud hurtling down the slope and then bursting upward over the new stone retaining wall, carrying with it a garden shed and a black Cadillac Escalade.

"Ah, shit," he said to the woman who couldn't stop screaming. "Kiss your ass goodbye."

"Here it is! Jump up!" Jaime shouted.

They leapt upward in full run and the wave caught them and the sudden surge was breathtaking, their heads snapping back and both of them clinging to the boards for dear life, their arms wrapped around them as they flew forward well off the ground.

What the hell, Twitch thought after a moment, when it all began to feel right somehow, and he clambered upright to balance on his board, so panicky he ended up goofy-foot like his Mexican pal. He gave a shout of exultation.

The obscene brown wave carried them far too fast toward the cliff edge.

"*¡Hijole, amigo! ¡Andale, pues! ¡Que mala onda!*"

"Surf the mother down!"


Just before the leading edge of the mudslide reached the cliff at Lunada Bay—carrying cars and people and broken houses and trees before it—a Palos Verdes Blue butterfly choose to flutter upward above the rattleweed where she'd laid her eggs the evening before. She had no idea about the strange phenomenon going on below her that she had to strain her wings so hard to rise above, but she had a sudden panic that it was destroying her all-important nest.

# A Scoundrel

THE WHOLE WORLD ROARED AND SPLINTERED AROUND THEM, AND THE BATHTUB BUCKED WITH EACH SOUND. Jack Liffey kept his eyes clamped shut, and his mouth, too, lest he panic Maeve, who was pressed hard against him. He could feel himself beginning to lose it. Because of that fall down a well as a child, he retained a true phobia of all confining situations.

When the rumble and smashing sounds seemed to decline, he thrust his shoulder up against the towels above them only to be met by yet one more vicious wallop, as if his exertions had set off this new blow. There was no give at all above him so he knew they had to be under something heavy, probably a lot of things, and a lot of dirt. Don't think about it, he told himself. Rescuers would be there soon, but . . . when?

From time to time there was another muffled thud out in some inaccessible world, and the air between them was becoming rank and damp.

"What do we do, Dad?" he heard Maeve's voice.

"I know some people." He stopped, realizing he wasn't making sense. By touch he found the pattern of holes of the tub drain and wondered if the sewer pipe had broken and might emerge somewhere into air. "Help! Two of us in here!" he called into the drain. The reverberations in their small sealed chamber were incredible.

"Honey," he said querulously.

"Yes?"

"If you can wriggle around here, just keep calling down the drain. I think I'm about to leave you for a while. It's nothing to worry about. Just my mind's defenses."

"Dad, don't pass out."

"I'll use less air— Love you."

And that was the last thing Jack Liffey would say for a very long time.


All at once, the tub shifted on its axis as if a giant had tried to spin it—Maeve could feel the wrenching—and something hard pounded their cage and thrust an elbow down onto them. She felt around in the dark and thought the projecting thing might have hit her father in the neck.

"Help us! Help my dad!"

But nothing changed. Quite a long time later, she was still shouting periodically down the drain when something poked her leg hard.

"Owww!"

All at once there were sounds of a commotion above them, and the barking of dogs alerting to something. In another moment, their ceiling of towels was ripped away along with the big intruding elbow, and light poured onto her. Fresh air rushed in like a precious gift. She sucked it in over and over, damp and full of life.

"Anyone alive there?"

When her eyes adjusted, she saw two firemen down on their knees, burrowing with their hands. A fine mist of rain wet her face.

"Help my dad. He was hit by something."

They yanked her out of the tub, and she looked back to see an oxygen mask going onto her father.

EMTs carried her to a plastic pad and began checking her vital signs. All around, there were dogs sniffing the ground and men poking long metal probes into the mud. In the distance some strange machine on a big-wheel dolly was being pushed across an amazing landscape of rubble. Beyond, a crane was just chugging into position, with workmen waving and yelling.

"You're in damn good shape, kid," an EMT said, monitoring the clothespin device they'd put on her index finger. "What's your name?"

"Maeve. How's my father?"

"He's breathing on his own. He'll make it. Smart of you two to get in the tub. A lot of the roof fell on you. Do you know if any other people were in the house?"

"Yeah, lots. Just before the mudslide hit, two boys smashed out the front window carrying surfboards. And there was a sheriff and a woman who went out the front door, I think. And another man was in a truck right over . . . Oh, God, over *there,* I think."

Everything was changed. She fought up onto an elbow and could see that nothing was visible of any of the houses on the block. She couldn't even tell where the road had been, and the whole hillside above, as far up as she could see, had been sheared off to reveal naked strata. It was like an open wound in the earth, plantless and striped in darker and lighter layers. Pipes stuck out of the earth here and there, and down below, the earth was lumpy with chunks of asphalt or pieces of house. Nearby, she could see the rear of a copper-colored Miata sticking straight up, as if planted where it might grow.

"Thank you, Maeve. You should relax now."

The EMT stood up and started giving directions to others. Once he was gone, Maeve ignored his orders and crawled across the rubble to where her dad lay unconscious on another plastic pad, an oxygen mask strapped to his face.

"Dad!"

A nurse tried to ward her off.

"Don't disturb him, please. I need to do an EKG."

"He's fine. He's fine. He is."

"I'm sure that's what we'll find, honey."

Maeve started weeping. "I'm sorry, Dad. I'm so sorry."


It took Gloria half an hour to get there from the Harbor Division Station, fighting other cops who kept trying to turn her back. She wore her badge on a neck chain now as she got out and picked her way across the mess. There was a kind of officious rage that often built up at a disaster scene, a need that cops and rescue workers had to push hard at anybody nearby, perhaps some unconscious urge to shove the whole disaster away. Her training officer had told her he was surprised more rubbernecks at plane crashes and hurricanes didn't get shot in a moment of zealous tidying up by overwrought cops.

Once Gloria had made sure Jack and Maeve were okay, she began helping out with the search for survivors—or bodies.

A full-size pickup truck had been seen by a little girl going over the cliff in the first thrust of the landslide, and there was no chance there'd be survivors, as the beach below was now under several thousand tons of mud and rock and trees plus odd sections of house and road. The same for a sheriff's Ford that had tumbled into the bay below. It had somehow gone sideways out of the debris and lay with all four wheels up like a dead bug. In fact the whole cliff face at Lunada Bay had a giant's bite gone from its former face. A grayhaired man in a suit muttered something to her about how this was really only what had been happening here for millions of years: one more slide, one more settling. A deputy corrected him, insisting this had been no part of a natural process. They were already certain that a large cache of explosives far above had touched it off.

"Deputy," Gloria said, holding out her badge.

"Yeah." She could see he was already exhausted, pale and on the edge of snapping.

"A pair of surfers, probably from the house here. Do we know anything?" It was a favor to Maeve.

He smiled wearily. "It'll be in the record books. Guinness, whatever. Somebody must've hooked up with a comedian."

Gloria waited.

"Those kids surfed the damn landslide all the way down to the water. A broken hip on one, a lot more broken on the other. But they're alive. Look."

She edged as near the new cliff edge as she could and saw an enclosed metal stretcher basket being drawn up the precipice by a half dozen firemen with ropes. She hoped, whoever he was, his injuries weren't too painful because he was getting a nice banging against the rock face.

She went back to Maeve, who was now snoring like an innocent, and then she hunted for Jack, who'd been moved away somewhere. She looked amid the debris and firetrucks, asking likely-looking rescuers, until at last she found him. They'd got him on a proper gurney that was waiting at the end of what was left of the road, but he seemed out cold.

"Jack!" she shouted. "Maeve's okay, and it looks like the boys are hurt pretty bad but alive. Nobody else in the area made it. You've used up a lot of your allotment of lives this morning."

He didn't open his eyes, but she thought she detected a spark of awareness in the movement beneath the lids. His right index finger moved oddly. She watched it like a mother bird and either saw or imagined that he was trying to spell something on the gurney. L-O-C-O.

"He's going to make it, too, Jack. For a while, anyway. It may not be very long, but he's with us. You know what he was burying?"

His head might have stirred, just slightly. But maybe not.

"It was your new phony FBI badge from that mail-order place in Japan." She laughed.

A corner of his lip spasmed. Was he trying to smile?

"Loco has no confidence in your good sense," she said. "What a scoundrel—he was trying to protect you from your own bad judgment."